Beasts Fr

C000314418

Beasts From The Dark

BEASTS
FROM THE
DARK

ROBERT LOW

CANELO

First published in the United Kingdom in 2020 by Canelo

This edition published in the United Kingdom in 2020 by

Canelo Digital Publishing Limited
Third Floor, 20 Mortimer Street
London W1T 3JW
United Kingdom

A CIP catalogue record for this book is available from the British Library.

Print ISBN 978 1 78863 769 5
Ebook ISBN 978 1 78863 699 5

Look for more great books at www.canelo.co

Printed and bound in Great Britain by Clays Ltd, Elcograf S.p.A.

Chapter One

*Province of Rhaetia, late summer, regnal year three of Marcus
Aurelius Severus Alexander Augustus*

You can find such a place anywhere and, when you do,
you are free to come and go to it as often as you choose
afterwards. It is yours alone, no matter how many others
may walk there, where you can find gods in the unseen
wind that drags fingers through trees, or in the sun
dancing on shiny water.

Drust and the Brothers had made shrines and obeisance
from one end of the Empire to the other, put one stone
on top of another, spilled wine, left food and asked for
forgiveness, favour or just to live through one more *harena*
fight. They knew you did not need stone pillars or altars or
priests – yet this was Rhaetia, whose woods were scattered
with such sacred places, lurking in the Dark, a place of
trees black with old blood and swirling with old gods who
breathed the mists and the sigh of wind in it.

Ugo honoured them with head bowed and mumbled
abject chants because some of his gods were here, while
the rest of them offered no more than a grudging nod or
two and a dash of salt in the sweat they flicked off their
faces – but they walked soft, as suspicious of these shaggy
deities as the deities were of them.

I

It was a temple with columns but they were all knotted boles and trunks leaning one way, away from the north wind – even old King Oak, who seldom bends to anything. There was water here too, leaping down a long stretch of deep cut; in winter it would freeze to a curtain of jewels, Drust thought. It looked like the right place, the place Headman Erco had told them of, but he could not believe it had been this easy...

Here even Jupiter walked quietly, politely asking permission of the old gods of this land, which knew Rome only slightly. And here all the Brothers stood, turning reverentially slowly, feeling cloistered by the heavy cylinders of the ten trees sacred to these wood folk – the alder, the apple, the ash, the beech, the crab, the elm, the hazel, the thorn, the yew and the willow.

And over them all, the eleventh tree, the one whose roots sucked love, family, life, everything...

The Blood Oak.

When the beasts of the wood came howling out around them, no one was surprised, and all of them turned, falling into the familiar gladiatorial stance, as worn as a whetted blade. Drust wanted to run, wanted to weep, and wasn't sure if he was doing the latter anyway – he took a swift look sideways at where Praeclarum stood, grinning her toothless grin, blade up and savage as fangs. Then the fire smothered all tears and fears in him and he crouched by the shoulder of his woman. His wife.

He moved to meet the beast who came at him, something with a twisted snarl in his boar's head, naked from the waist and wearing checked trousers whose colour was faded and stained. He had a spear and a shield like the lid of a wooden tomb.

Drust had no shield, but he had two vicious slices of *gladius*, the short sword the Army had once won an Empire with. And when the beast came at him, all foot-stamp and flurry of little stabs, he batted the spear sideways with one of them, rolled up the shaft and flung a fistful of steel into the man's face.

It hit the cheek-piece and grated sideways, caught the beast mask and wrenched it half off; blinded, the half-man shrieked and dropped the spear, clawing out a knife. For a moment he and Drust locked like stags; there was a glimpse of snarling, a flurry of wild stabs, growls and spits.

Then a blade burst from the man's neck, appeared and vanished, while the half a face Drust could see turned, astounded, until it fell away sideways, trailing rubies from the gaping wound. Praeclarum, her sword dripping, slapped Drust's shoulder.

'Out,' she yelled. 'We need to get out—'

Drust had no argument – he bawled it so loudly his head thundered – but he saw Asellio scowling back at him, standing over a writhing enemy. Drust thought it was to do with rank and fleetingly thought Asellio an arse for bothering with it at such a time – then he saw that he was wrong and Asellio was fuming at the fleeing backs of two men.

'I've got it, I've got it...'

He did. His name was Crispus and he had it in one blood-slippery hand, stumbling towards Drust with a big grin and the curly head that gave him his name stiff with blood. He held it up so that the tail of the *draco* standard fluttered – then he seemed to jerk forward and stop, staring at the bloody point which had splintered out of his chest. It vanished like some gory trick; when Crispus fell

3

forward onto his face, the owner of the spear shook the blood off it like a derisive spit, and he might have been snarling or laughing, it was hard to tell under the bland boy-face of the Roman parade helmet he wore.

They saw him crouch to grab the standard and Drust heard Kag yelling for someone to get it. The warrior had to drop his spear to pick it up, then brandished the standard over the heel-kicking body of Crispus. He might have bellowed triumph but the shrieks and screams of the struggling and bloody were loud and everywhere.

Drust saw Praeclarum leap forward and followed, cursing her even as he burned with admiration. He was panicked she would get sideswiped by some blade, hit by a spear flying out of nowhere – there were enough of them.

Instead, he saw the boy-mask of the helmet, leprous with lost gilding and splashed gore, suddenly cave in under the massive blow of a pickaxe. The entire side of the copper facemask seemed to crumple round the vicious point; Ugo followed it up with a savage kick that sent the body lurching away, helping him drag the weapon out.

He had a *dolabra* in either hand, two ugly mattock adzeheads backed by a sharp pick, the Army's favourite tool. He had long since lost his once-favoured long axe, but now the artist had found a new instrument...

Quintus appeared like a swirl of wind, plucked the *draco* from where it lay, then zephyred out, grinning.

'Away,' bawled Kag, and Dog, his terror of a face splashed with fresh blood, ducked and spun and ran towards them.

They fled like squirrels.

'Is he dead, then? Did we get the Dragon?'

4

Ugo was sure of it but had no breath to tell Kag that. They all stood, bent and panting, but Asellio eventually shook his head.

'Got the pole, but not the man.'

'I hit him in the face mask,' Ugo argued. 'He wore that fancy parade helmet from the cavalry, like we were told. I caved his fucking face in.'

'Not him,' Kisa said. 'Someone else.'

'Someone else,' Quintus echoed scathingly. 'You think? The Dragon's men are Romans who are said to have fallen far, but even so – that lot looked like tribal sister-fuckers to me, not Romans or anything that had once been so.'

Ugo chipped up the forest floor with a frustrated swipe of his pick and Kag patted his massive shoulder soothingly.

'We got the *draco* standard back, at least.'

'Not the right one,' Kisa pointed out, lifting the limp rag of the dragon's tail. 'This is old and rotted – look, the head gilding is all but worn off and the metal lappets—'

'Cost two men,' muttered the one they called Culleo, slumping down with a grimace.

'Four,' Asellio muttered, and everyone knew he was bitter that the other two were the ones who had fled, one of them his second in command. Drust said nothing, while men prowled about the wood and thatch of the huts – looking to see if any people were left, they would say, but looting was more truthful.

Quintus gave Kisa a harsh glance, picked up the standard and pitched it back towards the abandoned village. 'Should have known,' he said. 'Erco lied and Fortuna fucked us all yet again.'

None of the villagers had stayed to argue the point; the people of Lupinus had long since packed up their lives and trundled off south to the protection of the *limes*. Lupinus – Made of Wolfskin – was what the garrison and everyone else north of the *limes* called the place, but the score of tribals who had lived here had a different name for it, Drust was sure. He had never bothered to find out in all the times he had visited in the last few weeks; his only interest in the place was with the headman, Erco, and the hunters and trackers who provided wolf and bear pelts for the Army.

The true worth of Erco to Drust was that he knew a man who knew a man further north who knew where there was a white bear Drust had to take back to feed the amphitheatre in time for the Ludus Magnus.

It was that white bear which got them into this mess, he thought grimly.

Men came back from the huts, Culleo shaking his head. 'They have all pissed off,' he said. 'Back to the bridge probably.'

He spat. 'They are People of the Moss,' he added derisively, and Drust remembered that Culleo was from Rhaetia, practically a local, though from the Roman side. He was Helvetii and hated Tigurini, which was the Roman name for a clutch of tribes, among them the People of the Moss. They were tribals from north of the *limes* who clung close to it for profit and did not trust their own kind to be reasonable about that – but whoever they were in a village they called Lupinus, they had gathered up everything and run off.

'For the bridge,' Asellio pointed out, then gathered up his vine staff and clanked off determinedly. 'To the bridge, followed by those two runaway arse-sponges…'

6

It hit them all at the same moment and shredded all weariness. There were curses and a mad scrabble up the rutted track, stumbling over the frantic discards of the villagers – shards of broken pots, a spilled grain sack, even a whole cart whose wheel had buckled. They hadn't even stopped to fully empty it of stuff valuable and vital to them. Everyone who followed that trail knew what they'd find, even as they gasped for the gods to intercede.

The bridge was gone. On the far side, the engineers were gone, their oxen and chains and shovels and axes. All gone. Nothing remained but the wooden piles on one side and their counterparts on the other; the river below frothed and the balks spilled down into it were long sailed.

Asellio ripped off his helmet and flung it at the ground, cursing Stolo and Tubulus and the *optio* who had commanded the engineers.

'He should have known better, the shit trumpet,' he raged, but Drust had some sympathy – two of the *numeroi* of the Batavian came running up, screaming about being attacked, about beast men in the blood woods. And after them came a horde…

'They let the horde across,' Kag pointed out bitterly, and Drust had no argument for that. The *optio* had recognised the villagers and once the last gasper had staggered to the far side, he had whipped up his oxen and the chained supports, partly cut, had been torn up and allowed to fall. Drust knew it was because Stolo and Tubulus had told him everyone else was dead.

'They will wish for it to be true,' Asellio growled murderously, then wiped his face with a trembling hand that everyone noticed.

'What now?' demanded Scrofus, the thin, whining Pannonian and everyone looked at Asellio, because he was the commander of them all, even the Brothers. But Kag looked sideways at Drust, as if to say 'we should fuck them all and go our own way'.

Asellio found and picked up his helmet, absently wiping off the dirt. 'West,' he said. 'There is another bridge about a day and a half from here.'

'That will also be down,' Ugo grunted and Asellio scowled at him. Ugo spread his arms in apology and fell silent.

'We need food and water,' Drust pointed out, and Quintus grinned, looking at the sky.

'We have the river if we can get down to it and, besides, it will rain soon.'

'Give us less of your cheer, why don't you?' Asellio snapped, then seemed to lift himself a little. 'Culleo, take Tuditanus and watch our back trail – those inbred tree-lurkers are coming for us, I can feel it. I am going to check the watchtower – maybe there's something in it we can use.'

'We can't stay here long,' Scrofus whined. 'They will come here soon.'

'Then start running,' Manius offered and stared blackly. Scrofus moved away from him.

Kag and the rest of the Brothers moved to Drust, a pointed gesture not lost on the others. There were now only three of them – the thin Pannonian called Scrofus, which meant 'sow', Tuditanus, who was a local and named 'hammer' because he carried the communal tent and peg-hammer, and another local, Culleo. His name meant a wineskin, and his face showed how he had got it.

They were the lees of the Army, the lumber no one else wanted, their legs and backs marked by beatings from vine sticks, and so low they no longer even had real names. As a last resort they'd been shoved into the *exploratores*, the scouts of the *numeroi* of the Batavian Cohort. It meant they wore what they liked and got sent out to skulk, shirk and steal, commanded by one regular Army man – a *decanus* called Scaevola, nicknamed Asellio. It was a mark of his fallen status that the nickname had been given to him by his scornful peers – it meant 'donkey keeper'.

Drust knew these men were afraid now, because two of them were dead and two more had fled, leaving them outnumbered among the Brothers of the Sand, who were ex-gladiators and ex-slaves. Even to the likes of Culleo, slovenly drunk that he was, the seven Brothers and the woman with them were no better than shit on his shoe.

But Culleo also knew better than to voice it – these shits were hard-faced men with clear weapon skills. One of them, called Dog, had a horror of a face, skin-marked to look like a skull, and the grizzled stubble he had grown only added to the terror when he looked at you. It seemed to Culleo and Sow that Dog had climbed out of his own grave only yesterday after having been dead for a year.

Manius was a *mavro*, a swarthy streak of sneaking from the deserts far to the south of the Africas across the Middle Sea; Kag was a Thracian, wiry and deadly; Quintus was tall and lanky and never stopped smiling, even when cutting throats. Culleo said especially when cutting throats, but he said it quietly and only to Sow. Ugo, the giant Frisian, carried two *dolabrae* and knew what to do with them.

Then there was also one called Kisa – a Jew – and no one liked them, especially this one who knew everything about everything, never shut up about it and seemed inclined not to fight. He was also, Culleo and Sow thought, a *frumentarius*, a state spy, and they liked them even less.

But the ones that really made them outraged and uneasy began with the leader, Drust, who was nothing special to look at and yet somehow made even the mad Dog take orders – it unnerved them all when Asellio barked commands and all these so-called Brothers of the Sand turned and looked at Drust for confirmation. Then there was his wife, who was called 'Remarkable'. A woman gladiator. In the Army. Truly this was the end of days.

Kag saw them look and smiled back, which made them turn away and find something to do. 'We should get away from this lot,' he added quietly to Drust. 'They are the scum of the Army.'

'We are the scum of the Army,' Dog corrected, scratching his beard.

'We are not in the Army,' Kisa corrected pedantically. 'Technically. We are *numeroi*...'

Drust wasn't listening; he was squinting to see if Asellio was coming back, for they had a limited time here before the tree-fuckers came howling after them. Asellio was nominally in command and Drust hoped there would not come a point where that had to stop.

For now he sat on a stone listening to the river dance in the gorge, looking at the gap. Forty feet between the remains of timbers and it might as well have been forty miles – they weren't crossing to the safe south at this point.

He wondered whether Erco had fled with his flock of villagers, the smiling little traitor. He might lurk in the shadow of the Empire, trade with them, run to them when the rest of his warrior people ran amok, but Drust was sure the little man called Hercules had deliberately led them right into an ambush. He will have gone off with them, he thought. He'll be wearing a beast mask and dancing round Crispus's smouldering remains.

He felt sick at it all, looked over to Praeclarum for the comfort of her in his eyes; she smiled back, not showing her lack of teeth. It was scarcely six months since their wedding and he remembered the day, the joy. How had they ended up here?

He looked up at the watchtower, willing Asellio to hurry. The tower was a narrow, three-storey affair, the bottom made of stone, the rest timber and wooden shingle. The entrance was up a length of stone steps into a door on the middle floor, which made it defendable, but it was no more than a shelter for the luckless men who'd had to monitor the bridge beyond the Wall.

Asellio burst from the door cursing angrily and Drust saw his hands were empty – so nothing useful up there after all. He sighed, was turning back to the muttered argument when he saw Asellio fall. His worn regulation boot studs hit the top step and shot out from underneath him, and he crashed down onto the stairs, bounced down two and then rolled off the unbalustraded side and fell a dozen feet. In his banded armour he made an ugly sound, like tin pots clattering.

Ugo howled with laughter, bent over and slapping his thighs. They all did, until it became clear the *decanus* wasn't getting up in any hurry; then they ran over to him.

'Come on, come on – this is no time to snooze,' Kag said and took Asellio by the front to haul him up; it took all his strength because the *decanus* was cased in armour. The head lolled back and blood trickled out of his mouth; it was then Drust saw the back of his skull was all blood and mostly caved in from the half-buried stone it had landed on.

'Fuck,' Kag said and set Asellio back down gently, wiping his hands down his front and staring. They all did, with a sick sense of dread.

'Get him up,' Culleo said, his voice rising into panic.

'Only Pluto will get him up now,' Dog growled. He wiped his mouth with the back of one hand and they all stood and stared, frozen.

This was Asellio, *decanus* of the *Exploratores* of *Cohors nonae Batavorum*. Thirty years' service – when his first twenty-five years ended, he re-enlisted. He had fought the Alemanni all over Pannonia and Rhaetia, had come out of it with decorations and awards, wore his old *lorica segmentata* like a badge of honour, even though such armour was going out of style.

He had sired more sons and cuckolded more husbands, lost and made more wealth than most men would ever see, and had been promoted and broken too many times to count – his legs bore the old whitened weals of past punishments.

Dead from a fall down some worn steps.

It took a while yet for them all to truly believe that such a little matter could have carried off the likes of Asellio, but were forced to admit it as they carried him up onto the rutted road. Hammer even looked up at the grey-blue sky, as if expecting the mourning wrath of Jupiter.

The Brothers were less stunned by it. Dis Pater was practically one of them, and they had no fear of that deity or the deaths he had claimed of those closest to them, for they had lived with it daily for too long.

Culleo and the others were not so hand-clasped to Dis and had been longer with the *decanus*, long enough to have him as their bedrock. Drust saw the shock eventually slide off them, leaving them all with the gaping void of it under their feet.

They dragged him up and laid him down, then stared, then wiped their faces as if they could scrub the sight away. It stayed – an old man, head at an angle it should not be and blood drying round the grizzle of his beard.

They said what had happened. Then said it again. And again, as if it would somehow change, not be true.

'Fucken old bastard,' said Sow finally, bitterly. 'Just when we needed him.'

Kag bent, examined, then looked up. 'Anyone want his armour?'

It seemed like a slap in the face to them, an insult, almost a sacrilege, and they refused. None of the Brothers wanted it – they did not like to fight in such an oven.

'You'll need to be light and fast,' Praeclarum pointed out. 'There's some rough country if we are still headed west of here – and we are being hunted by those who run over it daily.'

'Well,' said Culleo slowly, hitching up his own tattered ring-coat. 'I am now senior here, so…'

'Shut up, you flap-sandalled gob of shite,' Kag said amiably and then looked at Drust. 'What now?'

'Roll him into the river as he is,' Drust answered. 'Otherwise the howlers will get his weapons, his nice armour and his head all in one.'

Hammer made a noise as if to protest, to argue for a decent burial, but Drust looked up at him and stopped the words in his mouth.

'You want to take the time to dig a hole? Or get as much between us and those who want their stolen dragon standard back?'

They hitched up their gear and got ready. Praeclarum moved up to Drust and kissed his cheek, taking the opportunity to put her soft lips against his ear, her breath stirring the hairs round it. He wanted endearment, at least an affirmation that he was working well on everyone's behalf.

'How the fuck did we get into this?' she whispered.

–

The usual way – by being in the wrong place at the wrong time. That was Quintus's wry take on it. Dog muttered vile threats at Cascus Minicius Audens, Beast Master of the Flavian, whose contract had taken them to the dark, wet woods of Rhaetia, and Kag shrugged and blamed Fortuna, fickle as ever.

Kisa muttered prayers to his one god, Ugo just looked grim as old rock. Manius said nothing, just whetted a knife and looked for the way out, but Praeclarum spoke, briefly and darkly, about divine retribution for having let an Empress and a Vestal die in a hole in the ground.

That was half a year ago – the day he and Praeclarum had been married, Drust recalled. The price for bringing the wayward former Vestal Empress of a dead Emperor from the dusty deserts of Syria back to her family so they could immure her, all right and proper, had let them pay for this enterprise. If it failed, they were broke as old pie crust. Again.

Drust knew the truth of how they had ended up out in the Dark and it was another goddess entirely, one they had ignored and so made angry. Fama, who spread your name far and wide, who lives at the centre of the world, where earth, sea and sky meet; from there she can see and hear everything that goes on and her home, on a tall peak, has no doors but a thousand windows and is made entirely of bronze, so that the slightest noise or whisper echoes and reverberates throughout.

He found this out from Legate Marcus Peperna Vento, in the *principia* of the fort at Biriciana, who had summoned them all.

'I am told that, despite how you appear, you are the very ones for this task,' he declared, stabbing a stubby finger at the painted scroll map on the desk in front of him. 'Here is where decent tribals raise crops of children and grain, sheep and cattle under the protection of Rome.'. Another stab. 'And here is where the only decent crop they raise is beards and hate for all of those on the other side.'

No one laughed.

They called him Legate, but Marcus Peperna Vento didn't have a legion – no one did these days. He had detachments from all over the Empire, the bulk of them from the Third Italica, and those were spread along a single stone wall and the fortlets studding it – this was the frontier in the north.

'This is the land of the tree worshippers, whose civilisation ended before the invention of the comb. They live in forests which the men call the blood woods, or just the Dark,' Peperna went on. 'Out there they curse Rome and get in more trouble than a dog eating a stolen pie. Like the dog, they end up beaten to death by the stick of the Army.'

He looked round them all, grim and unsmiling, a stubby man who wanted to get back to Rome with honour and a decent heap of coin and would do anything to achieve it. 'Now and then,' he said, his voice deepening to a bitter, half ashamed growl, 'they make enough of a fist of it to leap across the Wall and start pie-hunting on our side. Then we have to turn out and round them up.'

Again no one spoke, for they all knew such a fist had been made and that the only safe place on either side of the *limes* this summer was where they stood; the Army had the men, but seemed to lack the will to turn out and round anyone up.

Tribal raiders of Helvetii, Tigurini, Rhaeti and even Suebi, with their strange, knotted hair, were whooping and howling up and down the soft, rich south, looting, killing and raping. They weren't in big enough numbers to be a threat to the passes south into Cisalpine, but if it looked like they would become so, Peperna would have to turn out and march to stop them. Meanwhile, the Army had dropped all the serious bridges, the ones that could take livestock or wheeled vehicles – the raiders might pillage, but they'd be limited to what they could carry.

It was bad enough that all the roads from here south to Rome were now suicidally dangerous, Drust thought. The Brothers had carts and wagons waiting for a white bear and the feed for it but no safe way to get to the Beast Master of the Flavian.

Peperna knew this. He looked round them all and smiled a nasty smile. 'You have been brought to my attention. Fama has whispered in a high-placed ear on the

Palatine and so the word has come down to me. You call yourselves Brothers of the Sand – even the woman. You have skills the Army can use.'

'We are not in the Army,' Ugo growled warningly, 'and the "woman" is Drust's wife.'

Peperna's grin had widened like a steel trap – even Quintus had to be envious of that one, Drust thought uneasily.

'You are Army as of now,' he answered. 'You will shortly meet Decanus Scaevola. He is now your commander and you are now part of the *numeroi* of the Batavian Cohort. *Exploratores* of the Eighth Cohort – do you understand what that is?'

Drust knew – they all knew, for it wasn't the first time they had done such work, but never for the Batavian. Once this had been the German Guard of Emperors, until Galba had disbanded them, thinking they were too loyal to the deposed Nero. That had caused a major war with the outraged Batavii and, afterwards, some of the Germans had been reinstated.

But the *exploratores*, the scouts and informers, were still the most reviled unit in the Army.

'Of the Army, but not quite in the Army,' Kag said blankly. 'No uniforms, no drill, no parades – just a bit of scout and skulk.'

Peperna didn't grin back. 'You will assist Decanus Scaevola with your local knowledge. You will escort him and his men north of the *limes* and question your contacts as to the whereabouts of a Roman officer and the cavalry he has in his possession.'

The stun of that was a fist to all mouths and closed them.

Peperna nodded as if he had expected no less; he had a sharp and disturbing twist of a smile.

'You have had dealing with the limeheads north of here,' he said. 'The ones from that town by Bridge 41.'

Drust knew Peperna had made enquiries and there was no point denying anything – but all Drust knew was that the name of the headman was Erco, that his name was local-speak for 'Hercules' and almost certainly wasn't the name non-Romans knew him by. None of which made him a friend, let alone kin. He finally said so and pointed out that any of the detachment at the Bridge 41 watchtower would know as much.

'Besides,' he added desperately, 'we came here to fetch back a prize for the Emperor – a white bear for the big Games. I only know this Erco as a contact to the ones who have such a creature, brought down from the far north.'

Peperna rasped one hand on his stubble – when a man like that neglects his barbering, Kag pointed out later, you know there is trouble.

'There are no detachments at the watchtower. There are engineers at Bridge 41 preparing it for demolition, so here is what you will do, you so-called Brothers of the Sand. You will join the rest of the *numeroi* of Scaevola. We will care for your carts and gear until it is clear you aren't coming back. You should be very clear that the instructions regarding you come from the highest source – I have been told to mention the name Julius Yahya.'

He saw the reaction and smiled thinly. 'You can forget your white bear.'

'Fuck that,' Quintus growled sullenly, but it was a poor spark, quickly extinguished.

'At every order we stand ready,' Dog declared sardonically, and Peperna managed to look him in the eye for long enough to show he wasn't overawed by the face, but Drust knew it was a lie. He also knew Peperna was afraid; the atmosphere was reeking with it, a pervasive stink that you had to fight hard against to avoid infection.

Julius Yahya would do that, Drust thought, remembering the man from years before, when he had sent them north of the Britannia frontier. That had not turned out well…

'A slave,' Kag said suddenly and laughed with venom. Then he spread apologetic hands as he looked at Peperna. 'It always amuses me to see the likes of legates fawn over Julius Yahya.'

'He is a freedman nowadays,' Peperna said, seemingly unaffected by the barb. 'Advisor to the Emperor's mother. Does that give you a clue as to why legates fawn? As to how you will obey?'

Julia Avita Mamaea, Mother of the Empress, whose head was on coins and whose fingers were everywhere, pulling strings on behalf of her son. A woman who had organised the death of his cousin so her son could put his skinny boy arse on the throne. A woman who had organised a good Roman marriage for him, then grown jealous of it, banished the wife and executed her father for treason. Drust felt the greasy grey hand of it squeeze him into a hopelessness that bowed his head; he felt Praeclarum's fingers on his.

'What cannot be overcome must be endured,' she said.

No one had an answer to that or anything else, and Peperna hitched his official toga up like a big-ruffed wolf.

'Here's what you will do…'

He plucked a scroll from out of his sleeves and handed it to Kisa, a singular act that Drust did not miss. He knows us, he thought. He has made enquiries and he knows who can read best, who can write clearly, who does what.

'That is the history of Marcus Antonius Antyllus,' Peperna said, and the way he said it was like calling on a god for favours. 'He is a descendant of the great Anthony and a tribune *laticlavius*, former legate of the Third – when such appointments were made to senators.'

The last was said with bitterness and Drust knew that in recent times the senatorial rank had lost some power in Rome, emperors preferring to trust the Army to the lesser *equites*.

'You will go north,' Peperna said. 'Seek news of Marcus Antonius among those you know there, find him and let Scaevola and his men return him to his *castra*.'

'Is he lost then?' Kag asked, dark-voiced and dark-eyed, because he already knew the truth.

'Mislaid,' Peperna answered flatly. 'He always had radical ideas about taking the war to the enemy and now they are... unsound. You may have heard the name "The Dragon". That is Marcus Antonius. He is out there fighting an enemy he created by stirring up the limeheads. Now they have leaped the Wall to pie-hunt on our side, and no one knows if General Antyllus is alive or dead. Find out, and if he is alive you will inform him of Rome's displeasure and persuade him to return with the cavalry regiment and the *draco* standard he took with him. Rome does not want the blood priests of the Dark to have a noble head or a noble standard to stick it on.'

Fama had already whispered of the Dragon, a rogue Roman general leading a band of renegades under the *draco* standard of the Second Flavia cavalry, charging up and down and attacking anyone and anything that moved north of the Wall. This Antyllus had once commanded detachments equalling a legion, but took the disaffected of the Ala Flavia and made them his own. The rumour was that he thought cavalry a waste of men and resources in country like this, and wanted them retrained as wood-crawlers and secret fighters. The rumour was that he and his band had eaten all their horses in some perverse ritual.

They filed out of the *principia*, blinking in the light, standing in a whirl of movement as officers and clerks went back and forth clutching tablets and papyrus. Outside, men banged heels on hard ground and bawled '*Roma Invicta!*'. Everyone carried their fear like a pack they couldn't wriggle out of.

One man was stolid and unmoved, grizzled and staring at them from a face like a roofer's nail pouch. 'Scaevola,' he announced flatly. 'You'll hear me called Asellio, but it doesn't worry me one bit. Draw stores of what you need, within reason. Then follow me.'

'We stand ready for any order,' Quintus said, and Scaevola paused, then looked him up and down.

'I have been told of you and what you need to do. You have been told of me. Don't fuck with me or I will set you on fire and beat it out with a spade.'

They fell silent with admiration, then Drust said: 'We've been told of you. You know what we are here to do. What are you here to do?'

Scaevola squinted at him, then nodded. 'You'll be Drust, the leader. Well, as long as you can take orders from me we will do well. Once you find this high-born arsehole, me and my lads will persuade him of his error.'

'What if he does not want to be persuaded?' Praeclarum asked, all wide-eyed and sweet – Drust saw Scaevola's eyes flick to her and then back to Drust. Here it comes, he thought. But to a man nicknamed Asellio, Keeper of Donkeys, the inclusion of a woman gladiator in his command was just another *infamis* to add to the heap.

'He must be removed from command, Peperna said. By any means.'

'And then?' Dog responded, flat and sharp as new steel. Asellio studied the skull-tattooed face blandly and Drust admired that. Here was a man who had seen worse than Dog's face. He did not want to think on what that might be, but a shrieking mass of armed, muscled men with their hair limed up into white spikes would probably top the list. He shivered.

'You want us to murder the man,' Quintus added.

'I don't want you to do a fucking thing I don't tell you to do,' Asellio answered. 'Including murder.'

'What will Rome think of that?' Kisa demanded, his voice shrill with outraged astonishment. 'The murder of a senator?'

'You need not worry about that,' Asellio answered levelly. 'The biggest crime in Rome is to short-weight the grain dole.'

Drust laughed aloud when he heard it and all the others fell silent and looked at him, frowning as if pursing their eyebrows together would force out the bit he had seen and they had not. Eventually he told them that if the murder of a senator, even one with a headful of squirming snakes, was of no account, then only one person could have authorised it – the Imperial Consort herself, Mother of the Empire. Asellio nodded grudging admiration.

'You know not to eat fish with a spoon,' he growled.

'It is a beast hunt,' Drust said flatly, 'and most beast hunting is all spear and idiocy, which is why sensible people get others to do it.'

Dog hawked and spat, a singular insult to the steps of the *principia* that should have got him the worst of punishment pain; the scurriers who saw it pretended they didn't. Kag delivered his bitter verdict.

'The easiest animal to find is always the scapegoat.'

—

They got caught an hour later, scrambling along the steep rocks of the river, heading west with the water dancing uncaringly at the bottom of the gorge and the grey rocks on the other side slowly, slowly sliding down to meet the narrowing path.

Culleo had just said how this was a bad way, that it was too steep, that they should have gone back to the village called 'made by wolves' and then struck off into the forest. He had said it before and always in a whining grate of a voice, so no one paid him much heed.

The arrow that hit him drove the word 'forest' out of him in a high, plaintive squeal, then slammed him face first into the rocks he so hated. Drust was glad he had taken a shield and now slid it off his shoulder.

'Form, form,' Drust yelled and they turned, shields up. Sow and Hammer were dancing in little panicked baby steps, hovering on the edge of bolting.

'Should we stay here?' Hammer yelled in panic as another arrow whicked through the air and splintered on the rocks.

'Let's,' Ugo grunted scathingly, working his shoulders. 'We can plant flowers.'

They looked sideways at him, a big man with two mattock picks and no shield, scowling from out of a beard and hair whose braids seemed welded together. They might have streaks of grey in them, as if some bird had shit from the nest of his head, but those shoulders were massive and his roar was a blast of sound they could feel.

'Come on, you arse-sponges. Come and die.'

They came, but the first two seemed to trip and fall over, tipped off-balance by the sudden sprout of saplings from their chests – Manius nocked a third arrow and spitted one more before they closed on Drust and the others.

Drust dropped a shoulder and let the spear snick threads from his tunic, struck back but was too far for more than a pink of the point, enough to make the warrior rear back, his mouth an O under hair that looked dipped in frost, spiked with icicles of lime.

Kag bumped his shoulder – there is no room to move here, Drust thought. Not the way we fight.

Something slammed his shield, he saw a foot and slashed it with the *gladius*, honed to shaving sharp; the owner yelped and spun away, hopping. Drust turned a little when the corner of his eye flickered, blocked the solid thump of spear with his scarred egg of a shield, backhanded the *gladius* across the spearman's throat; the man gurgled, dropped the spear and clapped his hand against the spurt, as if he could shut the gape.

An arrow whicked so close to Drust's head that he felt the rasp of wind from the fletchings – the man he hadn't seen took it full in the face, just below the nose, and did not make a sound as his head snapped all the way back and his last thoughts burst bloodily from the great scab of scalp and skull that blew out down his back.

Manius, Drust thought, doing what he does best, though I wish he would do it a little further from me...

Ugo finished it, carving them with axe and pick, protected by Quintus from those he did not see and would not have cared about if he had. He blocked and stabbed and slashed to keep blade and point away from the big man, while the twin *dolabrae* sliced blood into the sour light of a dying day. The warriors realised, like dogs chasing a feral bull, just what they had sunk their teeth into; they let go and fled. None of them made more than a dozen steps.

There was a moment when no one spoke, just stood bent over and rasping for breath. Somewhere a man grunted and groaned. Behind Drust, Kisa told Culleo he hadn't been skewered, just had the breath knocked out of him by an arrow which had hit his slung forage bag and ring mail.

'They have no bows worth the name,' Manius added scornfully and brandished the Persian one he owned, a poem of curve in bone and wood. 'Silly little sticks they shoot are badly made and have no power.'

'At least one of them shut him up,' Dog said, glancing at the ashen Culleo briefly as he stepped over the sprawled dead, squinting down at them. 'These are not any kind of Romans. These are local woodlice – wouldn't you say, lads?'

He turned, innocent as a Vestal veil, to stare his horror face at Sow and Hammer, who were still half crouched, shields up. Sow licked his lips at the Rhaetian insults and looked as if he would tell Dog to fuck off, but Drust saw that resolve drain from him at the last.

'They never sat a horse,' Quintus confirmed. 'Same as the ones in that forest altar. No Romans of the Dragon here.'

'We were sold a three-legged horse by that headman,' Praeclarum confirmed. 'But the ones he sent word to still think us worth the effort.'

'Well, we stole a prize from their altar,' Kag growled. 'Killed a few, including one of their leaders if he wore a cavalry face mask. If they can replace it with some of our heads on a pole, I am thinking they will count that a trade.'

'We never should have come this way,' Culleo said hoarsely, levering himself up and rubbing where the arrow had smacked him. 'Look – the path has run out. Where do we go now?'

'Not back, as you have been whining on about for too long,' Dog fired at him. Drust looked round.

'Up,' he said, and everyone groaned. Culleo looked stricken.

'We'll never make it.'

'Shed your iron,' Drust said and Culleo's eyes threatened to pop; he was fresh from realising how that ring-coat had stopped him from being skewered.

'How will we protect ourselves in a fight?'

'Fight better,' Kag growled and dipped low to one of the corpses. Drust thought he was scavenging but the little Thracian turned.

'This one is alive.'

'Then change that state,' Dog answered. Drust ignored him, moved to the man and knelt. Kag was right – the man was alive, and under the desiccated muzzle of the wolf mask was a big warrior with a shock of tow-coloured hair and a beard done in two impressive braids, banded with tarnished silver rings.

He had a tunic coloured faintly blue, but mainly by mud and blood, trousers patterned in red and green squares, thonged from below the knee to where his torn leather shoes began. Manius had hit him with an arrow, but it had gone in low, just above the hip. Praeclarum arrived, looked, snapped the shaft and drew both ends out.

'He will live,' she said, rooting in her bag for packing and binding. 'Won't walk far, though.'

Manius appeared at her side and carefully took the broken shaft with the point still attached. He looked at her with dark, blank eyes and said: 'He will die. In a day, perhaps less.'

She looked at the barbed arrow, then back into the abyss eyes. 'You poison the points?'

'Not for anything I might eat,' he answered, and there was no laugh in his voice.

'Why would we care about whether he can walk?' demanded Ugo suspiciously. He had shaken a corpse free of most of its tunic and was using it to wipe the clots from his *dolabrae*.

'Because we cannot question him here and we need information,' Drust answered, straightening and wiping his palms clean on his tunic front. 'We will need all we can get but it won't come from this one, as I had hoped.'

He looked hard at Manius. 'One of your shafts almost kissed my cheek. I do not want such a lover, particularly

27

one with venomous lips. If Praeclarum had cut herself taking it out...'

Manius acknowledged it with a nod and loped off. Quintus followed him with silent eyes and no grin, then shook his head.

'Sib was right. He should never have been allowed out of the desert.'

Sib was dead, Drust wanted to point out, and though Manius swore it was not his arrow, no one could be sure. But then Sib might have tried to kill Manius earlier, believing he was some demon from the desert; their relationship, Drust recalled, had been complicated, even for Brothers.

'Pack up,' he said brusquely, then knelt and drew his knife, felt for the heart in the throat and thrust once. The warrior gugged and gurgled, then all Praeclarum's skill was wasted and only his heels worked, drumming furiously for a brief spasm before slumping to silence.

All that time in the undercroft of the Flavian, Drust thought wryly, learning from the Greek *medicus* how to do this. The Greek would be pleased that his voice still echoes in my ears... perhaps this is the true secret of immortality.

Quintus turned to Culleo and the other two. His grin was warm and wide and white, vicious as a feeding shark.

'Rid yourselves of all that useless metal, lads, or you will never make the climb. I'd throw away the tent too – not going to be of much use.'

'If I have to help carry any of you,' Dog added, 'I may have something to say on it.'

Culleo stood, working his mouth, and Drust knew the man wanted drink more than anything right then; he wondered if this was the moment the man would do something truly idiotic. Then Sow broke the knots of it with a resigned grunt, pitching the eight-man tent into the gorge.

'Let's get to it. Fastest way back to the *castra*.'

Kag nodded. 'Good move. That way you can get that rash on your balls treated.'

'You'd better tell your ma,' Sow shot back. 'That's where I got it.'

Kag and Quintus laughed and Ugo slapped Sow on the back hard enough to make him stumble and cough, but he was smiling when he got enough breath back to wriggle out of the ring-metal tunic.

They climbed for an hour, up the strewn rocks and loose scree to finally pop out on a boulder-studded escarpment studded with bushes that spewed down to a forest, ringing them on all sides.

'We have lost them,' Kag declared, wiping his greased face and flapping a hand at insects. 'Unless they come up through the forest.'

'What about it, you lads?' Quintus demanded, staring at Culleo, Sow and Hammer. 'You're from around here – Helvetii, right? Will they come up through the forest?'

Culleo spat, which Quintus did not like. 'Helvetii. What do you think that is? You are Roman in the same way – from the City? Apulia? Gaul?'

'He is trying to say,' Hammer interrupted, 'that he does not know any more than you. No one likes the Dark.'

'The Dark?'

'The forests round here are old as the first gods,' Hammer answered, his voice low, his eyes darting around. 'You step lightly here.'

Sow was hunkered, resting, but in a way that would let him spring up. 'You saw the sacred place where we stole that standard.' He paused and looked bitterly at Drust. 'Only to throw it away as if it was of no account.'

'It was as old as Varus,' Kag pointed out harshly. 'Rome has long forgotten it.'

'Not the tribe that took it, no matter when,' Culleo spat back. 'They are the ones who hunt us now.'

'Blame Erco for that,' Ugo rumbled. 'Little fuck lied, led us into an ambush. Thought we would all be killed and told that to the bridge engineers. Your tent-mates running up, screaming about hordes and blood and beast men didn't help, for sure.'

Culleo and the others fell silent, because there was no arguing with the truth. Praeclarum looked at Drust and he thought she looked pale and washed-out.

'We need a place to rest and hide,' she said. Drust nodded to Manius, who sucked in a deep breath which everyone noted, then loped out.

He does not like those forests any more than we do, Drust thought. Skilled tracker, silent killer – yet he is a desert man. Trees unnerve him. Only Ugo does not seem to care – he looked at the big Frisian and saw that he was wrong, that Ugo stood like an uneasy bull, shaggy head swinging this way and that, trying to use the corners of his eyes to spot the enemies sneaking up on them.

Manius was back not long after they had moved off, westward to the trees, which seemed to come at them too fast. He had found a place, an overhang that wasn't quite a

30

cave, though everyone eyed it apprehensively. Drust saw that it would let them light a fire unseen, allow them warmth and hot food, but he did not like the fact that they crouched under a single balanced slab of rock the size of a palace on the Hill.

'What if it falls?' Ugo asked, and Dog laughed as he squatted and began the makings of a fire.

'Then we are squashed,' he said, 'unless you are truly Hercules and can hold it up while we all escape.'

'Do not mention Hercules,' Kag put in, scowling. 'That Erco will suffer when I meet him.'

'Perhaps he did not run off to the safety of the *castra* with the rest of his village,' Kisa put in. 'Seems to me that he is more likely to join the howlers and screamers.'

'What say you?' Ugo demanded, looking at Culleo, who looked back at him, his pouched eyes black.

'I say you should stop asking me. I am Helvetii – which is the Roman word for it – the same way you are Frisii. If one of them walked up and offered his wrist to clasp, you would not know why.'

'Fair point,' Manius answered, laughing. 'Besides – you all look the same to me.'

He had set snares when he was out and went to check on them. The fire flourished, making them gather round it, hugging the warmth like a mother's embrace, and the talk was low and head to head.

'Julius Yahya,' Kag said wearily and Drust nodded, knowing exactly what he meant. Julius Yahya had been a slave when he had persuaded Drust and the others to go north of the Walls in Britannia to fetch back a Roman woman and her child – but he was a slave with the powers of a senator and more. The Roman woman and her son

31

turned out to be more than that, Drust recalled. He was probably the one behind them all ending up in the desert pursuing yet another high-born Roman woman, a Vestal no less.

'At least this time it is not a woman,' Kag muttered.

'That we know of,' Drust replied thoughtfully. 'Last time it was supposedly about Hyrcanian tigers and rescuing Dog and Manius.'

As if summoned, Manius loped in with a fistful of little squirrels which he started to gut and spit.

'You think that's it? Some woman?'

Drust sighed and looked wearily at Kag, while the sudden waft of cooking meat raked him with hunger pangs. 'How do I know? I know only that each time we succeed makes it certain Julius fucking Yahya will get us on another of his plots.'

He did not add what he suspected, that the woman in it was the Mother of Empire pulling her strings from the Palatine Hill.

'When I get back,' Dog said, shifting up to examine the squirrels with a ravenous eye, 'I will have words with Julius Yahya.'

'Get in the line,' Kag answered. They sat, smelling the squirrels and sorting out ways to eat them. In the end, they did what they always did – sauced their porridge with little bits of meat and wilted greens. They had wine, they had evaded their enemies and they were alive. It was enough for now.

'How far to the next bridge?' Kisa asked, and there was silence until Culleo realised everyone was looking at him.

He shrugged, picking at the scab on his purple nose. 'A day. Maybe more. Never travelled to it this way. Don't you know? You're the *frumentarius*.'

'Was,' Kisa pointed out flatly. 'Not now. Got too involved with this lot to be trusted as a State spy. Not that it was well paid, mind…'

'That bridge will be down too,' Sow offered. 'If they have pulled this one to pieces.'

'There has to be a crossing somewhere,' Quintus growled. 'All these limeheads seem to be flooding south easily enough. Got across the bloody Wall too.'

'They move light and can climb and swim,' Kag answered, then looked at Drust. 'There was no Spartacus mentioned,' he added thoughtfully.

'Gladiator?' Sow said scornfully. 'Not likely.'

'No big named leader that men will follow,' Drust explained. 'That means there is no conquest here, just a lot of little limeheads stirred up to go plundering. They will start south with what they have looted if it seems like they might have a serious fight on their hands.'

No one spoke for a long while; they had seen the Army here and it didn't seem any of them were up for a serious fight except with each other, over pay arrears or rations or privilege. Commanders were more concerned about not having their men try and make them Emperors than with leading them to fight raiders. When Drust said as much, Sow looked up sharply.

'Don't you worry, gladiator. The Army will sort them out.'

Dog laughed nastily, but Drust raised a hand as a warning; Culleo, Sow and Hammer were the lumber of the land, so bad they could not fit in the last century of the

33

last cohort of a Legion, but had been consigned to the *numeroi*, so far removed that they might just as well not have enlisted. Yet they still had pride.

They were, Drust thought, no different from the *laticlavius* they had been sent to find, this senatorial-ranked renegade. When the others had set themselves as sentry or rolled themselves up for sleep, Drust moved to Kisa with a lit torch and got him to move with him, away from the others.

'What of this senatorial general?' he asked, and Kisa, yawning, hauled out the scrolls he had been given, squinting blearily at them, though it was clear to Drust that he had consigned most of it to memory.

'Marcus Antonius Antyllus,' he recited. 'As we were told – a descendant of the great Anthony himself and so a member of one of the most powerful families in Rome. Did the usual career, appointed quaestor, praetor and the like. Tribune of the Fifteenth Apollonaris in Cappadocia, then the Second Adiutrix in Pannonia – this is where it began to change from the usual. Seems he muddied the floor of every *principia* he was sent to – got debts for gambling, arguing for a change of tactics, for more discipline, for more senators appointed to legion commands rather than *equites*. Made himself a nuisance to the Hill and was removed as legate of the Third Italica here in Rhaetia – either that or removed himself, the record is unclear. Became commander of the Flavia horse, which is a big step down for such a man – but he had ideas that the horse were of no account in the likes of Rhaetia and Pannonia and should be retrained as fast, light infantry. Actually, that is quite a sound idea given the mountains and forests—'

'Interesting but unimportant,' Drust growled, and Kag cleared his throat.

'Six months ago he led the better part of the Second Flavia horse out north, ostensibly as a show of force and against the wishes of the governor and the legate, who did not want the tribes north of the Wall stirred up – but he is a senator, so they couldn't do much other than complain to the Hill. Again.'

'He never came back?'

Kisa shook his head. 'According to the report here, he sent messages saying he was retraining his men, but some of them were nothing to do with the Flavia – legionaries and auxiliaries with grievances. That worried the generals and governor, as did the reports – second- and third-hand from the locals – that some strange Romans had sacrificed their horses or eaten them or both. Then they heard that this unit was raiding, waging war on the tribals north of the Wall, living off the land because the *castra* cut off supplies to try and force them to return. Led by someone called the Dragon, who wore ornate armour and a helmet with a face on it. That's cavalry parade armour, for sure. He had a *draco* standard, presumably of the Second Flavia.'

'Which is where we came in,' said a voice and Praeclarum slid out of the shadows, her smile warm in the torchlight. 'Are you even considering this still?'

Drust was not. All he wanted was to get back to the right side of the Wall and he said so. Kisa breathed out with relief and Praeclarum smiled more broadly, showing her gap and gums; her expensive pearl teeth were in a soft pouch round her neck.

'Make an inventory,' Drust said to her, 'of what supplies we have. Put Sow in charge of them – tell him he is quartermaster, which will get him to do it.'

'What of the other two?' Kisa asked softly. 'They are none of them to be trusted.'

'Culleo is cheating crucifixion by a ball-hair,' Praeclarum offered bleakly. 'Hammer is a looter and a brawler – lift his tunic and you will see the flog marks. Sow is not much better – the only fighting any of them has done is over a whore or a meat pie.'

'Keep a watch on them is all we can do,' Drust replied. 'Make it clear we are dependent one on the other, especially where we are going.'

'The Dark,' Kisa said mournfully.

The light faltered and sank to the earth. Shadow and fear slouched in, chasing sense and reason; the hiss of a leaf in the fetid wind made heads turn and hearts break into a ragged trot. The blackness was everywhere, it left nowhere to run, and everything became memory.

Chapter Two

Drust woke like a man falling upwards. I shouldn't have slept, he thought. Shouldn't have. But that's where dreams are and I find a lot in them. Dreams – they are who I am when I'm too tired to be me.

In the sullen overhang of rock, they moved quietly and with purpose, checking that blade, fixing this strap. Praeclarum came to him, squatted and offered him a thin wineskin; the liquid was resined but he drank it anyway.

'Those three are hoarding,' she said, and Drust levered himself to his feet. He didn't question her on it.

'Where are they?'

She jerked her head and he followed her out to where Culleo was fiddling with a bootstrap, Sow was arguing with Hammer over how best to fasten the neck of the bag they had made for the provisions. They'd used the waxed leather one Hammer had carried tent mallet and pegs in. All of them looked up guiltily as the pair came up.

'Empty your packs and pouches,' Drust said, and they looked calculatingly at one another while Praeclarum rested one hand on a hilt. Then their eyes drifted to somewhere behind Drust, who resisted the nag to turn; he'd had that one pulled on him before.

'Empty,' said the tomb-voice of Dog, and the three men looked sullen, then resentful, then resigned. Finally they began to pick stuff out of their packs until Dog walked forward, wrenched packs and pouches and began strewing stuff on the ground.

Four portions of twice-bake, the Army bread, and a ham bone with meat still on it. Drust jerked his head at Sow, who loaded it into the provisions sack and looked embarrassed about it.

'If you were back at the *castra*, you'd get beaten by clubs for this,' Drust pointed out. He looked at Culleo, whose pack was still intact. 'What else have you got?'

Culleo looked murderous for a moment, then reached in and drew out a wineskin, small but still fat. He raised it to his lips and began sucking until Drust tore it from him, the ruby drops flying like blood. Drust tasted it after pointedly wiping the neck with one hand, then handed it to Dog, who drank.

'Decent,' he said. 'Better than anyone else is drinking now.'

Drust looked at the three men. 'You can go your own way, you sorry sacks of shit. If you get back to the Wall I will make sure you clean the latrines forever using your own arse-sponges. I don't think you will get back on your own, so what I offer now is your last chance. Stay or go?'

They were silent for a second or two, then Sow stuffed the wineskin in the provisions bag and glared at Culleo. He looked ashamed.

'I'll stay. Hammer too, because he is an idiot on his own. Neither of us will make it, for sure, if left to ourselves.' He turned to Hammer. 'It's true, you know it.'

Drust and Culleo locked eyes. He was a raw-boned gangling man, Drust saw, spare and beaten by weather and

38

drink until his face looked like a broken-veined cliff with eyes. Finally he nodded.

'Join the others,' he said. As they lumbered off, Dog watched them go until he knew they could not hear.

'Cut their throats now,' he said mildly. 'It will save time later.'

'Three more fists with steel,' Drust pointed out, and Dog grudgingly admitted the worth of that with a curt nod.

They moved off until the scrub grew taller, became saplings. The sprawling forest of the Germanies wasn't all one, Drust knew, but lots of them linked by open areas, sometimes carved out for cultivation, sometimes just by the gods. The woods themselves were... different.

They swaggered in, as they would down any dark alley in Subura, shit-eating grins on their faces, shoulders moving in challenge, goading any watchers to make a move. In a dozen steps they had shrunk like emptying wineskins, started to crouch and walk soft; all talk became whispered or disappeared entirely, like the sun.

Under the shadows and canopy one tree followed another, one space succeeded another, without difference or progression. They walked through a place of eternal sameness, a hall of endless reflections, with neither direction nor distance, their footsteps reduced to soft hushes. The wind whispered messages to the trees, who passed it on with rustling lisps; somewhere a woodpecker drummed echoes and that made Kag blow out his lips and smile.

Drust knew why. The woodpecker was sacred to Mars, and while the she-wolf had nursed the Twins, the woodpecker had brought them food. It was a good sign.

They moved through a colonnaded temple of tall wooden pillars draped and smothered with hanging moss. It rained, sudden and fierce, but they only heard it at first, a snake-hiss in the canopy; later, it filtered through and sifted down on them. The heat sank on them like a blanket; insects pinged and whined, and there was no sun, just a haze of wet heat.

They stopped when Drust thought it might be noon, but Kag was sure he was late by an hour. Not that it mattered, for time itself seemed to creep like the tendrils of steam-mist rising up from the ground; they picked a fallen tree and the stump to perch on, eating twice-baked soaked in the thin wine to make it chewable, then passed round Culleo's hoarded wineskin of good stuff. Drust watched the man lick his lips and scowl; there would come a time, he thought.

'Poor feed this,' Sow growled.

'Go and hunt meat then,' Culleo spat back.

'The *mavro* has a bow – let him do it.'

'He only hunts men,' Dog said, grinning. The truth, Drust knew, was more to do with the dark wood than Manius's choice of victims. It was too enclosed for him, with too much underfoot to let him move quietly; he was a long-shooter from the desert, but here the prey could see and hear him long before he spotted them.

Still, he was adjusting and said so. He would find the Colour here, he said, and when he did – whatever it was – he would merge with the land, become one. Be far away and yet right here. Disappear. Quintus laughed and the rest of the Brothers joined in, making out that this was Manius just putting the frighteners on Culleo and Sow and Hammer. It was short and weak at best; they remembered Sib and how he had called Manius *jnoun*, a desert word for something dark out of Hades. They saw the lean, black-eyed dark man in the shadows and could believe it.

Manius fished in a pouch and came up with a small parcel of leaf made into a neat triangle shaped like a tiny pillow. He held it up and popped it into the corner of his mouth.

'Two left,' he said. No one answered, or looked at him, especially his eyes, which went strange and glassy and darker than ever, so that it was hard to tell where the pupil began. It was a mix that came from his own lands, deep in the desert south of Lepcis, and no one but him knew what was in it, only that the spit from it left a mark like blood.

'How long until we are out of this place?' Hammer wanted to know, his neck sunk down into his shoulders, peering up and round at the trees.

'When we get to the last trees, there we will be,' Ugo offered. 'I thought you were local lads – why so feared of this wood?'

Hammer gave him a sour look. 'They call you German, but I know you are Frisian. They have clumps of trees there but nothing like this. Swamps with small woods is what they have there, I have heard. I was born and raised far to the east of here and right on the edge of a place like this – which is really the same one, stretched out and up and down the mountains and valleys.'

He leaned forward. 'No one went more than a few paces inside, or stayed for long, or went anywhere near it at night. My village built a stockade against what might

41

come out of it. And made offerings to the gods when they cut it back to make more room for crops.'

'Cernunnos, stag-horned hunter, watch over us,' Sow whispered, and Culleo banged a fist on his shoulder.

'Hist on that, clod.'

'Cernunnos,' Ugo echoed suddenly, a bass rumble that tightened everyone's flesh. 'Spine of the Middleworld. Send Blackbird, Keeper of the Gate; Stag of the Seven Tines, Master of Time; Ancient Owl, Crone of the Night; Eagle, Lord of the Air, Eye of the Sun; and Salmon, Oldest of the Old, Wisest of the Wise, leaping from the juncture of the Five Springs. Watch over us.'

He spilled the good wine and not even Culleo made protest against it; a breeze shifted leaves and hissed whispers and no one dared move or breathe. When a bird churred from the depths, Sow whimpered.

Eventually, Kisa blew out his cheeks. 'Well – follow the wind and birds, like your god says.'

He got up and moved, muttering his own prayers, and Dog nodded admiringly at his back.

'Say what you like about that little Jew, he has Jupiter's own balls when he needs them.'

Kag and Praeclarum fell into step with Drust, and he knew they had things to say, so he waited.

'We might be in trouble when we get back,' Kag said eventually, and Drust said nothing. 'We have failed to find this Dragon, failed to recover the standard and lost Asellio and most of his men. It will only take those three to say it was all our fault and then…'

'Why would they?' Praeclarum demanded.

'Save their own hide,' Kag pointed out. 'Officially, Culleo is in charge and he will bring that grievance out from where he has stuffed it for now; he will claim we took over, which is not exactly wrong. He will do it because the Army will blame him otherwise.'

'So?' Praeclarum demanded and Kag spat meaningfully. 'So we kill the three of them before we get back,' she persisted.

Drust thought she was heat-struck a little, for the tone was fiery and she was beaded with sweat; he felt alarm at the idea of her having sucked in a vaporous fever from this dark wood.

'Ho – did I say that?' Kag protested and Praeclarum threw her hands in the air; since one of them held a naked *gladius*, it made the others rear back from the winking edge.

'Steady,' Drust said, and saw her blink and shake drops from her face. She looked pale and violet-eyed.

'I meant,' Kag said soothingly, 'that we might consider going after this Dragon. Talk with him. So we could say we did that, at least.'

'Are you sick?' Drust asked outright, and Praeclarum blew out her cheeks and then gave a short, nervous laugh. 'This place… the heat.'

Drust touched her face, felt the heat and the slick of her. 'We will be out of it soon.'

He turned to Kag. 'We won't be going after any fucking senator who eats his horse and has suborned most of his command into rebellion.'

—

They moved in snake-spurts, single files that shunted one another like a long train of camels and mules when the lead man stopped to take stock of something he didn't like.

43

Then they'd start off, stretching out like ribbon, getting into a space, then shunting to a halt, moving like a slow caterpillar.

It was weary and hot and sweat-drenched. Drust called a halt after two hours and they sank where they were. Manius came up, his teeth etched in scarlet when he grinned; his mouth looked like an old battlefield.

The sun slumped and the land began to lose colour, the virulent greens and stark browns and yellows bleeding out, the shadows creeping like assassins. They squatted, watching the draped moss turn to witch hair, listening to the night and trying to get some rest and food without the betrayal of a fire. Kag and Manius stood watch while the others chewed soaked bread. We will need to get food soon, Drust thought, feeling crushed by the whole affair. Or find a way across the river and avoid all the killers who prowled.

Praeclarum came to him in the cool night and they sat, shoulder to shoulder, listening to the creaks and the wind hiss in the canopy. No one spoke even if they had something to say; a whisper was a scream in this place.

In the velvet black, something small died with big shrieks and owls sang songs of mourning to the blood.

On watch, Drust's eyes felt gritted and he blinked for moisture, not wanting to shake his head, not wanting even that little movement to break him from cover, like a dappled deer moving in a glade. He squatted, alert, sweeping eyes in slow arcs, cutting the dark shadows of trees into sections like a pie, hearing the sound of his own heartbeat, the blood shushing.

He felt a moment of panic, of being watched, and turned his head slowly to it until he finally made out the outline of a vixen, staring hard and motionless like himself. She sat back, fixed her mask with delicate paws like a woman at a mirror, then vanished with a flick of tail. Drust breathed out while his stomach stopped flipping.

This is not our place, Drust thought. This was the Dark, which even the locals shunned save for the blood worshippers who moved boldly here, along trails used and reused and which we can't even find. There are no wolf cries, Drust suddenly realised. Probably no snuffling bears either – they have been hunted out of these woods and most of them are hanging from the shoulders of standard-bearers and horn-blowers of the Army in these parts. Perhaps the wood gods who lurk here will take revenge for that, he thought – and savagely quelled that idea with a fervent prayer to Fortuna.

The others slept, the ones Drust knew well – Ugo and Kag and Dog, his wife, and Manius, the dark-eyed killer. Even Kisa the Jew, who had never been a slave or a gladiator, who had never known what it was to wait in the dark for the cell door to be opened, to not go anywhere you were not ordered, to walk from the dim of the arena undercroft through the Gate of Life into the dazzle of what might be your last day in the world.

What a choice there was, Drust thought. What a sheer cornucopia of things to be afraid of – once he had thought that you would lose your anxiety when you realised how much of it there was, how expensive the worry was on your everyday life. He thought he had succeeded and preened to Kag about the knowledge, the new philosophy – anxiety was a luxury and you couldn't afford luxuries. It was a sad jest at best – the single mutilation, the worst wound any man wanted to avoid was losing their balls.

They'd pray for it – 'Fortuna, hear me, take my eyes, my legs, my hands – take my fucking life, great goddess. But spare those. Spare those…'

Once you get past fearing that…

Kag put me right, Drust remembered, because he knew real philosophy, courtesy of having to sit in class with a high-born squit he was bodyguarding. The squit learned nothing much, but Kag did, for all he could not read nor write.

You are only dealing with things that can kill or maim, he told Drust. What of the rest? You hold yourself responsible for all of us, the Brothers of the Sand, for bringing us safe out of every enterprise. That is the fear you can't kill…

We should be out, Drust thought. We should have pulled out as soon as the decision had been made to close the *castra* gates. Ducked out somehow, left everything and run for the passes back to Italia and fuck the white bear. That nagged him like a hangnail when he had time – like now – to brood on it.

Instead they were here looking for a ford or a bridge or a god who would get them across a river barrier to safety. And Kag wanted to go after this renegade – who was probably dead and certainly mad. Drust sat and felt his hand tremble for a bit, a new affair that he hid from everyone. He wondered if it was now fixed, a part of him, or would stop trembling when he reached true safety. More likely, he thought, years from now I'll be dining with friends, perhaps even family, and suddenly my hand will start to shake, all that old arena muscle remembering what it once was, but only enough to spill wine all over me while the ghosts of the people I failed to bring back looked on, but didn't laugh…

If I have years from now, that is.

There was a movement and a darker shadow rustled up to him, making Drust lurch with sudden panic until he realised it was Manius, come to stand his turn on watch.

'*Omnes ad stercus*,' Manius said, which was the password for the night; his teeth were still blood-lined white in the dim shadows.

'*Sodales, avete*,' Drust responded viciously. 'I almost fucking killed you.'

Manius ignored it, sank down, and even so close he simply seemed to vanish. 'I have found the Colour, I am not here,' said a dreaming voice. 'I'm somewhere else.'

'I know you are,' Drust said, hoping his voice sounded level. 'Keep watch anyway.'

—

Drust was awake to see the sun lance up into dawn through a canopy thick enough to deflect ballista bolts but which could only splinter the light to dapple. He lay, listening to the sleeping Praeclarum puffing through her soft lips, watched the red glow of the sun hit the bark of a tree, sliding slowly up the coarse trunk like an embered fire burned down to a bright crimson wrapped in a yellow glow. It briefly caught a squirrel, changed it to red-gold before the animal flicked off back into the shadows. He listened to a rasping sound, a slight pattering, on edge and wondering until Sow rustled up beside him and sat for a moment, head cocked.

'Badger,' he declared, 'scraping up new bedding. Squirrels cracking hazelnuts, or stripping the bark from

47

branches and letting it fall.' He broke off and frowned. 'Never found out why they do that – they don't eat it, just let it fall.'

Drust looked at him. 'How do you know this stuff?'

Sow shrugged. 'Told you – lived close to the dark wood as a lad. Not to say we weren't feared of it, for we went in a little way now and then – but there are bears and wolves, as you know. Well, not here, because Rome has paid for them all to be hunted out.'

He shifted a little. 'The *mavro* says he can smell something he don't like. That Kag said to come and tell you.'

Drust went to where Manius and Kag crouched in a stand of trees draped with green moss, tendrils of it trailing down; here the canopy was thick and the light made it look as if they were all underwater.

'Smoke,' Manius said as the others gathered, scarcely wanting to breathe aloud let alone speak. Now that he said it Drust could smell it, a mix of sharp woodsmoke – the sort that brought a pang for old comforts – and a harsher char. The memories that brought made the Brothers look from one to the other and it didn't go unmarked.

'What is it?' Culleo wanted to know, the note of his voice rising. Dog laid a surprisingly gentle hand on his shoulder.

'Something to make you stay quiet and soft, like you were trying to catch a monkey.'

Drust didn't think Culleo had ever seen a monkey, but the man got the gist of it all the same.

'Softly catches yer monkey,' Kag added, licking his lips.

Quintus grinned. 'See that? I never understood that. You can never creep up on a monkey – we tried, the gods know it. Down south of the Nile, you remember, lads?

48

You have to knock the little fucker over with a stone or a stick and net it while it's still dazed and on the ground. If you are catching it for the beast masters under the Flavian, that is. If it's just monkey meat, you get Manius and his bow.'

'That how you got your last woman?' Kag spat back. 'She looked like a monkey.'

'My last woman was your old ma,' Quintus whispered back, but he was already peering through the foliage.

Drust's last woman looked at him and smiled, rinsed her mouth with the vinegary wine and spat; he did not like the way she looked but said nothing, just indicated to Manius to lead them out towards the complex smell of cheer and death. The wind was soft, like a thin cry over stormy water, and it came with a sharpness, a hint of something, but so faint Drust couldn't drag out the memory. He glanced at Kag and caught him looking back; he nodded briefly, as if they had agreed something.

They crept on, to where the trees thinned and the grass seemed to rise up to their shoulders – all but Ugo. There were saplings here, but the grass was everything; then Kisa trailed seeds out of it, frowning.

'Some of this is wheat,' he declared and they all got the picture of it – old fields, given back to the woods, but the grass was the predator here, even choking the trees. Insects pinged and hummed and the heat seemed to sizzle; Drust almost wished for the dark shade of the forest they had left.

Then Ugo pointed and everyone squinted towards the misshapen tawny mounds they had thought were old fodder-stacks; they weren't, they were buildings, constructed low to the ground so that their thatched roofs came down almost to touch it.

Old, like the fields, Drust thought, blowing insects off his lips. He saw there was a longhouse, the roofbeam of it broken and sagged in the middle, and the other buildings clustered round it.

'Twenty folk,' Kisa whispered. 'Maybe more.'

'None now,' Manius answered, his voice normal enough to make everyone wince and cringe. 'Save for them.'

There were six, swinging and black with flies which droned up like baleful priests to reveal that the dead wore strip-skirts made from their own flayed flesh. Two were women, but it was hard to tell with the breasts cut off, and the rest were men pout-lipped from their own genitals. All had been there a long time, marbled and desiccated so that one had a leg fallen off.

Another had a piece of bark hung on a cord round the ravaged neck. The crude scrawl read: *Roma Invicta*.

'Here is your Dragon in action,' Praeclarum muttered and spat sideways.

'Weeks old,' Kag pointed out, but the cloud of flies was getting to him and he backed off, spitting and waving.

Culleo stood, arms dangling, his stare black. 'We were happy until the time of Sulla and Marius,' he growled to no one – or perhaps to the dangling dead. 'Then we found out we were barbarians, were naked, sinful and owed allegiance to another world and different gods from another sky.' He scoured them all with his mournful eyes. 'Good of the Romans to let us know.'

'You should watch him,' Kisa whispered like a hissing oracle, arriving at Drust's shoulder as Culleo crept out of earshot.

'The lack of drink has addled him,' Drust answered, though he had no conviction in it. Truthfully, he thought Culleo was infected with the Dark and, even after all his years as a Roman, was feeling old blood urges lurch up in him.

'He has seen the truth of Rome,' Kisa added.

'Which is?' Drust asked, though he was scanning, scanning...

'That the roads that never bend, the marble glories, the Flavian and their like are all impermanent as a dream at the crest of a dune, as if they were born of the cloudless sky. You go out to other folk's lands and force them to want finer shoes and carriages, cheap food from cookshops, free grain to make into free bread, and all they have to do to get it is be a fool in a toga.'

'Fuck you, Kisa – this is what happens when you are fed Greek philosophers.'

Quintus came up and Drust saw him scowl. He had never seen Quintus scowl. 'Rome is eternal,' he growled at Kisa. 'Athens is a goddess, Alexandria is a whore like Babylon, Jerusalem is a spade-beard with a secret knife – but Rome is a solid-chinned man, full of righteous anger and a good meat pie, drinking wine in a *taberna* before he goes out to add to the Empire.'

There was soft laughter and Drust saw the grin reappear on Quintus's gleaming face.

They had never wanted it more, Drust thought, the brick and marble and smoky skies; the cloacal stink of the Tiber and the spiced cookfires of a thousand nationalities.

They wanted to be down in the glow-lit dark of Subura, listening to the shrieks and arguments, the sharp, high cries that might have been deadly argument or fierce sex. Rome was the blare of trumpets and bloody death in the afternoon, the shrieking of women at market, the cries of all humanity, crowded on seven hills crusted with people from all four corners of an Empire spanned by straight roads and Law. They wanted it like a mother's hug.

Rome, Drust thought, is the pulsing heart of the world and would only be brought low by its own self…

'Might as well be a thousand miles away,' Kag grunted when Drust spat some of this out. 'Which is fuck all use to these Romans here.'

'You have to ask,' Praeclarum offered, looking round, 'why they left this message?'

'The Dragon,' Dog growled, 'marking his territory like any midden hound.'

'I understand that,' Praeclarum answered quietly, 'but why here? Look at it – no one has lived here for years. A message is only worth the effort if people see it.'

Drust felt the chill freeze the sweat on him. No one lived here, but people came. They met here, a landmark in a dark wood with no other features. They met here and went raiding… this message from Antyllus had been left for them.

The others had got to it as well, and Dog cursed, then nodded admiringly to Praeclarum. Ugo rolled his shoulders and said: 'eyes on stalks.' Suddenly, everyone felt that they were being watched.

'Manius,' Drust said, and the man raised an arm, then slid out into the tall grass and vanished, leaving only a small blob of blood-red spit.

'He is not here,' Quintus said, wiping his sweaty grin. 'He is far away.'

'His head is up his arse,' Dog answered moodily. 'That stuff he chews will get us all killed.'

Drust doubted it. What would get them killed would be vengeful men with sharp points and edges, and those they met an hour later, stumbling across old walls of thrown-down stones, no more than hip-height where once they had been taller than four men.

'The old frontier of Rome,' Culleo said pointedly. 'Before they pulled it back.'

'A hundred years ago at least,' Quintus said. 'And only a dozen miles of Rome given up. I would not look to seeing your tree-fucking friends at the gates of Rome before the world itself ends.'

'I meant nothing by it,' Culleo muttered. Drust had taken his helmet off to feel a breeze and mop the sweat from the leather lining. He had barely slid it greasily back when his world exploded into a star of light and a noise like he had been the clapper in a bell.

The part of him not muzzed by it said 'arrow' and 'helmet' and he could have sworn Fortuna said 'lucky bastard' in his ear – then Praeclarum hauled him sideways, away from the struggle. Dog and Kag stood shoulder to shoulder, Ugo lurched left and right, and where he carved blood flew, while Quintus danced and stabbed and blocked the blows directed at him.

'Are you here?' Praeclarum asked and Drust scrambled to his feet, weaving slightly and still hearing her voice as if from a long way off. He waved her into the fight and got his *gladius* out, though it felt heavier than it ever had;

since the last fight he had held onto the egg-shaped shield and was glad of it now.

He heard Dog roaring curses at them, saw Manius flitting to the flank, nocking an arrow as he did so. Hammer came reeling out of the tall grass screaming and bloody – the warrior who followed him saw Drust, checked and then lurched on, a spear in one hand and a long shield in the other. He had a silly helmet with horns, slightly askew, but Drust was fighting for sense and the spearman gave a foot-stamping assault, all blinding hand speed, so that the spear whicked and flicked and suddenly the *gladius* was gone.

Drust hadn't felt it leave him, but he managed to block with the shield, the spear smacking and scoring it, making him stagger and fall. The spearman was a plump, pimpled youth with a shock of red hair and a speckle of new beard, which let his triumphant grin show.

I am on my arse here, Drust thought, scrabbling backwards, looking at being skewered by a young ginger pig – he felt something under his fingers, managed to roll away with it when the spear stabbed.

Hammer's hammer, Drust realised wildly. The spearman lunged again and Drust let the point go over him and swung the tent hammer at his ankles, felt it jar, heard the crunch and saw him fall, screaming and writhing.

Drust rolled up to his feet, weaving like a tree in a wind, while the spearman screamed and flapped his empty hands at the white bone and bloody flesh where his shin should have been. Drust beat the man's silly horned helmet as if he worked at a forge making nails. It was poor work, that helmet; the segments split at the seams and blood came out the man's mouth.

There was fire, a sudden flare of heat and smoke and crackle, and Drust heard Kag yelling for everyone to get out of the field, that the grass was alight. He stumbled forward and saw two more spearmen – all beard-braids and slaver – look at him and shriek like girls. He realised he had become their worst nightmare, some great hammer-wielding god with fire and smoke at his back. He laughed; his head was iced but his back was flushed with heat.

The first one went down without so much as raising his spear; the hammer took him in the face with no more resistance than beating in a bird nest. The next waved the spear and tried a jab, but he was looking to run. Drust broke the shaft with one blow and then smacked him on the upswing, and his jaw flew off trailing blood and the middle of his last shriek of terror.

The next two tried to come at him together but one lost heart in it and ran off sideways, throwing away the spear he had in one hand and the torch he had in the other. Drust felled the second with a blow between neck and shoulder that gave a crack like a splitting tree.

There was a moment when he stood, turning this way and that in the smoke, looking for enemies, then Kag stepped up and squinted at him.

'You have Fortuna's own blessing at your call,' he said and pulled off Drust's helmet, handing it to him. 'I saw you put that war hat on an instant before the arrow struck it. One eyeblink slower and Praeclarum would be counting the inheritance.'

Drust laughed. Kag laughed. They stood, leaning against another and choking with smoke-wracked laughter until they saw Kisa kneeling beside Hammer. Drust became aware of the clotted horror he held and felt guilty about having made such a mess on it.

'Is he hurt?'

Which was the question of a *stupidus* from the Atellan Farces when you looked at where Hammer had clamped both hands on the open slash across his belly, as if he could hold in the blue-white entrails. He hoped so hard that his fingers had kept the grip even in death, and Kisa confirmed it when he looked up, blank-faced, and shook his head.

Culleo spat. Sow gave a low whimpering moan but no one else said much save Dog, who pointed out it might be a good idea to put some distance between them and the fire. They shifted away, leaving Sow and Culleo to ransack Hammer for anything useful, as if it was their right and no one else's.

'This one is alive,' Dog said suddenly, toeing a body; it moaned. Kag and Ugo hauled the man upright, where he stood, leaking blood from wounds on his head and arms. He was young and dark-haired, neatly cropped, clean-shaven. Drust saw the blood all over his tunic and the *braccae*, those trousers the northmen wore, loose and eye-watering with colour, tied at the ankles. He saw the man's scored shield lying nearby, an egg-shape of green and gold designs exactly like another not far away. Even the ginger pig, leaking blood from under his eyelids, was a Roman in a bad helmet.

The smoke stung eyes and the man hung between Ugo and Kag, limp and muttering, as Dog called Culleo and Sow to him.

'Ask him who they are and if there are any more.'

Culleo spat. 'They are from the Dark. They worship blood and should die...'

Drust slapped his shoulder, then looked pointedly at Dog and indicated the shields. The man's head lolled.

'He is no woodlouse,' Drust said. 'He is Roman – look at him.'

'Fortuna's fat tits, so he is,' Kag growled and slapped the man on his shoulder. 'Roman, are you? Speak up, you snail slime.'

'I am Roman, of the Ala Flavia,' the man said, puffing blood from his smashed lips. 'General Antyllus is a fount of mercy and bountifulness; be a source of mercy and bountifulness to him. If you will be such, you will find salvation. Otherwise you can go fuck a pig.'

Drust paused, considering; he needed information but thought this man wasn't about to give any. He looked round to where everything seemed to be burning and thought it might be a better idea to quit this place. Everywhere was shrieking and burning now.

The man spat, weak and bloody; it trailed down his chin.

'All the tribes of the Dark are out,' he managed in a voice like a soft sigh. 'They are coming – but we are *Roma Invicta*. Our anger is like fire. It burns it all clean. We are coming like fire...'

'You are a traitor, according to what we've heard,' Quintus said and shook the man. 'Roman – where is your famous general, Antyllus?'

'Bitterness is a god that gnaws its master,' the trooper said and then grinned bloodily at them. 'The Dragon is coming and he will bring the light of Mithras to the Dark... I am raven. I am the flame.'

'The Dragon has already tried with the fire thing,' Ugo grunted, looking at the flames and billowing smoke. 'Not very good, is he?'

'I remember a saying,' Dog said suddenly, picking up an extinguished torch and moving to where the flames flickered; they were growing too close, Drust thought.

'Make a fire for a man and he'll be warm for a day?' Kisa suggested scathingly. Dog laughed and ran the torch round the hem of the lolling Roman's tunic.

'Set a man on fire and he will be warm for the rest of his life.'

Kag and Ugo leaped back with curses, letting the man collapse, burning and shrieking, to the ground. He tried to get up and run, but his sinews were twisting and he simply flailed around, screaming through the flames until they ate his voice.

'Jupiter's fat cock, Dog – who pissed on your shoes?' Kag snarled, but Drust was sick of the heat and the flames and pork-sizzle stink of the man dying in fire.

'Manius – scout ahead. The rest of you, head west. Let's get out of this blood wood once and for all.'

They moved. 'Where's Praeclarum?' Drust asked, and when no one replied, asked it again.

There was no point in a third time; no one knew and she had simply vanished.

Chapter Three

He was cold, all the sweat on him a chill grease of fear and panic. Yet Drust burned with a furious anger and a need to be up and running after her, wherever she was, whatever direction, pick one, he would find her… The act of sitting still, fighting to think, trembled him in spasms, made him tighten his hands to fists so that the inked letters on his knuckles were stark against the clench.

They came to him silently. Dog laid a hand on his shoulder, Quintus on the back of his neck like he was a hound in need of calming. Ugo patted him briefly, awkwardly, then growled off to stand nearby, waiting like a fretting horse.

Kag knelt in front of him, forcing Drust to focus and look into determined eyes. 'We will get her back,' Kag said, putting out his hand, fingers splayed to show his own tattooed knuckles – E-S-S-S. *Ego sum servus Servillius* – I am a slave of Servillius. All slaves were marked somewhere and even freedom would not make these disappear; you lived with them either by hiding them, or wearing them like a curled lip. There were no hidden markings here.

Culleo and Sow looked on, squatting and sweating and uneasy. Angry, too.

'She's dead,' Culleo said harshly, and Ugo kicked him hard enough to set him rolling, but he climbed to his feet and glared against a backdrop of burning and black smoke.

'If they took her at all and she's not still lying dead in the grass,' he persisted, 'then she is dead now. They will slit her throat—'

'These are not your beast men of the Dark,' Kisa argued hotly. 'These are Romans.'

'Where's Manius?' Drust demanded, and Kisa jerked round to look at him, blinking sweat from his eyes.

'He went to look for signs,' he said. 'Do not listen to this one – we searched all around and did not find her. They took her, and if so, they meant it, so she lives. These are Romans.'

'Romans,' Sow declared and nodded grudgingly. 'Perhaps – but I am betting sure everyone here has seen what Romans can do with a woman in a war.'

'They meant it,' Kisa persisted, scowling. 'They came for her.'

'They came to snatch a woman?' Culleo countered incredulously.

'To take one of us prisoner,' Kisa corrected. 'And so alive, or why bother at all?'

'Why would they do that?' Quintus asked, but no one had an answer to it, even though Drust used the conundrum of it to whirl the gears in his head and stop them telling his legs to run. Then Manius came back, sweat-gleamed and dark as smoke.

'Four heading north,' he said. 'No mark I can recognise as Praeclarum, but they may be carrying her – the ground is not soft enough to tell her foot from another. There is blood, all the same, so someone is leaking.'

'Told you,' Culleo said and then scrabbled backwards as Ugo took a step.

'Lead the way,' Drust said, letting a little of his rage out as he rose. Culleo gave a growl and stood up.

'You want to follow these? Further into the Dark? The way to safety lies westward...'

'Then take it. We go north,' Kag spat and Culleo flung down his helmet.

'Hammer lies a little way off with a hole through him you couldn't block with your ink-marked fist, but no one here cares a fuck for that. Oh, no – we are all to charge off in pursuit of one of your own, the doxy of your leader—'

Ugo sprang surprisingly quickly for a big man and Culleo had no chance other than to yelp before he was hauled up into the squinting grimace that was Ugo's face.

'I will crush your skull until the inside pops out,' he rumbled and then stopped because a blade was at his neck. When he followed it, he found a determined Sow at the other end.

'Let him down, giant. Too many of the Batavii have died on this enterprise.'

'Do it,' Drust ordered, feeling the angry burn at this delay. 'Kag – give them water and bread enough to get them on their way.'

'Alone?' Sow demanded.

'Your choice,' Kag answered. 'We go north.'

Sow sheathed the sword and blew out his cheeks, then looked at Culleo. 'Not much choice, is there? Die west or die north.'

'I am working on a new way,' Culleo answered, massaging where Ugo had gripped him, the sweat-spikes of his hair ragged as his scowl. 'Called not dying at all.'

Ugo wiped his palms down his tunic and nodded admiringly at Sow. 'You have large bags, little man – but if you point that sticker at me again I will take it from you and use it to remove those large bags.'

'Well, you have to get a pair from somewhere,' Sow answered, staring back.

Kag thrust out his hand, knuckles up and fingers splayed. One by one, the others who knew of this added their hands until, finally, Kag looked at Sow and Culleo.

'You have your own marks somewhere – the idiot ones you Army farts always get. *SPQR* on a shoulder blade, where an *optio* can't see it on parade. *Roma Invicta* across the belly – which is fine when you have one flat and hard, a lot less so when it swells with retirement. No matter – you are no different from us.'

'Former slaves?' Culleo spat, his face a bag of blood. 'Gladiators? I never was a slave – and I am a soldier of Rome, not some fancy-dancing Greek poncing around in an amphitheatre.'

'You were once Helvetii,' Drust answered harshly, 'and now deny them. Your father's father and beyond belonged to a Roman, for sure, until one of your breed worked out what a spoon was for, crawled up a notch and made himself free. Now you have taken that inheritance, marked yourself with the insignia of the Rome you have enslaved yourself to, and deny you were ever anything else.'

He thrust out his own hand, the letters seemingly more stark than usual. 'This is how a slave is made – not birth, not breeding, not any whim of Mars Ultor or the carved gods of this blood wood. A pound of Egyptian pinewood bark, two ounces of corroded bronze, two ounces of gall, an ounce of vitriol. Add anger and pain and humiliation as you will. Mix well and sift, wash knuckles with leek juice, prick in the design with pointed needles until blood is drawn. Then rub in the ink.'

He looked at them all, one face at a time. 'You either show them or hide them.'

'Brothers of the Sand,' Dog said, 'forged in a ring.'

One by one the others repeated it while Culleo and Sow looked on, wondering why the heat had gone out of the day and their skin crawled as if under a chilled wind.

–

They made plans between kisses. About coming out of Subura and living as husband and wife in the light, so it was right that they ended up strolling like they were ordinary people and planning the wedding under the Colossus Solis.

Drust liked the shade of old Nero's narcissism. Vespasianus Augustus had sensibly added a rayed crown to the head and renamed the giant affair Colossus Solis, but it was still old Nero, naked and as tall as twenty men, leaning on a pedestal and holding a rudder piercing a globe, though few people knew why.

Praeclarum was fretted by the Vestal whose fate was about to be sealed in a tomb, the proper punishment for having betrayed your vows. She thought the Vestal had been punished enough and did not like the idea of their own future paid for by the price of bringing the woman, once an Empress, back to Rome to die.

Two boys fell past Drust, pushing and shoving one another, laughing. An elegance of perfume and kohl swayed on her way, heading for the fetid dim of the Flavian's pillars. Hucksters selling seats for twice the price, thieves, sausage sellers – all human life was there, and some that didn't look as if it was. They poured in from the suburbs and outlying farms to make money or lose it but determined to enjoy themselves. For a moment he felt at one with it, a glorious commune with what it meant to live in the whole of the City instead of the lowest, darkest part of it. He was them and they were him...

Except for the grim men who came from four points round Drust. He knew them at once – hired men, hard men. It did not matter why, for there were too many who held grudges or wanted vengeance. You could not leave Subura because no matter where you went, you dragged it with you.

The four thugs closing in on them was the truth, all of it, right there, and they stood, sucked dry of dreams and fumbling for weapons they did not have.

There was a flurry and one of the men went down, people ebbing away from the affair like ripples from a thrown stone. Ugo, grinning, kicked the downed man in the head while his mates turned to stare. Another went down and Kag was there with a wooden cudgel. A third yelped and fell when Quintus cracked both sides of his knees with an expert wrist flick and a wooden training sword.

'Move,' said Dog, grinning at them both as the last man fled from his unveiled face. 'I hear there is a wedding and Great Solis's shadow has brought your family to celebrate.'

He woke into twilight, had a moment of confusion about bulk and shadow until he sorted it out – the bulk was a fallen tree and the shadows were using it for shelter and concealment, a cold camp of whispers and little movement.

Manius had found it when the light grew too bad to track further and Drust had looked at the big tree, an oak which had finally given up the fight against wind and age. The roots had been ripped out of the ground, clutching desperately at earth and stones, and now showed the bones of the ground-world. How deep do roots go in this forest?

He laid his cheek against the loam and the cool moss, felt the deep, searing panic of her loss, of where she was, how she was…

Owls and the moon paired up in the killing of voles and shrews, the unseen birds sounding their flute-notes, such a soothing thing for a murder. Somewhere a fox screamed and something small and in terror shrieked; this whole forest was a slaughter.

He rose and made himself move from shape to shape, sometimes speaking a word or two, mostly just letting his own shadow fall on them, let them know he was there. He got responses, from a grunt to a querulous note from Kisa.

'Problem?'

The man was hesitant and wanted to say something; Drust felt a barbed hook of unease.

'Praeclarum,' he said, and Drust felt the hook twist.

'What woman calls herself "Remarkable"?' Culleo's sullen voice was too loud and Dog made him aware of it by thrusting his horror of a face out of the shadows; Culleo shrank and muttered.

'She is called that because she is that,' Dog growled, and Drust blinked once or twice, frankly amazed. Dog had always been the one who spat and clawed and fought any of Drust's attempts to make them finer than they had started out. He had wanted to be leader at one time – Drust was not sure that ambition was cold or still smouldered.

'They are all like that,' Sow added, laying a hand on Culleo's shoulder. 'Dog here is a man who had his face ink-marked in pursuit of a woman, I heard. Quintus and Kag and Manius and Ugo are all long-time *harena* fighters

– you know how the Legion changes you, Culleo? The amphitheatre is the same, I suspect.'

'Never saw a woman fight in it,' Culleo said. 'Don't seem right.'

'Isn't now,' Ugo said, coming up on the talk as if it was a fire. 'Old Severus Augustus put a stop to it and not before time – women weren't trained right, didn't fight right. Slaughtered *tiro* dwarves or the unarmed condemned. Got put in naked mostly, so the sweaties in the crowd could see tits and cunt.'

He leaned forward a little, his face seeming to shine like a small moon. 'But she is better now. A proper woman, married and everything. Done right – we were all there. We are all better because of it...'

He tailed off because that was as much as he could manage about how he felt. Kag laid a hand on his shoulder.

'Is anyone on watch?' Drust asked drily, but he was filled with the glow of them, as if he sat at a fire.

Birds stopped them midway through the next morning, just as they filed out in a half-crouch of sweating anxiety, clenched as curls, into where the trees thinned and the ground dipped. The birds wheeled in easy spirals, swooping down suddenly then soaring up again. Higher still were lazier shapes against the sun-dazzled sky, looking like black crosses endlessly falling.

There was a long slide of open land, a clearing maybe used as grazing once but now overrun with a choke of shrubs, old stumps sprouting new saplings. They squatted and tallied it up, each man making his point based on what he saw.

'Ravine,' said Kag, 'where that line of green is. Land runs down to it from here and it is tight-fitted with trees, which means water.'

'Maybe this is where the river narrows,' Kisa offered, but Quintus looked at the sun and then the slope and shook his head.

'Unlikely – we are strayed too far north now. This is a feeder stream.' He added a grin to sugar the disappointment. 'We could follow it, find the main river and a way across.'

'Birds is on something dead,' Ugo added, and Manius wiped his dark, greased face and agreed.

'Maybe a dead deer,' he said, 'maybe not. But they made us find them, and if we can…'

Then others can too, Drust finished to himself. He looked at the shape of the land, the thickness of the trees all around and in the ravine, worked out how long it would take to traverse it and how best to do it. All the time a part of him was shrieking at what they might find there.

Loving her had been fiery and full and I should have been well happy, Drust thought, with her and me both. Instead, I was fretted by the idea that the gods laughed at what the pair of us imagined would be our life together. There was something about it all made my heart thunder, he thought, and it wasn't joy, it was fear. Our lives trembled, always at the edge of something terrible.

The ravine was gentle, the moss and rocks of it embedded to make descent and climb-out easy; the riverbed was dry, rotted with fallen trees and choked with thorn which they had to hack through. The depth of it held the heat, sultry and thick with dead air, where insects seemed barely able to fly.

Up on the far lip of it, they emerged sweating and gasping into a copse of birch and a clotted undergrowth of tangled branches and roots which seemed to claw upwards like dead fingers. The birds flapped off, all of them crows and rooks and black kites, voicing harsh displeasure.

The body was easy to find, shrouded by a veil of clouded insects which broke and scattered reluctantly in angry humming; Manius bent to it, though people wondered at how he suffered the stink. Drust did too, but no one wondered at that and they all held their breath for that reason as much as the smell and the flies.

Not her. The relief of it almost made Drust keel over, but he managed to fight the swimming in his head and stood up.

It was a man in a linen tunic and trousers gathered at the ankles, yet he wore Army boots. The shoulders and back of the tunic were thick with black runnels of old blood and what had been done to him after that was by beak and talon.

He had nothing else on him, but the ruined face had a clear line across the forehead, so far ignored by the birds when they went for his eyes, which marked where sun and weather had not reached because of his helmet.

'They took helmet and weapons and anything else he carried,' Manius confirmed, waving away flies. He spat one out. 'Left his *signaculum*. Lucius Claudius Silanus, five feet seven, *Ala II Flavia pia fidelis milliaria*.'

He rooted around in the leather pouch and produced a fold of papyrus, handed it to Drust.

It was decent stuff, not the coarse fibres for everyday, and had been much folded so that it was cracked along the creases and the already faded words were even harder to read. In the end, Drust passed it to Kisa.

'That's a good cut,' Ugo said almost mournfully as he peered at the corpse. 'That's the slice of a *gladius*.'

'Praeclarum was fighting,' Kag replied. 'The lad did well to keep moving this far then, giant of the Germanies.'

Culleo went to the body and everyone assumed he was looking for loot, but he didn't stay long and came back flapping flies from around his head and spitting.

'I remember him,' he said. 'One of those fancy boys who rode out with our rogue general.'

Drust and Kag exchanged glances which said the same – why are men of this Roman renegade going to the trouble of lifting a woman from them, like she was a prized mare?

'This is a letter from a sweetheart,' Kisa said sadly, carefully refolding it. 'Lucia wonders why she hasn't heard from her darling and is worried because his last letter was so strange.'

She would wonder and worry for only a little longer, Drust thought, and for a brief moment shared the grief of her loss before throwing it savagely from him. Praeclarum is not dead, he raged to himself – *quando tu Gaius, ego Gaia*. Where you are Gaius, there am I Gaia – her traditional vow at the wedding, with her fake pearled teeth making her smile brilliant and her wreath of flowers making her chap-cheeked face a glory to him.

'This is not the right man,' Manius said, his voice dull as old pewter; he wiped his face with a swift gesture, shaking his head. 'They left this one because he slowed them down – there is another, wounded but not badly enough to stop them moving. This one has been dead for an hour, no more.'

'How can you tell that?' Culleo scoffed, and Manius favoured him with his black-eyed stare.

'The birds have not had time to do more damage and they would not come until he was dead and alone. His colleagues stayed until he died, then stripped the body and went on. Left his *signaculum* so those who found him and could read would know he was Roman and a soldier. They are an hour away.'

Culleo had nothing left to say, but Drust looked hard at Manius. 'Can you follow the right trail?'

Manius looked uneasy, on the verge of a lie. Then he nodded. 'I still have the Colour.' He uncoiled and loped off, looking for tracks.

Sow wiped his streaming face and looked at the sky through the thinned branches to the clouds building up to hide the sun.

'Getting cooler too,' he offered. 'So it's all good.'

Ugo patted him like a wayward hound. 'Praise day at evening, a weapon when tried, a maid when married, ice when it has been crossed, and wine when it has been drunk.'

It was a rutted old saying he trotted out now and then, claiming it to be part of his Frisian past, and they all knew it well. Well enough for Drust to appreciate that Ugo had been quick-witted enough to miss out the part of it which said, 'a wife when dead'.

Chapter Four

The blessing of cloud, like all god-gifts, quickly became a curse. It grew dark and even more sultry, until suddenly a wind rushed in without warning, storming through the trees with a sound like surf. Then the air trembled with the deep drum of thunder, and Ugo looked up, spread his arms wide, each with a *dolabra* at the end, and called out 'Wōðanaz'.

Culleo and Sow edged away from him, and when the first dazzling blast lit the world into stark relief, they edged even further. Drust was blinking – they all were, for the light had seared through the eyelids.

Not long after, the rain started but not as sheets. It came down in a shroud of grey-white, a soaking mist that cut vision down to vague shapes, even when the sky flashed.

Manius lost the trail, confessing that the rain and the dark and the mist had made it impossible. Movement was also impossible, so they hunkered down, close together for the warmth, and waited it out, panting and whimpering like a pack of wild dogs. In the end they could not tell whether it was day or night.

After too long a time, the mist sank to snake coils in and out of the trees and that let them see through the murk of what was, they realised, a dying day. Manius moved off again, the milk-mist swirling as he passed; the thunder still growled, but the flashing had died.

'I wish the sodding rain would,' Kag muttered when Ugo mentioned the latter as a gift from Wōðanaz, and the big man nodded drips off his shaggy eyebrows, frowning.

'He will make it by and by – you should be patient. And more appreciative.'

Kag smacked him on the arm, raising splashes from the sodden cloth. 'You need to remember you spent almost all your life in a slave cell or Subura. You have been getting far too friendly with the tree gods up here, giant of the Germanies. Next thing you will be wearing a necklace of skulls and dancing round bloody altars.'

'You are thinking of the *harena*,' Ugo responded, scowling. 'The only Germans you saw there were big men wearing such silly danglers as skulls on chains and blond wigs. Most of them were not German at all but Gauls pretending to be what the Flavian fondly believes are Germans. Most of the real Germans never made it as far as the *harena*; they were strangled in Triumphs for generals.'

Quintus gave a mock moan at the memory. 'This must be the time of the Victoriae Caesaris,' he said. 'We always had a good time around then.'

'You forget much,' Dog spat back. 'Does "good time" include the undercroft of the Flavian, waiting to fight? Watching friends die?'

Quintus realised the marsh he had walked into and fell silent. Octavian's Games in Honour of Caesar's Victory had become an annual event, with a festival to honour Venus Genetrix, Caesar's patron deity and divine matriarch of the Julian family. The festival, with food and wine and access to women, was what Quintus had remembered – but it was those Games, Drust recalled, that had seen too many of their brothers dragged off by the heels through the Gate of Death. The Emperor was rich enough to pay for deaths.

Manius came back, sliding in through the mist which came up to his waist and swirled round him like a cloak, so that Drust had a moment of cold chill at the sight of him, eldritch as a wraith. He told of old walls and a tower and led them to it while the rain sifted down, soft as baby hair.

Drust felt eyes and he was not alone in that; they were all scratched by them and even the sudden soft wind that blew away insects and offered the balm of the rain failed to make them easier. They stopped, keeping shields and weapons up as they turned their ravaged faces to the wet and grinned. The fortress loomed like a black scowl, but there was nothing watching them save a frown of hunched-up crows.

The fortlet was small, no more than four walls and a high tower, but it was stone and so the fires that had been made in it had eaten the wood and only blackened the rest. It was not the first time this had been done, for the walls had collapsed in old ruins in places, replaced by earthworks topped with pointed stakes, so old they now had moss.

The main gates were gone and there had been stables inside and probably a bakehouse and cookhouse, but they were tumbled into the courtyard they had once surrounded – a chestnut tree had grown up to twice the height of a man and torn apart the stones.

The roof of what had probably been a main hall had collapsed when its timber frame burned away, but the tower had arched stone supports on its six floors and was all intact, save for the doors. There was a faded inscription above one, a dedication – *To Mars Victor the First Cohort of Breucorum under the command of Titus Caninius a.u.c. 874.*

'This place is a hundred years old and more,' Kisa said in a low breath, as if he feared to move even the air. Drust was not surprised – the whole place stank of musty stone and old death.

'Those Breucorum lads were up on the Wall in Britannia,' Dog pointed out, running his calloused fingers along the inscription after tearing free the moss and vines. 'Didn't get much relief when they moved from here.'

No one laughed, because they were now here and looked like staying. 'Now I am sleeping in a charcoal pit,' Culleo spat moodily.

'It is not a good place,' Sow agreed, hugging his drenched cloak as he turned this way and that. 'The dead are here.'

Drust had no time for any of them now and was flustered and frustrated by the collapse of their attempt to close in on Praeclarum's kidnappers – an hour, by the gods. Just an hour away from them…

'The dead are here,' Ugo echoed, looking around and up, and that finally sparked Drust.

'Good,' he snarled. 'Go find them and ask them something useful – call on Woden-arse if all else fails.'

It was harsh – more than he had intended. Ugo looked steadily back at him with the agate eyes of a dog kicked once too often until they were hard to meet.

Kag said, 'Come, giant of the Germanies – let's see if we can find a part of this ruin with enough roof for shelter.' Ugo nodded, hefted his twin *dolabrae* to rest on each shoulder and moved off. It was only when he was twenty paces away that Drust let his breath out.

I have seven men, Drust thought, and a woman who belongs with us. They were grim and strong, but like a team of mules who had to be cajoled, forced or lured into moving in the same direction on the one purpose.

We've been lucky, Drust thought. A crew who'd come out of the ring alive, even if they had never been in the top rankings – probably because of it, since that was where the deaths were most paid for. Surviving being taken by Rome as mewling babes had been a gift from the gods, surviving the childhood that followed had been a dice game, and even when freed, their life afterwards had been a stumble from one miracle to another.

On the surface, they had always looked like oak-hard dirty swords, which hid almost all of the finer truth beneath. But now even the surface was melting into grey streaks and lines and muscle gone stringy. He watched them moving purposefully, sorting gear, making a camp – all the worn business that they could do and still keep the edges of their eyes on the forest and what might come out of it. They were all ripped and decayed under layers of dull mud, all that old dust turning to silt rivulets, leather bleached out.

'You feeling fine?'

Kag was trying to be offhand, but the concern showed like blue veins and Drust could see why; here I am, the man they have followed for years, the one they've relied on to get them out of this shit, and I am standing like an ox in a slaughterhouse, staring into the misted wood with eyes like peeled eggs.

He grinned and lied, but he was not feeling fine. I will never be feeling fine again, he thought, even when Praeclarum is back with me, because the feeling of her loss will always be there and will colour me for the rest of my days. He would not put her at risk again – yet what else could he and she and the others do to make a life?

Drust had nowhere to go and was just realising it.

They found a dry spot and made a fire, for they were all sure that they were watched, and so warmth, hot food and a dry place to sleep was a blessed luxury from Fortuna. What the watchers would do was what occupied them as they huddled round the fire, hoping their own watchers were better.

'Well,' said Kag, 'they have her secure now, for sure. I cannot see them coming down on us for slaughter – else why run off with Praeclarum at all? She was a target.'

'Why?' Ugo asked, fretting his brows. 'It makes no sense. Romans took her – I cannot see what for.'

'Sacrifice,' Culleo said flatly, and Kag nudged him hard.

'Spare no feelings, why don't you? We are all stones here.'

'Not sacrifice,' Kisa added scornfully. 'Even the barbarians would not bother with that. Oh, they would nail all our heads to a tree once they had beaten us in a fight. But swooping in and running off with a woman? Not sacrifice.'

'What else?' demanded Sow. 'Though I agree with the little Jew.'

'Trade,' Kisa said, looking at Drust and shifting uneasily. 'Perhaps this Dragon wants to get us to go home and leave him alone.'

Quintus grinned his steel-trap grin. 'He does not need Praeclarum to do that. He has a great many men. He could swat us like flies. Besides, he must have seen that we were going south before he rushed us.'

'Then he wants something else,' Drust said, staring at the fire, his eyes blinded by flames. We are traders and no matter what we carry, what we deal in, it is always about desire…

They talked round it for a long time while the guards changed, but no one could work out what it was. All that was decided before sleep took them was that they would stay here; sooner or later the Dragon would let them know.

Drust sat for a long time while the fire sank to embers. He stared at the dark now, thinking of her out there, and only broke his stare from it when a shadow shifted to join him. To his surprise, he saw it was Kisa.

'She will be unarmed. Angry, but unhurt,' Kisa said. Drust agreed – he did not think she would be cold or wet, but she was alone.

There was a heartbeat and an intake of breath from Kisa that made Drust's heart flip; he looked at the shadowed face, saw the eyes fretted with concern and… secrets.

'She is not alone,' Kisa said.

She is not alone. Kisa had used the traditional phrase – 'I am not alone' – that Roman wives used to announce a pregnancy to their husbands, and Drust was stunned by it, the whole idea of it, so much so that he forgot entirely that Kisa must have known this for a long time and said nothing. When he exploded with it, everyone else came up, concerned and wary.

'It was not my place to say,' Kisa argued, spreading his hands, his face miserable. 'It was for Praeclarum. She spoke to me only because she thought I had some way of telling if it was male or female.'

'So she could announce you were to have a son,' Ugo added, seeing it at once. 'A very great matter.'

Jewish magic, Drust thought wildly. He looked at Kisa. 'Did you?' he asked and his voice sounded hoarse and somehow not his own. A kidnapped Praeclarum was one thing. A kidnapped Praeclarum with child – my child, he thought, was entirely another. Kisa shook his head and shrugged.

Dog stood stolid as a post, but Drust could see his scathe even from deep in the pits of those skull eyes. Dog did not have to say a thing and Drust would have had no reply to it if he had.

He set them to clear the courtyard, helped cut small trees to make a good log barrier at the gate and another for the tower, which is where they would all lair.

All the time he was remembering long ago, remembering the fighter from the group calling themselves Amazon, the dark dusty ruin she had lain in, whimpering and writhing as she spilled her half-made babe into the dust. While the *medicus* went to his elbows in her gore trying to save her, he marvelled at how a slave *gladiatrix* had managed to conceive at all, let alone carry it this far.

Yet Praeclarum wasn't a slave and she was longer in the *harena*, Drust thought, so there is a chance she will be a mother. And I will be a father.

The revelation washed over them all, left them all changed. Dog sat silent in his disapproval, saying nothing but making it clear he thought it a clear vindication of all the warnings about gladiators and women.

'You drank a bucket of Falernian at the wedding,' Quintus pointed out, suddenly and with no seeming reason, but no one needed context.

'An excuse to drink a bucket of Falernian,' Dog replied sourly. 'Any will do.'

'You kissed her,' Kag added with a wry twist of smile, 'and she let you, which was good of her, given the face that loomed too close. You wished her well, long life and happiness.'

'Convention,' Dog muttered. Then he realised Drust was listening and looked like Death ashamed. 'I do not mean you ill, Drust, but a mind is distracted when you have someone else you care for more than yourself. You get dangerous. You take risks – witness this, where we have charged after a pack of wolves, right to where they want us to be.'

'A killing ground,' Manius said blackly from the shadows. Ugo growled at him.

'Why go to all this trouble and then kill us all? They could have done that anywhere.'

'They knew our mission,' Kisa said suddenly, and glanced meaningfully at Culleo and Sow. 'Someone informed.'

'You, being the prince of informers, would know all about it,' Culleo spat back. '*Frumentarius*.'

'The entire *castra* leaks like a rotten aqueduct,' Kag answered soothingly. 'Besides – if you believe Culleo did it, ask yourself why he is here, in the cold and wet and danger with everyone else.'

There was silence, then Quintus said, 'What do you think, Drust?'

Drust felt as if he was someone else, floating above his own body listening to the owls call.

'I think I will be a father,' he said in a slow, blissed grin of a voice. He turned to Kisa. 'If your Jewish magic worked, never tell me what she carries.'

'We will find out soon enough,' Kag echoed grimly. 'When we get her back.'

They ate around fires made with wood that barely smoked, but no one thought it much mattered now. They wanted to be found, they wanted Praeclarum back and they had chased the men who took her to here.

Sow sat with a knife he had put a better edge on and shaved his head until he looked like a thumb from the back, while Culleo watched, trembling now and then with the lack of decent drink. Drust liked Sow with his new-shaved head and quiet calm. He was considered to be more of a local than Roman back in the *castra*, but he was no woodsman at all; as Kag said, he'd get lost crossing the forum of any Roman town.

Now he looked as grim and blood-dyed as the rest of us, Drust thought, but everyone knew he slept badly, had heard his dreams of the forest dead crawling up to him with eye-gouging knives. Manius had some of that, but his worst fear was being woken up in a hurry and slashing a friend to ruin with one of the knives he always had in his fist while he slept. He was also drifting off, or so Kag said, and Drust knew what he meant. Still alert as a wind-chime, Manius would spit blood from his chewing leaf, look at you with eyes like holes in darkness and tell you how he was far away. Manius could smell the enemy and went scouting because of it; so far, the talent had not let him down, but even he knew that it would, this day or the next.

Quintus was still a tall man, still with the grace of a long-legged spider soft-stepping through the woods, and age had not wrecked all of that yet, nor stopped his grin.

There were the others – Kag with his dark, wet, nervous eyes, always looking for a way out, a way round, an angle. Kisa, who trembled at the idea of anything to do with fighting, who gave every sign of being the rankest coward – yet he had followed them in and out of every terror.

He was like all of us, Drust thought, the Brothers whose footprints were filled with blood. A man can walk this life and laugh through chattering teeth, but if he has any sense at all, he knows fortune cannot last and only the gods will help them in the end.

He wondered where Praeclarum was and how she fared and offered impossible promises to any god who would keep her safe.

Chapter Five

The forest beyond their ruined walls was a brooding of shade and morning dapple. It was more of the Dark, the trees like pillars in a temple, the bird calls sinister, even the fluting of woodpigeon seemed mournful. When they stopped, however, everyone gripped weapons and watched, crouched and curled behind shields.

A slap of wings brought down leaves and the pigeon that made it fled from the new moving shapes filtering in knots and clumps through the trees until they were a good bowshot away. There they stopped, a man-length apart, shields up and weapons ready. They had good helmets and ring-coats, spears and swords; the shields, Drust saw, were battered and needed the green and gold laurels touched up, but it was the design the *Ala II Flavia pia fidelis milliaria* had always used.

'No horses,' Ugo said, a statement of the glaringly obvious that made everyone look at him and Dog snort with derision.

'Well spotted,' he said and Quintus turned to him, grinning.

'Look – all neat in their ranks, like they would if they did have horses.'

Drust saw it was true – they had spaced themselves to allow for the horse. Kag laughed and shook his head.

'Well, we have them where we want them. Now their horses have gone, who will do the thinking for them?'

Kag simply crouched, hands on his knees, and sang softly in Greek. No one else understood much of it save the refrain, which was '*erreto, erreto, erreto.*' Kag had told them it meant 'let it go to Hades' and the song was about some contrite Greek warrior from long ago who had left his shield with his courage and legged it during a battle; now he mourned the loss of both.

'*Erreto* to all of them,' Dog muttered.

'They look fierce enough,' Sow agreed, scrubbing his lengthening stubble with worry. To everyone's surprise, Culleo hawked up a greasy gob and spat it sideways.

'I have chewed tougher mutton than these.'

It made them laugh, a sound as feral as slavering wolves, but Drust watched as a bigger knot of men stepped closer, to where a decent shout would drift to them. They surrounded a man in bronzed ring mail and a helmet with two large yellow plumes and a face mask, a bronzed, shiny likeness of a smooth-cheeked youth. He was draped in a cloak the colour of old wine – all scrollwork and plumes – and beside him walked a standard-bearer holding a pole with a long *draco* of green metal lappets and silk. It would have been more impressive, Drust thought, if they'd been riding hard enough to make a wind catch it and make it dance.

'The Dragon,' Kisa breathed, but Drust had no time for him; he was searching, eyes like frantic squirrels, for any sight of her. Found none.

'The Dragon wants to talk,' Kag said. 'Now the dance begins.'

Drust heard it, but it meant little – his belly lurched sickeningly and ice formed in the sweat down his spine. The man with the standard raised it high and cleared his throat.

'Marcus Antonius Antyllus Augustus, Vir Ementissimus, Defender of Rome.'

'Oh fuck,' Kisa said. Drust looked quizzically at him and Kisa bowed his head and sighed wearily.

'They're about to throw purple over him,' Kag said grimly. 'Salute your new Emperor, lads – at least until the Legions get to him and make him a god.'

'No wonder they wanted him dead,' Quintus said and they watched as the Dragon stepped out of the ruck of guards and peeled off the helmet.

Underneath he was a menagerie of man, with a beard like a badger's arse, the glaucous eyes of a fish, a corvine nose. He grinned horse teeth, wiped the gleam from his face and blew out his cheeks.

'That will do for that,' he said in a slightly high-pitched voice. 'Too hot for ceremony, but the lads love it.'

The lads looked as if they would love a bucket of wine and a decent meal, Drust thought, but he was walking cautiously; Marcus Antonius Antyllus might look like a collection of harmless animals, but Drust had seen his work and it was every bit as crazed and bloody as a barbarian altar. Besides – he had Praeclarum, he was sure of it.

Antyllus thrust one arm out with the helmet clutched in its fist; the standard-bearer took it. Antyllus did not look at him but up at the rotten-tooth tower and then right and left of it.

'This was Rome,' he shouted in an aloes voice. 'This was the Empire before those who should have known better gave it up and left it to rot.'

His men agreed with shouts and a rattle of weapons on shields. Antyllus looked at Drust and the others. 'Good men died here and those who left them behind feel the betrayal still in their sons and grandsons. Now this boy, this Alexander in name only, is looking to do the same – pull back, shrink the Empire.'

'Is he?' Quintus bawled, thumbing snot from his nose and inspecting it. He wiped it casually on his tunic and grinned his big grin. 'I never knew that. Did you know that, Kag? Ugo?'

'Have some respect,' the standard-bearer growled, his voice metallic under his own face-masked helmet. Dog thrust his stubbled death's head at him.

'You must be boiling in that head-cauldron,' he shouted. 'Take it off so I can see your face and mark it to be ripped off later.'

'What do you want?' Drust asked Antyllus. It was as if a pile of anvils had fallen from a cart. There was silence for a moment, then the birds seemed to come back to life and an owl fluted deep in the dark trees.

'You were sent to kill me,' Antyllus replied.

'To persuade you to return. They said you were unsound,' Drust responded. 'That your methods were… suspect.'

'Makes Caligula look like a model of rectitude was what they said,' Kag confirmed. Antyllus turned and looked from one to the other and they all saw it, those glaucous fish-eyes changing to something that seemed to resemble the reflection of fire on sharp steel.

'I am unsound to those who have no love for Rome,' he answered and then took a brief, shuddering breath – to still the rant boiling up in him, Drust saw. 'Do you think my methods are unsound?'

'I see no method at all,' Drust said, looking round. 'I see troopers with no horses running around the woods where they have no right to be, stirring up the tribes.'

'Now we have seen what those tribes will do,' Antyllus replied softly. 'What they are capable of and what the Army's response will be. Is it to your liking?'

He waved a hand vaguely southwards. 'There, a few weeks' march away, is Italia. A week or two beyond that is Rome. While this boy-emperor dilutes the soldiers with gluttony and greed, the wolves of these woods whet their fangs and prowl.'

Culleo made a noise that might have been agreement and then fell silent.

'Rome,' Kag said mournfully and Drust wanted to turn and tell him to shut up because he did not like the look in those fish-eyes and Praeclarum was in his clutches. 'Rome won't care for you,' Kag went on. 'They have had enough of usurpers.'

Antyllus flung up one hand as if swatting away a fly, then looked up at the trees and the sky. 'Well, you have come to kill me and failed. Now I need you to help me instead, and I hold your wife. You have until the sun touches the top of that great oak. If you have not thrown down your weapons and come out to kneel at my feet, I will show you what I have learned from the blood altars in these woods. I do not need all of you.'

'Why does he wait?' Dog demanded as they crouched like feral foxes, laired up and looking for a way out.

'Because he has a use for us,' Drust answered, though he did not know what it might be.

Manius came loping up and he looked stricken, a face like a blinking calf, new-born to the world; it frightened Drust more than Dog's ever had.

'I can't smell them,' he said. 'I can't hear them, can't see them – but I know they are there... I know it. I need to find...'

Dog loomed over him, all set to snarl, but saw Drust's face and clicked his teeth shut. Kag gave Manius water and everyone else walked away from them.

'He is done up,' Quintus said.

'Surprised he lasted this long,' Dog said. 'That leaf he chews has finally addled him.'

The Dark has addled him, Drust thought, a man from the slow, rolling sea of desert sands, trapped in a labyrinth of pillars and shadows.

'We should go out,' Culleo pleaded, sweating and shaking as the lack of drink eroded everything in him, crumbling it like surf on a sand wall. 'Talk to him. Agree to whatever he wants. He is a senator of Rome—'

'And you think... what?' demanded Dog. 'This makes him any less savage than a *haruspex* of the woodlice tribals round here? You should stand, just once, in the middle of the *harena* and look round at the expensive seats down the front. You will see your senators there, howling for blood like any tree-humping German or Gaul.'

No one answered, because they wanted to make a fist of it, though they did not want to die. In the end,

Drust thought wearily, we will have to throw down our weapons, otherwise we will never rescue Praeclarum.

Antyllus gave away his true nature when he sent men in before the sun touched the oak, shifting them in sudden as a bowstring snap, heralded only by the crashing of undergrowth and the snarls. They had retrained well, Drust thought admiringly.

Drust heard Kag bellow out 'Jupiter's balls', but he barely had time even for that before the figures crashed down and Drust, with the flicker of them at the edge of vision, crouched, hunched and spun, so that the one who came at him realised too late that his powerful spear-lunge had left him open as a whorehouse door.

Drust's *gladius* pinked him, a sickening tug that he tore away from, shrieking with the shock of it rather than the pain; there would be no pain for him yet, Drust thought, so he would fight on, not knowing he was already dead.

The foolishness of this man, a Roman when all said and done, angered Drust, who took the *gladius* and his shield and beat him like an evil stepchild. Kept smashing down until something flitted once more at the corner of one eye and he spun away, crouched and snarling.

Dog went past, looking like the lost son of Dis, though there was slaver spuming from his mouth and bristle beard. He had no shield, two swords and went rolling into the pack of fighters, screaming spittle.

Quintus was with him, guarding his back, but he paused and looked Drust up and down. 'There are more and that one is assuredly dead,' he offered quietly. Then he trotted on.

Ashamed, Drust clenched his sticky hand on the hilt and took a moment to look round, seeing too many enemies and the poor cover of the ruined walls. He lurched into the fight, came up behind the man fighting Kag, the pair of them trading blows and looking for openings while two more looked to come against Kag's back. Drust hit the man in the back with the shield edge and heard a crack like splitting wood. He fell like a lopped tree. Kag, panting, blinked at him as if he could not believe what he was seeing.

'Form, form...'

Kag bawled out an echo of it amid the shouts and curses. One by one the Brothers backed off, breaking in pairs to move to the cover of old stones and spiked earth, where Manius had his bow.

There was a horn blast that stopped the renegade Romans; they turned and trotted off while many lay like ragdolls and one or two limped or crawled – at least one, unseen in the bloody grass, called out in a voice high and thin with fear. Drust did not need the language to know a plea not to be left behind.

His comrade heard it, turned and darted back – Drust heard Quintus yell out admiringly at this act of Roman courage, but Drust wanted to do something, a gesture to stop the man in his tracks, because one man moving forward at speed could drag another and another until the bastards had turned and then the Brothers were all dead.

He brought up the sword and swept it down, roaring *Roma Invicta!* and meaning to point it at the running man, save that it was greased with the redhead's blood and flew out of his hand, while he stood and gaped, appalled at the loss.

It went out and away like an arrow, spun once and smacked the running warrior in the face, hilt first, with a sound like a wet clot thrown at a wall. The man went backwards as if hauled off his feet – Drust darted up to him, afraid he might get up and run off with the *gladius*.

He got to the man as he struggled up half blinded and spurting blood from a ruined nose. Drust went for the sword, slipped and fell in bloody mulch, got it in his hand and swung from where he lay. It cracked the warrior's naked knee and he howled and fell over again while Drust gasped and slavered for air, almost done.

He half rose, slipped and fell on the crawling, mewling warrior as he struck out again, aiming for his head and missing by most of the length of it. The point went in the back of the man's neck while Drust's vision circled and shrank to pinholes of murky twilight. He lay face down on top of the man he had killed, sucking the last gasps of the warrior's breath, jerking as the man kicked and flailed to final stillness.

They dragged Drust off the body, turned his face to the sky and slapped it sharply once or twice until sense came back. He found he was looking at Quintus, who beamed.

'Back, are you? Well, that's a good thing – that was as flashy a move as any I have seen practised. I would not use it in the *harena*, mind – no one will believe it isn't faked.'

'You couldn't do it twice,' Dog echoed flatly. 'Is this your new *harena* name – the Butcher?'

'Ho,' Kag said scornfully. 'This from a man who set a prisoner on fire?'

'Enemy?' Drust managed and Kag helped haul him up to weave on legs that were not his own, it seemed.

'Out there still, making demands.'

'Well,' said Quintus thoughtfully, 'this Antyllus lad is happy to throw just enough men at us to make us think and let him know what we can do.'

—

'Throw down your weapons and come out,' the standard-bearer bellowed. 'You cannot stand against us.'

'I heard this only an hour since,' Kag said, just loud enough for those around him to hear and they laughed even louder, which did not please the shouter. He was a scowler now that his face mask was up and his accent, Sow was sure, put him somewhere in Gaul.

'There are a lot like him,' Culleo pointed out. 'They have bows too.'

'We have a bow,' Quintus replied, but even as he spoke he was looking round. 'Where is Manius?'

'Far away,' Dog answered, bitter as lye. Drust hoped that the *mavro* was close but well hidden – or had found the Colour again, whatever it was. He looked round at their fortress, a half fallen tower of rotten stones splintered with ivy and saplings. Bad place to fight, he thought – but at least these are the ones who hold Praeclarum; he searched, hoping to find she was with them.

'Come out. The general has promised no harm to you if you do. We have your warrior woman...'

'There are more plots among the trees here than in the palaces of the Palatine,' Dog observed moodily. 'What do these ones truly want?'

The standard-bearer waved one hand and Drust's heart kicked up into his mouth as a huddle of men moved forward, shields up and spears ready. In their midst, walking unsteadily, was Praeclarum; Ugo roared and banged one *dolabra* on his own helmet, chewing the air in a frothing fury. The standard-bearer had his helmet off, the better to be heard, and showed that he was too fair for heat; his face was a bag of blood with blue eyes. He waved one hand at the men surrounding Praeclarum, his eyes fixed on Drust.

'Your wife,' he said. 'If you and your men do not throw down your weapons, the general will have her ride the sapling. This is a method we learned from these woodlice.'

Drust did not know what it meant, but was certain it wasn't a good thing – Sow told him in a few terse words that it involved tying her between two young, bent-over trees and then cutting the ties so that they sprang apart in opposite directions.

'Fortuna's tits,' Kag growled. 'That's barbarian for you.'

'Did you miss the crucifixions in the *harena*?' Quintus demanded and Kag fell silent. Drust looked from one to the other and then dropped his sword and shield at his feet. The others said nothing but did the same – only Culleo hesitated, licking his lips until Dog's stare made him curse and throw down his sword.

'Now we are fucked,' Dog spat bitterly, looking at Drust.

'Fortuna favours us,' Kag replied firmly, and Quintus grinned and shook his head.

'Fama is the goddess in this. Let's see if her hand holds true over us.'

'She is not a goddess,' Kisa muttered, outraged. 'She is a literary conceit, no more. Ovid made her.'

Quintus looked at the men coming up, spears ready, to collect the discarded weapons, while the standard-bearer swaggered forward, his grin greasy on his sweat-smeared face.

'Now you have insulted her,' Quintus said wearily to Kisa, 'and that is why your name will never be known even to the wind.'

Drust tried to move towards Praeclarum but found men with spears blocking his way. Antyllus stepped up, grinning and wagging a finger.

'Not yet, gladiator. Once we have spoken and made agreement, but not before.'

Drust didn't like the little tick, but he held all the sharp edges and the lives of his Brothers and, above all, the life of Praeclarum, so he merely nodded.

'Let's get to it then.'

Antyllus scowled, not liking this disregard and having planned to throw more fear into them. Instead, he was forced to bawl out for his men to move off, and contented himself with getting the standard-bearer to shove Drust a few staggering steps.

When he had recovered, Drust found Kag's sweaty face at his ear with a brief, urgent whisper.

'Manius is missing.'

They moved off through the trees and Drust tried to keep the group surrounding Praeclarum in sight – tried to keep her in sight. Everything else disappeared to the edge of his vision, so that when they ground to a panting stop, he knew only that Praeclarum was hurt.

'Let me see her,' he called out to the standard-bearer, who simply looked back and shook his head.

'He is worse with his bloody mask off,' Kisa whispered, wiping sweat from his face. Kag squatted and looked at the ground to hide his moving lips.

'These are not the ones we fought in that grove with the *draco* standard,' he said. 'Those are the barbarians of the Dark. Erco sent us to them, which means he was in the pay of this Antyllus.'

'Which means this Antyllus knew everything about us and our mission the minute we stepped from the gates,' Quintus said, and Ugo, fiddling awkwardly with little twigs and his belt, nodded. He was missing the heft of his two weapons and it made him fretted.

All Drust's attention was on the knot of men with Praeclarum in the centre. Drust finally tore his eyes from her as she sat, head bent and breathing hard. The men were small – cavalrymen usually were, because the horses were small – with large shields, all of them marked exactly the same, though scarred and in need of new paint. Most had kept to clean chins and short hair, Army-style, but some had beards and had started braiding them. They still had large spears and small, broad-bladed throwing ones, ringed coats and the longswords of cavalry; these were not the beast men they had fought at the altar.

If he'd had any more thoughts on it, they were driven out of Drust by Praeclarum tilting sideways like a half-emptied bag of grain. He sprang up and took two steps, only to be met by one of the soldiers using his spear like a door. Drust never broke stride, simply shifted into fighting stance, dipped a shoulder and heaved; the man went backwards and there was a sudden boiling of movement and shouting.

Ugo hauled Drust to a halt while men formed a barrier of spears around all the Brothers; Antyllus came up, scowling and sweating, helmet in the crook of his arm.

'Do not do that again. I need you alive, but there will be pain if you persist.'

'She's sick,' Drust said, struggling in Ugo's grip.

Antyllus looked across and then uneasily back at Drust. 'She will be attended to when we reach our destination.'

'I can attend her,' Kisa said suddenly and slapped his chest. '*Medicus*. One of your own is injured – I can look at him too.'

Antyllus glanced over to where the injured soldier sat, holding his arm. Then he nodded. Kisa smiled briefly at Drust and went across.

'Manius is following us,' Dog whispered in Drust's ear, then glanced to where Kisa squatted with the wounded warrior. 'I hope our Jew doesn't kill anyone – he is no more a *medicus* than I can fart coins.'

'He has magic,' Kag said, and not all of his tone was ironic.

Not long after, a sharp order started everyone moving. Kisa loped back to them and Drust seized him by both arms.

'Well?'

Kisa winced at the pressure and Drust let go. 'She was beaten – badly. She was grabbed by six of them and wounded two before they overpowered her. One bled out and died as they escaped – he was the one we tracked – and the one I bound up got his thigh slashed open. The remainder were angry at that. They knew that she had to be brought alive, but unharmed was not specified. So they beat her.'

Drust's eyes told everyone more than any words. Ugo laid a hand on his shoulder. 'There will be a reckoning there,' he promised.

'What do they want – did you learn that?' Kag demanded and Drust shook the storms from his head guiltily. I should be asking that, he thought dully.

'Only that Antyllus ordered it and is not happy that they beat her – I do not think those who did it will remain unpunished,' Kisa replied and paused. 'But you should be careful here. These men have reasons for turning their back on the Rome they know, and the only way back for them is if Rome is remade in the image of their general.'

Culleo slithered in to join them. He was licking his lips and looked as if he had been drenched in a rainstorm; his hands shook.

'The soldiers are arguing. Some want to head a little south and west, to go around what lies ahead. Others are scathing them and say they should go straight through. All of them are afraid.'

'Straight through what?' Kag demanded, and Ugo threw up his empty, fretting hands.

'You had to ask.'

Culleo licked his lips again. 'The worst part of the Dark.'

There was no sudden transition from the light to the shadows, but warriors who had been walking stolidly, shields on backs, spears on shoulders, suddenly started to hunch themselves and then crouch.

The light slowly filtered away from dapple to splintered shafts through a blue-green dim; Drust made the mistake of looking up and grew dizzy with it, panicked at the sudden idea that they were underwater, drowning.

The ground between the great trunks of crushing trees was a carpet of wriggling ivy and mulch, roots that caught the foot if you tried to walk normally, so everyone had to step carefully and deliberately. The trees were shrouded in moss, hanging like witch hair; mighty oaks wore it like a barbarian king does furs, Drust thought. This was not a good place.

When the distant, eldritch clacking started, echoing among the shadows, everyone grew more tense still, even Ugo, who wanted a weapon in his hand and kept clenching round the hilt that wasn't there.

'*Auerhahn*,' he said to them. 'A cock bird, no more. Mating call. Heard it before.'

It soothed only a little because no one knew what an *auerhahn* was, while it seemed there were a great many mating cocks in the Dark, and Kag said as much.

'That's because you and Romans like you have stripped these woods of creatures that eat them – wolves and bears,' Culleo responded sullenly. 'There is scarce any of those animals left in these woods, thanks to you – the foxes are not enough.'

'Even so,' Ugo answered, frowning, 'there are a lot of *auerhahn* out there.'

They were surrounded by a hundred soldiers of the Army, but the Brothers did not feel safe all the way through that wood, and when finally the light grew to dapple and the bird calls to flutes and chirps, they all found themselves wiping sweat and taking great relieved gulps of air.

'I do not care for the Dark,' Quintus growled as the other warriors grinned and made noises like men who had never doubted their own courage or that they would get

97

through without incident. The standard-bearer strutted – like one of the clacking birds, Kag offered, and that made for laughter.

The trees thinned to saplings and scrub, then spilled into swathes of long-overgrown pasture land with a few grazing cows and sheep. Drust's eyes leaped ahead like running deer, almost dizzied at being free of the narrow sightline of trees.

It also let everyone see the smoke and the distant buildings and the powerful stockade around it. At one end was a square of stone walls, partially repaired with timber and earth, surrounding a single square tower the height of six or seven men.

'That's a Roman fort, for sure,' Dog hissed. 'Hard to get in or out.'

'Give us time,' Quintus answered, grinning.

'You have no time,' Culleo spat back. 'This is the end, thanks to that woman.'

Dog had no answer to it, but Drust merely shrugged. 'Have you never been in love?' he asked and Culleo considered it, ferreting in his beard for what itched him.

'Was married once, but she left me for a farrier.'

'Love is for fools. It's a surging of blood in the loins.'

Dog was looking ahead, but everyone knew he was speaking to Drust. 'There is little mystery and less magic in it,' he added. Then he turned and looked Drust in the face, using his own, like he always did, as a club.

'She is now a slave, like all of us. We will be worked like oxen until we die and she will be raped. She may even find she likes it in preference to being worked like an ox. That's what being a slave does to you – makes you grateful for shit you would rave at as a free man. I remember it well. I thought never to be returned to that state.'

Drust's face drained and everyone saw it. Ugo pinioned him in both arms and Kag lunged forward to put himself between them, glaring at Dog. Before he could speak – and to everyone's astonishment – Kisa stuck his own face in Dog's eyeline, red and angry, his words spitting out like knives.

'You whoreson,' he hissed. 'She saved your life at least once – I saw it happen. You kissed her on both cheeks on the day she and Drust were wed, and would defend her in a fight. Yet here you are, snarling out this old putrescence when you know it to be falsehood, when you know you love her as much as anyone here, save Drust.'

Dog opened and closed his mouth with astonishment.

'Without the rest of us, you are weary, stale, flat and unprofitable as all of us are on our own. You are grimy, squalid, nasty and profane, a foul and disgusting excrescence with a self-inflicted horror of a face, who can set a man on fire and joke about it. Monkeys look down on you. Dogs piss on your shoes. Even sheep won't have sex with you. You are unreservedly pathetic, starved for attention, a fool, an ignoramus, Dog; and the sooner you realise it, the better for everyone, including yourself.'

'Ho,' said Kag admiringly and clapped his hands like a lawyer at a trial. Dog stared, fixed and silent, while Kisa, half ashamed, turned away.

'*Missus*,' Quintus said, looking at Dog warningly, and whether he would have upheld that call for a let-off or not was taken from him by men with spears shoving them into moving.

They came up through small clumps of cattle that Drust was sure were stolen beasts, for he realised that no one lived here and had not done so for a long time. There were patrols, cautious as foxes, horn calls to announce the arrival of Antyllus, but the stockade village was a crumble of ancient buildings, some of them ominous with old char. Everyone seemed watchful, on edge.

'Rome,' Kag said laconically, while the only ones not armed watched them come up. They were slaves, locals taken in raids – they could be home in a day, perhaps two if they ran, Drust thought. Ugo put him right on that.

'They are from the other side of that forest,' he said. 'If they flee north, they will just become slaves of another tribe. If they try to get home they must go through the Dark. They are not yet desperate enough for freedom.'

The older slaves stared with that silent tolerance for misery that caused people who noticed them at all to drop their heads or look away. The younger ones looked with naked contempt, risking the lash.

Drust and the others were marched to a large round hut whose daub walls let in light and whose roof looked like a whore fresh-kicked out of bed. It had the must of old, rank straw and death.

Praeclarum, Drust saw, was taken up to the distant arched entrance of the stone fort – it had a wooden gate and, he was sure, a spiked drop gate as well. They would put her in the tower, at the top, he thought. That's what I would do.

'She will not give in to despair,' Kag said, coming to squat next to him. 'Neither should you.'

'Can you see her again?' Drust asked Kisa, and the Jew shook his head sadly.

'That door is closed. They have their own *medicus* here, Frontinus by name. It is clear this Antyllus will feed your desire to see and talk to her, yet never fulfil it.'

And so get me to do anything he asks, Drust finished for him. He nodded admittance of it.

They'd hardly become used to the splintered dim before men arrived to huckle them out and down the rutted road to the largest building, the one which had once been the meeting house, the longhouse. It was solid with timbers, but the roof was thatch and sprouting spikes like a harridan's bad wig.

Inside, even in the bright of day, you needed torches, which was why they found Antyllus outside, sitting in a chair and lathered while a man shaved him. They stood while his cheeks were razored and wiped clean of excess soap.

'This is Lentulus,' he said, nodding to the man with the razor. 'He does hair too – when we are done here, he will attend to you. You look like barbarians – but I suppose that was the point when you were sent into the forest to find and kill me.'

'To find you,' Drust corrected. He felt like a slave again, standing with his hands behind his back facing the master of his destiny. He did not like the feeling.

'The *castra* has no secrets,' Antyllus said, taking a clean cloth to his chin. He wore a simple tunic with a broad purple stripe on it and the blood-red boots of a senator; the message was not lost. 'I knew of your mission almost as soon as you and the rest moved north out of the gates. Erco was told to lead you to the lair of the beast-masks and finish you off.'

Drust said nothing, but Dog grunted like a boar sensing a rival. Antyllus felt his chin critically, then nodded his satisfaction to Lentulus; it puzzled Drust, because there was a strange deference in it.

'Yes,' he went on, 'you showed some resilience, which made me think on matters again. I thought it unlikely you would fall in with my plans without some incentive – which is why your woman is now in my tower.'

He pulled a pouch out from under his tunic belt and Drust's breath caught in his throat; he knew it well.

'I have her smile,' he said and dangled the pouch which held Praeclarum's pearled teeth. 'If you want it and her returned, you must do something for me. The river crossing you have sought for so long is a day away to the south. The river shallows there and the bridge is still up, too small for cart or beast, which is why it will be unused. All the savages will try to find a way to bring back the livestock they have stolen, and only when they realise that cannot be done will they turn them loose, drop the carts and pack for walking. You must use that bridge to travel to the *castra*, to Marcus Peperna Vento, and tell him how I am persuaded to return to the fold, with all my men and the standard of the Ala Flavia.'

'Jupiter's hairy balls,' Kag spat. 'Leave us alone, can't you? Just walk up to the gate and announce it. Then the pair of you can wag your cocks at one another.'

Antyllus gave a nod and there was a slight movement behind Kag, who reacted too late; the spear butt caught him on the back of the calf and flung him forward, hopping and cursing.

'You will do as I say. I have four hundred men, hardened and trained as light infantry, and Marcus Peperna

Vento should want to grab them with both hands – the lands all around him are swarming with raiding enemy. If he vacillates, you will know he means for my death, not my redemption. In which case, find a way to open the gates. Thereafter what happens is down to me and you need have nothing more to do with it. You will have your woman, her teeth, and whatever carts and beasts are left to you – I suspect not many since Peperna has heard that you are dead.'

'Fortuna fuck me sideways,' Quintus muttered. 'We did as asked. Well done is ill paid.'

'The price of fame,' Antyllus answered levelly, uncoiling from the chair. 'If you would go into the Dark of the north for strange beasts, I am thinking you will enter Hades for a woman who is one of you, even one with no teeth.'

He stopped and his smile grew wider. 'I do not ask for Hades. Just the gates of the *castra*.'

He stopped, looking uneasy, and his hand strayed to his forehead before dropping. 'If you listen,' he said wearily, 'you will hear the dice rattle on the table. Once they have ceased to bounce we will know.'

No one spoke. There were answers all of them wanted to give, but none that could be said. Antyllus nodded, satisfied.

'Tonight there is a small dinner, myself and my officers. You will attend. Try and be… tidier.'

He made to move off, then paused and turned to them.

'One of you is missing,' he added. 'The *mavro*, the Libyan. If you have any way of getting him to join you, I strongly advise it. This is not a place to be skulking alone – Cernunnos will get him, as sure as death.'

Chapter Six

A small dinner for officers. Well, the longhouse was no *triclinium*, even if everyone was arranged around three sides of a long table. Nor would you find larks' tongues, sterile sows' wombs and milk-fed snails – here was mutton from four-horned sheep, cheese and wrinkled winter apples, wild boar and a huge cauldron full of boiling beef; it was the table a barbarian chieftain would keep, arranged in Roman style.

There was ale by the bucket, which only added to the strangeness – but there was a lot of decent red wine, cheering, shouts, and a desperate kind of libation to the gods of Rome, as if to caulk the cracks in something unnatural. If there were those who thought it wasn't fitting for this sort of native display to have stamped across a decent Roman dinner, they were not eating here, Drust thought.

Antyllus lay on a decent divan, as did the senior officers, with the standard-bearer, Drust now knew was called Marcellus, on one side and, peculiarly, Lentulus on the other. Even Kisa did not know whether Lentulus was simply a barber, or even a slave – but it was clear he had the influence of a favourite.

'They do not care for us at all, Drust,' Dog said out of the corner of his mouth, though he didn't need to be low-spoken; there was noise enough to drown out a shout. 'We should have let the barber shave one of us at least, it appears.'

Drust had no answer to what was patently right – Lentulus had come, obedient to his general's wishes, and been told to sod off, so had to return and admit failure. Nothing came of it, which further annoyed the man, who clearly believed his complaint deserved action.

Drust and the others ate sparingly and drank less, not knowing what Fortuna might suddenly spring on them. They watched Antyllus lolling on his divan, resplendent in white and senatorial purple and looking down his nose at those he considered lesser folk. Which was everyone.

He was open-handed and smiling like a boiled cod at those he had invited, his own Chosen, just like some barbarian chieftain sitting in a High Seat, with Lentulus and Marcellus like hounds at his feet. It was clear to Drust that the pair were a lounging slouch of no good who shared only scowls and, he was sure, a mutual fear of Antyllus.

Drust watched Antyllus and felt like a sacrificial horse, the instant he feels the blade – but the anger at what had been done to Praeclarum burned that away. It flared and consumed everything. Those next to him seemed to feel some of the uncomfortable heat of it; Dog shifted sideways on the bench a little and took a long swallow from his bowl. Then another.

Kag held his place but he bent to Drust's ear. 'Be wary. This is still a Roman dinner and for a general too, but these men of his are strung on tight wires. They are more slaves than we were.'

Then Antyllus ordered in the *dinos*, which Drust knew was a big Greek cup for holding wine – but what came in was carried by two men. It was heavy and bronze, worked with scrolls and bunches of grapes, all the trappings. But men came and filled it with wheat beer, which formed a scum like sea foam. They learned later that it had been found here and had clearly been part of some German warlord's household, long abandoned.

'To the Army,' Antyllus called, standing up and toasting with his cup. Everyone did the same, including Drust and the others, because they thought it best. When the racket died a little, Lentulus sneered across at them.

'Are they Army, then?'

'They are,' Antyllus confirmed.

'What army?' someone shouted, and that burst the rafters until Antyllus held his hands up for silence and cocked his head at Drust.

'Well – tell them what you do in the Legions,' he said, wryly mocking. He wanted them to admit they had been sent to kill him, to make his officers see how long and gripping his reach was. He wanted to be imperious and unafraid; Drust was not about to be his mammet.

'I can tell you what we don't do,' he replied levelly. 'We don't salute, we don't work and we don't march.'

'We fight,' Dog added.

'I had heard that,' Lentulus said. 'Gladiators, I had heard. Who look like slave scum still and refuse to let me alter their condition.'

'Hard to explain to the *castra* how we came to be neatly barbered,' Drust announced, and Antyllus did not want discussion on them returning to the *castra*, on what he wanted them to do, so he stopped it. Lentulus, however, was vicious with drink and looking for an excuse to use it.

'Well, gladiators still, though I had heard you were poor at best and are now well past that. Just the thing for an entertainment at a Roman dinner.'

'Not this dinner,' Antyllus said firmly and the fire and steel edge in the voice cut through Lentulus's fog. Marcellus smiled.

'I thought to see them do what they claim to do best,' Lentulus persisted sullenly. 'Fight.'

'Something strange to you, so I don't doubt it,' Kag said loudly. 'Whose callouses come from gripping a pole – oh, wait. That's the other pederast.'

There was a moth-flutter of indrawn breath at this.

That was it, Drust thought. The end of all their lives here. He was aware of all the eyes swinging to the stricken men, wondering and waiting gleefully for what might be done to them now. Ugo rumbled in the deep of his throat while Kag wryly offered his cup in toast to Lentulus, who was struggling to stand and making poor work of it.

'Enough,' Antyllus said and Lentulus gave up. Marcellus, on the other hand, was a little dagger of vicious spite.

'Of course,' he said silkily, 'it would not do for such an insult to go unanswered.'

'Marcellus,' Antyllus said warningly. Lentulus looked like a confused horse feeling four hands on the reins and Marcellus shrugged idly.

'I thought only of the cauldron. The loser begs forgiveness. On his knees.'

The cauldron. It went round the hall like a rustle of sour wind. They set up a thumping chant and others just demanded it, out loud and drunken. Lentulus looked sick; Marcellus grinned ferally at Drust.

'Let the pair lift the cauldron then...'

'Neither of them can manage that,' Antyllus answered sharply, and Marcellus shrugged.

'Let them choose champions then – that big fellow looks capable. Match him with Mus.'

The others caught the name and started to bang the table and shout it out like a chant – 'Mus, Mus, Mus...'

He was no mouse when he finally ducked into the feral reek of the longhouse, a giant in a sweat-stained tunic. He was bigger and wider than Ugo, who looked round at Drust, then grinned and shrugged.

It was then that the others caught the gleam in Drust's sideways flick of an eye, a glint of anger and cunning. Like seeing a bear come out of the cave you had just wandered up to, Ugo told everyone afterwards.

'I need no champion,' Drust said, and that silenced the howlers for a long minute. Then he grinned at them.

'Five *denarii* on the Son of Mars,' yelled someone, and there was howling and betting in equal measure. A small Roman dinner, Drust thought scornfully.

He stepped up to the cauldron and saw that once it had been burnished and might have looked like gold, but it wasn't even bronze but gilded iron, worn to the truth in the inside by the stirring of the ladle. The beer sloshed in it, heady with the reek of fermented wheat.

The important – the vital – part of it was that it weighed enough for two men to have to carry it when it was empty. When it was made into a swimming pool of wheat beer it couldn't be moved at all save by four, so stewards or slaves took folk's cups and filled them using a heavy iron ladle that had come with it.

'Mus isn't strong enough…'

They took serious bets on it now and the shouts went back and forth, the odds flying with them. Few were for Drust, even from those who had enjoyed the wit about being a 'Son of Mars' – every soldier in the Army was a Son of Mars.

Mus, on the other hand, flexed biceps to the roars of the crowd; the cauldron sat like a dark doom, sweated with slopping beer, sour with possibility.

'He should never have been in the cavalry,' Ugo growled. 'Look at him. His legs would dig troughs in the ground and the pony he rides would sag in the middle.'

'He rode no horse,' Kisa agreed. 'He has comrades here of the same stripe. Look at them – every one is a grumbler, a misfit, and they are not all cavalrymen. I say "stripe" advisedly – look at their legs.'

They saw it, the weals and slashes made from the vine sticks of centurions and delivered to the greybacks, the foot soldiers of the Army, as casual punishments for not doing their perceived duty. These were the ones who thought themselves badly handled.

'Remind me of the rules?' Drust demanded, slashing through the calls. He sounded desperate and Lentulus, his eyes piggy and his face red as a smacked arse, laughed aloud.

'Rules?' he blurted out. 'You lift, you carry, and whoever carries it further wins.'

'So,' Drust said, frowning as if he was having trouble with it, 'if your big Mouse there doesn't carry it further than I can, I win?'

One or two laughed. Lentulus blinked, frowned and nodded; Drust saw Antyllus's eyes narrow and wondered if he had worked it out – but he stayed silent, stroking his chin.

The odds changed and flew like birds; Lentulus leered and Marcellus watched with a fixed stare, his face dark and eager. Antyllus was trying for stoical calm but fell short of it; he did not like matters getting away from him as badly as they had. Get used to it, Drust thought savagely, for you believe you are leading these Sons of Mars, but they are leading you. That purple cloak they will eventually throw over your shoulders may seem like a vindication of greatness, but you will find the weight is crushing.

'You first,' he said, looking thoughtfully at Mus and the cauldron. 'I may need a little time to work up to it. You may spill a little too, and make it lighter for me.'

Mus had a chin like a reef and a grin that showed too many bad teeth. He bent his knees and hugged the cauldron. 'I won't spill any,' he said, and Drust nodded, looked mournful. Kag and the others watched, bemused; they knew Drust would never lift the affair at all and even Kag could not work out what he had in mind.

Mus was into the task and already straining while the crowd roared him on, faces gleaming with sweat and the lust of the moment. Kag and the others watched Drust step forward and take the ladle out; the lightly frosted curls of his clenched hair fluttered in the heat from the torches.

'Just to make it a little lighter,' he said, waving the ladle. Mus could only manage a grunt but people laughed and shouted more encouragement. 'Go on,' they shouted – all the ones with bets on him. 'Lift it, shift it…'

Mus growled and strained, the muscles bunching on him like something alive fighting to get out of his body. When he got the cauldron off the floor he would try and shuffle a few steps with it, and Kag saw Drust cock his head to one side, as if appreciating the grunting effort. He looked like a curious bird from the dark of the forest.

He let Mus get the bite of it. Let him get it a finger-length up off the floor and into the urgent shouts of his supporters in the crowd.

Then he drew back and hit him in the forehead with the ladle.

Mus gave a grunt and fell like a sacrificed sheep; the cauldron clanged heavily to the flags, teetered and slopped, and people ebbed away from it. Then it rocked itself steady on its tripod legs and Drust carefully put the ladle back. He looked at Mus, who was struggling like a stricken beetle on the floor, his eyes crossed slightly and a red mark on his forehead. Everyone else gawped, equally stunned; the silence fell like a black mantle.

'No rules,' Drust called out, and looked down again at the glazed Mus. 'You have carried it no further than I could.' He smiled like a drawn dagger at the green-tinged Lentulus. 'I win. I will wait until the wine returns your wits before I hear your apology. Tomorrow will do.'

Ugo stepped down and held out one hand, which the dazed Mus took; it was a strain on them both to get him back to his feet and he was weaving after he had done it.

'If you sit, someone will bring you beer and a cool cloth,' Ugo said. 'You use one on your belly and the other on your head – I will help if you have trouble getting it the right way round.'

There was a pause while folk worked out what had happened and why and then got the sheer jest in it. They howled and beat the table and laughed; Mus, dazed, nodded and wavered off to sit down, head hanging.

Kag saw Lentulus's face – and then felt Antyllus's eyes rest on him like blowflies; they flitted from one to the other out of a face like a stone idol and Kag did not like it. Drust, smiling stiffly, dipped the ladle in the cauldron beer and called out: 'A toast to General Marcus Antonius Antyllus – three times long life.'

There was nothing the hall could do but echo him – *Vivat. Vivat. Vivat.*

Dog tugged at Drust's hem until he pulled him back to the bench.

'Well, you sent him a message, for sure, but I do not think we should stay here long,' he said. 'We should get our weapons, find a way into the tower, get Praeclarum and run for that bridge.'

'Or cut our fucking throats here,' Culleo growled blearily, swallowing more beer and belching the fumes in both their faces. 'Save all that effort and thinking, because we will be just as dead at the end of it. Us and your precious bloody wife.'

Antyllus was as good as his word, which surprised everyone; as soon as the desperate dinner party lurched to a close, two soldiers led Drust through the dim, rutted streets with their looming ruined shadows to the fortress.

It was a drop gate, he noted as he passed under, spiked and solid, but only part of him registered it, while his heart was beating at its cage like a mad bird. They led him up the stair of the tower into a room flickering with lurid torchlight, and turned him over to more guards, dicing at a wooden table.

Up another wind of steps the air grew fetid and Drust knew the fevered stink of it well, wafted with memories of the dying in the undercrofts of amphitheatres up and down the Empire; the maddened bird threatened to try and escape out of his throat.

She lay on stained straw but at least they had given her blankets and a cup with, when he tasted it, water with a little vinegary wine in it – *posca*, the Army's favourite marching drink.

She stirred when she felt the rim of it on her lips, flicking open her eyes with a moment of panic which subsided to softness when she recognised it.

'Easy,' she said in a voice husky with fever, 'I still have a few teeth left.'

'I have seen them. Antyllus has them in a sleeve of his toga, but we will get them back.'

'I was taken so easily,' she murmured bitterly. 'I let them take me so easily...'

'We let them take you,' he said, 'and you did not make it easy – one died and another will remember the day every time he limps.'

'They beat me,' she said and the memory of the pain was thick in her voice, so that Drust almost crushed the cup with his anger. Instead, he smoothed the sweat-greased brow and she smiled.

'If I had hair it would look like Medusa. There are still blessings to be had, it seems.'

'The *posca* is nice and cool.'

'Lovely,' she said.

'We will get you out of here,' he said. 'And go home. Everything will be as before.'

She stirred and he saw a gleam where her eyes were. Realised it was light on tears.

'The baby,' she said.

'Kisa told me.'

'The trouble with Kisa is that he lacks the power of conversation but retains the power of speech.'

'He is young enough to know everything,' he countered, and heard her chuckle, then cough. The sound was wet and alarmed him.

'I think I lost it,' she said simply, and the knell of it fell on them both, so that he bowed his head and tried to keep the tears from crushing out of his eyes like pips from an apple.

He heard the guards clumping up and knew their time was nearly gone.

'I love you,' he said desperately.

'Tscha,' she said scornfully. 'Marry me, you said, and you will never look at another horse.'

'I feel so miserable without you,' he countered, grinning. 'It's almost like having you there.'

The guards arrived, twin shadows looming like temple columns. He felt a hand on his shoulder.

'I will get you out of here,' he said to her, 'no matter what.'

Antyllus was there when Drust came out of the tower into the courtyard; a rain had started, soft as tears.

'You have seen her,' he said. 'Now it is time to fulfil your bargain.'

'She is sick,' Drust declared. 'She may have lost our child.'

'Not the case,' Antyllus answered firmly. 'My *medicus* assures me and is making offerings to Asclepius to avoid such a terrible fate.' He paused, frowning. 'I did not know she was with child when I arranged for her to be... intercepted.'

'Would it have mattered?'

Antyllus said nothing and Drust leaped on that. 'Then let her go. Let us take her – we will do as you ask.'

Antyllus shook his head. 'Of those sent to fetch her, one is dead and one is crippled. What would they – and their comrades – think if I reduced their efforts and sacrifice to nothing?'

Drust nodded; he had known that before he asked, but he'd had to ask. The anger burned in him, the way ice felt sometimes in the coldest winters. He said nothing but promised much to the gods who would save her.

–

The others did the same when he reported it all, but they also said nothing within earshot of the hundred or so men who took them a day south, to the river. It had run out of dance and spray, spilling wearily into a gentle slide through a meadowed plain, but it was deep and black and cold. The bridge was small and wooden with an abandoned watchtower.

'You won't get a cart or an ox or any pack animal across that, right enough,' Kag said, watching Antyllus's men watching them.

'Which is why no one cares for it and so it is still intact,' Culleo said, grinning. 'We can be across and back to a decent bath and a cup or two of wine.'

'If we don't walk into some of the plunderers going home,' Sow answered, and Culleo spat sullenly.

'Hist on that, lest a god who hates us hears it.'

'The only god who doesn't hate you is Bacchus,' Dog answered, and walked across the bridge followed by the others. Once there, he turned and raised one hand in farewell to the watching men.

After they had plodded down the trail and round a bend out of sight, Drust stopped and turned to them. They knew what he was about before he spoke.

'I can't ask it of you, but I am going back once those escorts have left off watching for it. She will not last without help, so I plan to sneak back and find a way to get her out. You should go on and tell Peperna everything – make sure he knows none of you will open any gates.'

Dog and Kag looked at one another, and Dog shifted from one foot to the other and looked from Kag to Drust, then round at the others.

'I will come,' he said. Kag laughed, shaking his head mockingly. Quintus just grinned his huge wide grin.

'There's noble,' he declared, and Dog scowled at him.

'I am not noble, nor ever have been. But you will want to know why, Drust, given what I have said before.'

He took a breath and glared round at them all before shrugging. 'I look like Death and now I feel it as well. My bones ache in winter and I have to roll out of a sleep to take a piss. I don't like folk much and they feel the same.'

He stopped, looked at the ground, then defiantly up. 'I was born with nothing and still have much of it left. I have no blood relatives, no loves old or new, and I mostly know a few bar owners I can spend an evening with. Kisa was right – you are the only ones I can be with and who will be with me, which is a sad statement to make on a life. You are the closest I have to a family and Drust made that possible – you all know it. So I will follow and save his woman.'

'Well said, Pluto,' Ugo declared, beaming. 'For my part there was never any doubt.'

'Nor mine,' Quintus added, and Kag merely nodded. Culleo spat sideways and ran off, scurrying down the track. No one was surprised – but they were when Sow stood his ground.

'Don't ask,' he said wearily. 'I could not tell you. Perhaps because everyone in my unit is dead save that running rat. Perhaps because I like your woman, Drust, and really don't like this overblown senator.' He stopped and shrugged. 'Perhaps I don't know myself.'

Ugo clapped him on one shoulder and laughed. 'Perhaps you will change your mind when you see where we have to go.'

Drust looked at him; sometimes you forget that the big Frisian is not the ox he appears, he thought. He looked around them, this family, these Brothers of the Sand.

Then he nodded and led them back across the bridge and into the Dark.

Chapter Seven

They moved south, swiftly at first, gliding through the scrub and sparse saplings to where the trees began to crowd. As the sun lowered, the shadows thickened and then, as if a blanket had been thrown on them, they were in the Dark.

The last light of day speared through the canopy in glorious golden shafts, one by one winking out until there was only shadow and fear. They came to a halt, not because they were weary, but because it seemed they were pushing against the blackness, as if the very ground under their feet might be solid or a chasm.

Eventually they hunkered, pretending to gnaw hard bread and swill thin wine round their mouths to soften it enough to chew.

'What will Culleo do?' Kisa asked Sow, who shrugged.

'Blame us. Make himself look like a hero and us like tools of this Antyllus. He will betray everyone.'

'Ratfuck,' Quintus said, then gleamed his grin from the shadows. 'He and I will have a reckoning this day or the next.'

'Join the line,' Dog muttered, then lifted his head at a bird call.

'Blackbird,' Kisa declared, and Dog snorted.

'It's an ouzel.'

'Blackbird.'

'Do either sing at night?' Kag flung in and that silenced everyone.

Then there was a sound that hackled up the hair on their neck and arms, sent cold running up and down them. Low and mournful and distant, immediately repeated somewhere behind them.

'Wolves?' Kisa asked tremulously.

'Thought we had rid these woods of them all,' Kag said.

'All space gets filled,' Sow said.

'Wolf calls don't echo,' Ugo said suddenly. Dog shook his head in mock amazement.

'All sound echoes if the place allows it.'

'This isn't the place.'

He was right, Drust thought. There's no echo and perhaps no wolves – he told them to check weapons and be ready.

They had edge and point but no bow. No one mentioned the missing Manius or where he might be, but Drust did not think the man was dead. He was sure he would know and the gods would not allow him to pass lightly.

'I can use a knife,' Kisa offered and Sow grunted in the dark; it was now a blackness where you could not see anyone beyond touching range unless they had a grin like Quintus.

'You can only use that close up,' Sow pointed out. 'You don't want to be close up to anything in this place. When it gets light I will cut you a staff. You can hit with a stick can't you?'

Drust almost heard Kisa hackling up then. It might not be his preferred place, he said, and he might not know the ways of the forest, or how to move in it, or whether he looked at ouzel or blackbird. But he knew a tit when he saw one.

It made everyone laugh, but it was all too loud and Drust hissed urgently at them to leave off. Kag's voice, low and soft, drifted from a little way away.

'Stick with me, little Jew, and do as I say and we should be fine.'

He'd managed a small laugh, adding, 'It's a ring ouzel, not a blackbird.'

'Arse,' Dog growled.

'It's a merle,' Ugo said.

They stayed crouched and silent and sweating all through the night, which fretted them with rustles and squeaks, owl calls, and the howls of what might have been wolves. In the morning, they worked the stiffness out, pissed in brief spurts; Sow cut Kisa a stout branch, the noise of the work making everyone wince. They moved on, swinging their heads from side to side like blinded beasts. Peculiarly, Ugo took the front position.

'I was barely walking when my da' took me on the hunt,' he said as they walked, looking everywhere but at the others just behind him, 'and he taught me some of it. I have forgot a lot, but some of it sticks. We used piss to hunt. Hinds' is best, though not when they're carrying, o' course – but there's better eating in a doe. Stags' is easier to get – all you need is hind piss if you want to take one in the rut, but you needs must be good and hungered, for it is poor eating – stringy and tough. Too full of black phlegm humours, thin because it forgets to eat. You can use stag piss at any time – even if he has no interest in a hind, a stag will come at the smell of a strange male in his lands, just to find out…'

He stopped, listening; those nearest saw his hands clench and unclench on the shaft of each *dolabra*. They stood in wary half-crouch; Ugo went on.

'All that's bow and stable,' he said, speaking soft and low and almost to himself. 'The game driven or lured to where you stand – noble-born would scorn it in favour of thrashing about with horses and dogs, blowing horns. They weren't hunting for to survive, mind, just for sport.'

He knelt briefly, peered, rose up and prowled on.

'Best way,' he said, 'is use a stick, scuff the leaves off of an area about the size of a man's head. Drop some fewmet and add some piss – you get it everywhere if you look, they marks boundaries with it. Then you wait. A stag will come, thinking it is a scrape from a rival. Sometimes a hind, though the scent of a stag usually means nothing to them.'

'You can track boar too, though that is harder,' he went on softly. 'Look for scraped-up mast as a starting point. That's where they have snouted for food. They might even come back, so waiting is best. You can never move quiet enough to fool a woodland creature – and smell is your enemy. Never believe the wind is right. Never.'

He stopped again, glanced around, then up at the sky, judging the wind by the movement of the branches and leaves. They had all scorned Ugo's claims of knowing the forests, because he had been a mere boy when plucked up as a slave. No one scorned now, for he was something dark and feral.

It started to rain, brief and savage and only touching them after it had stopped, the memory of it sifting through the canopy to the deep green-blue where they moved.

'Birch,' Ugo said, nodding to the surrounding trees. They were wet, the colour of mottled cream. 'Lady of the Woods, that's birch. You make brooms from birch, for they sweep out evil with the dust.'

He went on like that for a little while, muttering soft as if he prayed – talking past his fear, Drust saw. They slunk past sprouting stands of hazel – 'the nuts has wisdom in them and if you make a seeking-rod from the wood, you can find lost things.'

Oak was the gate into the secret heart-places of the woods, they learned, and when they came on one spreading a canopy over a clearing, Ugo stopped and took a breath; it was now so dark they saw him only as a shadow and brief gleams of sheened sweat.

'There will be willow soon,' he said. 'Which means grief – you knows what willow looks like?'

They all nodded and Ugo worked spit into his mouth and swallowed it; his throat is dry, Drust realised. It made his own shrivel.

'The oak is the gate,' he went on. 'The willow is the guardian. After will come elm, which grows from stakes put in corpses. Gallows trees and coffins is made from elm. This is how you make a holy place, a sacred place. We will find the Blood Tree soon.'

'We are moving towards one of their sacred places?' demanded Kisa fearfully.

'That's what the giant of the Germanies has said,' Quintus replied. 'I shall never question him again on the ways of the Dark, except perhaps to ask how the fuck we got to this part of it.'

'Fortuna guides our steps, the fickle bitch,' Kag added in low, bitter tones; Dog spat.

'Fortuna is nowhere near here, nor any other god of Rome,' Ugo said. 'This is the land of Cernunnos, stag-headed god of the Gauls and Germans. We are here because you followed me and I followed the... pull. I tell you this because I will not say another word, nor make a sound from now on, and neither will you.'

They moved on, with the whistle and call of birds as incongruous as a helmet on a donkey. As if they were not being hunted by monsters...

The woods unnerved Drust more and more; they seemed braided, knotted, twisted as if tortured and silently screaming. Trunks split and ran horizontally, offshoots like snakes. The rain sifted down on mulch while unseen needle beaks stitched songs into the fractured sky; an eyelash in a sliver of granite sky through the canopy became a swooping fret-winged crow.

Drust saw watching eyes everywhere. They came past willow, almost bare as claws and clumped with a hanging of leaves like patched hair, seeming to bow, polite mourners, as they passed. There was a sighing, like regret.

Then Ugo stopped and stood still. Drust felt the blood surge and pound in him; he watched as Ugo pointed and every heart lurched at the sight, the shift of shadows, eldritch in the weak light splintering through the foliage.

A fox face, tall even for one raised up to stand on two legs. Tall as a man, peering through hawthorn with the dark slender of its shadowed body barely visible. To the left was a bear; beyond that some other animal Drust could not identify.

Then they came in a silent rush, shadows like splinters of the dark detaching and so fast that Drust could only sweep the *gladius* across his front to divert the cut; there was a deep toll of doom as it hit another blade and the push of it spun Drust sideways. He kept it going, turned full circle as he stepped past one side of the plunging attacker and used his shield like a swinging door to slam him in the back so he shot forward into a trunk face first.

There was another coming at him and he slashed him on a wildly upthrown arm, heard bone break and a howling yelp. Not unworldly beasts then – they could be hurt. If they could be hurt they could be killed. Drust started to move on… then recoiled as the same man came at him.

The warrior stumbled forwards, snarled from a withered wolf's face with a man's eyes. He should be writhing in pain, blind with it. Or dead. He should have had one shattered arm flopping uselessly, yet he had a pair of axes in his fists and smelled rank, like mouse piss.

Drust avoided a swinging axe slash from the broken arm, but there was no grip in the hand and the axe sailed away into the shadows; the man never seemed to notice it, just kept swinging as if he still had it in his fist. Drust backed away, mouth dry and the sweat on him like a cold sluice – then he felt anger burn in him. He was Drust, a fighting man of the amphitheatre, not some spear-waver from an arse-end kingdom, made witless by a man smelling of rodent piss.

He slammed the shield like a fist into the shape, heard it grunt and saw it fall, then followed it up, banging and scoring ruts in the mulch as the man rolled away. He missed with two, hit him with two and stopped, panting with the effort and covered in sluices of blood; the man was pulped to the shoulders and, just as Drust saw he was *still* moving, another figure lunged from behind.

The shield was buckled from his frenzy and he was already too late to use it and knew it – but he whirled and snarled the sword up in a last desperate block. The arc of a *dolabra* passed over him like a rolling wheel and thundered into the black figure Drust had missed entirely. The one he had sent flying into the tree, he thought, dully. The one who should have been out of the fight or dead.

Ugo lumbered after the weapon, gave a final chop to the figure, then stuck out a hand to help Drust up. He was scowling.

'They die hard, these beast-masks. Fuck the foul mothers that made them.'

They came flitting out of the blue dark, scuffing through the mulch and witch hair moss, leaping and growling and howling like the animals their masks made them. They were terrifying, eldritch… But the Brothers knew this game, had seen all the ways of it in the *harena*, from the elaborate face-mask *secutor* helmets to the full lion-head Persian 'barbarians'.

It had probably worked well for these men before – a lot of howling beasts from the Dark would have made even hardened legionaries shriek like girls and lose their innards – but Drust watched a fox-pelt go down under a flurry of vicious *gladius* stabs from Dog, saw a stag-face stagger and fall in front of Kag and Quintus, as if dragged down by wolves. Sow's sword broke the shins of a running figure but lodged in the bone of it; he grabbed up the man's fallen spear and rammed it into the belly of another so that he jerked on the end like a gaffed salmon.

Kisa, to Drust's astonishment, leaped on the back of a wolf-masked figure, one of the four Ugo was slashing and hacking at; he stabbed a little knife in the man's eye and fell with him – they rolled into the flurry of leaves and mulch and blood and struggling, roaring madness. Vanished from sight.

Drust knew what to do. He did not care for it, but he knew, twirled the *gladius* as if it was part of his arm and then lunged forward, banged a man off his feet with the remains of his shield, stabbed another away and headed straight for a knot of them, the ones round the black oak – the Blood Tree.

The air went like a spoon in gruel, thick and slow. An axe flashed and he blocked it, the jar through the shield almost ripping it from his grip; splinters flew. Someone hurled forward, snarling high and yowling like a cat, his fingers like claws on the edge of the shield and his weight dragging it down and Drust with it. He wrenched most of it free and booted the man hard when he fell, missed him with a sword swing. Ploughed on. Got smacked in the side of his head by something hard or sharp or both; white light blew sense away and he stumbled and staggered through it until focus came back.

Another axe flashed and he hit the wrist that held it with the shield boss, about all that was left to him, stabbed into the withered wolf-face and tore the weapon free as the man fell away, trailing blood.

He saw Praeclarum. Saw her, clear as if on a summer's day against the blue of a clear sky, standing high on a stone tower. She smiled like a mother watching her child do something clever – then reached out and took him, down and down into a harsh embrace. He felt it, grinned a bloody smile at the slow – so slow – crowd in front of him. The side of his head hurt. Felt like ice.

'Come,' he said to them and did not wait, moved forward as if through a hayfield, the battered remains of a broken shield in one hand, the *gladius* in the other, circling like a sickle of light and chaff flying away from it. He cut, struck and spun, moved as a maiden does at a dance, and the blades whicked past him like horseflies while those that held them fell away.

He laughed for the joy of it. Then the great stag loomed up and he blocked his blow, scorning it, though the last of the shield was sheared and left him with a fistful of metal boss and ragged splinters. The great stag bellowed, the horns of it wide and terrible, the axe seeming to make the air scream as it hissed around.

Drust gave him no chance and fell on him like the wrath of an avalanche, slamming him with the last remains of the shield; if the gods had been kinder, a jagged stick of it should have gone in his eye, but his haired face with its dark pits of eyes jerked to one side and it went in his cheek. It drove him down to the ground and Drust with him. Then he drew back the *gladius* and pegged him to the ground like a curing hide.

Men roared, the sound like the rush of an approaching wind. They surged away from him then, backed away until he was in a half-circle, the hem of which heaved and struggled with other fights – but they were distant matters to Drust who only saw the circle of horned stagmen. The one at his feet shrieked and writhed, but he was fastened by the face; men moved to get to him and Drust saw them.

There was one, larger than the rest, who closed swiftly, head lowered as if about to ram Drust with the spread of strange horns. He was fast and hard and had a great club, like Hercules – but Drust was woven war and red death and to touch him was doom.

That lasted until the stag-man smacked him so hard Drust's helmet strap broke and it flew off. So hard, his head almost turned completely around and he found himself in the bloody mud of the forest floor, mouth full of old leaf, grunting and mewling. He rolled, because it had been practised and practised; the club slammed a spray of blood and twigs into his face, just where he had been.

The stag-man was bellowing in a rut of rage. Drust rolled and he kept slamming, kept missing, cursing with frustration. Drust had lost the *gladius*, threw the metal boss of the shield and it smacked his attacker, though it was as if he threw a pine cone at a great oak.

Then the horned man was closing and Drust had nothing in his fists but clenched mud and blood and knew he was doomed.

The arrow came out of nowhere, struck the man hard; Drust saw him gasp with the power of it, reeling – but not falling. A second punched between the horns and blew brains out of the back of his head. He barely yelped, but went down on one knee.

Then, as Drust watched in sick fascination and terror, the stag-man rose up, rose right up over him and he knew what the club would do. The stag-man roared out and rushed forward the last few steps – or so his ruined mind believed. He went sideways like a crab, hit a tree and fell, mumbling and burbling.

There was a series of wails and a horn blast; in another few seconds the Brothers were panting and slashing at shadows.

Ugo bawled challenge like a bull. Quintus and Kag stood, slathered in bloody sweat and gasping, wild-eyed, and still trying to work out how badly they were injured. Kisa puked while Dog uncoupled himself from his fighting crouch and grinned his bloody death grin at a shadow.

'Timely,' he said. 'Good shot too.'

Manius slid from the Dark, unnocking an arrow. He looked round at everyone from the dark pits where his eyes were.

'I found the Colour of this place,' he said. 'I have been tracking them and you. I know where the tower is from here. I am here. I am far away.'

No one spoke, just concentrated on breathing and examining one another for wounds. Drust stared at the dead, the monstrous army of Cernunnos; the stink of mouse piss was strong.

'They bled only a little,' Kag said, and Kisa, wiping his mouth and spitting, looked up and then around in a dazed sweep of eyes.

'Some foul brew. I have heard of this — they can feel no pain, do not bleed, and if you kill them you also have to push them over before you can say they are dead.'

Drust blinked, swallowed the dry rasp in his throat and dashed sweat from his eyes, despite the sudden chill; a wind washed through the black-shadowed glade. He turned to Manius, who was crouched like a hound.

'My thanks,' he said. 'That was a good shot – where have you been?'

Manius shrugged. 'Far away.'

Dog laughed and looked at Drust pointedly; he might just as well have put a finger to the side of his head and made little circles.

'Monsters...' Kisa managed, looking round. Dog laughed and toed the stag-man over as far as Manius's arrow would allow. Ugo muttered some prayer or spell.

Even in the dim, this Cernunnos was revealed as old, his matted grey-white hair worked into antlers with twigs, his beard full of woven-in leaves, more twigs, little bones, coloured ribbons. His skin felt cold and normal as any fresh-killed man would. Yet he had fought like a man a decade younger, using only a knotted club; Drust's head still throbbed.

'They died hard,' Kag reminded them. 'Is anyone hurt badly here?'

They had slashes and cuts and bruising, some that needed needle and gut. Dog had the worst of it, a slash across his midriff that gaped like a lipless mouth. Kisa did his best with needle and poor thread, apologising the while. Dog simply grunted. 'An inch deeper and you would not need to bother.'

Ugo clapped Kisa on the shoulder and declared him winner of the Games. 'That knife in the eye trick,' he said and shook his head admiringly. Kisa looked sicker than ever.

'We should lay the stag-horns out on their altar,' Ugo added. 'In honour of the gods here.'

'Fuck their gods,' Dog spat back. 'Let the birds and animals have him then. Fitting, for these forests beasts to return to the Dark.'

'Besides,' Sow pointed out wearily, 'you killed them in droves, for all their brews and forest strength.'

It was true enough. They had been no warriors, just priests, potioned with secret brew and desperation. Protecting their own, as Sow said.

Kag looked scathe at him. Shrugged.

'The world is like that, isn't it? Two peasants fight each other over some patch of land that gets ridden and ravaged flat next day by a warlord and his Chosen. Who are slaughtered to a man the day after that by Rome and the Army. Merchants ruin folk out of their houses, their livelihoods and their very lives. A man who had a homestead and a wife and a son and a decent plough ox cuts the same merchant's throat for revenge. Thus is the world ruled, by gods above and below in turn.'

Everyone was silent and Kag seemed a little ashamed of his outburst. He spat.

'Now,' he said, looking at Manius, 'how far away are you – can you lead us to Praeclarum?'

Chapter Eight

The passing of centuries had created this sacred grove, the huge oaks clawing ever skywards, growing in power and girth until they touched, fused like pouring stone, the *opus caementicium* that built the Empire. Now the trunks were bloated into buttresses big as those in any *basilica*, while the branches above formed snaking bridges a hundred feet and more over their heads.

At some point there had been fire, deliberate or accidental, and now there were blackened caves, charred chambers and holes looking like mere shadows in the blue-green dim under a canopy boiling like a thunderhead. Yet they could hide anything, including the nailed-up skulls of the dead, as Dog discovered.

'This one is nailed up through the eyes,' he said, pointing it out. 'A statement, do you think? On sending spies out into the Dark?'

'Just two handy holes for nails,' Kag growled back and nodded to the crouching Manius; Dog acknowledged it and tossed the blackened skull casually away.

'What of it, Manius?' he asked. 'Can you find a way to Praeclarum?'

'How did you avoid these... horrors?' Kisa interrupted before Manius could speak, then drew back as the *mavro* turned his head; it looked as if he had no eyes at all, just sockets like the skull Dog had thrown away. Waiting to be nailed, Kisa thought wildly, and suddenly became aware of the fly-buzzing dead he stood among.

'I found the Colour,' Manius said. 'I found my father. He wore a collar made from the mane of a lion he had killed himself with his bare hands – he had the mark of a single claw swipe to prove it.'

'Right,' Kag said hesitantly.

'I wore no such collar, though I wanted one. I had a kirtle of leopard and javelins suited to my size and I knew I would kill a lion, this day or the next. I knew the secrets of every *wadi*, every oasis, of the vulture and the hyena, the spoor of eland, the fewmet of giraffe. I slept with the smell of sand and the wheel of stars... all of it making a pigment I could recognise anywhere. I knew the Colour of my land.'

He stopped and bowed his head, a mercy for Kisa. 'Then the Romans came and made me a slave...'

Drust laid a hand on the matted braids of his hair. 'Slave no longer. Brother of the Sand. Lead us to Praeclarum.'

Manius uncoiled, nodded and loped off. They watched him go and then started to follow, though Kag and Drust exchanged looks on the nature of Manius and did not need to say a word for both of them to hear the long-dead Sib speak fearfully about *jnoun* and how Manius should never be allowed out of the desert into the world.

Other people had different concerns.

'I hate trees,' Quintus muttered fearfully.

'You hate everything that isn't a *taberna* in Rome,' Kag pointed out. 'Squint a little – doesn't this remind you of night on any street down Subura? The *insulae*? The shadows? The pillars of the Basilica?'

'What it reminds me of,' Kisa said firmly, 'is the need to get out of it before those... creatures... come back.'

They kept moving, stiff and sore, while the fat, morbid trees gave way to straight-growing mountain ash, tall pillars that were spaced like those in a ceremonial portico; the light splintered down in a dapple that was a balm of relief.

When they found themselves sliding out to sparser woodland, where the light was stronger and bathed clearings in sunshine, they stopped and crouched, sweating and panting. Distantly, a horn blared which brought heads up; Kisa whimpered. Dog had him rebind his wound, which was leaking fresh blood.

'Do not worry, little Jew,' Ugo declared firmly. 'That has nothing to do with Cernunnos or these death warriors. That's a good Roman horn.'

It was the *cornicen* blowing orders. Antyllus was on the march south to the gates of the fortress at Biriciana, where he expected to be let in one way or the other.

'When he is opposed,' Drust added as he laid all this out, 'he will know it's all up with him. He will then send word to his little fortress here...'

He did not need to add what the word would order; they all nodded and hefted weapons, then Dog put his splayed hand out, face down, and one by one the others added to it until they had a circle.

'Brothers of the Sand,' Drust said, 'forged in a ring.'

'There are men,' said a voice, and instantly the ring broke. Manius flitted back, turned his head and pointed south. 'Six or seven. Moving quickly.'

They were a last patrol from Antyllus's fortress, scurrying back across the ravaged fields before night fell; no one who was not drunk or addled or us wanted to be out in the night, surrounded by the Dark, as Kag laconically pointed out.

But the scurriers were hurrying shadows that could be followed, and they did, right up until they were close to the ruined walls. Far too close, as Sow scathingly observed. 'Have they no sentries at all?'

'Let us hope not,' Kag whispered back.

They squatted in the brush and scrub of what had once been fields, listening to the night birds call and hoping what they heard were really birds; around them the blackness pressed and the Dark with it, the trees seeming to lean in. Manius slithered in and spoke in low whispers only to Drust – but no one missed the way he jerked now and then, as if gaffed. When he ceased speaking, he simply stopped, squatting and silent as a shade.

Drust told the others what Manius had found. 'There are many men to defend the place – Antyllus has taken a strong force to wave at Castra Biriciana, but he has left enough to hold this. The foragers don't want to spend a single second longer beyond the walls they have, so they made an opening on this side. It is no more than a slit in a tumbled wall, Manius says, with a wicker barrier stuck in it which the foragers remove and replace each time they go through.'

'Horsemen,' Sow said with disgust. 'They have no idea of making a marching camp.'

'Fortuna smiles on us, then,' Kag declared, and Dog nodded agreement.

Drust took a breath and let it out, long and slow as if it pained him. When he spoke his voice was low and hoarse.

'We must get to her quickly and get her out. Quick and silent because once someone hammers on an alarm iron the place will boil; they fear the Dark and will be all edge and panic. We will not last long.'

Manius was sure the foragers' slit-gate came out in one of the courtyard shelters, where wood was stacked for fires. There would be shadow and cover enough initially, but then they'd have to get across the yard to the tall tower itself, whose door was no doubt guarded. Here Drust looked at Manius and simply said, 'arrow'. Manius managed a manic grin, his teeth bright in the dim.

'I will not be far away,' he declared and that brought some tense chuckles.

'What then?' Kisa wanted to know and everyone told him almost at once.

'We run.'

There was little time to spare, Drust thought, as he fought panic. Antyllus would parade in front of the *castra* walls, waiting for shouts of approval when those inside saw his new purple cloak. If there were jeers instead, he would expect Drust and his men to open the gate, and when that didn't happen he would curse and send a runner back to the tower to carry out his threat and kill Praeclarum. Drust and the others would need to pluck Praeclarum from her prison and then run for it – though Drust had not said it aloud, everyone knew they'd have to go back through the Dark.

So they moved swiftly, goaded by what they had to do and who it was for. Even as they did, the rain started in slow, fat drips, warm as blood. Then the wind rose a little and rushed the trees; when the distant grumble of thunder rolled out, Ugo stood proud, stretched his arms out to either side and raised his head to the sky.

'Wōðanaz,' he called, and Dog slapped his big shoulder angrily.

'If you call that out again, giant of the Germanies, I will shove one of those road-makers up your nethers.'

'What part of silent did you miss, you *stupidus*,' Kag added savagely and Ugo subsided guiltily, loping along at the back.

The rain came down like a mist by the time they crept up to the lee of the old walls, unseen and unchallenged. By then the thunder was louder and stabbed with flashes; in the shelter of the lean-to it drummed. The Brothers crouched, hearts stuttering and blinking at each lighthouse blast of lightning.

The inside of the fortress was no more a comfort than the view from outside, where it was all a shadow of tall walls and gates. Daylight would reveal the truth of ruin and crumble, but the garrison had repaired a deal of it with timber and it looked solid and grim; in the stark light of one flash, Drust saw something hanging from the tower and everyone squinted to try and make it out. No one could, but it seemed sinister and Drust did not want to think on what it might be, though he had to fight the urge to run and find out.

There was no sign of anyone, guards or otherwise.

'They won't like to roll out of their shelters unless the roof is falling,' Kag assured the others. 'A good time to make a dash for the tower. Can you see a guard, Manius?'

'I have him. I am far away.'

'Then fucking get closer, you mammet.'

There was another flash, a brief, blinding image, starker than daylight, of Manius and his full-stretched bow. There was a dull thrum and then they heard him exhale.

'Did you get him?'

'Do you hear him yell?' Manius countered mildly.

'Move,' Drust ordered, because there was no choice, because the thing hanging on the tower walls was still there and it filled him with dread.

They were halfway across the yard, moving like a dog pack, when a flower of flame blossomed on the gatehouse to their left, making them all crouch. There was a larger flare, of a more powerful brazier being lit, and like a chain, others went off all round the walls.

'Did you think it would be so easy, you bitch-ticks?'

The voice boomed out from the top of the gatehouse, the figure no more than a black shadow outlined against the red flames. Kag gave a weary curse and Manius spun and shot but no one knew if it was even close.

'Run for it,' Drust bawled and sprinted in a mad lumbering run for the tower they had been heading towards. As he started forward, he heard shouts, and arrows clattered and zipped; one plucked his tattered cloak as he lurched into the tower doorway, following Dog. As the sky split with light, he had a frozen moment that showed a man on the gatehouse roof; there were more, armed and milling in the yard.

Dog struck and cursed, bellowing like a balls-cut bull. Two more armed men spun away from him, one clutching an arm – Drust stepped in and slashed him to bloody ruin and then followed on; the others piled on through the doorway, Sow high-stepping like a goosed priestess as an arrow whicked between his feet.

Quintus was punching steel into a body on the ground and Drust saw the doorway could not be barred. 'Up,' he ordered and led the way round a wind of stairs, and then had to flatten against the wall as a figure rolled and screamed down it like a boulder, ribboning blood behind him. He plunged on and found Dog panting and watching the steps above; ahead, more armed men were coming down on them. The place was too narrow for such a fight.

'Steel to the front,' Dog growled and Drust heard the burst of shouting and the clang of metal below them – more men were coming in the door.

'Sharps to the back,' he said – and Dog yelled a warning that made him jerk his head back. There was a dull clang and the world went red and reeled madly; Drust felt sick and sat down on the worn stones, hearing Dog curse.

Then, as if a dirty pool suddenly sucked itself to the sides, his mind went clear. He saw Dog heft his shield, just as another spear arced down and clattered off it. The shaft of one had hit him in the head, bouncing off his helmet and skittering down the steps. Somewhere, in the midst of those snarling men at the top of the stairs, Drust saw a figure in a white light.

'Praeclarum,' he said and embraced her; she was like a glowing mist, the world slowed to a thick light, and he had all the time in the world to move forward, feeling the savagery, the frenzy, the rising tide of it carrying him on as if he was the point of a thrown spear.

They were slow, so slow. Drust cut and crouched, ducked and leaned on the narrow steps, easily avoided every painful lethargy of stab. Then he reaped them and every one that fell fed him with more desire to do it again. And again. And again… all the way up the curve of stairs.

No place to escape, he roared at one as he cut the throat from him. No way to run but up and I am coming there and death laughs wifh me…

It was not their tongue he roared in, but they understood and he felt them tumble behind him like scree down a slope and it was magnificent; he turned at the top and looked down on new faces, vaguely remembered. 'Good,' he told them, 'it is good you come to me to die…'

Then the world fell on his head and the white light went out like a pinched candle. He felt like a king, before falling.

–

Drust was sick and trembling weak, but he was alive and knew where he was – top of a tower, the one they had charged into and stunned the ambushers, the one where he had…

'Killed everyone.'

Quintus shoved his grin into the light and squinted, took Drust by the chin and turned him this way and that; a ball of blood-pain seemed to roll from one side to the other inside his head and he felt sicker than ever.

'Don't… I will vomit.'

'You'll live,' Kisa said grimly over Quintus's shoulder and then grinned. 'Eight men you killed and it had to be a good blow to stop you falling on everyone left. That is a god-gift you have, but it does not know when to leave off.'

'Did I… hurt anyone of ours?'

'You did not, only by the blessings of Mars Ultor – but I had to whack you to be sure of it.' He looked contrite and afraid. 'Sorry,' he added.

Drust ignored him and tried to stand, felt hands gripping him and a voice said, 'Hold him steady.'

'Praeclarum…'

'Below,' Kag said, his face looming in front of Drust and wavering slightly, as if seen through water. 'I'll help you. The fort's *medicus* is there – we managed to keep him alive.'

'Good trick that, sprinting for the tower,' Dog added. 'It's put their ambush out of joint.'

'How did they know we were coming?' Ugo wanted to know and Drust could have told him easily enough if his mouth worked as it should have. No spy, just the cunning of a man like Antyllus, who played two moves ahead of most other people – and yet gambled like a drunk.

The room beneath was fetid with fever-stink. Quintus was outside, watching the stairs, and the *medicus* was crouched like a whipped dog, staring fearfully round, his face sheened with sweat and blood-dyed by torchlight.

But Praeclarum was all of it, a blanket-wrapped figure on a swathe of barely clean straw. She stirred when he went to her, her eyelids fluttered like bees on a flower.

'I have lost our baby.'

'Hush,' Drust managed, though it sounded hollow and empty. He had stood on the last step outside the doorway, roaring defiance, red with other people's blood; the thought of what he might have done inside if he had not been stopped made him feel sicker than ever. He saw her move slightly and wince, and turned to the *medicus*. 'What have you treated her with?'

He bobbed his head and spat it out as if it was a report.

'Anis, wolfsbane – the one that isn't venomous – centaury, fox clote, vervain. All good for wounds and bruises, but not in quantity for a woman in child—'

He stopped, took a deeper breath and ploughed on into the morass. 'Since she lost the child, white willow to kill the pain – and some chervil to promote rest. She has birthing fever and has lost a deal of blood besides.'

'How long since the child was... lost?' Drust demanded, seeing Praeclarum's eyelids close, seeing how she fought to keep them open.

'Six days,' the *medicus* said and shook his head bitterly. 'I said she should be taken to Biriciana, but Antyllus wanted her here.'

So we would come for her if we proved false to him, Drust thought. He had expected it – but not the mad rush we made right to the heart of his trap.

He laid a hand on her raggled sweat-spiked hair; she was a tallow flame in a wet wind, every ragged draw of breath into her only serving to make him wince, each exhale leaking like blood.

'If you hope to escape here,' the *medicus* added quietly, 'she will not survive the journey.'

'What's your name?' Quintus demanded from the doorway.

'Frontinus,' the *medicus* replied. 'Gaius Fabius Frontinus.'

'Well, Frontinus, when we escape,' Quintus said, 'you will be coming with us to make sure that doesn't happen.'

'I have no medicines left,' the man answered miserably. 'Antyllus made sure of it. In the event you achieved the

142

miracle of Fortuna and lifted her from here, he wanted her dead. If you doubt it, see who hangs on the tower wall.'

'Who?' Quintus demanded sourly.

'Mus, the one you hit with the ladle. He failed Antyllus, made him look less and was throat-slit for it. Hung on the tower as a warning.'

'No Army punishment that,' Drust managed, to take his mind off Praeclarum's breathing. 'I am sorry it ended badly for him – there will be others who feel the same, I am sure.'

The *medicus* looked sharply back. 'A few. Not enough. We have all cut our ties here. The only way back is to be the favoured of an Emperor. He rode out covered in purple to make sure of that.'

'I thought you had all eaten your horses,' Quintus laughed.

'Sacrificed to Mars Ultor,' Frontinus corrected. 'Save for the general's own. No Roman general walks these days – and certainly not an Emperor.'

Kag slithered wetly down from the roof. 'Who is hanging off the tower?' he demanded and Drust tore himself from watching Praeclarum to tell him. Kag grunted.

'If we can work out a way to haul him up without getting stuck with arrows, we can get him off it and use the rope to get ourselves down the far side, maybe.'

Down was dangerous, Dog answered tersely. What he did not say involved Praeclarum. The top of the tower was the last safe place and it was higher than anywhere around it, so could not be shot into accurately by arrows. Quintus watched the door and the stairs that led to the outside; the others were above, hunkered in the lee of the raised lip of

143

wall. The yard below had torches sputtering in the rain and shadows flitting between them.

'Trapped,' Drust said and spat.

'No one was expecting us to do this,' Kag growled, then clapped Drust on one shoulder. 'They had enough men in the tower to prevent it, they thought – never imagined Spartacus would be here.'

'If I had known you were so good,' he added, 'I would have worried more when you and I walked into the *harena*.' He found a torch and managed to spark it into life with a damp striker and flint. Then he raised it over Praeclarum and examined her carefully.

He withdrew the light from her eventually and sat back, looking at Frontinus, then Drust. 'Does not look as if she should be out in weather like this.'

Drust said nothing, but misery leached from him like sour heat. Kag looked him over in the torchlight. 'You don't seem bad hurt – this *medicus* will confirm it, won't you?'

The *medicus* nodded as if his head would fall off.

'Mind you,' Kag went on, 'it was as well you were stopped before you turned us all into meat. You put Macedonicus to shame.'

They both grinned at the memory of the beast hunter who managed to emulate the fabled Carpophorus by slaying one of every type of beast in the world. On one bloody afternoon he slaughtered a hundred, some with teeth and claws enough to fight back.

A ragged whisper of a voice broke their reverie. 'Mark me, lads, I am thinking it is no good matter to be always hitting my man on the head…'

They stared. Kag smiled and said softly, 'Welcome, lady.'

'It will do him no harm,' Quintus added, grinning brightly in the torch glow. 'Knock some sense in.'

Drust felt too sick to be annoyed, and besides, Praeclarum was awake and talking lucidly.

'Never thought this would be where it ended,' she said.

'It isn't ended.'

'So you're a *medicus* as well as a gladiator?'

'Merchant,' he corrected. 'And you are drugged, so what do you know?'

'The baby is gone. I can feel the blood sloshing around. I have pissed myself, right? Not piss, though. Not all of it.'

'You tell me what to do and I can do it. If I can't, this *medicus* can.'

'Just because you have expertise with a *gladius*,' she said, 'doesn't make you a surgeon. Frontinus is a good man, though, so don't kill him with it.'

Drust said nothing and she sighed a little, slipping into sleep — or death.

'You came for me,' she said before she went out. 'Fool.'

She was asleep, no more. Drust wobbled to his feet, feeling weariness snagged to the bone.

'I will watch her,' Frontinus said. It was clear he had been doing that for some time and that he did not like what his general had done. Drust heard Dog call his name from above and reluctantly left Praeclarum to climb into the night and the rain.

'Look there,' he said, peering cautiously through the crenellations. Drust did and saw a figure waving and shouting; he wore a red cloak and a helmet with a centurion's transverse crest. Marcellus. There were others around him, arguing and moving back and forth like squat dancing bears. The voices were harsh and angry.

'He has made a cat's arse of it,' Dog said, sitting with his back to the wall and his bared face turned to the rain. His death-face gleamed and slithered with runnels, the short stubble of greying beard only adding to the horror. He laughed with bitter satisfaction. 'He thought to have us all snicked off, like threads on a frayed hem. Antyllus will put him up beside Mus when he gets back.'

'If he gets back,' Drust said. 'And regarding that – cut Mus free.'

Fortuna would need to be smiling like an open drain for Antyllus to arrive back here in splendour, he thought. By the look of the men here, the ones tied to him like a dog to a blood sausage, the savour of rebellion was leaching out.

'They won't follow the likes of Marcellus,' Sow added, as if he had read Drust's mind. 'Antyllus is expecting the centurions of Biriciana to rise up and join him, but that won't happen. If he tries to force it, there will be a fight and he will lose. He may even die in it.'

'If Antyllus succeeds,' Drust countered, 'he will send men back to let these ones know they have a new Emperor. If he fails and escapes, he may come marching back to here as his last refuge. Either way, we all die.'

Dog wiped the rain from his face and flicked it away. 'Well, boss – what is your plan for this?'

'Run at them screaming, I always say,' Ugo called out, and those on the roof laughed – save Kisa, who was shivering; Drust sent him down to the dry with instructions to watch over Praeclarum.

'The simplest plan is always the best,' Dog agreed. 'At least we will arrive in Elysium together.'

'Optimist,' Sow growled. 'Dis Pater has his eye on you. Mithras, Lord of Light, will hold his hand over me.'

Dog laughed. 'We will find out soon enough.'

Drust wondered how long it would take Marcellus to persuade men to attack the stairs. He got Kag to replace Quintus, looked at bringing Dog and Manius down into the shelter of the tower, but Manius shook his head when given the offer. He had his bow ready but unstrung; the cord for it was coiled under his hat to keep it dry and Drust knew it would be the work of a second for him to brace it if needed.

'When I was barely up to my father's knee,' he said, his eyes the only thing visible in the night, 'I could already stalk the wild duck in the oasis reeds. I wanted to do the same with a lion, but my father laughed and said my little bow would not distress the desert king.'

Drust waited for more, but none came, so he left Manius there and took watch on the other side.

Then he heard Kag bellow that they were coming up the stairs.

'Stay here,' he told the others. 'Watch for hook-ropes or ladders.'

Then he plunged down the rickety ladder to the room below, hearing the clash of steel and the bellows from outside the door. The *medicus* crouched, grim-faced, and Drust pointed the *gladius* at him.

'One twitch from you,' he warned but got no further; a dark shape lunged up and into the room, panting heavily and scattering drops of rain which flew molten in the torchlight. He had a *spatha*, the longsword the legionaries

147

preferred these days, and had lost his shield, if he ever had one.

Drust sprang forward before the man had a chance to start slashing, locked fingers round his slippery wrist and brought the *gladius* up, only to find his own wrist locked in a hard grasp. They lurched and Drust banged him into the far wall, but all he could hear was a low growling sound like some backed-up lion in the *harena*.

It's me, he realised, just as the man tried to butt him in the face, forcing Drust to jerk his head and take it on the cheek. The blow speared ice into Drust's head, made him fighting mad, as he had been before, though now he couldn't seem to make a sound when he went for him with his teeth.

He got him down on the jawbone, just where the jowl is, though he was aiming to get in his neck. He wanted to rip the jugular from him, wanted it so bad he could taste the iron and copper blood long before his teeth clamped on his jaw and went to the bone.

The man thrashed madly as if he was a fish hooked out of a stream, and now Drust could hear him screaming, faint and as if from down a corridor, behind a closed door. The man bucked and kicked and turned Drust in a half-circle, slamming him into the wall. His only sense was the stink of the man, sweat and fear and shit and the faint, faraway sound of his whimpering howls.

The man tried to wrench his sword arm free, and Drust spun him in turn; they rolled along the wall until there was none, then went through the door and crashed down the stairs. The sword pommel banged the side of Drust's head but he saw the *spatha* fly up and away into the dark and lost his grip as the man lost his. They rolled on the stairs and scrambled up, Drust two steps lower and between him and his friends.

'Mithras,' the man yelled. 'Lord of Light!'

It was muffled to Drust's ears, but he knew a man called on the gods when he thought he was losing, so he got the *gladius* up to hip level and went for him, low and fast like a snake from under a rock. Gladiator.

The man shrieked like a child and spun half round, looking for his sword or a place to run, and Drust drove the weapon into his exposed back, low on one side. It went in like there was nothing there, so that the bang of his hand on the man's back muscle came as a surprise and he almost let go of the hilt.

The man screamed again and tore free, the *gladius* coming out with an obscene slide and sucking sound. They both felt it; he stopped and turned, trying to look as he clamped a hand on it. Felt the blood and panicked, started to babble.

Drust drove the *gladius* again, straight for the heart and parallel to his ribs, a perfect stroke. He felt it burst the bag of the man's heart, lancing upwards and inwards until it grated on the shoulder blade at the back and flexed. As Drust started to draw it out, it sprang back so hard it almost tore from his grip.

The man was gone anyway, sunk to the steps with Drust half on top of him, hearing him gasping. He tried to get off the man, saw a hand come up and thought the man was trying some last, desperate attack, but his eyes were all dreamy and gone.

Sow stumbled up, panting and bent over, hands on his knees. Drust, surprised, craned round and saw Sow flap one hand.

'Sorry. Bastard slipped past me. Hit me in the ribs and slipped past me...'

Drust saw him wince, saw the hilt of the dagger and the last half-inch of the blade. Sow fell forward just as Dog loped up to join them; he bent, felt the neck, gave a grunt which could have meant anything.

'He's sixed. You hurt?'

Sick to vomiting, weak, wobbly, but there was nothing like a wound on him; he levered himself off the dead man, glanced at Sow and followed Dog back into the tower room. Quintus came down to take over, grinning his big teeth at them all.

'They never tried to climb to the top of the tower,' he said, disappointed.

'There are four of them dead at the foot of the stairs,' Dog said. 'They won't be trying that again either.'

Then he rubbed his slick death-face.

'We lost Sow.'

No one said much. Quintus and Dog tumbled Sow and the dead warrior down the steps to join the others and Dog paused before he came back into the room.

'I hope he was right about Mithras.'

Drust wanted to say that the man he had killed had been a follower too, but it would have made no sense to Dog – half the Army worshipped Mithras, the soldiers' god.

He had never seen the man's face, or had a name, but the final fingers had fluttered on Drust's cheek, trailed down it like a lover's caress, like a mother's last touch.

He felt them long afterwards in the darkness.

Chapter Nine

It was a soft morning according to Ugo, some memory from his ma. All the others knew was that a mist sat tight on the hills and flowed into the dark of the trees like a stream in spate. Everything dripped, but the sun was there, a gold coin of promise.

'You still here?' she asked, her voice a rustle of straws.

'No, lady. It's a dream brought on by over-medication.'

'What did you give me? Frontinus said he had nothing.'

'Little-known Roman remedy. Powerful stuff called watered wine. For better effects, use less water.'

'Never become a doctor. Your bedside manner appals.'

'At least I am here.'

'And to think once I thought you might be afraid of commitment.'

'You mistook me for a Vestal,' he answered and then bit his lip. Wrong thing to say, bringing that up, the Vestal who had gone into the punishment tomb on the very day he and Praeclarum had been married.

'This is punishment for that deed,' she said, and he gripped her hand.

'It is not. She paid the price for arrogance and greed. There's no curse on you, lady.'

She shifted slightly. 'I would smile, but he took my teeth.'

'I will get them back.'

'Don't have time,' she murmured, and wheezed in and out for a bit until the idea of breathing caught and stayed. Then she slept.

Drust climbed wearily back up the ladder onto the roof, where Quintus and Manius watched cautiously over the edge of the crenellations; below was movement, like a disturbed nest of ants.

'Something has happened,' Quintus said, peering. 'Lots of shouting but I can't make anything of it.'

Manius nodded agreement. 'I think a messenger came. I think it was not good news.'

We can only hope, Drust thought to himself, but he did not know where that would leave the Brothers in all this. After a while, Quintus raised himself up, high enough for Drust to feel a stab of anxiety. Then he hunkered down again and grinned.

'They are leaving. Look.'

They were. Men were streaming out of the fort, out of the raddled village that had grown up around it, men in a hurry and carrying anything they could pack. Quintus was beaming and Dog stuck his head out of the tower trapdoor.

'They are all leaving in a running hurry,' he said.

'Whatever is coming at them,' Drust answered, 'it is not Antyllus in triumph. Keep watch.'

'It is not even Roman,' Manius declared and took off his leather helmet, uncoiling the bowstring. Drust risked a look and saw the fringes of the forest spew loping figures. Saw something with horns.

'Juno's tits,' he swore. The Dark was coming on them.

Ugo's soft day dragged itself up higher, all silvered milk and wet heat. Kag came to the top of the tower and joined in the careful watch, saw the beast-masked warriors leaping round the tower and the village, pursuing the running Romans. More of them filtered carefully up through the village, poking in houses.

'They have bows,' Dog noted, and Manius grunted.

'They have sticks with string,' he corrected scornfully. 'I have the only real bow in this land.'

Drust went down to the filtered dim of the tower room, where Kisa had started a fire near the door, so the smoke would be sucked out. It had not entirely worked, but the blue reek was worth it for the smell of hot soup. Ugo was outside the door, hunkered on the steps and watching; he looked up as Drust stuck his head out.

'Nothing yet. They will know by the smoke that someone is here.'

Drust moved to where Praeclarum lay in a thick miasma of smells. Kisa looked up from where he was stirring.

'She drifts in and out,' he said. 'I thought to get some food in her, some heat and strength.'

'I keep coming back,' she said, making them both turn; the voice was a flutter of sound, no more.

'It's a good habit. Keep it going.'

'Is it day or night?'

'Sun's up.'

She moved, gasped with the pain and tried weakly to feel under the blankets. Drust stopped her, shook his head.

'No need. I cleaned you up.'

'How many times?'

Too many was the real answer, but he shrugged. She smiled a little, not showing her lack of teeth, and it was a good thing to see.

'You should get away while you can,' she said.

'Leave you here alone? I am your latest lover, not your last.'

'That was the wife of the *lanista*. She loved me, or so she said. Threw a vase at me once – was as big as my head.'

'That sort of size? Doesn't seem like romance to me.'

'There *were* flowers in it. I didn't help as much as I should have. Might have had something to do with the way I let her fall out of a window into the street.'

'You didn't kill her, she did that all on her own.'

'That's noble. Like the Vestal. Now you are a priest as well as a *medicus*. How's that working out for you?'

'I might take up the work. Convince gullible matrons that their lives are not worthless and their husbands faithful. Just for practice, let me tell you that you're an attractive woman.'

'Is that a proposal? No, wait. I am already married to you. One of those gullible matrons.'

'I did consider stealing a kiss from you, for all your lack of sugar. I put it down to the fact you are ill – oh, Juno save me, I will anyway.'

Her lips were cracked and hot, but she smiled when it was done. 'You should go. Give me iron and leave here, for I am done here.'

'Hist on that,' Drust ordered severely, as Kisa came up with a bowl.

'Here, drink this.'

'Hemlock?'

'A gruel of leeks and onions. I found some in a corner and they were not all rotted.'

The blissed look on her face made them all smile. She sank back and licked her lips a little, then looked up at them and it was all different in her eyes.

'Thank you,' she whispered. 'For the soup. And the kiss. And for staying. They will come for you, you know.'

'I know. But I am from the *harena*. I throw sparks like a sacked village.'

'I can smell the smoke,' she answered, then she fell asleep.

–

Fat grey-bellies sagged in a dull sky and spat rain that was danced across clinging grass. A lone blackbird started from cover and whirred away in a blur. No sign of a mate, Ugo said morosely, which is a bad omen.

There were no good omens, Drust thought. The village burned, but badly because it was too wet. It smouldered and smoked, blew choking reek this way and that.

'I am sorry for Sow,' Ugo said mournfully, not taking his eyes off the curve of stair. 'A good man and a strong heart.'

'It was until a dagger burst it,' Kisa noted moodily. He stopped, clouded like haar on a sea. 'Culleo will be ashamed of himself, if he has the capability at all.'

'Ho the tower!'

It was called in Latin. Drust looked at Ugo and levered himself away from Praeclarum, wiping his hands together. He climbed the rickety ladder to the tower top, where faces looked at him expectantly.

'Now it begins,' he said, then went to the nearest merlon.

'Ho yourself.'

It was Erco, the little headman of the village called Lupinus, bulked out in leather and metal and with men on either side with bows and the arrows nocked in them.

'You seem to be here and there and everywhere,' Drust called out, keeping his own head down. 'But I am not surprised you favour these beast men – you sent us to them to be killed.'

'Not enough of you died,' Erco replied savagely. 'You should come down. It is wet and you have nowhere to go.'

'As if you had planned it,' Drust answered. 'But you did not see this. Some matters a treacherous Druid cannot foretell, though they are thick with perverted magics.'

Erco scowled. 'Druid? There's no Druid in this. There is, however, the Lord of the Forest.'

Drust heard the warriors hoom deep in the back of their throats, a hackle-raising drone that made everyone look around to make sure men were not clawing up over the rim of the tower. Drust saw the tall horned figure step forward and raise his arms, chanting. His was the full head of a stag, horned tines and all, not some matted hair worked with twigs and branches. Even when they knew it was no more than a beast-head on human shoulders it still chilled.

'We've already killed a few of those fakers,' Drust called out.

'Not this one. This is the Lord of the Forest. Come down, otherwise he will come and scour you out.'

'You may dream of it,' Drust answered. 'I am happy enough here.'

'Throw down your weapons,' Erco persisted.

Dog loomed tall, standing in dangerous view of the bowmen. 'Come and take them if you think you are strong enough.'

Kag dragged him down, scowling. 'Nicely done.'

'Some old Greek said it first,' Dog admitted. 'I saw a play about it once, as part of the Games in Corinth.'

'Spartan,' Kag corrected. 'King Leonidas to the Persians at the Hot Gates. They were slaughtered to a man.'

'Last chance,' Erco bawled. 'Come down, or men will come up and make you.'

Drust laughed. 'Tell your hairy horned faker that I came into this world kicking and screaming and covered in someone else's blood. I will go out the same way. I hope you lead, you treacherer, because I want you to be first to die.'

There was a growl from Ugo and a loud boom of laughter from Quintus. Dog nodded and spread his hands. 'That takes the palm, for sure. Did a Spartan say that, Kag?'

'A gladiator said that,' Kisa answered before Kag could speak, and it astonished everyone else to silence. 'Personally, I prefer to believe the sayings of my god, who makes good out of the storms that devastate your life.'

'This is because you are old,' Ugo growled. 'Like Dog here, who has to piss in the middle of the night.'

'I do,' Dog agreed solemnly, 'but so do you. I know this because I can hear your knees creak when you are rising.'

Drust drew his cloak tighter at a sudden rogue breeze, smiling as he sent them both down to the doorway. It was good to be home among old friends.

They came ahead, under a shower of stones and arrows, carrying makeshift ladders of crosspieces lashed to a single long trunk. There were, Drust had to admit, a deal more of them than he had thought, and he remembered how hard they'd been to kill.

Ugo was on the stairs and Drust heard him roaring about 'Donar' and 'Mars Ultor'. Drust was looking to where the nearest ladder would land when arrows skittered and spat off the crenellations; Kag yelped and ducked.

The beast men of the Dark swarmed up to the walls and flung up their ladders; a few started climbing the stones, which were rough enough to permit it – there was even a curl of ivy up one side to help them – and Drust moved to where a hand slapped on the top of the wall and a festering wolf-face looked over.

The man was looking down to find his next foothold, pulling the mask to one side to see better; then became aware of the presence above him and glanced up, his mouth open in a bearded face, his skin cap askew and the sweat sheening his weather-brown brow.

Drust brought the *gladius* down; the man shrieked and hurled himself backwards before it landed, and all Drust did was blow chips from the stone as the man fell, shouting and flailing. An arrow clattered close to Drust's head in reply.

He walked along the wall, ignoring the scatter of arrows, shot high and blind to drop onto the tower top – it was not any leader-strut he did either, he really did not care. He burned with the fire of anger at them, all the treachery and hate, the fickleness of Fortuna and the curse of Fama, if indeed she was a goddess at all.

He stopped, put a foot against a ladder and pushed. It went out, then sideways, while he listened to their falling screams.

Men shrieked and bellowed; a spear twittered like a bird as it sped past, lobbed up from below. Someone clawed up onto the wall and Drust walked to him, casual as a stroll down a path, and gave him iron, the gladiator's final stroke, straight down through the flesh between neck and shoulder, rammed through to the heart. There was a crunch of sound and the man yelped, jerked away from it and fell back over the wall.

Another figure slithered over, sprang to his feet and flung a short spear which Drust avoided. Dog had gone below to help Ugo, but Kag hacked another warrior two-handed with a long *spatha*, then found time to shunt sideways and bundle the latest climber off his feet. Drust gave the man no more chances, ran forward and slashed like a woman with a skillet gone past reasonable argument. Left, right and left again, the keen edge staggering the man with each cut so that he reeled backwards; his rough-woven shirt, his wolfskin coat and his paunch flushed and he fell against the merlons, trying for breath that would not be sucked in. Drust shoved him, smelling the high, sharp stink of mouse piss; the man went over, flailing and silent.

On the other side, Quintus whirled on his heel and planted a blow in the back of a man and the blood streaks flew. Kag, blood all over his face and beard, smashed a man with his shoulder and then moved after him, repeating and repeating it until the man finally went out and over the edge.

There were too many. Drust knew it, even as he saw that they were as before, men dosed with some potion, used to fighting a wolf but not a pack and certainly not trained ring fighters. They had no armour save pelts and no weapons beyond axes, little spears and bows.

They had numbers. Numbers would do it.

The next warrior over the lip of stone was not alone and he was not like the others. He had a face matted with hair, but that was his mask, it seemed. He had no helmet, just wild hair like a bush, was big enough to loom like a rock over Drust. Kag made to block his way; the warrior slammed him with the butt of a long axe and Kag went backwards, falling on his arse. He was up in an eyeblink, but now he had warriors of his own to fight.

Drust thought of her, languishing in the darkness below him, hearing the shouts and the screams and waiting for some beast man to come at her. He went for the axe-giant, yelling. The man backed off, slashed once, slashed twice, making Drust rear away in turn, then he bored in. Drust caught the strike with the sword – and was back on the Ludus training ground, being taught how to fight a man with an axe.

'You'll get them from time to time,' the lanista said, strolling up and down while Marius stood opposite, playing the mad Gaul to the hilt with growls and gnashing up a froth. 'Crowds love a mad German with a big axe – but listen up. Rule one – never block an axe strike with a sword. Never.'

The mad German whirled his wrist and the blade spun out of Drust's hand, casual as if a baby had lost a toy. The German had no mask, but there was a wolfish look to the eyes that blazed out of all that hair; a quick look over his shoulder told them both that more men were coming up,

160

but he did not want help to kill Drust, all the same. That was for him alone...

'Here's what you do,' the lanista had said, and then stepped sideways as Marius bored in, a light, easy movement of his whole body, like a dancer avoiding a bull. Then he struck with his wooden stave and Marius yelped, dropped the axe and sucked his fingers.

The axe-giant came at Drust, all fast feet and hands; he felt the wind of the axe, heard the hiss of it, tried to move sideways, light as a dancer, and collided with someone else, fell on his arse like a *tiro* and watched death rear above him. The axe went up like the hammer of Dis and the big warrior started a long bellow of triumph.

There was a birdwing whirr of sound and the man yelped and staggered. Manius did not bother nocking a second arrow, but stepped forward – light as a dancer, Drust saw dully – and slammed it in the bewildered eye of the axe-giant. The big man reeled away, but he seemed more angry than in pain, pawing at the arrow through his neck, then the ruin of his eye. Kag, fresh from killing his own man, saw it and lashed out a vicious kick that took the axe-giant in the belly; the man made a noise like a dying sheep and vanished over the edge of the tower.

'Fuck you,' Kag said wearily, and dragged Drust up. 'Try and stay off your arse, Brother.'

Drust tore free of him and scrabbled for his sword. Quintus was slumped in a corner, panting and being sick alternately. There was the sound of a horn and Kag blew snot from one nostril.

'More of them,' he grunted. Quintus levered himself up, wobbling a little, still grinning his wide, mad grin.

'Fight to the finger...'

Drust looked at the bodies on the tower roof and bent to tug one to the edge, smelling the iron stink of blood and that mouse-piss reek. They bleed after all, he thought; Kag helped him roll the body off the tower.

They did three more, then Ugo's wild, bloody face appeared out of the trapdoor.

'Horns,' he said gleefully.

'We heard,' Quintus answered. 'Only you are happy at hearing more enemies.'

'Not enemies,' Ugo said. 'Listen closely.'

The horns blew again, regular blasts that raked up memories. Kag slapped one thigh and laughed.

'The Army is here,' he said. 'That's them being told how to form up.'

They saw them through the trees, trotting off the road and slotting into place like some cunning toy, with their standards and their *cornicen* and their centurions. The Army had come, following what was left of Antyllus's failed rebellion, to make sure none of it was left to further stain the Empire.

'The Third,' Quintus called out, then ducked as an arrow flicked close to his head. 'Jupiter's hairy cock – that was close.'

'These woodlice will make a fist of it and fight the greybacks, it seems,' Kag said. 'More fool them.'

Drust eyed the Army ranks appraisingly. There were vexallation standards from a dozen different units, mostly the Third Italica. *Antoniniana* it was called now, an honour by Caracalla after it had fought for him against the Alemanni. It had fought for Elagabalus too, against the Dacii and the Helvetii and the Suebi, and any other tree-huggers they were pointed at.

They were good, though not the power they'd once been. Even from where he stood Drust could see the men wearing ring-coats, the ones still clinging to the banded armour of old, the egg shields and spears. The lack of archers. The lack of horse. No artillery at all.

The smoke from the festering fires that seemed reluctant to burst into flame drifted like funeral feathers, blocking his view. On the other side, the man with the antlered head waved his arms, pointing with some club or staff.

'They are going to make a fight of it,' Kag repeated sullenly, and then winced as an arrow dropped and shattered on the stones next to him. 'Those bowmen might do a bit of damage.'

'They are not bowmen.' Manius looked at them all, one by one. 'I am a bowman. I have the Colour of this place. I am here and I am far away.'

Then he rose up in full view and stepped right up onto the edge of the crenellations, nocking an arrow as he did so.

'Get down, you mad bastard,' Quintus yelled, but Manius balanced like a bull-leaper, drew and shot without seeming to take aim.

They watched the flight of it, a drop shot which seemed the length of the back run of the Circus Maximus, a long, arcing flight that slammed into the antlered man, just below the nose of the mask. He went backwards as if hauled by a rope, flailed once and was still.

There was a silence so profound it seemed like a shriek. In the pause, Kag saw Manius step down, casual as an easy smile. Out beyond their sight came the shouts of 'Roma Invicta!'.

No one spoke, but they kept their eyes on Manius as he coiled back up in a corner and stared at the sky. Drust looked at Kag, who shook his head. Then Drust went down the ladder to Praeclarum.

Frontinus was there, had managed to make more light, which let Drust see his face, set and grim and miserable when he shook his head in wordless answer to Drust's unspoken question.

He fumbled back to where Praeclarum was, knowing now that Dis Pater had claimed her. He came in bloody, with a *gladius* in his hand and the reek of fight on him, but she looked at him like he was a messenger from the gods.

'I thought you had gone,' she said and her voice was like a small animal. He knelt, cradled her head, and she looked at him and whimpered like something in a trap.

'I'm afraid.'

'I know, lady.'

He pulled her up and into him, his grip tight. It was a strange feeling in this dark with the tease of a bright day, the last she would ever know, with no sun, no clouds and no future in it. The lips Drust touched were dry and cracked, yet they flickered on his. Her hands fluttered on his arm.

'You should stop hating yourself for what you are. Hating all those who are not. Yours is a noble profession.'

'The fuck we are,' he replied softly. 'We are the dregs of society, no more to be considered than old tree stumps. The most pathetic people who ever fell out of Pluto's arse. Know why? Because we let the likes of Rome pen us up, steal our dignity and our future.'

'You are not some barbarian from beyond the frontier. You are Roman. You know no other way.'

'It's a fucked-up situation, wife, that no amount of gods or drink can solve. The only faith left to us is one another and we knew that a score of years ago.'

'I will be gone soon. I am sorry I cannot come with you further… but don't leave me here just yet. Not yet…'

Not yet. She was a strong woman still and would take a long time dying…

'Wife,' he said, 'there's no need to fear now. I am here.'

She sighed a little. He waited until the Army stormed in – about an hour. She still sucked in one ragged breath after another, but it was reflex, no more. She wanted to fall but the habit of life was too ingrained and she was gladiator to the end. When it came, he was smoothing her matted tangle of hair; she stirred a little, smiled the way she must have done when she had been a girl and her ma brushed her hair.

Then life stole out of her.

Chapter Ten

Rome, weeks later

They came down the Flaminia and into the City by the gate under the Capitoline, the escort troops beating aside the grain carts and stone carts and all the other four-wheeled transport anxious to make the gate before daylight stopped them.

A few enterprising two-wheelers filled with farm produce had no worries about the law on big four-wheeled carts in a daylight Rome, but they were also jostled aside and made their irritation known until the escort growled at them.

Those who had given up the race and parked themselves off the road, near the wine and sausage sellers, watched with faces as grim and sullen as the oxen they had unshackled while Drust and the others crunched past. The carts, they saw, were heavy timber, with sliding doors on either side open to show the iron bars and the men slumped inside. They were beast cages, but those in them were men.

'Close those,' demanded Rutilus, 'they are exciting too much attention.'

'It's hot,' Kag countered. 'If you shut them in, they will just need water sooner and they haven't had that for hours, since you insisted on making the gate before daylight.'

'Close the shutters and we'll have to stop and water them,' Ugo agreed, 'or they will die.'

The commander of the escort troops looked from one to the other. He was called Rutilus because of his washed-out sandy hair and beard, though 'red' was hardly the colour it brought to mind. He had a face browned by weather, incongruously pale blue eyes, and wore the centurion's transverse helmet crest like a twisted cockscomb.

'You mistake me,' he growled back. 'I do not give a fuck for them. Close the shutters.'

'Leave them open.'

Drust's voice sounded strange, even to him. He hadn't used it much on the whole journey from the north, through the mountains, down the west coast to Ariminum, and now to here. He had sat on the side seat of the middle cart, hugging the urn with his wife's remains, hugging his memories of her; Rutilus and the rest of the escort thought him crazed at best, so his actual speaking came as a surprise that clamped Rutilus's mouth tight.

'They are not permitted to die,' Drust went on, flat and cold, 'until the *harena* says so.'

Rutilus started to argue, then saw the one they called Dog arrive at the wheel of the cart, throwing back his hood and his veil to offer a death grin. Rutilus knew it was only a horrendous skin-mark the man had, but it always chilled him to the bone when he looked on it.

He gave up and stamped off, bawling extra-loud orders to his men to clear the way. Dog grinned at Drust, then turned as a weak voice pleaded for water from the fetid depths of the cart.

'Is that you, Culleo? I hope it is. Go thirsty, you shit-breath.'

They ground on through the dimly lit Forum of a city asleep, the silence broken by dog-barks and cries that might have been lust or panic. There were few people out and about, even when they reached their final goal, the bulked edifice of the Flavian and the Ludus Magnus gates.

Rutilus was savage with the tousled porter, forcing him to go and fetch the commander of the Urban cohort.

'Dunno if he's up and about, yer honour.'

'He'd better be. Get Aurelius Scaurus here – he knows we're coming.'

'See if you can find Cascus Minicius Audens,' Drust called out. 'Kick the old bugger awake and tell him Drust and the Brothers of the Sand are back.'

'He'll come at the gallop,' Kag added, grinning. 'If only to get his wagons back.'

He came faster than the Urban cohort commander, faster than anyone would have credited for a man of his age. He had thrown on a tunic and a cloak against the night chill, but his hair was a puff of white wisps and his face glowed fiery in the torchlight. He came rubbing his hands together and beaming, then stopped and stared.

Quintus came around the head of the stolid oxen, saw the look and burst into laughter; Audens shook himself from his astonishment.

'I sent you to get a white bear,' he said, then beamed even wider. 'This is better – who are they?'

'Traitors to Rome,' Rutilus said before anyone else could speak. 'Deserters from the Army who have been stripped of their rights and condemned.'

'Traitors and deserters,' Audens echoed and rubbed his hands. 'Better and better. Nothing the crowd likes better than watching Romans who have betrayed them being justly punished. And they are former soldiers too, so they won't be bumbling about with no idea how to use a sword, like the rest of the *noxii*.'

'Glad you are pleased,' Drust growled. 'We also brought your wagons and oxen, so all's good – now pay what you owe.'

'Hold up,' Audens said. 'These caged were not trapped by you, I presume. These are from the Army, sent by the Law, and cost nothing.'

'Read this,' Drust answered. 'If you can.'

Audens snorted indignantly. 'I could read before you could pass a solid stool.'

'I meant in the poor light, old one.'

Mollified, Audens subsided, took the parchment and weighed the seal, squinting to see the stamp on it. When he did his face changed. By the time he had finished reading it, he was nodding and frowning seriously. Then he looked up at Drust.

'Pay in full, it says – and find a place in the Collegium for an urn? What's that about? One of your lot die up north then?'

Drust shifted the urn so Audens could see the name on it. 'My wife.'

Audens looked stunned. He knew how recently we were married, Drust thought dully. He wonders how I have managed to gain her a place in the crowded burial niches of the Collegium Armariorum, the gladiators' club. He has seen the stamp and knows who has authorised it.

Julius Yahya was not a name you questioned.

He sat in the *principia* as if he were a legate, but that would have been a step down for him. When Drust had first met him, Julius Yahya had been a slave, though one who owned great houses and had his thumb on the rich and powerful. He had been the favoured of old Emperor Servillius Severus, then his son Caracalla, then freed by Elagabalus, and now he was advisor to Alexander's mother, the true power of Rome. The Severans had been good to Julius Yahya.

He had the same leathery face, brown with ethnicity rather than exposure to the elements – the likes of Julius Yahya seldom exposed himself to anything as common as the elements. He was average height, still had muscle that age had not turned to string, still had the face of a bland merchant – and the eyes which held a controlled violence.

Legend had given him a lion's fangs and roar, a tiger's claws, the powers of some ancient Hercules, Drust recalled. Now a freedman and no doubt a citizen, he was more powerful than ever before. As powerful as an Emperor.

He sat, with age-mottled hands and wattled neck, smelling faintly of salt-sweat and expensive perfumed oils. Beside him on the wide desk lay a huge open hand of gilded iron with a scrollwork inscription Drust could not read at this angle.

'You may wonder if I came all this way to the wilds to find out if you had succeeded in the task I set for you,' Julius Yahya said, his voice low and rheumy. 'In fact, I came here to deliver this gift from the Emperor.'

They perched in a half-circle around the desk, staying wisely silent, looking at the open-hand on a pole.

'The inscription you are all straining to decipher reads "Severiana", which title the Consors Imperii has graciously decided to bestow on the Third Italica,' he went on. 'To which end there will be a formal parade to present it and a reaffirmation of oaths from all vexallations.'

Again no one spoke. *Consors imperii* – Partner in Rule – was just one of the titles of Julia Mamaea, but the gilded hand was neither here nor there; the oaths were almost all of it, the rest being donatives for doing so. In the aftermath of a rebellion by a Roman senator and elements of the Flavian cavalry, this was as standard as the crucifixions on the road leading all the way to Biriciana. Scores of them and all Roman.

'We have a few prisoners condemned to the amphitheatre,' Julius Yahya said and pushed a scroll at Drust. 'To let Rome see how rebellion is punished by the Mother of the Empire. Ex-soldiers and ex-citizens, now traitors, picked by lot from those still awaiting crucifixion. If it pleases you, know that one Culleo and a lower-ranking centurion called Marcellus are among those bound for the amphitheatre. Your carts will convey them to the Ludus Magnus, to the Urban Cohort commander there. You need not worry about your bear-hunting task – your carts now belong to the Army. You will have a full century as escort.'

How rebellion is punished by the Mother, Drust thought. Not the boy-emperor...

'Audens won't pay us for men,' Kag said flatly. 'He wanted a white bear.'

'Show him that seal and he will pay and thank you for it.'

No one argued. Julius Yahya tapped the desk and a slave slippered in; Drust wondered what had happened to Verus, the pale, cold-eyed killer they had seen at Julius Yahya's back last time they'd met. It was a bowlful of years ago, Drust thought. Perhaps he is dead.

The slave left more scrolls, which Julius Yahya unrolled in the light of a strong lamp; outside the dim of the office they heard the cadence of marching.

'I am sorry for your loss,' Julius Yahya said suddenly. 'The entire unit – and your wife among them. I rather think your term as *numeroi* in the *Cohors nonae Batavorum* is complete, don't you?'

He waved the scroll. 'Honourable discharges. They will be set in copper too, which is fancy for some almost-unit of the Army, but I am doing well by you for your labours.'

There was silence – relief for the most part, Drust thought. No one had liked being part of the Army, however tenuous, and now that they were out of it, Drust wondered why Julius Yahya was doing so well by them. A sense of responsibility, perhaps, for how the last couple of enterprises had turned out? He stared at the sign on the wall behind Julius Yahya's head: 'The *Legatus* knows how to do it by knowing who can do it.'

'Which brings me to your next task,' Julius Yahya said. 'Antyllus.'

'That was our last task,' Kag pointed out. 'It did not go well.'

Julius Yahya shifted and smiled, though it did not go further north than his thin lips.

'It went as I planned. I included you because I wanted *apokalypsis* – you know this word?'

He was looking at Kag when he asked, and Drust had to either admire his marvellous memory from years before, or admit that Julius Yahya still had dossiers on them all, which revealed – among other things – that Kag knew some finer points of philosophy.

'Change,' Kag answered, and Julius Yahya made a little sideways motion of his head.

'Not quite. A revelation, an unveiling of the truth, if you like.'

'Like I said,' Kag growled. 'Change. Brought about violently.'

'No matter, it worked. The truth was unveiled. Antyllus was forced to move before he was ready, and colour himself purple, he believed, in order to prevent further attempts on his life from gladiators and the like. He has served his purpose.'

Drust thought fleetingly on what that purpose was, on the weary voice that spoke of the dice in the cup, but didn't say it. Instead he asked the obvious. 'Where is Antyllus?'

Julius Yahya smiled his threadbare smile. 'Escaped on a fine horse. In Rome, I suspect.'

'Rome – why there? Is he not sought as a traitor?' demanded Kisa in an outraged voice.

'He is. Rome is safer than anywhere for him. He has friends there still, though they will have their loyalty tested now that he is a failed rebel. However, he has information I need, so I want him alive. I have dispatched Verus – you recall the man from before?'

'Pale. Wasted. Looked like a backstabber in a dark alley,' Dog declared, and Julius favoured him with a cool stare.

173

'Indeed. He is knowledgeable in certain areas of Rome – the Hills and the better parts. He is at a disadvantage in others – the parts you know well. The darker areas.'

'Subura?' Drust said dismissively. 'Why would the likes of Antyllus go there? He'd stand out like a whore at a wedding.'

'Perhaps. But Marcus Antonius Antyllus is descended from Julius Antonius, second son of the great Anthony who was defeated and destroyed by the Divine Augustus. He is called after his namesake, Julius Antonius's son, executed at seventeen by said Augustus.'

'All the more reason for him not to be in Rome. I understand the east is popular with those trying to outrun the State's wrath,' Kag replied wryly.

'Or the north, beyond the Walls,' Julius Yahya added, with a wintery smile at the shared memory of their first encounter and the reason for it. It was a brief flicker, dying in the cold recall of that bad time.

'The key here is the Julii connection,' Julius Yahya went on. 'The unfortunate General Marcus Antonius was the loyal right hand of Caius Julius Caesar, even after the stabbing in the Senate, even after the whole business with Cleopatra. The *gens* Julii and the *gens* Antonii are still tight.'

'And the Julii still have their house in Subura,' Drust finished.

'That old place?' Quintus interrupted. 'Subura grew up around it – the Julii moved out when the great Caesar became richer and more powerful. No one lives there now, I think.'

'That will be for you to find out,' Julius Yahya said. 'You will have money and documents allowing you to travel

174

freely, but your best asset is how you can move in that place. That and the people you know there.'

He leaned forward. 'Ferret him out of the dark. Bring him to me in Rome. I want *apokalypsis*.'

I want teeth, Drust thought, softly placing the urn in the dark, dusty niche. He had made a promise to her and would keep it; she was not complete until she had her smile back. He came out of the dim recesses of the Collegium ossuary into the dim light of a puling morning where the others stood patiently. Kag sat on the stone marking the *pomerium*, the boundary between the dead and the living of Rome. It had originally, according to legend, been the line ploughed by Romulus to mark the walls of the city, but it had been extended many times since. One more, Drust noted, would swallow the *Collegium Armariorum* and it would end up being demolished.

The others had small offerings – bread and fruit mainly, because they knew it would not benefit the dead but the scores of living who inhabited the tombs, truly destitute and usually fled. Escaped slaves mostly, Drust thought, who could not risk the grain dole of the City, but depended on the offerings for Dis Pater.

'What now?' Ugo rumbled, hitching up his toga. He wasn't used to it and it was as incongruous on him, Kag had noted, as a silk gown on a pig. On them all, if truth be known. They'd bought them from traders on the road down, along with better tunics and proper shoes, but their hair and beards were still wild.

'We find a place to stay, a base — Quintus, didn't you have a house somewhere in Subura?' Drust demanded. Quintus had a wide grin and a shrug in reply.

'I did. Just before we left for the Germanies I came home to collect my gear and found everything I owned pilfered and the most of the house in the road. The Vigiles were clearing it up. Those little bucket bastards had pulled the whole *insula* down as a firebreak to prevent some blaze spreading.'

It surprised no one. The tenement *insulae* of Subura were thrown up by speculators and survived a few years until the cheap materials mouldered and even the rats quit. At some point it would collapse and the Vigiles would rush in to make sure no fires started — fires in Subura were as endemic as the rats and more feared. Once firefighting had been the primary role of the Vigiles but now they policed the streets — at least in the better parts; in Subura law and order was dispatched by thug gangs.

Once that was us, Drust thought, working for Servillius Structus; but now his power is gone and what empire he had made in Subura was broken up among many other, lesser, sharks.

'Then let's find Milo's,' he said and the others nodded and growled agreement. It was a wine shop near where they had all worked when Servillius Structus had been alive, no more than a long walk from his *domus* and stronghold. The mere mention brought memories back to those who had been part of it; everyone fell silent, speculating on what it looked like now and not wanting to know.

Drust stuck out his hand, palm down to show the inked letters on the knuckles — E-S-S-S, the mark of when he had been a slave of Servillius. The others followed, even Kisa who had never been a slave and had no such marks; it made a ring of hands and they all intoned the worn words.

'Brothers of the Sand, forged in the ring.'

They filtered back into the City, trying not to be as outlandish as before, though it was difficult for men wearing the toga and with the wild hair and beards of barbarians. It did not help that Ugo had wrapped his *dolabrae* to make them inconspicuous and simply succeeded in making them look like cloth-covered axes.

'I could grab a bucket,' he offered helpfully, 'and then I would look like one of the Vigiles.'

Kag shook a scornful head. 'You would look like what you are — a fucking mad German in a toga. At some point you will need to rid yourself of those bloody pick-axes or we will end up staring at the seepage from the drains in prison.'

Those that bothered to notice crossed the street as the Brothers made their way to the Quirinal, moving down the High Footpath to greet an old friend, Theogenes the fist-fighter. They stood for a while, reaching out to touch the bronze fingers, shined from so many other times. Theogenes was the greatest hero of the *harena*, though he never fought in it, for he was a Greek from the time before Socrates and Plato. He did the *pankration* and *pygmachia* and served under the patronage of a cruel nobleman, a prince who took great delight in bloody spectacles. He had two victories at the Games, won three times at the Pythian, once in the Isthmian, and a thousand other times in lesser *munera*.

He sat at the head of the High Footpath on the Quirinal, a road into Rome which was venerable when the twins were cuddling wolves and being fed treats by woodpeckers. He was bronzed by Apollonius. Or Lysippos, no one was sure. Next to him stood a proud and haughty ruler – mostly ignored by those who came to see the real hero, the boxer. It was his last great victory, the Brothers thought.

The pugilist sat on a stone, a man running hard into his middle years with a thick beard and a full head of curly hair. He had a broken nose and flattened gristle ears, the slanted, drooping brows that told of too many blows, and a forehead furrowed with scars more than age.

All lovingly rendered in bronze, save for the blood, which was copper. He sat with his forearms balanced on his thighs and his head turned as if he were looking over his shoulder – as if someone had just whispered something to him.

We came here on our wedding day, Drust remembered, to polish his *caestus*-wrapped fingers, for we are him and he is us. The loss of Praeclarum was sharp as a cold edge then; the others saw it and stayed silent on the fringes of his grief.

The journey from the Quirinal was long, broken only by a stop at a cookshop for bread and chickpeas and some *lora*, the wine of slaves, made from the leftover grape pulp mixed with water and then pressed a second or third time. It was like an old friend all the same, and they were refreshed enough to plunge into the Subura.

The day was well on by the time they reached Milo's, better known as the *Dioscuri* after the shrine to Castor and Pollux which stood on one side of the crossroads. At night this was the realm of cut-throats and thugs, every alley, every shadowed recess a potential hiding place. Back in our day, Drust thought, we were the ones who kept the law, the ones the casual thugs feared.

In the day it was thronged with merchants and customers, hucksters, whores and drunks of all sorts; it reeked of fried cooking and poor oil and the *Dioscuri* was just one of many wine shops, sandwiched between a cloth-seller and a hand-miller, who would grind your dole grain for a consideration.

Milo had been a decent four-horse driver in his day – he had taught Sib a few things, but Sib went off to drive for the Reds, and Milo was Green through and through and barely forgave the betrayal. His *taberna* was decked in green tiles, plastered with graffiti about Green drivers and even their horses. There was a pungent curse along one wall, faded but still legible if you squinted: 'I call upon you, oh Demon, whoever you are, to ask that from this hour, from this day, from this moment, you torture and kill the horses of the Red and White factions and that you kill and crush completely the drivers Calrice, Felix, Primulus and Romanus, and that you leave not a breath in their bodies.'

The names were old and all of them long gone to the dust, and only the State-sponsored teams – Red and White – were mentioned, though he might equally have included the Blue. Milo was short and still skinny, though not as muscled as he had been in his day, when he was lashed by the reins to a four-horse, with only a whip and his skill to get them round the turns and a dagger to cut himself free if a pile-up happened – the 'shipwreck', as every driver called it.

179

But he had made money and made it to freedom, then bought an entire *insula* – three floors, twelve dwellings and the street level reserved for his *taberna*.

It was like every other such establishment – a block of counter on two sides, holed to take *amphorae*, a fire and oven for making flatbread and sausages in the back, which was all the food the drinkers needed as they bellied up to the counter and ordered *albanum*, dry or sweet, or *massilitanum* – called 'smoke' because of the taste – which was cheaper and reputedly healthy but an acquired taste.

The biggest difference was that it had a cellar, converted into a decent dining area with tables and benches, where you could eat quality food if you had the money. It had three fireplaces giving light and heat when they were used and both the Vigiles and the charioteers loved it; both had money to afford it. The Brothers ostentatiously swaggered down into it, making the slave girl smile.

Milo was there attending to a trio of Vigiles in a corner. He saw them, stopped, then grinned and spread his arms, making noises like a welcoming friend even though they had not seen him in a long time, preferring to stay away from where Servillius Structus had been strongest before he died – their old headquarters, The Place, was a spit away up the street. As they filed in, Milo lost the smile and a V appeared between his brows; he took Drust by the hand, clasping it between both his own.

'I am sorry for your loss.'

News travels fast, Drust thought, but he nodded and said nothing.

'He was a good driver in his day and might have been something, save that he liked an easy life too much. Broke my heart when he joined the Reds, fuck them. What happened?'

Drust and the others realised that Milo was talking about Sib; he did not know of Drust's wife or her death. Manius scraped a chair across the worn tiles and sat.

'Drifted when he should have gone straight,' he answered blankly. 'Shipwrecked.'

Milo spread his arms and said 'What can you do?' then beamed again and asked them all what they'd like to drink.

'*Falernian*,' Drust said, knowing the inevitable answer.

'In your dreams,' Milo replied. 'I have some *calenum*, though – four assēs with some bread and sausage thrown in.'

'Ho – I want a drink, not to own the vineyard,' Kag responded and Milo laughed.

'*Conditum*,' Drust said, and everyone nodded agreement. Milo stroked his stubbled chin.

'I heard you had been out east – acquired a taste for it, I see.'

Conditum was a wine mixed with pepper, honey and seawater – mainly a Greek affair, though Milo was right about it being a favourite of the desert dwellers. The slave girl brought it and Quintus found her name was Calida because of her red hair. Or, as Kag suggested later in a whisper, because she had a rash.

'Now, lads,' Milo declared like an avuncular grandfather. 'You will want food. I have a beautiful *suppli*, which you can have white or with a *garum* sauce.'

They ate and drank and talked, sharing a few asides with the three Vigiles their buckets and axes neatly stacked, enjoying the cool of the cellar. Above, the rattle of chatter drifted down, clattering with the red plates and cups.

'Do you have rooms?' Drust asked and Milo frowned.

'In the building? No. Fully stocked, I am glad to say. And no temporary Games tourists either – long-term renters with decent jobs.'

'Point taken,' Kag answered wryly, and Milo apologised.

'I did not mean you lads, though you are inclined to up and leave in an eyeblink. It was better when you were with old Servillius Structus.'

'Speaking of that – who controls it now?' Quintus wanted to know and Milo made a flap of weary hands.

'Many. It's all broken up. Marcus Flaminius has this crossroads and the streets down it for about a mile. And The Place.'

'Flaminius? Didn't he used to be a carter?' Dog asked. 'Servillius Structus employed him and his wagons from time to time.

The name lurched Drust in his seat. Marcus's father, Clodius Flaminius had outraged Servillius Structus and he had set Drust at him. It was the first time I killed for him out of the *harena*, Drust remembered. He also remembered how he had made a mess of it, failed to neck-slice the man cleanly, who had fallen to the ground and let go the reins of his big dray horses, which had jerked the cart to motion. No one could stop it – the iron wheels ground Clodius's lolling head; the crunch and splinter and blood spurt had made a slave throw up.

'He died,' Milo said and did not elaborate – which means my involvement is a common rumour, Drust thought.

'So the son has ripped out a living from the ruins of old Servillius Structus, eh?' Kag mused, then glanced at Milo. 'Fair, is he? A shepherd who fleeces rather than one who skins?'

'The latter,' Milo growled morosely. 'And the one he sends, Cossus, is a fuck. He always asks for more, which he keeps for sure. And a free go at Calida. And he pisses where he chooses, rather than in the fuller's bucket outside.'

It was not new and not surprising. This was the way of it in Subura and Milo would pay or the entire *insula* would burn to the ground and the Vigiles would tear down the rest to prevent it spreading.

'Well, we need a place to sleep,' Drust said, 'so we had better find one.'

'You can sleep here for a few nights,' Milo said, indicating the cellar room. 'When we close, you can push the tables to one side and I have some straw pallets you can use. Not much…'

'But welcome,' Drust said, and they clasped wrists; Drust leaned in so the Vigiles could not hear. 'Now tell me what you know of Caesar's house.'

'The old villa?'

'The same. Occupied, is it?'

'Not since the owner got his liver pierced in a dozen places on the floor of the Senate. Been abandoned for decades.'

'No one lives there?' demanded Kisa, and Milo frowned and shrugged.

'No idea – I haven't been around there for years, though there was a decent baker I used to go to, but the journey isn't worth it. I am too busy. Ask the Vigiles;

they have the power to enter any building, to make sure the proper fire prevention is in place. They can impose fines, so no one gainsays them.'

Drust did not want them to know, but Milo did not know that and turned, beaming, then repeated what Drust had asked. The men were a stubbled, rough-looking trio – the entire Vigiles was one step above thug and not a big one. The oldest of them, who claimed to be called Ahala – 'armpit' – nodded sagely.

'Went there once with some of the lads, oh, a year back at least. Old porter at the gate by the name of… wait, it will come to me. And a woman who cooks. Might have been his wife. No one else I saw – just enough to stop the scum coming over the walls and camping out in the garden.'

'So there are people there?'

'Slaves, like I say,' Ahala confirmed. 'Carbo, that was the porter's name.'

It meant 'charcoal' and Manius stirred.

'*Mavro* was he?' he asked and grinned his white grin. 'Like me?'

'Darker. Nubian, I thought. Big, bald and old, but he looked capable of using the club he had. Otherwise folk would have moved in from the surrounding *insulae* and made it a home for many, ignoring the spirits.'

'Spirits?' Ugo demanded, and Milo nodded.

'The Divine Julius's ghost walks the atrium, they say.'

There was a clatter, a crash of breaking pottery and loud voices from above; Milo hurried to see. Kag sent Kisa to order some wine for the obliging Vigiles a move which went down well.

'Well, since we have a place to bed down,' Kag said softly in Drust's ear, 'I am supposing the next task is to go and talk with Caesar's ghost.'

'Do not even say such a thing,' Ugo growled, close enough to overhear.

'The first task,' Drust said firmly, 'is the baths and a barber. Trim or lose those beards, get the braids off. Start to look like a Roman freedman and citizen – that is, nothing at all to anyone who cares to glance our way.'

Calida came down with cups for the Vigiles, smiling back at the comments; she had just gone back upstairs when Milo clattered down, flustered and uneasy. He went into the back of the cellar room and came out with a fat pouch, which he tossed in one hand while he smiled laconically.

'Payday,' Kag said as he passed. 'They causing trouble?'

'The usual,' Milo answered over his shoulder. Calida came hurrying down the steps and launched herself into Quintus's lap; she trembled like a rousted rabbit.

A minute later, a big shadow blocked the light from the stairwell and some muscle with a blade came down, walking slowly. He glanced at the Vigiles, who pretended not to see him, then at Calida, who clearly did not want to see him.

'Come on, you. Don't fuck me about.'

'I won't fuck you at all,' she spat back.

He reached out a hand to grab her arm and had it slapped away by Quintus, which made muscle-man smile.

'I am Cossus. You'd do well to stay out of this – all of you.'

The Vigiles were willing, noses in their wine cups and pretending to discuss the chances of the Greens at the next meet. Cossus glared round the rest; he thinks he has the measure of us, Drust thought, and who could blame him? A bunch of salt-haired people with no barbering and bad clothes, more worn than old shoes. Looked like a threadbare patch, unravelling slowly.

Cossus thought about it again when Ugo lifted one of his *dolabrae* and thumped it naked on the table. It was a brute, the shaft of it all in one piece and carved round the knotholes to keep the integrity of the wood; it made it appear crude and vicious, which was all of the truth.

Cossus saw what he thought was some ex-Army on their uppers – or more Vigiles. Either way, he was still not impressed enough to back off and the smirk proved it. He said, 'Dug a few holes with that?'

'I will dig you a new arsehole,' Ugo answered, which made Cossus stop, then grin. He stood, legs apart and one hand at his belt, from which dangled the vicious smile of a *sica*, black with old sin, the wooden handle worn smooth.

'You diggin' any holes here?' he demanded.

'We don't get paid to dig holes,' Drust said.

A pause, another grin. 'What do you get paid for, then?'

'Keep order.'

'Do order need keepin' here?'

'You tell me,' answered Drust and brought up the *gladius*, laying it on the table with a soft thump, echoed by the others slapping their own edges out on the tables. Cossus did not like it and neither did his friends, peering over his shoulder on the steps.

'At this range I can rip you through your belly, back-bone and beyond,' Drust said. Cossus blinked and his teeth stuck to his lips, but he did not want to back down.

'If you manage such a strike,' he pointed out, and Drust shrugged.

'Oh, I will manage it. We are all of the *harena* here, so once you are dead one of us will use his blade to kill that one with the red scarf. Then him with the big belt. We'll dice to see who kills those left. We aren't fussy about that sort of thing.'

He leaned forward a little, aware of the men he had mentioned edging away.

'No matter who is left standing,' he said, looking Cossus straight in the face, 'you will not be.'

'*Never hesitate over killing*,' he heard the *lanista* as if he stood at his shoulder. '*Don't look as if you were forced into it, look as if you can't wait to do it, as if only the gods above and below can stay your hand. Look as if those gods are of no account in it at all. Look as if you are a son of Dis.*'

There was a scrape as the Vigiles moved away; Cossus was aware of it, but he plastered a smile on and raised his hands. Gladiators was something he had not considered and he was rightly wary.

'Hey, ho – what's all this? No one is causing trouble here. Are we, lads?'

'Jupiter's hairy cock,' Drust said thoughtfully. 'I thought you were. Hey-ho...'

'*There are two ways to bend people to your will*,' he heard the *lanista* say. '*Love and fear. In the short term you have in the* harena*, you cannot make folk love you...*'

A tongue flicked Cossus's teeth and the smile wavered slightly. 'I did not come here to have some steel pointed at me. I think I prefer it down the street.'

'I imagine so,' Drust answered, and watched Cossus back up the steps to join his men. They made a lot of noise as they sauntered out, but were less jaunty than when they had come in. The silence hung for a moment, like the end of a play. Cue applause, Drust thought.

'That went well,' Kag said, and the others laughed. The Vigiles scraped back their chairs and got up, pretending they had important fires to fight.

Milo came down, wiping his nervous hands on his apron and smiling in a twitched coney sort of way; he eyed the hurrying Vigiles sourly. 'That will be all round the neighbourhood in an hour. Cossus won't like the way you made him look.'

'No, he won't.'

'It is likely he will come at you again.'

'He will.'

Milo looked from one to the other.

'What will you do when he does?'

Drust looked Milo steadily in the eye.

'We will kill him.'

'You do not know what Cossus is like,' Milo said, and Kag laughed aloud.

'No – but I know what we are like.'

Chapter Eleven

Exhaustion took Drust at the Baths of Agrippa and he fell asleep after a massage by a slave with expert fingers, kneading his back and his legs. He recalled, muzzily, questions about his wounds and whether he had served, but then it was all grey, heaving sea.

That was what loss was, Drust was realising. Adrift in a grey, heaving sea, watching the swell grow and grow until it crashed on you, took you down, spinning and spinning and gasping for breath until, at the point where you were sure you would die, you were launched back into sunlight and air. Then you floated, waiting for the next wave, almost knowing what would trigger it – a snatch of song, a scent, a comment.

By the time he woke and joined the others, the day was well advanced and the baths were growing busy – these were the oldest baths in Rome, always kept refurbished in gleaming white marble, and close to the Campius Martius. That hallowed field was now built over by temples including the Pantheon, which Agrippa had also commissioned, but there was always a lingering whiff of dank smoke which let people know that Pompeii and Herculaneum were not the only places at risk from the fires of the Underworld.

They were all shaved, shorn and blissed by hot water and the feeling of clean, watching the naked bodybuilders lift lead weights with loud grunts, or playing some game with a ball which involved a lot of arguing. A handful of young boys in loincloths watched while trying not to be seen doing it, but now and then they would put their heads together and giggle.

The only one not here was Manius, who had suffered to be shorn, shaved and briefly soaked, then gone sliding off to Caesar's house.

'Think he will find anything?' Kisa asked.

'Just what we know already. I don't think Antyllus is there,' Drust replied.

'If not – what do we do?' Ugo demanded, feeling his head cautiously; he did not like being so close-shorn, for hair was a mark of a warrior, a symbol of respect. He had been a Roman for long enough not to let it bother him unduly, but he was missing his lice.

No one spoke while they pondered on it, but in truth there was nothing much they could do save make it known they were searching for a Marcus Antonius Antyllus.

'With luck he'll get to hear of it and flee to Tarsus,' Quintus observed. 'Or the City of Sharp-Nosed Fishes, or even further east or south, where Rome's fingers do not easily pry.'

'What then for us?' Kisa asked, and that hung in the air like a fart at a feast. What indeed, Drust thought. Would Julius Yahya be content to know his prey had slipped him? Let it go – let the Brothers go?

He did not like the nag about Antyllus in all of this. He had not looked much like a man determined to assume the Purple and overthrow the boy-emperor and his mother.

He had looked, if Drust was truthful with himself, like a man backed into a corner and desperate.

'Lentulus,' Kisa said suddenly, and that lifted heads. The little Jew felt the eyes and stared round them all. 'Didn't he also escape?'

'He did, you clever man,' Kag said, grinning. 'We forgot about him, because he is only a barber.'

'That's what reminded me,' Kisa said. 'Getting shaved. I thought he might be plying his trade here in Rome.'

'Pah,' Kag declared dismissively, 'Lentulus is the one most likely to have run for the east or the south. You will find him oiling his way into society in Alexandria, or even Palmyra. Your Ptolemy loves a good primper.'

'He was fiercely loyal to Antyllus,' Kisa pointed out and then smiled slyly. 'Like a bed slave would be.'

'There is that,' Quintus agreed, fingering his smooth chin. 'Perhaps we should look for him too – if we find him here, it is certain he will lead us to Antyllus.'

'We'll know more when Manius returns,' Kisa said, yawning sleepily. 'Though he is taking his time.'

'Hunting out some of that leaf he chews,' Dog growled.

'He is far away,' Kag agreed and they laughed.

The noise grew intrusive; barbers, masseurs, the pluckers and preeners vied with their customers in raised voices. The hucksters of sausage and cheese snacks, bread and wine, all roared out their spurious adverts until it made quiet conversation impossible. The middle of the pool might have done for secrecy, but it now had a rainbow sheen of old oil and what looked suspiciously like a turd.

They wandered out, hitching their togas and muttering about the feel of them. In the end, they took them off and bought cloaks with hoods from a merchant – the same Gallic cloaks that had given Caracalla his name. They wandered in tunics, the toga looped and wrapped round one arm, or held like a bundle of washing so that they could conceal their blades; Dog walked with his hood up to hide the worst of his face.

'You can't fight wearing one of these affairs,' Ugo growled disgustedly, thrashing his toga-clad arm.

'Not going to fight, are we?' Kag pointed out as they went past a line of coffered slaves being touted at reasonable prices. They looked, partly because they had been in that position and some could even recall it, partly because of curiosity; they had once bought and sold for the Ludus of Servillius Structus now long gone.

It was Kag who spotted him, who turned and whispered, smiling, to Drust. 'That one. The one with the scar on his right arm. That's Stolo.'

He was right. They stared until the dealer spotted a potential sale and moved across, smiling, looking them up and down, assessing their wealth and likelihood. Then his grin shone like a lighthouse flare.

'Drusus, isn't it?' he said and slapped his chest. 'Marcus Octavius Balba – we did business when old Servillius Structus had the Ludus Ferrata.'

Drust remembered him and said so, which made the man beam. He was short, stout and with a clench of curls salted with age. He indicated the line of slaves.

'These are on their way to the Graecostadium, but I can sell them *sub hasta* for a while if you have an interest.'

Sub hasta, 'under the spear', was an auction wherever the dealer stood, as opposed to the official version at the Graecostadium.

Kag moved to Stolo, who looked at him dull-eyed. Kag kept his face steady and close until recognition dawned – and when Dog drew back his hood and stepped up into Stolo's eyeline, the man whimpered and drew back.

'Ho, ho,' Balba said, clearly taken aback by the sight himself. 'This is a valuable property. I don't want it dropping dead thinking Dis Pater has come for his due.' He tried looking round to encourage a laugh, but none came.

Kisa lifted the placard round Stolo's neck and read it aloud. 'Age – 26. Sex – male. Physical attributes – strong and fit, former soldier. State of health – fit. Good looks – personable. Skills – former soldier. Intelligence and education – above average. Can read and write.'

'You lie like a fallen tree,' Kag spat out. 'Add ten years to his age. Don't forget to point out the strongest parts of him are his legs, which carried him away from the fighting.'

'Ho – I am an honest dealer here—'

'Shut the fuck up, you *mangone* bastard,' Quintus growled. 'This is one condemned to the *harena* – if he had been caught and delivered with the others we brought from the Army up north, in chains and shackles and bound for the *noxii* executions at the start of the Ludus Magnus.'

His voice turned heads and people paused to listen; this was better entertainment than some Sibylline faker of prophecies or a snake-charmer with a flute. '*Mangone*' was a reasonable name for a slave dealer, but delivered in the way it was seemed destined to start a fight.

Balba thought so, for he turned and started waving for his strong-arms to close in; Drust took him by the front of his tunic, while Ugo moved like a huge boulder that stopped the strong-arms dead while they considered it.

'Do you want me to call for the Urban Cohort?' Drust demanded, soft and sibilant. 'Tell them you harbour an escaped deserter, condemned *in absentio* to the Flavian?'

Balba blinked once or twice, then tried to wrench himself free. When that failed, he gave up and shook his head miserably.

'Unshackle him, turn him over to us and we will deliver him to where he should be.'

'You are just stealing a slave,' Balba blustered. 'Worth a thousand sesterces at least—'

Drust shook him and Balba gave in. Stolo was unshackled and Quintus took him by the neck of his filthy tunic. 'Try to run and I will cut you down.'

They moved swiftly off, one on either side with a hand under Stolo's armpit, walking hard enough for him to have to trot, and because he was weak and had been beaten, he frequently lost his footing and was dragged until he recovered. Drust chivvied them on; he did not want to wait and see if Balba finally worked up enough courage to call for the law. Probably not, he concluded, since he almost certainly had a couple more in his coffer that would not stand scrutiny.

By the time they reached Milo's bar Stolo's toes were battered and he whimpered a lot, so they stopped at the fountain outside the temple to Castor and Pollux, dashed water in his face and on his feet, then let him drink.

'What will you do with me?' he managed to gasp.

'Think of the worst,' Dog growled, shoving that face at him again. 'Then double it.'

Stolo moaned and shook his head. 'When the gods decide to fuck you, you are truly lost. I mean – in the whole of the Empire, we end up on the same street in Rome.'

They lifted him up and carried him into Milo's, laughing and pretending he was one of them and already drunk while they dragged him past the leaners on the bar and down the stairs. There were a couple of people at a table who decided elsewhere was better when Dog glared at them and told them to fuck off.

'You are death to custom,' Milo declared bitterly, but was interested in what had been brought in.

'Bring him wine,' Drust said. '*Mulsum*. Put some life in him.'

'So we can take it back later,' Dog answered. Stolo, drank the sweet wine in three gulps and lolled back, blowing out his cheeks.

'I did nothing to you,' he declared mournfully, and Quintus laughed out his astonishment.

'You left us on the wrong side of the river, you and that fuck Tubulus. You ran back to the bridge screaming that everyone else was dead, so the engineers cut it.'

'We ran, for sure,' Stolo admitted wearily. 'Like a four-horse from the tape drop – but by the time we got to the centurion he was coping with a flood of runaways from that village. I tried to tell him the headman there had been a traitorous fuck, but he was too busy.'

'So who ordered the bridge cut?' Ugo demanded disbelievingly.

'Some tribune arrived with a detachment of men and a funny-looker in a hooded cloak. Not Army, but the tribune practically sucked his cock. They spoke to the centurion and then to Tubulus. I fancied I was next and didn't like it, so I made myself scarce behind some oxen. Then Tubulus shouted that everyone else was dead, the centurion ordered the bridge cut, and that was that.'

Kag squinted and scowled. 'A tribune? A funny-looker in a cloak? You expect us to believe this horseshit? Everyone from your old unit did die and it was only the blessings of gods above and below that we didn't.'

'Save for one,' Drust said quietly, and everyone looked ashamed at having omitted her. 'What did the cloaked one look like?'

'Like a week-old corpse,' Stolo replied sullenly, then glanced at Dog. 'Not as much of a frightener as him, mind, but bad enough. Pale. I mean, like the colour had been sucked out of him. Eyelashes and hair too. Made me determined not to go with him like Tubulus did, the skinny arse. I slipped off then and kept slipping. Don't know what happened to Tubulus – never heard or saw him again.'

Kag looked at Drust. No one else spoke and then Drust took Stolo under the chin.

'We know this man. His name is Verus and he is more dangerous than plague. I will give you one chance. I have a toga I can give you. Here is enough for a decent tunic and some shoes – your feet are too fucked for you to run far on them naked.'

Stolo looked from one to the other, astounded, then licked his lips. Drust saw it and smiled; Stolo didn't like that smile and showed it in his fearful eyes.

'I know, I know – you are wondering how far you can run. Well, you can try it. I give you the toga to hide those ridiculous skin-marks – SPQR is the folly of youth and at least you had it done on the chest, since anywhere that can be seen is a violation of regulations.'

Drust reached out a finger and touched the faded lettering on Stolo's forearm. 'But *Roma Invicta* here is just a fuck you to regulations.'

'I was broken for it,' Stolo admitted. 'Got passed over for rightful promotion then got drunk and then got the skin-mark and then got broken from the rank I had.' He shook his head. 'I was truly a *stupidus* back then. That's when the gods decided they'd had enough of me. I could not do worse.'

'Ho,' Kag declared. 'Says the man who ran off and left his comrades.'

Stolo dipped his head and stared at the floor. He knew what the punishment was and everyone saw him tremble at the anticipation. Drust took Stolo by the stubbled chin and forced him to lock eyes.

'Well, here's why the gods above and below put us on the same street in the greatest city in the world. I give you this one chance. You can run until you do something foolish that will reveal you are probably a deserter. Or you can go out, quiet and slow, keeping your head down and sure in the knowledge that here, in this place, you have a refuge and friends.'

'Friends?' Stolo repeated. 'A refuge? How can I trust you?'

Dog snarled at him. 'You got his wife killed,' he said harshly. 'If Drust hands you this lifeline instead of wrapping it round your treacherous neck and strangling you, then you had better take it.'

'And if you betray it again,' Quintus added, with a grin that his eyes had no part in, 'then we will queue up to cut pieces off you.'

Stolo flicked out his tongue, looked at the wine cup as if willing it to refill. 'What do I have to do?'

'Pick up any trace of this Verus. He is in Rome. Be careful – he is more than just a fright to look at.'

Stolo looked round them all, then nodded briefly. 'I felt bad about them cutting that bridge.'

'Never felt bad about running, though,' Kag pointed out. Stolo had no answer. He drank another cup of *mulsum*, ate a sausage, and then left with Kisa to buy shoes and a decent tunic; they both wore the toga like gentlemen.

Kisa came back in an hour and joined the quiet throng round the table. They ate chickpea stew and bread, drank watered wine, and talked.

'He has shoes and a tunic,' Kisa told them, 'so that's the last you will see of Stolo.'

'Perhaps so,' Drust answered. 'But if he comes up with word of Verus it will be a worthwhile wager.'

'You think Verus came down to the bridge to make sure we stayed on the wrong side of it?' Kag demanded.

'You know anyone else who looks like that?' Quintus countered. 'He was making sure Julius Yahya got his due.'

'Stolo might have seen him before and just lied to us,' Dog pointed out, but even he did not sound convinced by that.

Verus was there at the bridge, Drust thought sourly, and he had it cut to make sure we would not return to safety. He had been told to leave us out there to accomplish his master's plans.

Apokalypsis.

–

He slept, but the waves kept coming so he was not surprised when the ghosts turned up a little later. He was almost pleased to see them, or so he told himself, if they were all old friends come to escort him quietly to the core of the dream, because he knew that's what it was. He was walking across some parched desert to somewhere, yet he felt bone-weary and unable to resist anything, so he might well be about to stand in front of Jupiter or Mars Ultor, or the entire pantheon.

Fine for you, who had a life.

Lupus Gallus was gloomy as he walked alongside, in the same patched tunic he had worn on the day he'd died. City of Tibur, Drust recalled, and a long time ago, when Lupus Gallus and a host of others had fought as, supposedly, the Roman legions of Caesar against the tribes of Britannia – sixteen light chariots with javelin-thrower and driver.

They won, Drust remembered hearing, and were lauded for it, all but Lupus Gallus – silly fucking name only a tiro would use. Wolf of Gaul. More like a foolish pup. *Last time I spoke to him was just before we escaped under the Flavian. I told him his footwork was still awful and would get him killed… the scythes on the chariot he failed to dodge cut the legs out from beneath him.*

Yet I wept for him, Drust recalled, *the last time I ever did for anyone until Praeclarum. I could not tell you why – he was hardly my last best friend.*

I owed you money – besides, your tears were nearly all relief that you still had both legs.

Drust had no answer and wondered why Lupus Gallus had come to haunt him in the first place. At least, he saw, he had his legs back in death, but he was nowhere near my best friend…

That would be your wife, as is proper.

The lilting accent made him turn, head heavy as a slaughter-stunned ox so that he could feel it wobble on his neck as watched his mother step forward, arms clasped round her to hold the palla he remembered, the one she had got off — as he found later — Servillius Structus. Black and fringed, with a swirl of red flowers and firebirds — silk, she had insisted, from Parthia. So exotic and outlandish she did not dare wear it, as a slave, beyond the privacy of Servillius Structus's home.

I never had anything as beautiful, save you, my son — and my memories of home. Better things to keep in your head than spirits, Drusus.

You loved your Britannia home, Drust remembered. Even though it was far away and long gone for me. Few there would have known you if you'd gone back — and none would know me.

Ach — that's just family. You think you know them, Drusus, but you do not.

Back on you with that, ma, he mocked — you think you know me, but you don't.

She laid a hand on his shoulder, staring into his face from beyond the grave with that old, familiar look that ripped the heart from him.

Every little lad thinks his ma does not understand him. Silly Drusus...

Then the wave truly hit.

When I saw her lying there, after the last breath had sighed from her, all pale and ravaged, I cried out for it and could see it and nothing else for a time, so beautiful and so broken; I would tear out my eyes if I could but she'd be there in the holes, painted with blood in the holes; I can see her, all white and her eyes gone fish-dead, cold stare frosted like old stars, and me like the splintered club used by Hercules...

He woke to the shouts and hammering blows on the shutters of the *taberna*. Milo lived on the first floor and had stuck his head out of the window to rain curses on whoever thought they would get a drink at *conticinium*, the time when even animals had the decency to shut up.

'It is Ahala,' Drust heard. 'I need to speak with Drust.'

Milo bawled for Salvius, the kitchen slave; Drust imagined it was because Calida was already in the room with him and in no condition to answer a door. By the time the shutters had been raised and lamps lit, Drust and the others had roused up and found some light that allowed them to see Ahala, followed by Milo and Salvius, come down the stairs.

'Fetch some wine for everyone. *Conditum*, the good stuff,' Milo said tersely, and Salvius scurried to obey, wiping sleep from his eyes.

All of them saw Ahala's face as he looked round them, one after the other. Then he sat heavily and Drust's heart seemed to turn over in his chest.

'Come from Caesar's house,' Ahala said. 'Got word that there was a disturbance up there. Noises and stuff. The baker has a shop and feared he'd be broken into, so he sent a slave for the Vigiles...'

He stopped, shook his head. 'Commander Scarpio took my section and we went up and hammered on the door, demanding entrance as Vigiles on duty. Got no answer. Commander says break it down, so we did.'

The wine arrived and he grabbed the nearest one and drank it off. Everyone waited, fretting with impatience but saying nothing.

'Porter was dead. Big lad, too – I fell over him in the dark because I couldn't see him. Black as Hades he was, but his throat was slit. Female slave, similar, in the atrium.'

He stopped and looked at them all, then shook his head again.

'There was another. Scarpio sent me because I said I knew who he was, who his friends were. Said I should bring you at once because he's never seen anything like this in his life.'

'Manius,' Kag said dully.

They went along the Via Argiletum at a fast walk, a ground-eater they had used before on long journeys when time was of the essence – the closing of a city's gates, or a curfew on leaving – right into Tartarus, the heart of Subura's darkness.

'He might have been born a *nobile*,' Kag muttered as Ugo brandished a torch and snarled at the shadows, 'but the Divine Julius spent a deal of time among the *populus Romanus*.'

'This is like the Dark,' Ugo growled. 'Without trees.'

The villa stood on a corner of the Argiletum, a spit away from the Temple of Peace and the Forum Nervae. It was hard to believe that in daylight this was a place of markets and strollers. It was hard to believe they were standing in it, panting and sweated and peering broodingly at the shadows, listening to the shouts and shrill, the night sounds of Subura; this district belonged to someone else, with his own thugs wondering what all the fuss was about.

The *domus* was typical – it had been built to look inward and the walls, though peeling and slathered with

202

signs and graffiti, were solid blank bulwarks against the *populus Romanus* in the streets surrounding it. It had been here before any *insulae* and just in case anyone had ideas, the Julii had at some point added long iron spikes to the top of the walls and fixed them in concrete.

The double doors of the entrance were flung wide and two hard-eyed Vigiles stood, spears ready, buckets and axes stowed neatly behind them. On either side, the inset shops were also unshuttered – a cloth-seller and what Drust took to be the baker Milo admired. Everywhere blazed with torchlight.

Ahala got them through to the atrium, which had been fashionable in its day, when the Divine Julius lived here. He had quit the place when he was made *Flamen Dialis*, a High Priest of Jupiter, and was married to the daughter of Cornelius Cinna. The tree in the atrium fountain had been an unseen root then, struggling under the tiles.

Still, the robbers and raiders had not got to the place, so the columns still had marble and peeling gilding; there was even a mosaic with only a few leprous patches of missing tiles, enough to show an elephant dying gloriously to a single hunter. Drust recalled that the family name of Caesar had originated from some myth of an ancestor single-handedly killing such a beast far out in the Africas – *caesai* in Mauri tongue. Or so folk said.

Lying on it, staining the tiles with a slow, insidious shadow of viscous clot, lay a woman, her white hair straggled in gore; insects fluttered and imprisoned themselves in the sticky blood.

'The kitchen slave,' Ahala pointed out and Kisa bent to study the body.

'Oi,' said a sharp voice. 'Leave off there. The Urbans are coming and bringing some official *medicus* who will study the bodies. I am not going to piss them off by having some amateur fingering around in it. Besides – the one you want to see is over here.'

'You'll be Scarpio,' Drust said, and the man acknowledged it with a curt nod.

'You'll be Drust.'

He was tall, broad-shouldered and made more martial by the polished leather armour and the crested helmet. He was aiming for efficiency so as to throw that in the face of the Urbans when they arrived and told him to fuck off out of it since he was only a little bucket boy. The Urban Cohorts were the city guards, the only armed unit permitted in Rome besides the Vigiles, but the latter considered themselves good as legionaries and disparaged the Vigiles.

The corpse Scarpio led them to was on one of the square pillars of the portico. They were stone faced with wood whose red and black paint had peeled, giving them the look of lepers begging in a queue.

On one of them hung a body. It took them a while to realise it hung there, because it had been nailed to the pillar through the eyes. It took them no time at all to see that the tongue had been drawn out and cut off – the withered discard of it lay like a dead fish in the large pool of Manius's blood.

'Thought you should see this before the Urbans close it all down,' Scarpio said. 'Since this is a message, no mistake. Was your man out on the scout? I never saw the like of this before, but I heard of it in my days with the Fifteenth out around the Parthian capital, which we were burning at the time. We sent scouts out and had to go and chase them; found two of them like that. Message was clear to us, as I suspect it is to you – no eyes to see, no tongue to tell. Send more and we will do them the same way.'

'Fifteenth Apollonaris,' Kag muttered, not looking at Scarpio. 'Good outfit.'

'We all thought so,' Scarpio said, then waved the torch to sizzle away some of the night insects, flocking to drone like priests on their feast.

'Can I look at this one?' Kisa asked pointedly. 'I am not entirely without skill.'

Scarpio nodded, then turned away and drew a wine-skin out of his bucket, drank, rinsed it round his mouth and spat it sideways into the overgrown garden. He offered it to Drust, who took it gratefully.

'That's a sick sight,' Scarpio said, then nodded to where more torches bloomed like strange flowers. 'Over there is the porter. Not in the first flush of youth but a fucking big Nubian with a fucking big stick. Dead from a sharp point stuck in his ear. Just like that. Didn't look as if he knew much about it.'

Drust spat out the thin wine and nodded, then handed it round, which Scarpio noted with a bilious stare.

'If you have any idea who might have done it,' Scarpio began, and Drust shook his head and lied, though he didn't like to do it to this man.

'No.'

Might have been 'no, I don't know' or 'no, don't ask' or 'no, I won't tell you'. Whatever it was, Scarpio decided not to pursue it.

'Once the Urbans are done you can claim the body. They'll take it to the Mamertine, I suspect – or maybe hand it to us because they can't be bothered to carry it. Leave it a day and check with me again. Leave it longer and I will have it burned – it stinks the headquarters out by then.'

Drust nodded. He was stunned, bewildered, felt rushed – was rushed, because Scarpio warned that the Urban Cohort was arriving and it might be best if Drust and the others weren't here; he didn't want to have to admit that he had summoned these strangers.

They slid off, silent and stumbling a little, back down to Milo's. He and the others were up and about, bread was baking, and the kitchen slave worked sausages in a large pan, smiling cheerfully at them.

They sat, chewing on bread and tasting ash. Manius was gone. Another branch from the withering tree – Drust wondered if there was anyone in the City who was a *mavro* like Manius, who could sing his song.

Once, when they had dipped down as far south in the Africas as Romans had ever gone and tried to hide there, hunting strange beasts, Manius told them of his people. Round the fire he revealed that the date of birth of a male child is fixed, not at the time of its arrival in the world, nor in its design, but much earlier: since the day the child is thought of in his mother's mind.

When a woman wants to have a child, she settles down and listens until she can hear the song of the child who wants to be born. She sings it up as a boy, because girls are a lesser breed. And after she has done this, she comes to the man who will be the father of the child and teaches him the song. When they make this child, they sing the song, to invite him into the world.

When the mother is pregnant, she teaches the song of this child to the rest of the women of the village, for all must know it and sing the song to welcome the boy's arrival.

If the child gets hurt, gets ill, gets sad, he always finds someone to soothe him and sing his song. And when he is ready to die, all the villagers sing, for the last time, his song.

Drust told them all this, quiet and in the dark; he heard Calida softly weeping and Kisa cleared his throat.

'I do not know the song he was made with or born with, but I know the one he sang in my heart. It was dark and made me afraid – yet now that it is fading, I miss it.'

Chapter Twelve

They waited a day, sullen and talking quietly about what they had seen and what it might mean.

'He was hit hard on the back of the head. Knew little of it and when he woke up it was because he was nailed up alive through his eyes,' Kisa told them. 'He died from blood loss. To do all that was done requires skills and instruments – the marks of pincers were on that tongue, used to pull it as far from his mouth as possible before it was sliced off. And who carries crucifixion nails, casual as a money purse?'

'No one normal,' Kag growled. 'But a man like Verus would. Those are torturer's implements – I knew him for a bad one the first time I laid eyes on him. You remember, Drust?'

It was not something you forgot, that dark shadow at the back of Julius Yahya, sinister as a wraith, white as new bone and with the eyes of a leopard.

'Did no one hear?' Ugo demanded. 'Even with no tongue a man can scream.'

Kisa lowered his head and spat, which was a foul obscenity from such a fastidious little man.

'His throat was cut, just enough to ruin the voice. He would have no breathing either.'

They were all silent, thinking on what had been done and what kind of man would do it. Everyone had a different tale to tell about Verus – that he was born of an egg from a manticore, that he was a Parthian from some sect of trained killers, that he was not right in the head. That last everyone could agree on – what had been done to Manius was not for information but to silence what Manius had obtained; Drust had to assume that whatever Manius had learned Verus now knew. There was a message, for sure, but there was more – a sick delight.

'Why does a man like Verus kill Manius? Are we not on the same side?' Kisa demanded.

'It is a clear message to stop looking,' Quintus pointed out. 'Is this from Julius Yahya, who now does not want Antyllus found? If so, could he not have sent a note?'

'It is from Julius Yahya,' Drust answered. 'Manius saw something, heard something, was on his way back to tell us and was killed to prevent it. Verus knew that Julius Yahya would not want it known, so there is something here that can hurt him.'

He paused, wiped his mouth and thought about the sort of skill that could take the likes of Manius unaware. He had lost the Colour, for sure and now he was far away...

He took a breath. 'But much of what was done here was done for the pleasure it gave him who did it.'

'This stinks like a week-old corpse,' Ugo growled, then realised what he had said and fell sullenly silent with embarrassment.

'It means,' Dog said, 'that Julius Yahya can't be trusted. Something has changed. We have to assume that he has set his pale hound to find us too.'

'I hate that Parthian fuck,' Ugo growled, shaking his head, his hands clenched into fists. 'If I get my hands on his scrawny neck...'

Quintus laid a soothing hand on the big man's shoulder. 'First – let's deal with Manius.'

They all trooped off to find Scarpio, who released to them the swaddled body of Manius.

'The Urbans' *medicus* found sod all as to who might have done it,' he told them. 'They have listed it as "unsolved murder", and since it was in Subura, that's the way it will stay.'

He handed Drust a wax mask. 'I got this made for the funeral, after the nails were taken out. Smoothed it round the eyes so it doesn't look too bad...'

Drust took the pale wax, the swaddled body and a deal of coin up to the Grove of Libitina on the Esquiline, found a funeral arranger and handed over the body and the coin – almost all they had left of the latter.

It was enough for a simple funeral, at night and accompanied by a pyre and the ashes in an urn with the face mask fixed to it. No wailing procession of horns and banging cymbals, no weeping 'mourners', nor herald to announce the name of the deceased.

'Wouldn't be his song,' Ugo noted, remembering Drust's tale. The funeral arranger tried his best to sell them more – it was two days before the official start of the Ludi Romani and the City was already well into performances of plays and music, so actors of all sorts abounded and could be got cheap.

The pyre, soaked with fragrant oils, was expensive enough, and when it was burned out on the second day, they went back and collected the urn. Drust could not help but think that if this had happened out in the desert, as Sib's death had, Manius would have been rolled in a hole, with a rock scratched with his name and some epigram to show a Roman lay there.

Instead, he was shoehorned into the same niche as Praeclarum, because they only had the one space in in the crowded niches of the Collegiam Armorium.

'Won't matter to either of them,' Drust said. 'In life we shared the same floor space. Death is no different to the Brothers.'

It *was* different, though. Coming so close after Praeclarum, the death of Manius seemed like Fortuna had finally forsaken the Brothers of the Sands, so it was a sombre crew who trooped wearily down the dawn street to the *taberna*.

There was a big crowd, for all that the sun wasn't yet over the horizon, and that stopped Drust and the others in their tracks. Then they saw Cossus and slowly the mosaic formed.

The crowd had been dragged out of their *insulae* and shops – mostly women and kids because the men were away working unless they had a business here. They were sullen and growling, but hemmed in by thugs with clubs and knives – about twenty of them, Drust assessed – and Cossus himself was armed with a meat cleaver, held at the neck of an angry Milo.

'Cossus,' Drust said wearily. 'We have been through this. It will turn out badly for you – what will Flaminius say?'

'Ask him,' Cossus sneered, and men parted to allow the big boss through. He was built like a brick temple – solid pillars for legs, a basilica for a body and a tiny votive offering of a head. He wore a gold medallion on a chain; the Twins Castor and Pollux, Drust saw. He was exactly what he had been brought up to be – a haulier, working at heaving horses in and out of traces, loading and unloading four-wheelers.

'Wait for me,' Ugo shouted suddenly and trundled towards the entrance to the *taberna*, catching everyone by surprise. A man stepped in front to stop him and Ugo gave a bear-growl and smashed him sideways with a shoulder, then vanished into the dark maw of the entrance. Cossus laughed.

'Well, one less of an already pathetic band.'

'Get off me, you keg of shit…'

Milo's struggle and rage were cut off by a crack on the head from the flat of Cossus's cleaver. Flaminius stepped forward and raised his hands.

'All of you here,' he began, turning in a slow circle to encompass them all, 'all of you have heard how these men defied me and think they are heroes, saviours that will prevent me from taking my rightful dues, prevent me from imposing punishment. Look on now.'

He stopped for effect, started to speak, and had it cut off by a series of crashes from inside the *taberna*, followed by a shriek and a body flying through the door to hit and roll, scattering others like pins.

'I am here to show you what happens when you defy me…' Flaminius began again, and Drust had had enough. The funeral, Praeclarum, the sleepless night – he'd had enough.

'Listen to me, Marcus Flaminius. You are a cart driver, no more. You got lucky when old Servillius Structus died and you grabbed the least little part of what he owned,

212

and now you think you're the Emperor. I know a lot of your lads… Silanus there. We dragged grain carts down to Ostia. Marcus. Gaius. Bubulca – did that rash ever clear up? Vatia – I introduced you to your wife.'

'Yeah – thanks for that,' the man shouted back sullenly, and the crowd laughed.

'Scaeva,' Quintus called out. 'We played dice with those seamen from the Flavian that night and won enough money for you to pay off your debts.'

'I found more,' the man shouted back, and again the crowd laughed. Flaminius turned this way and that, sensing things were slipping. He raised his hands again and started to speak, but Drust shouted over him.

'You know who we are. You know what we are…'

'You killed my father,' Flaminius snarled, and that silenced Drust because it was true.

'Hearsay,' Kag spat back. 'Rumour.'

Dog had slipped his toga to puddle at his feet, revealing a length of wicked *gladius*. He smiled his Dis Pater face at Flaminius and winked.

'I heard it was one of his own wheels. Turned his head into broken egg.'

Flaminius worked his mouth like a gaffed fish, his face flushing. He was on the point of screaming his way to Dog when someone burst from the door of the *taberna* with screams of her own. The man pitched out of it moments before was still finding his feet as Calida shrieked her way to him, swung the monstrous copper pan she carried and smashed it into his face with a noise like a temple bell.

Women in the crowd cheered, knowing instinctively what must have happened inside and why the man had been pitched through the door by Ugo. Men spilled away from Calida uneasily, but one stepped forward, club raised. Then Ugo burst from the doorway, a *dolabra* in either hand. The first blow took the club swinger low on the back, the crack of it like a pry-bar on a locked door. The second, with the mattock head, split him from crown to neck.

'You can start now, lads,' he yelled, waving his picks.

The crowd burst like a nest of wasps. Cossus thrust Milo out at arm's length and raised the cleaver, only to reel back when Dog sprang at him; he let Milo go and frantically flailed with the cleaver to try and keep Dog off.

It was futile. Dog leaned sideways a little, slashed, leaned the other way and stabbed. Cossus, hamstrung and wondering why one leg was pitching him to the ground, had time only to see the inside of him spill in a blue-white rush from his belly as he fell. He rolled sideways, whimpering and trying vainly to put the coils back.

Drust went for Flaminius, ducked a slash from another man and saw Kag stab the same man in the throat. Quintus came in from behind him, a long, lean wraith flailing his unshrugged toga like a net. It slapped a thug in the face, made him reel back, and before he could recover, Quintus had stabbed him in a flurry of blows that flushed red over his tunic.

Another snarling man stuck himself in the way, right in Drust's face, so close he could see the pockmarks on his nose and that it was no one he knew. He also saw the cudgel with the nail in it, poised to strike, and managed to slip a shoulder. It wasn't enough and the nail raked through tunic and skin, a searing pain like a brand.

Drust howled, fell to his knees, grabbed the man's ankle and hauled hard; the man fell backwards in the dust, yelping and trying to scrabble away through the haze and milling legs, but Drust swarmed after him like some giant spider. He had lost the sword, but his hands found the man's neck, his knee drove the wind out, and he leaned his whole weight on the delicate bird-flutter he felt in the man's throat.

The man kicked and gasped, managed to roll Drust off him and half crawled away. Drust scrabbled in the opposite direction, was kicked hard in the ribs and stuck out a hand to balance himself; he felt something hard in the dust, closed fingers on it and wrenched his *gladius* out of the dirt.

The man saw it, shrieked and turned to run, but Drust banged his way past a struggling pair and fell on the man, working his elbow furiously, feeling the tug as the blade went in and out.

He crawled over the man when he had stopped moving, wobbled wearily to his feet and came face to face with Flaminius. The world seemed to slow; Drust closed in like a relentless wind, his head howling like a blizzard wind. Enough. He'd had enough...

Flaminius had a sword and blocked, but he had no aptitude. He was a killer from the shadows, a thumper, a strong-arm. When Drust cut through his wrist and slashed a bloody score across his chest he shrieked, but not from pain, only from seeing his hand hanging by a scrap of bloody skin from his bloody wrist.

Someone collided with Drust then, and he turned, trying to slash, but was foiled, felt someone catch him by the hem at his neck and haul him backwards onto his arse.

He recognised Kisa through a haze of dust, realised that he had tried to slice one of the crowd and let himself be dragged wearily up, almost into an embrace.

'Easy,' Kisa panted. 'Find your head before you hurt someone you know.'

'Flaminius…'

'I wouldn't worry.'

Flaminius was gone, reeling out of the crowd, which parted to let him. He got as far as Castor and Pollux, sank down by the fountain and watched his heart's blood slowing to a trickle from the stump. Drust lost sight of him as the crowd closed in and blocked him from view.

The noise was ragged and ugly – men were running, women were screaming curses. Ugo had stopped in a circle of bodies, his *dolabrae* dangling and clotted with gore, all the way to his elbows.

Dog appeared, blew out a short, dismissive breath and grinned. 'They are broken. That was easy – the crowd are chasing what's left.'

Flaminius was still alive, kicked and punched and beaten by those he had terrorised; a white-haired harridan who sold cabbages up the street was hitting his head with a stone and fled when Drust moved to him. Flaminius had just enough sense left to know a shadow blotted out the sun. Perhaps he thought it was death…

'I said it would end badly for you.'

Flaminius spat little blood drops from smashed teeth and lips like blubber. Whatever he said made no sense, but Drust got onto one knee and gave him iron, as neat a stroke as he had been taught years before by the Sardinian in the undercroft of the Flavian. The heart in the throat –

when he drew the *gladius* out, the blood scarcely made a spurt and did not last long.

Quintus had moved to comfort Calida, who was now shaking and weeping. Milo, trembling and pasted with sweat, picked up the pan and turned it this way and that, examining the dent.

'I shall have to buy a new one,' he said morosely.

'You'll have more money to do it now,' Kisa pointed out. 'Think yourself lucky it was not you that made the dent – you can't buy a new head.'

Milo did not want to look at the broken, leaking ruin of the man who had outraged Calida; he had not realised his bedmate was capable of anything like that, and Drust could see him making plans to sell her as soon as was safely possible.

The crowd had gone, scampering back to the safety of their homes, because they knew the Vigiles would come at a gallop when they heard the word 'riot'. Riot meant the danger of fire and since they were responsible for controlling both, it would not take long. The Urbans would be close on their heels.

Besides that, the good people of the district had to deal with the shock and shame that would follow the exultation of having struck a bloody blow on the thugs who had terrorised them for so long. Drust and the Brothers knew that sickness like an old friend and rarely let it bother them now – but they saw Calida's hysterics and heard others vomit as they trailed off.

Yet there was a strange peace on them. Drust felt it and Kag, as ever, found the words for it.

'We held our own funeral fights to the memory of Manius,' he said, and the others agreed as they leaned on the bar counter and sucked up *conditum*.

The Vigiles arrived, led by Scarpio, and only when they had judged it safe, that the riot was done and no fires started. They eyed the bodies and asked the questions, but Ahala was among them and had filled in most of the answers anyway. Scarpio nodded, ignoring the fresh wound-bindings on Ugo's arm and Dog's thigh, and the bruises and scratches on everyone else. If they saw the bloody rent in Drust's tunic and the bandages beneath, they pretended not to notice.

'Well, there are eight dead men here, Flaminius and Cossus among them, so I am guessing a fight broke out between them. We'll clean up the bodies and make a report. If the Urbans come, which I doubt, give them some free wine and sausages and let them know the district is in good hands.'

Drust nodded and smiled. He knew what Scarpio meant, but did not want to tell the man, when he was being so helpful, that he had no intention of taking over. That resolve faded when a handful of men appeared later, when day had gone and the bodies had gone and the blood had been dusted over.

Silanus was there, sporting bruises and a cut; Scaeva was untouched and smiling about it. The rest were also men the Brothers knew – some of them the ones Drust had pointed out earlier – all standing and shuffling from one foot to the other.

'Thing is,' Silanus said awkwardly, 'now there is a hole where Flaminius was and no one can seem to fill it proper like, not without a fight which we don't want. If left, someone from outside will come and you might get this shit all over again. Not good.'

'Not for you,' Dog growled, and Silanus flapped a hand.

'I knows it. Thing is, though – you beat him. Killed him and Cossus dead. You are from the old times and knows how matters work. You keeps what you corpse. Unwritten law, isn't it?'

'And if we do?' Kag demanded. 'We are supposed to keep you lot on? Trust you, who just tried to kill us?'

'Business,' Scaeva answered flatly. 'Earning for that wife you got Vatia and the kids that came with it. All our other bad habits.'

That brought laughter and nodding.

'Fact is,' Silanus said, 'that's why we're here. You knows it, knows how it works. We'll be your men now and it will be better – like you said, Flaminius was a carter and no more. He didn't know… the way of it. He has no wife, no son, no family left, just a whore he liked who has fled. The Place is standing empty, save for us. Besides…' He broke off and shuffled, twisting his nervous hands this way and that. 'They say you is his son. Old Servillius Structus.'

It wasn't true and Drust thanked the gods daily for it – but it seemed it was a legend set here.

–

They followed Silanus and the others up to the Place, stood at the gates of it. Drust took a deep breath as if about to plunge underwater.

The Place was achingly familiar, all high blank walls and one large main gate with double doors to allow the four-wheelers in. It had big raised warehouses, four in all, and stabling for twenty or thirty muscled horses, quarters for slaves and freedmen workers. It had a *domus*, with an atrium and a peristyle and all the rest. A shed for Servillius Structus's fancy litter which made everyone grunt, recalling how life had started to turn that night in Subura when they'd escorted him from the annual Ludus Magnus dinner.

They knew it well, were almost brought to their knees by it; here was where they had come to get their orders from Servillius Structus, where they had slept and eaten. Here was where the tally-men had worked, where the little empire in Subura had been administered. Here was where the Fat Man of Subura had ruled.

'Fuck me,' Kag said, looking round. No one spoke, no one said it – but it was like coming to their old home, though the shade of Servillius Structus still flitted through it. They spent the night there trying not to feel like thieves and, by the morning, had realised what they had fallen into, had bowed to the skin-prickling workings of the gods, who had clearly arranged for them to sit at the centre of their old boss's spiderweb.

In the slanted morning rays, they sat round a familiar, scarred table and looked at one another.

'What now?' Kag asked, and Kisa looked up from the scrolls he had been poring over. Next to him was a square, solid wooden box with iron bands and at least three locks; the sight of it had made everyone queasy, reluctant to touch it, never mind open it. They knew it well.

Kisa, who had no qualms, found the keys and cracked the locks. Inside were neatly rolled scrolls, leather purses heavy with coins, and even more coin – in gold – stacked sideways in neat rolls.

'Surprised this lot didn't sack the place,' Kisa muttered.

'It's the same for them as us,' Drust answered. 'This is their home, the only one they know.'

'Well,' Kisa said after a while, 'Flaminius has contracts – so we have contracts – for carrying grain and sand for the *harena* here. Meat too, and animal feed. I am guessing all this was carried over from when your old boss worked it, and I suspect the folk needing their goods hauled won't put up much of a fuss if we now do it. There's also a tally of what he had been milking from the locals.'

'Do we carry on?' Kag asked. 'With this?'

'The contracts are all the ones old Servillius Structus had – Flaminius just strong-armed his way into them when the Fat Man died. Kisa can sort out all the scrolls of what needs doing,' Drust said, seeing it clearly as for the first time. 'We can all make it work. Rather us than more strangers, more bad arses on old Servillius Structus's seat.'

'Save for the milking,' Quintus said. 'We should stop that – you saw what happened.'

'Halve it,' Dog growled. 'Sheep need shearing – Flaminius got that right. Halving it will have people cheering and they know whoever is here needs to have their beaks wettened. They like us, at least for now. Get rid of it entirely and you'll cause trouble with the other district bosses.'

They worked it out through the rest of the morning, until another of the old crew, called Papa, came up with bread and chickpeas, hot mushrooms and wine.

'From Milo's,' he said, beaming, and everyone looked at one another; this was the way of it, then. The district had accepted it and suddenly, without warning, they were men of substance and virtually the law here.

'Got a man at the gate,' Papa went on, sorting out the tray. 'Came to Milo's and was sent on here. Name of Stolo. Says he's found who you are looking for, boss.'

Chapter Thirteen

Stolo was amazed. He turned this way and that in bewildered, slow circles, and said it so often that they eventually told him to shut up and tell them what he had found.

'But look at this,' he enthused, spreading his arms wide. 'I went away and you were all sharing one room in that *taberna*. Now look… it's amazing.'

'Not nearly as amazing as you coming back,' Kisa declared morosely. 'Now I owe a big German a fistful of coin.'

Stolo shrugged and then unfolded himself from the top of his toga and helped himself to drink and olives and bread. 'I thought about it,' he admitted, 'but where would I go? What would I do? Not much call in Rome for being able to march in step for thirty miles and throw a straight javelin at the end of it. Not much call for my Army talents – save with you.'

'What talents are they, then?' Quintus demanded sourly. 'All the animal attributes of a warrior – a chicken heart and legs like a hare.'

'Ha. I was eighteen years in, you lanky fuck. I got drunk, got some bad tattoos, got the vine stick a few times, won a few big pots at dice and lost far too many more. I fought shoulder to shoulder a lot of times and never ran until that day…'

He wiped his mouth with the back of one hand. 'Wouldn't have that day, either,' he muttered, ashamed, 'save that Tubulus ordered it. He outranked me — remember?'

'And you always obey an order...'

'Enough,' Drust said. 'What did you find?'

'Do I get a billet here?'

'Depending on what you found,' Drust answered, and Stolo chewed bread and swallowed it with wine.

'Well, I went back to Caesar's house and started asking around about a pale man with white hair. Had to sleep in doorways, and a temple once — thought I would end up throat-slit.'

Drust looked at Stolo with a new and grudging respect. 'What did you find?'

'There had been comings and goings all week at that place — not just the Nubian porter and the scraggy old cook. The baker had seen a pale man and one black as night, or so he said — I am guessing that was your Manius — but no one knows where the pale man is now. Or even who he is. So I thought I would try around the baths — a man like that would need washing at some point, if only to get all the blood off. I wasn't keen, mind you, seeing as what happened to your lad.'

'What did you find?' Kag demanded, and Stolo looked sideways at him.

'Do I get a billet here? Regular coin? Food and all that?'

'What the fuck did you find out?' Dog demanded menacingly, and Stolo stopped chewing, then swallowed with difficulty.

'Long story short — and, believe me, this took a lot of doing — I discovered your pale killer is looking for someone called Lentulus. So I found out where this Lentulus was, thinking you can stake him out and grab your pale man when he comes.'

'Not bad,' Ugo said admiringly and laughed. Stolo grinned.

'Where is Lentulus? At what baths?'

'Baths? No baths. He's trying to bury himself as a *sparsore* for the Greens.'

'A chariot driver? Him?' Quintus exploded incredulously. 'He's a barber.'

Not a driver, Drust thought, but a *sparsore*. It meant 'sprinkler' and the job entailed caring for the horses. The worst part of that was positioning yourself during a race so as to dash water in the faces of your team's horses as they rounded a turn – it cooled them and got rid of the choke of dust, making breathing easier. Added a stride or two and that was worth it to a driver.

'Is this the same Lentulus?' Dog wanted to know. 'A primper of hair and beards?'

'Big fan of the Greens,' Stolo said. 'And hiding out.'

'Not well, if you found him,' Kisa muttered and Stolo bridled.

'I have been wandering for days on the trail of him, sleeping rough, eating shit. I could have just jogged off, but I thought Drust here might actually honour his pledge. I thought I might actually have friends,' he finished bitterly.

Drust nodded and called Scaeva, told him who Stolo was and what he had done. 'Find him a bed and treat him equally with you all. If he fucks up, tell me.'

225

Scaeva nodded grimly, and Stolo got up and glanced sourly at Kisa, who was bent over, noting his name on the list.

'What now?' Quintus asked, and Dog fetched his cloak and drew it round him, for all that it was a sultry day.

'We are off to the Circus, lads.'

–

The City heaved like a poked ants' nest – this was the first day of the Ludi Romani and everyone, it seemed, was heading in skeins of barely contained riot towards the Flavian and the gladiators.

There had been plays and recitals in venues all over the city for a week at least, while the athletes had been running and jumping in the Circus Agonalis, a stadium built by Divine Domitian nearly two hundred years before.

There were athletes now at the Maximus too, the long-distance lads who were built like spotted panthers and could run on and on forever. They swaggered, half-naked, cloaks thrown over one shoulder to show off ridges of muscle and long legs, and even the Circus Agonalis couldn't hold them – the Maximus was the venue for their endurance races, in honour of some Greek.

Not today, though. The Circus races didn't start until ten days after the Ludi Romani, but the fever was already intense and each faction got their chance to practise, to acclimatise horses and work the chariots a little. Today was the turn of the Greens, and the fans, the hucksters of faction merchandise, the odds-makers all swarmed in; when Drust and the others got close, it seemed as if a patch of Elysium's emerald fields had fallen on Rome.

They got in because they knew people – and it was clear word had spread about the Brothers of the Sand taking over the *Dioscuri* district from Flaminius. It seemed no one had liked that haulier and thug much.

'Isn't that how everyone starts off?' Dog growled aside to Kag.

They came down trackside, to the starting area which was already thick with horses and chariots being tacked, un-tacked or up-ended for more work. They found a familiar face – Caepio, the *conditor*.

He had a face like an old burned boot and no more than three teeth set in a jaw of silvered stubble. His eyes peered out from the furrows of a ploughed field of face, and he had been a slave of the Greens for as long as anyone could remember. Slave or not, he was a valued *conditor*, a builder and fixer of chariots; he looked up from slathering foul-smelling grease on an axle and grinned as if he had seen the Brothers only the day before.

'Drust. Kag. How goes it?'

'Well enough, old one,' Drust said, squatting down and offering a skin of decent wine they had purchased on the way, together with bread and olives. Caepio drank, passed it back and Drust drank from it too – he did not wipe the neck first and he knew Caepio had seen that.

'Looking for a lad called Lentulus,' he said mildly. 'Barber by trade who now works as a *sparsore*, it seems.'

'I know him,' Caepio answered. 'Popular lad – you are not the first to ask.'

'Who asked – a tall man? Strange hair, strange skin, strange eyes?'

'Nix – a little man trying to wear a toga the way he used to wear armour. Shifty look to him.'

'Stolo,' Kag muttered out of the side of his mouth. Old Caepio scooped up another slather of evil-smelling brown-black grease and started working it into the hub.

'There was yet another – Brasus the Dacian.'

'Who in the name of Jupiter's hairy cock is Brasus the Dacian?'

'*Retiarius*,' Caepio said, absently smearing black streaks down his filthy tunic. 'One of the *familia* of the Ludus Ulpius Ralla. Won a few and is highly rated, or so I hear.'

'Ludus Ulpius Ralla?' Kag queried, squinting with bewilderment. 'I never heard of that School.'

'There was a Senator Gaius Ulpius Ralla,' Drust said. 'Got himself executed under the old Emperor Severus. His son got himself sixed under Caracalla, as I remember.'

'Unhappy lot,' Quintus growled. 'Proof that you can only survive when great men hate you if you are so little you can easily hide. Like us.'

'Senator Marcus Ulpius Ralla,' Caepio confirmed, and finally rolled the wheel and axle to one side, straightening and rubbing his back. 'Latest in that sorry line and crawling up the arse of the current Emperor – and elsewhere on the Empress, if you believe rumours – by sponsoring a day's racing here and the gladiator bouts between them.'

'What the fuck has he to do with Lentulus?' Dog demanded, scowling with frustration.

'Ask him,' Caepio said and grinned gum at them. 'He's trackside, mooning over Murena. He volunteered to be Murena's *sparsore* – it will get him killed this month or the next.'

Murena – the Eel – was one of the Greens' rising stars, a wasp-waisted, wide-shouldered youth from Cyprus where, so the story went, as a boy he had leaped bulls for a living until rich Greeks stuck him in a chariot.

Caepio took them down through the crowd of grim-faced guards, gladiators and wrestlers there to make sure neither horses, drivers nor carts were tampered with, and the betting touts kept their distance. There was no barrier, it seemed, to the gushing girls – and boys – in green who clamoured for the attention of the charioteers.

'That's Murena,' Caepio said, indicating an olive-skinned youth with short curls of blue-black hair. He was ignoring the fawning, jostling girls trying to get close, attract his attention and leap the last barrier; any who tried it found themselves in the embrace of a bear-like guard and put back struggling and kicking where they had started.

Murena never even glanced up. He had his racing leathers on, was inspecting a wheel on the chariot and, evidently satisfied, stepped into the affair and wrapped the reins around his waist, lashing them tight in a complex weave. Attendants started to lead the horses to the stalls and he finally deigned to wave to the adoring fans. His name was the same for a woman and a man and that was all part of it, why the boys were here as well as the girls.

'There's Lentulus,' Kag said suddenly, and they all saw the man helping lead Murena's team to the starting stalls. Nearby, three other teams were being led in, the animals gleaming and restless, but amid the hiss and spit of men at work, the mutter and growl and occasional squeals, the horses were surprisingly silent.

'Two to one on Murena,' Quintus said, smiling. Caepio stroked his stubble.

'I'd take that if you were serious,' he said, 'because the Eel won't slip past today. He has rigged his team Roman-style with a twist – usually the strongest horses are in the central paired yoke, with the steady ones on loose traces on each outside line. But he has put one of the strongest pullers on the inside trace and put a drifting wheel on the right side – see it?'

They saw it, a wheel with a thick rim and a smaller radius, which made the cart look lopsided.

'It is smaller, thicker, and has an iron rim to take the stress of drifting round the top end of the *spina*,' Caepio pointed out, 'which makes it slower – Murena is trying out an inside hauler to see if that will compensate.'

'You don't think so?'

Caepio shrugged. 'Seen all the combinations. The driver makes the difference and it means Murena has to put his balls out to make it work. High risk, that. Lad won't make old bones at this rate.'

He nodded to another chariot with yet another fright-eningly young driver wrapping reins around his gleaming black waist. 'That's Scipio the Blemmye. They call him Scipio Africanus as a joke, but he's not a funny man to get in front of. Ruthless, that one, and few like him – he'll never make it to twenty either, but it will be the knife in the alley that takes him to Dis Pater.'

He pointed again. 'See? He has his cart rigged Greek-style – strong ones on the traces, steadies in the yoke. The outside horse is called Hieron and is worth more than the rest of the team put together.'

They were only practising but, as Caepio said, there was a good-going rivalry within the Greens – and all the other factions – to make it a decent show for those who had inveigled themselves into the stands.

'No shipwrecks,' Caepio said, 'but the racing is fierce.'

Out on the track, slaves raked the sand, fine, white and imported at vast cost. Horns blared and the Eel made a show of selecting a whip; barely able to work up a face fuzz, Drust thought, and winner of one hundred and twenty-two races.

The girls shrieked; someone had chalked up '*Vincas, non vincas, te amamus Murena*' on a piece of board and was waving it like a flag – 'Win or lose, we love you, Murena'.

Four chariots burst from the stall and raced for the rope stretched hoof-high across from the *spina* to the stands at the start of the first turn. If there was a bad start, a shipwreck straight out of the stalls, the judge would not drop the rope and the race would be deemed not to have started at all.

The problem was that you made the choice to go balls-out for the rope, or to hang back and risk being accused of being in league with a bribed judge who would not drop the rope in time, entangling the leading chariot horses.

But that was on race days. On practice days, the rope dropped and the chariots, like missiles fired from some giant ballistae, vanished into dust and faint screams; on race days you would not hear yourself breathing for the sheer level of noise.

'Did you see?' Caepio announced triumphantly. 'The Eel didn't get the inside line, for all his rig. The Blemmye has it...'

Drust searched for Lentulus, saw the man scuttle to the right side of the track, swathed in a haze of dust and carrying a gape-mouthed leather bucket. He jostled with others all doing the same; on race days, it would be rival factions, the Red and White and Blue, trying to shove you from a prime point – even into the path of the chariots.

They came round the bottom turn, the horses at full extension, necks stretched, manes bobbed and ribboned in green. Behind came the chariot, not rolling but leaping through the dust. It would be like riding a plunging dolphin, standing on its back… Sib had done this.

'Sib did this,' Drust managed aloud, and Caepio turned and nodded sadly.

'Good driver. Not in the class of these, mind, but a good one. Sorry to hear he died – on the track, was it?'

'A shipwreck with horses,' Drust replied tersely, and the old slave wisely did not push further. Instead, he pointed out Lentulus, dashing forward with his bucket and flinging water in the faces of Murena's speeding horses. It was a blur of movement and, for a sickening moment, Drust thought Lentulus had been struck and gone under the wheels.

Then the dust, swirling in strange swoops and curls in the aftermath of the *quadrigae*, cleared to reveal him, hands in the air and the bucket still held, but upside down to show he had been successful. He was grinning.

'Jupiter,' Kag muttered. 'Our barber has more balls than I allowed him.'

'Let's see what he has to say – Ugo, see if you can cut him off.'

They moved through the throng. Slaves waited to dart out to rake the sand smooth and scoop up the debris thrown from the stands – bits of bread and fruit hurled down in fury. Even in a practice, fans would try and pelt their favourites' rivals; on race days, every rival faction would try to put off the opposition, and the Urban Cohorts was there to make sure it was nothing heavier than an apple core.

The water-throwers were refilling, talking animatedly about how close they had come, the chariot-builders and horse carers were already working on the next four *quadrigae* that would run, as Drust and the others closed in on Lentulus.

They were balked by *lictores*, big men with a bundle of rods and an axe-head making sure their master was not impeded. The master was a patrician, still young but galloping towards corpulence, moving like a whale and flanked by the pilot fish of equestrians. He was certainly rich and he was probably a *curule aedile* – they were permitted two *lictores* – an office rapidly disappearing. The *curule aedile* stopped in front of old Caepio the slave and smiled with a look Drust knew well.

Here was a man responsible for regulating public entertainments among other obsolete functions, but who had probably only accepted the unloved role because of his undying passionate absorption with horses and chariots, the driving force of his life, far more important than regulating baths and brothels or registering prostitutes.

'Well, Caepio – what's your reckoning?'

There was no sense that he spoke to a slave; his tone, in fact, was deferential, for Caepio was the master here.

'Murena is running well, but he'll have to stick his neck out to make his rig work,' Caepio explained. 'Scipio Africanus is flying.'

Lentulus had seen Drust and his mouth was open, his face drained of colour. Drust cursed and started to move, only to be blocked by one of the *lictores*.

'It's him I want,' Drust said into the stony face.

'Don't care. Go round.'

The *lictores* were all hired men and stolid as pillars when on duty; Drust cursed and went sideways, seeing Ugo had already manoeuvred into position and was closing in.

Then the racers came round the bottom bend and a great roar went up from everyone, a surge forward that almost flung Drust to the ground – Murena had somehow got a nose in front and was skid-turning in a shower of dust and fine sand like a storm in a desert.

There was a moment when everything was just a golden haze of choke and splutter, where shadows flitted; then the swirling vortices the chariots had created dragged it all away, leaving Drust looking at the engorged, excited face of one of the grooms, eyes pink-rimmed from too much exposure to sand and dust.

Lentulus was nowhere to be seen.

'Where could he have gone?' Kag demanded, but there was no reasonable answer to that other than the stables and workshops under the Circus and reached by ramps from where they stood. But even Caepio wasn't about to get them down there.

They milled moodily around under the grim, tight gaze of the *lictores*, but there was no getting round them or the Urbans at the entrance to the Circus under-gallery.

'We've lost him,' Quintus admitted eventually, and Dog growled moodily.

'What now?' demanded Ugo, and Drust tried to think, but it was Kisa who spoke, his voice quiet and soft so that only they could hear.

'Brasus the Dacian,' he said, as the chariots slid round the bottom bend for the second time; there was a great cry of *Prasina, Prasina* – 'Greens, Greens' – and an even bigger one for Scipio, who had managed to cut Murena on the top turn.

This was no major race and neither man was about to force the issue, so they started to haul up and would trot the last circuit to wind the horses down; they were nodding and shouting back and forth to each other, grinning and acknowledging the hoots and squeals from the stands with waves.

'Like to see what they'd do one-on-one with a *gladius* and a crowd that wants to see their guts,' Kag growled moodily.

'Let's find out about Brasus and this Ludus Ulpius Ralla,' Drust said, his mind starting to work, oiled by the grease of fear of what Verus might do. He no longer felt safe out in the streets of Rome and he did not like the feeling.

'Quintus – stay here with Caepio. See if you can get to talk with Murena and find out where Lentulus might be. At worst, you might get a message to Lentulus, telling him we mean him no harm.'

Kag looked sharply sideways at Drust. 'That true?'

'I want to know what the fuck is going on and how to come out of it alive,' Drust answered, equally edged. Kag acknowledged it with a nod.

'Well,' he said, rubbing his chin. 'Let's head for the baths and wait – this is the first day of the Flavian, so everyone will troop in after dark for a splash and a shave and a gossip. Trying to get to anyone we know now will be futile.'

It was good advice; the Baths of Titus sat not far from the amphitheatre, under the Esquiline Hill and huddled in the shadow of the much more extensive baths built by Trajan. Consequently, they were a little run-down and not much used – perfect for the filthy spill of gladiators, beast handlers and worse from the Flavian.

They went off, pushed by the cries and shrieks of the Greens. Kag looked back briefly, then at Drust, and did not have to say anything about Quintus being on his own. Drust tapped Dog on the shoulder and jerked his head; the man looped up his hood, grinned death at them and trotted off to find Quintus.

That's the measure of things now, Drust thought. We dare not walk alone in the City we once strode in like kings, for fear of the beast from the Dark...

Chapter Fourteen

The baths generally opened around lunchtime and stayed that way until dusk. The Baths of Titus lit copious oil lamps when the shadows started to crowd in, because they knew when the custom from the *harena* would arrive. Decent customers would stay away, since they'd have to share with the gladiators and other scum.

Kisa had his hot soak and splash and then wanted to return to The Place, so Drust sent Ugo with him. That left Kag to sit with Drust, waiting while the insects killed themselves in sizzling ecstasy.

The customers arrived slowly in knots. The gladiators swaggered in – they had survived the first day of the Games and were pumped by the feeling, talking loudly, making big splashes when they dived in, though no one spent any time reliving their contests; they had come here to do the opposite, before trooping back to their lonely cells to wait for the following day.

Drust and Kag watched and listened for a while, then moved in and asked questions of those they knew, however slightly. They bought wine and sweet cakes, were flattered by those who remembered their names – but got no information on Brasus; none of the rest of the School he belonged to were here, but expected any moment.

When the breakthrough happened it came quickly. One minute Kag and Drust were sitting wincing at the newly arrived *venatores* vying with one another as to who could take the scorch of the *laconica*, the dry-heat room. The gladiators, as ever, made scathing comments at these animal handlers and hunters, who responded with pig noises, an old insult. It was because gladiators ate a porridge gruel as standard fare when in training – the same stuff *venatores* claimed farmers fed to their pigs.

It was good-natured enough, unlikely to spill over to anything worse; both sides had had enough of blood for one day and even the arguments about racing factions were tepid.

Then, suddenly, Drust looked up into a face from memory. It was a ploughed field of old ruts, with brows that threatened to throw long hairs into his wet eyes, and the old *lanista* stood there hipshot in a bland tunic, his legs gnarled and twisted with veins.

'I heard someone was looking for one of my lads,' Curtius growled.

Drust recovered enough to find a voice. 'I thought you'd be dead.'

'It's worse than that,' Curtius answered, levering himself down on the seat next to them. 'I have discovered you are alive.'

'One of your lads?' Kag asked and the *lanista* cocked his head at him.

'You have grown older and skilled in venality. I hear you have taken over The Place from the arse who sat in it. That was well done. I miss Servillius Structus and the old Ludus Ferrata.'

'You weren't in the cells of it,' Kag responded, then smiled. 'Good to see you are still alive.'

'*Uri, vinciri, verberari, ferroque necari*,' Curtius replied laconically.

I will endure, to be burned, to be bound, to be beaten, and to be slain. It was the oath every gladiator swore – and the one the Brothers had tossed aside when they'd been freed, determined never to say it again. They had their own oath now.

'Last time I saw you lads,' Curtius said slowly, looking from one to the other, 'you were bound for the *harena* to die like Christians. I heard you escaped, were run down and killed. I also heard you threw a future Emperor into the Tiber.'

Macrinus. Drust remembered the man, then a Praetorian officer, pinwheeling off the aqueduct. Should have thrown him off over land, not the water, he thought.

'As you see,' Kag replied and smiled. 'Now you are *lanista* for this Ludus Ulpius affair.'

'*Summa rudis*,' Curtius corrected. 'One must eat, even with few teeth. For instance, I hear Cascus Minicius Audens sent you north to fetch back a white bear.'

Drust felt unaccountably pleased that old Curtius had been made a *summa rudis*, a freedman referee of the contests. He had been around when they were slave gladiators – even if he had scowled at Servillius Structus freeing them. He never thought we deserved it, Drust thought. Perhaps he was right.

'So he said,' Drust agreed. 'We found no white bear but enough beasts to make us bloody. Not all of them were tree-fucking barbarians either.'

'Why do you want Brasus the Dacian?' Curtius demanded.

'He's looking for someone we are also seeking,' Drust replied, and Curtius rasped calloused fingers over his stubble and cocked his head enquiringly. Drust told him.

'I never liked the task he was set,' Curtius growled. 'Stank like a bad privy.'

'What task was that?' Drust asked, and the old *lanista* hesitated a moment, then called for Brasus.

He was big, fattened on gruels of grain and leeks, but with shoulders like a meat carcass heaver and hair all shaved off save for a dark-red pad on the top of his head. He had startling blue eyes and the expression of a child; he could not have been more than twenty.

'Tell these men why you are looking for Lentulus.'

Brasus's brows made a V and he looked at Curtius. 'All of it?'

'This is Drust and Kag,' Curtius said easily. 'The ones who escaped the Flavian.'

Brasus's eyes widened and he grinned and stuck out a hand to clasp them, one by one, by the wrist. Drust felt awkward and flushed; he'd had no idea they had forged a legend.

'Fama,' Kag muttered sullenly.

'Not a goddess,' Drust responded.

'A literary conceit,' Kag finished, and they both laughed. Brasus looked at them, bewildered.

'Lentulus?' Kag prompted.

'I was told by Curtius to escort this Lentulus to the old Caesar house,' Brasus said. 'Curtius told me I was not to go in, but wait outside the porter's gate and then escort him wherever he wanted to go after that.'

'Who told you?' Drust asked Curtius, who squinted at him.

'Marcus Ulpius Ralla,' he said quietly.

'Himself?'

Curtius nodded. 'Came down to the *Ludus* in the dead of night, alone save for a torchman and a single *lictor*. Asked me to send a fighter with the man he brought with him, this Lentulus. I was to ask no questions and obey the instructions of Lentulus to the last syllable.'

A senator comes down to the Flavian training schools in the dark, practically alone. That in itself would make what he wanted stink like a privy, as Curtius had noted.

'What happened?' Kag asked the big Dacian, who shrugged.

'I took him to Caesar's house and waited. He was inside only a few minutes…'

'He had no trouble getting in?' Kag asked thoughtfully.

'Na. Porter opened the gate soon as he said his name.'

'Then what?'

'I had to take him down to the Circus. He spoke to the guards and got in the gate. Then I come back here and told Curtius.'

'The Circus? At night?'

Brasus shrugged. 'I thought he was living there. Didn't talk like a slave, mind, and didn't look like a driver. I thought he was a groom or a horse dealer.'

'It circles round and eats its own tail,' Kag muttered gloomily.

'Tell him all of it,' Curtius prompted sharply, and Brasus looked guiltily around, then fell into a whisper.

'When this Lentulus came back to the porter's gate there was someone with him. Big man, who patted

Lentulus on the cheek like he was a clever dog or a favourite son and told him to hurry, that there were men out and about round the *domus*.'

'Did you see any?' Kag demanded, and Brasus shook his head.

'What did this man look like?' Drust asked, and Brasus glanced once more at Curtius as if for approval.

'I knowed who it was, yer honours. It was a general and a senator called Antyllus. I'd seen him before when he'd come to a dinner Ulpius Ralla put on. I fought Serpicus at it – you remember, Curtius? Put on a good show.'

'You did,' Curtius agreed and then jerked his head in the direction of the other gladiators. 'My thanks, lad. Go and enjoy yourself – not a word, mind. Not one word to anyone else.'

The Dacian lumbered off and Curtius watched him go, then sighed.

'*Hoplomachus*,' Kag declared and Curtius confirmed it. Of all the gladiator styles, the *hoplomachus* was the most armoured, the slowest.

'Tried him at everything else,' Curtius went on moodily. 'He's won a few, but his footwork is leaden.'

'Why is he set to look for Lentulus now?' Drust asked and Curtius frowned.

'Because the same man who ordered him to escort Lentulus now wants him found. It seems everyone at the Caesar house died the same night.'

He looked at them with his watery eyes. 'That you?'

Drust shook his head. 'One of ours got caught in it. Manius – you recall him?'

Curtius nodded. 'Sorry for your loss. Heard about your wife too – you have had a sore time of it.'

'No Antyllus at the Caesar house, though,' Kag said softly and Curtius acknowledged it.

'Want me to ask around?'

Drust shook his head. 'That will bring the attention of the man who did them all at the Caesar house. Pale man, white-haired, not nearly as old as he looks and deadlier than Cleopatra's asp. If you hear of him, keep clear and send word to us.'

Curtius nodded sombrely, then squinted at them.

'I can get word to Lentulus all the same. Through the drivers. Tell him you mean him no harm.'

Drust nodded acknowledgement. 'I mean him no harm.'

Kag said nothing and his silence shrieked like a library; Curtius either ignored it or did not notice, just held out his cup and had it filled. He beamed.

Drust toasted him. 'Fortuna smile on your men these games.'

Curtius frowned. 'Unlikely. Two days from now, the racing starts at the Maximus and the Emperor is determined to keep the crowds in the Flavian. He has ordered twenty pairs to fight to the last pair standing – a *perfidiae harenam*.'

'A circle of treachery,' Kag said softly. 'No rules, no referees.'

Curtius shrugged bony shoulders.

'What can you do?'

They walked warily back to The Place and Drust was pleased to find men on the gates and in the grounds, alert and ready. He was less pleased at how fretted he was, how every shadow held the beast of Verus.

The others, back from the Circus, agreed.

'I felt naked all the way here,' Quintus confessed.

'Didn't find Lentulus,' Dog said moodily, pouring wine. 'You?'

'A sniff of something,' Kag said, 'but when it was laid out it was a threadbare weave.'

'So – we wait for Lentulus to bang on the door and remind us of how we made a promise not to cut his throat for what he did to us?'

Ugo shook his head with disbelief. 'That's the plan?' he added.

There was a thundering bang on the double gates. Then another. And another. Vatia came skidding up, eyes wide.

'People at the gate.'

'You say so?' Kag spat back scathingly.

'Names?' demanded Dog, and Vatia worked his mouth a few times and then said, 'Fish.'

'Gaius Tullus,' Silanus interrupted, cuffing Vatia back to the gate. 'Some of his lads with him – he has the area for a mile all round the Basilica Aemilia.'

'Fish?' demanded Kag and Silanus shrugged.

'He's a fish merchant. Has a shop in the Basilica.'

Gaius Tullus was a burly man with a fringe of hair round a bald pate. He had chins, a nose that wobbled and – what Drust found strangest of all – the glaucous eyes of a fresh-landed fish. Perhaps you get to look like them after a while, he thought.

There were four others with him, a sensible precaution in a Suburan night, all of them hump-shouldered, bellied, crook-noses whose weapons had been removed at the door. They did not seem much bothered by that, which soothed Drust a little. Gaius Tullus came right to the point, tossing a fat leather purse onto the table; it chinked heavily.

'This is the time for dues to be paid,' he said.

'For what?'

Gaius Tullus shrugged. 'For wagons to transport fish from Ostia. For permission to roll them through this area up to the Basilica. For the keeping of the accord.'

The accord turned out to be Flaminius extorting coin on the promise of not hijacking fish or beating up the transport drivers, no more. Kisa went through the scrolls and lists and came up with the numbers, which were eye-watering. Drust made no sign of that, simply nodded then stood up; Gaius Tullus and his retinue eyed him warily.

'Flaminius is dead, so is this debt. For the wagons, I will take an honourable price as is proper for rental. For the continuation of the accord – only this.'

He stuck out his arm and, slowly, Gaius clasped it by the wrist. Drust called for wine, they talked about this and that, and finally Gaius Tullus stood up and looped his cloak round one arm, signalling to one of his men to light up a torch for the journey home.

'I had heard you were a fair man,' he said, 'and now have it proved. I give you this, then, as a measure of friendship – men came to me with your name in their mouths. They wore homespun and tried to look bland as old dust, but if anyone had bawled out "Attention!" they'd have stiffened and banged their studs.'

'Vigiles?' Kag asked tentatively. Gaius snorted.

'Neither that rabble nor the Urbans. These were Praetorian or I do not know *garum* from *allec*.'

He smiled. 'Any time you want either of those fish sauces, let me know.'

They watched the double gates close on him and then looked from one to the other.

'We should double the door guards,' Dog growled. 'Put more men patrolling the grounds.'

'Unlikely to need them,' Kag responded. 'You heard the man – bland as dust and talking quietly. They wanted to find out more; if they wanted to drag us off, they'd have a ram at the gates.'

Kag was right – but the ram might be on the way, so Dog wasn't wrong. Drust said as much, then declared he was tired and would sleep, which was only half a lie.

He lay in Servillius Structus's old bed, feeling the strangeness of it; here was where his mother had lain. Perhaps it was where she had died giving birth to her stillborn son – Servillius Structus's son. My half-brother…

Like Praeclarum, he thought suddenly, if birth was what you could call what happened to her. He felt her all that night as a chill loss all down the side she had favoured to lie next to him.

Sleep was crushed out of him by all of that and the weight of everything that had happened, occupying The Place, dealing with other gang leaders, becoming a power, unlooked for but – Drust was forced to admit it – less unwanted day by day. He sat in the chair of the man who had once held him as a slave. He slept in his bed, counted his money, dealt with his old contracts. He felt the presence of the Fat Man everywhere he turned.

Morning brought relief – and Lentulus.

He arrived alone at the big front gates and was let in by Stolo, who brought him into the main room where people yawned and threw grumbles and olive stones. All talk stopped when they saw him.

'Lentulus,' Stolo announced with a sneer, though he was least qualified, Drust thought, to have such a grimace.

'I was told I would be unharmed.'

His voice shook like the rest of him, though he was trying hard not to hunch like a cursed dog; he kept glancing over one shoulder until Drust realised it was an act worn to a nub by repetition. Here was a hunted man who trembled like a fly-bitten horse.

'You are safer here than out there,' Drust pointed out, and had it confirmed with a nod like a nervous tic.

'I know it.'

'You could have saved all this by coming with us at the Circus,' Kag added, and again there was that quick, birdlike nod.

'I know it,' he answered and raised his hands to let them fall back to his sides. They shook, Drust saw – I would not want to be shaved by this man now.

'Well, you know whom we seek,' Dog growled, but he shoved a bowl of wine forward; Lentulus took it, drank it down in one and shoved it back for a refill.

'I can take you to Antyllus,' he said. 'He is at a villa on the Ostia road – do you have horses?'

'About a dozen,' Kisa chimed in. 'Drays, though, with no proper riding tack.'

'We have straddled worse,' Quintus noted.

'Get them all ready,' Drust ordered. I will not go out with fewer men than I can muster, he thought. Not with

Verus, Praetorians, the gods know what else lining up to stick us with sharpness…

'Why is Verus hunting you down?' Kag demanded.

'He hunts Antyllus and anyone who had knowledge of what the general knows. Like your friend…'

He stopped, shook his head and wiped fingers across his face as if trying to tear free a veil or a vision.

'They fought at Caesar's house. Your *mavro* was spying on all of us, but was ambushed. Carbo the porter and Antyllus himself rushed in to tackle the man who did it, wanting to know more – but Carbo was killed and Antyllus got cut. I got him away.'

He stopped, stared unseeingly for a moment or two. 'That creature…'

'Why is Verus doing this?' Drust demanded.

'He has been set to it, of course. By his master.'

'Why?'

Lentulus shook his head. 'I will let Antyllus tell it. If he wants to reveal all, so be it. If not, then I will not speak on it either.'

'You little fuck,' Kag exploded. 'If you don't tell all you know, I will hang you by the heels and flay you with a blunt knife…'

Drust laid a calming hand on Kag's shoulder and he stilled to silence and laboured breathing, but the point had been made. Lentulus wobbled but Drust had to admire the way he rocked back to steadiness.

'Antyllus has asked for this meeting,' he said. 'He is dying, I think, so we had best waste no time.'

They had ten mounts in the end and Drust picked men to come with the Brothers – all but Kisa, who was left in charge of the Place. The rest plodded off, kicking the unyielding flanks of the big cart-pullers and managing scarcely more than a reluctant trot.

At the Ostian Gate, Drust half expected to be hailed and stopped by the Urban guards, but they were too busy coping with the melee of four-wheelers, beasts, drivers, hauliers and traders all waiting for dark to enter the City. It helped that several of them belonged to Drust now, along with the men that crewed them.

It took them most of the rest of the day to get down the road, with the Tiber looping back and forth, and they stopped only once, to feed and water the horses and themselves. On the way, Lentulus was not as tight-lipped as he had promised, but almost all of it was about Antyllus.

He had inherited the mad, bad and bold of his illustrious ancestor and his father, Drust learned. Gambling had ruined the family, be it on the races, the *munera* or just dice – well, they had inherited all that from the master of the bad gamble, Marcus Antonius himself. Thanks to him and the ones who came after, the family estates were all gone and this villa had been little more than an overseer's house for the last resource of the *gens*, the salt pans outside Ostia.

The day was sliding to blue dim by the time they reached it, just where the road started across the raised causeway of the salt flats into Ostia proper. A wind had risen, low and mourning to itself, hissing and whining through stunted shrubs dotting a landscape of raised earthworks and stinking pools of saltmarsh mud.

The villa itself was in darkness; there were no slaves left, no attendants of any sort, Lentulus declared, and Antyllus relied only on secrecy to keep him safe. Kag, as always, was unconvinced and kept looking backwards. If you are leaving tracks, you are being followed…

Lentulus agreed, not only by his now well-worn nervous tic of looking over his shoulder, but with terse words. 'Julius Yahya has persuaded the Mother to set Praetorians on me. They will have been watching.'

The villa porter's gate was broken to matchwood long since, which allowed them to lead the big, tired horses in. Drust had Silanus take charge of the four men brought with them, while the rest of the Brothers and Lentulus started towards the atrium of the main building.

Leaves whirled in the sighing wind and it was dark; they had torches but did not want to light them until they found out if anything lurked in wait. Weapons up, they crept forward, following Lentulus into a room until all of them caught a tendril of a smell they knew well enough – sweet and rotted.

'Spark up that torch,' Drust ordered, and Kag worked his firestarter, the big wheels of sparks scarring their eyes. The torch flared, the flames twisting in the wind and throwing lurid shadows of themselves everywhere. Something clacked, so disturbingly like those birds in the Dark of the north that Ugo gave a grunt and stiffened.

'Reeds and the remains of the garden,' said a voice, and everyone froze in place, weapons up and ready. It was a wisp of what had once been, Drust thought. The voice of a man with his ankle grabbed firmly by Dis Pater…

'Nothing grows well here,' the voice went on tiredly. 'The salt kills it. You can taste it on the wind…'

All Drust could taste was the stink of rot. He moved forward and gestured to Kag to bring the torch. When the flickering light fell on the bed and the figure, no one spoke or moved for what seemed the longest time.

The face was a ravaged hawk, the skin stretched too thin over the bone, so that it looked painful, as if it might split at any moment. The eyes were laired deeply in their sockets, and in daylight he would be the colour of old cream; in the light from the torch he looked like a mummer's mask left too long in the rain.

Kag flicked back the fetid bedcover and they all blanched at the reek, at the sight of the belly wound, red-lipped like a poxed whore. There is no coming back from this, Drust thought, and it must have shown in his face, for the figure on the bed groaned with what everyone realised was laughter.

'You are too late,' he said. 'Your revenge has been done for you.'

'Justified,' Drust responded blankly. 'But that's only half the reason I came all this way.'

Antyllus tried to raise a hand but was too weak; Drust saw he did not have long.

'Good men died because of me – Mus for one. Your wife for another. I am sorry for them all.'

'Keep that for the gods you will stand and face,' Kag spat back.

'It was my idea to take her as a hostage,' Antyllus said, as if he had not heard Kag at all. 'Otherwise you would all be dead, which was the preferred option of my staff.'

Here Lentulus shifted uncomfortably.

'I was told, of course, that a deputation was on the way to me, to find out what I was actually doing. Then I heard what the headman Erco did, and how you all fought out of it. That was when I knew what Julius Yahya had done to me.'

'Julius Yahya?'

'Of course. He arranged it all.'

'Arranged what?'

Antyllus groaned his bitter laugh. 'You don't play the game, do you?'

'What fucking game? Stop speaking in riddles, curse you...'

Quintus stilled Dog with a slight touch, but it was as if Antyllus was unaware of anyone other than himself and Drust.

'I am a senator,' he said, his voice suddenly strengthening. 'Do you know how those are made?'

'Bile, greed and viciousness,' Drust answered.

'That and coin — more than a million sesterces. Men who need help meeting this requirement are given grants. Should they mismanage their funds, they are expected to step down.'

He stopped and his thin, cracked lips tightened in pain; for a terrifying moment Drust thought he had died. Then he sucked in a gasping breath.

'No one has mismanaged their funds more spectacularly than I,' he added and coughed out another laugh. 'Save, perhaps, my father.'

'So Julius Yahya bought your debts,' Dog said grimly. 'Bonded servitude we know well. What did he want you to do?'

'Play the game,' he answered.

'A game? That's what all this is to you?'

'Of course. The board consists of seas and kingdoms, the men in them are counters, placed and struck from it according to the skill of the players.'

'Gambling,' Quintus replied slowly. 'That's what got you into this mess.'

'Of the highest sort,' Antyllus answered. 'Julius Yahya wanted me as a player on the board, or so I thought, and so that's what I became. I had a moment when I thought I might be the one to exercise his will, but I was not sure who I was playing with – or against.'

'You never play any game with the likes of Julius Yahya,' Dog growled, while Antyllus took some thin wine from a skin brought by Ugo. When he had finished sipping from it, the big German dropped it on the bed close to Antyllus's wasted hand.

'In the end, I realised I was not a player at all, just a counter. I was to take out a force, to make a core of loyalty – I was told the Mother of the Empire wanted a new candidate for the Purple.'

'You believed that?' Kag demanded with disgust, and Antyllus coughed out a bitter laugh.

'Of course. Why not? You have Julius Yahya telling you, and the nature of the woman herself – she had the last Severan to claim the title dragged out in chains to die and he was her own kin. She did the same with his mother – again her own kin.'

He fought for breath, giving time for the others to admit all of the truth in that.

'Still,' Quintus said, 'I wouldn't have put my life on it – and I am a fucking gladiator who once had no choice.'

Antyllus nodded weakly. 'You and I are the same, then. I had no choice in the end. I suddenly started to get letters from senators I did not know well nor had written to. They were all polite and offering help – I learned later they'd been told this was to do with my possible censure by the senate for having gone off into the north with a lot of Romans. And all of them were from supporters of the Emperor. I found out more. I wrote my own letters in secret to those I trusted and a few answered; some of them sent word of offered bribes to implicate colleagues, some even spoke of Julius Yahya, and I knew I was caught in a plot. In the end, Julius Yahya caught a whisper of it and grew suspicious. He sent you, so I was forced to move.'

'*Apokalypsis*,' Drust said and Antyllus groaned agreement.

'I adopted the Purple but I knew it was a wild cast of the dice. When it failed, I fled to what friends I thought I could trust, hoping to find time to use what I knew. In the end, even the likes of Ulpius Ralla betrayed me, when he realised what I had.'

Drust felt a prickle of excitement. 'Which was what?'

'Documents. Letters, replies, admissions of bribes, of payments made, of coercion – all confirming that Julius Yahya has organised a plot to implicate the Emperor's supporters, backed by the Mother.'

There was a stunned silence, then Dog snorted derisively. 'Julius Yahya is the Emperor's man – why would he plot against him?'

'In a day or two,' Antyllus answered, his voice gone dreamy, 'the Circus will start the races. Presiding over the opening will be Julia Mamaea, Mother of the Emperor.'

'And?' demanded Kag. 'This is nothing sinister – she is there every year.'

'Not alone. Always with her son, the Emperor. It's a statement. A move in the game. But this year she is alone and Alexander will be at the Flavian. He has organised, for that same day, a *castra dolo*. Twenty pairs, to the last pair standing.'

Drust had never seen a 'circle of treachery', when paired fighters fought to the death with no referees, making and breaking fleeting alliances for advantage. It was a fabulously expensive undertaking – but it would suck all but diehard racing fans from the Circus Maximus, leaving Julia Mamaea looking down on a threadbare crowd and made to look a distant second to her son.

Antyllus saw that Drust had got to it and he racked out another painful wheeze.

'You see? Julius Yahya does not work for the Emperor, but the Mother. She sees her power being challenged by a boy becoming a man and less inclined to give in to her. This is how the game is played in Rome.'

So she had organised a little rebellion as a counter. A nothing spasm of coup in a distant German forest, easily dealt with and with an aftermath of proscriptions which would include the innocent supporters of the Emperor as well as the guilty greedy. A statement, a message as unsubtle as nailing someone to a post through the eyes and cutting out their tongue, and from a woman who could kill her own son's wife as easily as stepping on a roach.

Little or not, it was a dangerous and reckless move. Such small beginnings could easily spill out of control, like a fire in Subura…

Outside was a flurry of noise. Inside was a last wheezing gasp.

'I was sending the documents with Lentulus to a place of safety when this Verus arrived. I did not know your Manius was there – I thought only that I was under attack and that Carbo the porter had fallen.'

He stopped, fighting pain and oblivion. 'He was fast, that Verus...'

'He has done for you,' Drust said. Then added viciously, 'Now you know how my wife spent her final moments.'

There was a soft puff of sound from the bed, a voice scarcely more than the mourn of the wind. 'My neck. I kept it...'

Silanus burst through the door, eyes wide with shock. 'Riders – a dozen or so.'

'Ha,' Kag declared savagely. 'Now we make a fist of it.'

Drust thought swiftly, whirling to Lentulus. 'Tell us where these documents are.'

'Keep me safe and I will show you.'

He was a rat in a drain and Drust wanted to six him then and there; the little barber saw it and blenched, taking a step back. Drust fought the urge to ram his *gladius* in the man's neck, a struggle that left him trembling as he turned back to Dog.

'Make sure he stays alive,' he ordered, and then went to where there was shouting and the clash of steel; he thought he heard a gurgle of bitter laughter from the bed.

In the peristyle and atrium men fought, stumbling over the fallen statues and twisted roots of a place in ruins, the tiles uneven, the ground pocked. Steel clashed and shadows lurched in the sparking torchlight.

Watch for Verus, watch for Verus, watch for the back-stabber...

A man came at Drust, stabbing with a *gladius*; Drust sidestepped, thrust the torch into the man's face and heard him scream, saw the beard catch fire. He did not wait for more, simply slid his own blade in and out of the neck like an adder bite.

There was another to fill the hole, slashing left and right and left again, scattering sparks from the torch as Drust used it to fend off the strokes. The man thinks he has a *spatha*, has been trained to use that longer sword. He has a beard like the other one, is big and strong, and though the tunic is the colour of oatmeal, he is not some hired thug, gladiator or anything like it.

He was Army and almost certainly Praetorian; for a moment the thought chilled Drust almost to a standstill and the man saw it, gave a growl of satisfaction at what he thought was an enemy on the point of wetting himself, and bored in.

A figure came speeding past trailing the sparks from a torch, dipped briefly and made a movement, then rushed on, heading for the door. Drust had a brief moment of insight – Stolo. Chicken heart, legs of a hare.

Still, he had expertly hamstrung the Praetorian with a single stroke; the man found he had no working legs and collapsed in a limp heap, bemused. Drust gave him no time to mourn, gave him iron into the neck, the heart in the throat.

Even as he brought the blade out he caught a flicker at the edge of vision, enough to know it was a sliver of pale in the dark, moving round all the fighters, heading for the sickroom.

'Dog!'

Dog had seen it and sprang forward, two swords moving like silver bars of light; then he gave a scream and reeled away, one sword falling to allow the hand to clutch his face. Drust tried to run to help, but another of the Praetorians closed in on him, forcing him to parry and strike; their blades rang high and thin.

He had time only for a brief glance as Ugo grappled with an opponent and hurled him away; the man gave a despairing shriek as he pinwheeled through the air, and the pale-haired Verus had time to throw up one flapping hand before he was struck, the pair of them tumbling away into the dark.

There were shrieks from horses and the sound of hooves flailing away into the distance. Someone bawled an order, had it repeated, and suddenly Drust's opponent stepped back, then again. He pointed the blade in a word-less gesture and backed off.

Drust let him. He saw that the fighting had stopped and moved as fast as he could stumble to where Dog raved and cursed, his face covered in blood. Quintus was with him, trying to get him to stop clutching with his hand so something could be done.

'Lentulus?'

Dog spat blood in a burbling curse and indicated the ground at his feet; he was sitting on the little barber, whose face was purple in the torchlight. Drust forced Dog's hand away and saw the extent of the damage – a deep cut from the left of the jaw all the way up the cheek to the hairline, washing his skull face with crimson.

'Need to stitch that,' Quintus said, 'when I can see.'

He set to do what he could while Dog cursed him for inflicting more pain. Ugo lumbered back, growling about how Verus was nowhere to be seen. 'I saw him struck by a fucking big beefy palace rat – but there's not even a splash of blood.'

Kag came in and, to Drust's surprise, Stolo was with him, minus the torch and with his teeth clenched to stop them chattering.

'They are all Praetorians,' Kag announced disgustedly. 'Luckily those Palace turds are well removed from any fighting other than over coin or quim.'

'How can Verus summon up a dozen of that lot?' Ugo rumbled and rolled a shoulder. 'I think I might have strained something throwing him.'

'Poor fucking you,' Dog managed between pain grunts.

'He clearly has one of those sealed scrolls Julius Yahya hands out and the Mother of the Emperor to back it up,' Quintus muttered, busy trying to staunch the blood from Dog's face. 'Gods above and below, that's a deep one – I can see your back teeth.'

'I saved you from worse,' Ugo pointed out, and Dog acknowledged it with a weary flap of one hand, then winced free of Quintus.

'Jupiter's cock, you fumble-handed fuck – are you trying to peel my face off?'

'Hard to see where your face actually is,' Quintus spat back. 'Hold still or bleed to death.'

'Fourteen Praetorians, all of them time-served,' Kag said. 'A little flabby here and there, but nonetheless Praetorians. We should be cheering, for six of them are dead – well, three were dead and three were hurt but are dead now. The rest are gone, running.'

He stopped, slapped Stolo on one shoulder, staggering the man forward a step. 'You have this to thank for it – he cut their horses free and waved fire at them until they ran off. Their owners panicked, thinking more gladiators were coming down on them.'

Drust nodded, feeling a wash of relief. Their own horses were slow, but quicker than walking; they could make a run back to the City…

'We lost Quadratus,' Silanus said grimly. 'And Sura has a wounded arm.'

If Sura could ride, then he would be safe. Quadratus had taken a slash across the throat and Drust was sure that was Verus's work. They brought him in and Drust, half ashamed to admit it to himself, did not recognise the man and made a mental note to look more closely at the faces of those who now worked for him; just one more matter in an endless list. It seemed the burden of family was growing day by day.

They laid the dead Quadratus beside the mumbling Antyllus.

'What about him?' Kag asked.

'Let him die,' Dog mushed through the rags soaking up the blood of his face. 'I will drag that fucker Verus back here and lay him at the feet of his master.'

Ugo frowned. 'You would not do that to a sick rat.'

Dog, who knew he owed his life to the big German, stayed silent and sullen, while Drust looked at the clotted *gladius* in his hand as if he had just spotted it. He saw he hand tremble, wondered if it had been doing that since he first noticed it, or had stopped and was now starting again. Not that it mattered…

He looked at Antyllus, the venal, reckless gambler who had killed his wife and unborn child as part of his 'game'.

The wind whined, tearing up leaves and whirling them in mad circles over the corpses, scattering the desperate insects, bringing the cloacal stink of wet mud and salt.

A dying man in a dead land, Drust thought. Fitting enough. Then a thought struck him, the words Antyllus had said right at the last: 'My neck. I kept it…'

He reached down, felt the thong and cut it, bringing up the pouch with Praeclarum's pearl teeth inside. The sight of them made his eyes blur, but he knew where to find the heart in the throat just by touch now.

The bloodied sword, with no moon on it, stayed secret and silent all the way in and out. Then they set fire to the bed and rode out, beating the fat drays into a semblance of gallop.

Chapter Fifteen

On the ride back Lentulus was strapped to the horse, though he protested. 'I will lead you to what you need,' he claimed, 'if I can be assured of my safety. Have I not already proved this?'

As if to offer some reinforcement of his good intent, he spilled the story of Antyllus out, a bilious vomit of greed and ambition. Antyllus had continued to add to the debts of the family and then found them mysteriously gone and a benefactor offering help. By the time he discovered it to be Julius Yahya, it was too late – but he was dazzled by what seemed to be the regard of this powerful man.

'He encouraged the general,' Lentulus told them. 'Got him to lead the disaffected of the Army out into the wilderness and Julius Yahya's influence prevented trouble over it. For a while, the general thought he was appreciated in the highest circles – then letters started arriving. They came from senators and quaestors, all professing to be friends of the family, of him. Offering support. None of them solicited by Antyllus.

'The general grew alarmed. He realised this was not just fawners seeking to ingratiate themselves into his good graces – someone had prompted them, coerced them even, but they were all of the blandest sort. None mentioned rebellion and few confirmed help; those that did professed to assist him in rehabilitating himself to his peers for what he had already done. The one thing that struck him was that they were all people who supported the young Emperor rather than his mother. Or had offered Julius Yahya resistance and slight.'

'So Antyllus rebelled?' Drust demanded incredulously.

'He wrote some quiet letters of his own and discovered what Julius Yahya was up to.'

'So he rebelled?' Drust echoed incredulously. 'That was his best plan?'

'He was about to return to the *castra* when he had word of a plot to have him killed,' Lentulus added bitterly. 'Then Erco intervened, and when that failed he had no choice. You know the rest – save for the fact that he knew Julius Yahya had marked him and that his only recourse – in his own eyes anyway – was a last throw of the dice.'

'Idiot,' Kag muttered and no one disagreed – though Lentulus provided some contest.

'He thought he had a loaded die in the throw.'

'The letters,' Drust said. Lentulus nodded.

'A scroll case stuffed with them and other notes. As long as he had them hidden, he thought he had leverage with Julius Yahya – he was giving them to me the night that… creature… Verus came at us in Caesar's house.'

'Why you?' Drust demanded and Lentulus drew himself up a little.

'He had his reasons.'

Drust did not let it go loose, all the same. Back at The Place, they sat round the table, gnawing hard cheese, olives and twice-baked Army bread. Lentulus, miserable as twenty miles of bad road, sat like a condemned man and refused to tell where the scroll case had been taken –

263

though he would lead them to it. He also refused to tell why he had been charged with the task of hiding it. In the end Drust let him fall silent, but no one could come up with an answer as to why the likes of a barber in the Army should be so trusted by the likes of Antyllus.

Still – if he led them to the prize…

'What then?' Kag demanded, and they looked at each other until Drust blew out his cheeks and said what they all already knew.

'We hand it to the Emperor.'

'Of course,' Quintus declared, beaming. 'Why didn't I think of that?'

Drust savaged him with a glare. 'I say it because that's what must happen. Not anyone else – the Emperor's own hand. Even then, there is no guarantee we will be safe.'

No one said the obvious, though it hung there like a bad smell – how do you get to the Emperor without going through all the court officials, the Praetorian and the rest? It was impossible.

'First,' Drust said, looking at Lentulus, 'we had better get to the scrolls.'

'I said I would take you. It was a promise made to a dying man.'

'Whom you left to die, alone and in the dark,' Drust pointed out, which made Lentulus lick his lips.

'He was shaved,' Drust added. 'Last time I saw him he had a good-going beard. But you were at the villa and shaved him. Then left him.'

Lentulus flapped one weary hand. 'What else could I do? I am no *medicus*. I can pull a tooth, bind a wound – or give you a trim and a shave. I learned that to avoid fatigues. I write a decent script and that got me out of building roads or marching camps. But nothing I learned would let me save the general. So I shaved him, my number one best job, then left him with watered wine to hand if he needed it, safe and in the dark.'

He stopped and took a breath. 'I also gave him the rites.'

'Rites? What rites?'

'Is it far, this hole you dug?' interrupted Dog, and Lentulus hesitated, then sagged a little.

'The Maximus.'

They stared at him, disbelieving. 'You dug a hole in the Circus?' Kag demanded and Lentulus fluttered one dismissive hand.

'No, no – I will say no more on it. I will take you, all the same.'

Drust was grit-eyed and felt sheened with a layer of scum and sweat which even a clean tunic could not alleviate. It did not help that the day was overcast and sultry; the crowds thronging the street kept looking at the sky and, closer to the Circus, muttering about rain.

There was no more practice, just the ants' nest boil of people sorting out the Maximus for race day – which was in two days, Drust realised. Slaves polished the dolphins along the *spina*, fresh white sand was being spread and raked, and the public was only allowed into the shops under the stands. They felt prickled in a familiar way, which wasn't helped by Kag muttering about leaving tracks and being followed. Twice he swore he had seen the same figures dogging them through the streets. It was likely, Drust thought; the Praetorian would be watching, hoping to be led to what they sought. Which is exactly what we are doing.

Lentulus led the way to the right, where the dim of the Circus undercroft was split by bright lanterns so no one would miss the wares. Drust knew there were at least sixty shops here, selling everything from sausages to souvenirs – and they were the acceptable ones. In little niches and shadowed holes you could find the unofficial ones, selling sex and drugs. It seemed the perfect place to lose any trackers.

They went past a shoe seller, his wares on wooden benches and his place marked with curtains hung between columns. Next to him a slave sold bread for his baker master, and next to him a lantern bobbed on a stalk over a table thick with vegetables; somewhere meat was cooking.

They gave up trying to talk; the noise was loud, relentless and echoed. Lentulus pushed past some cages containing a stock of chickens and hares. On the counter were two bowls of fruit – figs, Drust saw – and a barrel containing cooked milk-fed snails for the customers to snack on while they chose livestock from a fat woman with a colony of chins.

Kag laughed aloud at the sight of two monkeys chained to the stall which sold boiled chickpeas, eggs and onions, their antics designed to attract a crowd to these race-day snacks. The monkey owner displayed his eggs and onions floating in glass bowls of water so that they looked larger than their actual size. He had a set of scales, universally known as 'ambushers' – as in 'lying in weight'.

Suddenly Lentulus stopped and everyone had to dance to avoid walking up someone else's heels. A matron gave a pungent curse, which Dog answered by dropping his cloak hood just long enough to make her squeal and rush off; his face now had the new attraction of a roughly stitched scar.

'Here,' Lentulus said, and they stared and made faces at a reek they could taste and which they knew well enough – the dye of *murex*, those tiny shellfish that cost an Emperor's ransom. The shop sold cloth for the upper end of the market – the *murex* made the purple of a senator's broad stripe, the narrower one of an equestrian – and the man standing in it, wearing a striped desert robe and a quiet smile, was a *mavro* from Carthago.

'Lentulus,' the man said and bowed.

'Philosir,' Lentulus replied, then added: 'These men are friends. They are with me.'

'Are they initiates?'

'All men strive for the Light,' Lentulus replied, and Philosir frowned and shook his head.

'The rule is clear—'

'Am I *pater* or not?'

Philosir paused, then inclined his head in agreement; Lentulus pushed past him into the back of the shop, through the hangings of cloth in all colours. Drust and the others followed after him and Kag clicked his fingers derisively.

'He's the *pater*, Phoenician,' he said, though he had no idea what that meant.

There was a door, solid and heavy and yet opened with a simple push; they followed Lentulus inside, then down some dimly lit steps. They stopped and stared, up and around.

It was a domed undercroft, lit with sputtering torches and seemingly empty of everything save echoes. For a moment Drust felt he was back in the Dark, the columned pillars on either side like the fat trees of some sacred glade.

Then he saw the panel at the far end, lit by two lanterns. A figure in a Phrygian cap was kneeling on an exhausted bull, holding it by the nostrils with his left hand and stabbing it with his right. As he did so, he looked over his shoulder towards the figure of Sol, while a dog and a snake reached up towards the blood and a scorpion seized the bull's genitals.

'Mithras,' Kag breathed.

'Unconquered Sun,' Dog echoed, and Drust remembered the rayed amulet he wore. Dog had been a Sun worshipper since the start and had, though he would not admit it now, once revered Elagabalus, the boy they'd rescued from the far north and who became as infamous as Nero when he was made Emperor.

Lentulus moved forward, stopped and bowed his head, muttering to the panel. Then he moved in behind the massive slab of it and came out with a leather bucket-shaped scroll case.

Drust and the others stared; it had just been sitting there, practically in plain sight. He could not help but say it, wincing at the boom of his voice in that cavernous bell of a temple.

'Its safety was assured,' Lentulus said and indicated the mosaic squares on the floor, each one with a different symbol. Kag got to it first and gave a short grunt of awed realisation.

'You are *pater* – the Father,' he said, and Lentulus nodded sombrely. They all knew at once what that meant – they had seen and heard the Mithras worshippers out east, almost all of them legionaries of the Army, the most devout working their way up the grades from the lowly Raven to the Soldier, and up the rest of the rankings to the Father.

Drust looked at Lentulus in a new light – here was what passed for a high priest of Mithras, and now he knew why he had been so favoured by Antyllus.

'What rank was the general?' he asked, and Lentulus paused in the act of handing over the case.

'He had received the mysteries of the Lion,' he said. 'One day he would have made a Father himself.'

'And you were his guide and teacher,' Kag finished. There was a muffled shout from behind the entrance door which made them all turn. Lentulus bowed his head.

'I have not been back here since the day I left the case,' he said. 'Those hunting me would come here and find only the god – but they have followed us today since we began walking.'

'Then we had better shift out of here,' Quintus growled.

'My work here is done,' Lentulus said. 'Go behind the panel and you will find a door in the floor. It is heavy, but once opened you will access the old tunnels that run from the Maximus to the Flavian. I will close it behind you – but it will be no barrier to the determined, mark me.'

There was a loud splintering crash. 'What about you?' Drust asked and Lentulus smiled. There was no longer the nervous over-the-shoulder tic, no shaking. No fear. It was a startling enough change to make everyone stare.

Lentulus knelt. 'My duty is fulfilled. I am here, where Mithras is being born from the rock, with the water miracle, the hunting and riding of the bull, where he is meeting Sol who kneels to him, where he is ascending to the heavens in a chariot.'

He looked at Drust and smiled. 'If these soldiers are crass enough to harm a *pater* in the temple of Mithras, sully the holy of holies and bring down the wrath of the god on them, then I am well placed to beg a lift on the chariot of the god.'

'Fortuna smile on you,' Kag muttered as they hurried off, chased by the sound of the door breaking.

'Does he know these are probably all Germans of the Palace Hounds, who don't give a fuck for Mithras?' Ugo hissed as they strained at the ring of the door. It came up surprisingly easily, revealing darkness and no clear way down, even when Drust held a torch over it.

'Probably not,' Kag growled back and thrust an unlit horn-panelled lantern at him. 'Now get in that hole.'

Ugo, scowling, sat on the lip, took the lantern and dropped himself into the dark. One by one the others followed, and when Drust dropped in last, he heard the grate of stone, the dull thump of it closing and a last breath of voice that said, 'The Lord of Light go with you.'

They turned slowly in a circle of torchlight where a faint breeze set shadows to dance on the brick walls and the curved roof of a barrel-shaped tunnel. It stretched in both directions and the flickering flame only made the dark more sinister – four or five steps further on, the torch barely showed the outline of the roof above them.

'Which way?' Ugo demanded, and Drust looked up and around.

'Away from here – if I have it right in my head, this way leads to the Flavian.'

No one argued, but that was because none of them knew any better, so they moved steadily through the dark, pooled by the light of a single torch; and if anyone thought of the time they had crept through the corridors of a similarly black temple they did not want to summon up the memory aloud.

Ugo did mention how this resembled the Dark when they came upon a section dappled with light from far above them, splintered through what appeared to be gratings on both sides. Below it, attached to the wall, was a solid-looking tank of lead. The light, coupled with the half-columns of pillars like giant trees, the shadows and the plants that seemed to have flourished, all made them nod and agree uneasily.

'This is a piece of work,' Dog muttered, trying not to waggle his jaw as he spoke, keeping the sentences short and terse.

It had been built over a drain that leached rain off the streets and into the sewers and then down into Father Tiber. That had been ancient when all the workers came down here to carve out a roadstead, building a tunnel over the drain big enough to take four-wheelers with cages and the oxen to haul them.

It had been built just after the Flavian was finished – a faded inscription confirmed it – when the Maximus was still used for combats and shows. Twenty years later, the Flavian dominated all of that and the Maximus concentrated on the races, for which it was purpose-built and better suited.

'This place was left to moulder,' Kag added when they had talked this back and forth a bit. 'It hasn't been used for a hundred years. Longer.'

They prowled, looking at the shadows and the strange spidery growths of plants – from seeds spilled out of the grain and fodder and dung of all the exotic creatures that came down, Drust realised. Quintus confirmed it by pointing out shrubs they all knew from the deserts of the Africas.

They saw a half of wheel, splintered and cobwebbed, crumbling next to a rusted cage which had been abandoned. Ugo peered cautiously at it.

'Might be beasts down here.'

It had occurred to them all, though no one wanted it said out loud. Drust thought it unlikely anything had survived and bred through generations. No tigers or bears, he said. Or river lizards.

'So those are not the eyes of a hunting beast then,' Ugo replied, and pointed back the way they had come. Everyone froze, seeing the red eyes Ugo had spotted. Then Drust gave a curse.

'We have been too busy sightseeing,' he growled, 'and have forgotten what pursues us. Those are torches in the hands of enemies.'

Dog drew out both of his swords and spat blood onto the dusty roadway. 'Fight or run?'

'Run, *stupidus*,' Kag spat back and set off at a fast jog. With only the briefest of pauses, the rest followed him along the trackway until Kag suddenly gave a yelp and stopped, pointing.

They all looked. A dog-sized rat skulked to one side, pausing only to turn and hiss at them, all red eyes and yellow incisors. Another followed it and another after that.

'Gods above and below,' Quintus said, wiping his mouth with the back of one hand. 'Bad enough the two-legged kind, but this – do you see the size of them?'

'Hard to miss,' Kag offered wryly, 'but they are all running as we are.'

'Perhaps they don't like Praetorians either. Sensible beasts...'

Drust glanced around, seeing the wreck of a big wagon, the timbers all collapsed and the wheels broken. It looked like the bones of a giant beast – but it narrowed the walkway.

'Here,' he said, and the rest of them got it, turned and set themselves. Never run in the *harena*, Drust thought. You only arrive back where you started, too tired to fight.

The torches danced closer, like fireflies. For a moment Drust felt his head swim, seeing what appeared to be a lake behind them, boiling up bubbles. He shook his head to clear the vision as the shadows materialised into figures, advancing steadily and falling into a wedge.

They had tunics, hooded cloaks and the usual weapons you could hide so as not to cause comment on the streets of Rome. Knives and the *gladius* then, Drust thought. No better armed than us and we are masters in the craft.

There were a dozen of them, perhaps more, and they were confident – they were Praetorian, after all, the last forging of the best of the Army – so they came in hard and fast, left arm up with a bundled cloak-end as shield, right arm drawn back for the thrust. They were veterans and trained in the way of the *gladius*, even if it had fallen out of favour.

Drust slashed, saw the returning thrust, the left arm up, and he knew what the weakness was – they fought like they had their big shields. He ducked a shoulder so that the enemy point hissed past his ear, drove his own point through the man's protective forearm, cloak padding and all. He saw him go open-mouthed and wide-eyed with shock and pain, then slammed his open palm into the man's chest, sending him backwards into the one behind.

Dog weaved and ducked, twin points flicking out; a man screamed and reeled away. Kag punched a man in the face, failed to move out of the way of another, and Drust saw the point of a *gladius* go in the fleshy muscle of his left arm and burst out the far side.

Ugo saw it too and bulled his way to Kag's side, slamming into the enemy with one massive shoulder; the man went sideways with a deep oofing sound, losing his grip on the *gladius* and leaving it waggling from Kag's arm.

Quintus completed the ruin with a slash across the man's eyes and then thrust his torch into the tunic. His nearest mates pounced and beat out the flames, then suddenly they were standing panting, with the Praetorians a few steps back doing the same. Three of them were down and a fourth was half crouched, moaning and holding his face, smelling of char.

'Give it up,' one of them called out hoarsely, and Drust took this for the leader. He was about to tell the man to fuck off when he saw Quintus staring and frowning, followed his gaze and squinted.

The boiling water was closer, popping little bubbles. He couldn't understand it, but Dog, his face leaking blood, suddenly kicked out at something, then backed off a few steps and shook one arm furiously. A spider popped to the ground and then seemed to spring up, waist height. It did it again.

'Run,' Kag said through teeth gritted with pain. 'Run like Dis Pater was chewing your arse.'

They ran. The Praetorians saw it – and gave loud bellows of victory until their leader demanded they follow. It was too late.

Drust heard the yells and then the screams of utter terror, remembered the dog-sized rats that had been scuttling in a panic, and he did not look back, just pumped his arms and legs and sprinted, careless of debris, careless of the dark, caring only for what was behind them.

He followed Quintus's torch until it stopped and they huddled in the pooled light, hands on thighs, retching and trying to breathe at the same time.

'What the fuck?' demanded Dog, and Kag, wincing as Ugo worked the *gladius* out of his arm, put them right.

'Another legacy from this beast tunnel,' he growled. 'You remember them from the desert – the jumping spiders?'

Drust remembered them at once. Body the size of a *denarius*, long legs, and the ability to pop into the air if disturbed. They had scared everyone at least once – but Drust had only ever seen one or two.

'Well, here they are the size of my palm,' Dog muttered, worrying his scar with probing fingers. 'And there are more than a few...'

'Nothing here that eats them, not even those dog-rats,' Ugo said, looking back.

'They must hate the light, which starts them moving,' Kag decided, using teeth and his good hand to bind up the wound in his arm. He worked the elbow a few times and frowned. 'Our torch wasn't much but all of the Praetorians' woke them up. I would wager there are a few shops and *insulae* above here complaining about fucking big spiders… This arm will get stiffer in an hour.'

'This is not a good place,' Ugo muttered, glancing round uneasily.

'You think?' Dog countered viciously.

'Keep moving,' Drust ordered. 'We will come up to the entrance to the Flavian soon.'

'If it is an entrance,' Quintus pointed out morosely. 'They probably blocked it up.'

'More cheer, that's what we need – we should sell you for a *fossor*,' Dog muttered, and Quintus slapped his hand away from his scar.

'Stop grubbing in that – and stop talking or the scar will be as broad as your face. And we will need a *fossor* to get out of here.'

It was a weak jest at best – *fossor* was the name for a clown in the farces, but it also meant 'gravedigger'. They laughed all the same, making it another light in the darkness.

We are like a stick in the hands of a child with a knife, Drust thought as they hurried off. Whittled less and less with every stroke and to no purpose.

They came up to a place where the road seemed to cross a huge open area. The shadows prevented them seeing the extent of it, but they all felt as if they stood in a basilica; they tasted the musty air and the strange dust in it.

'I do not like this place,' Ugo muttered. 'Who knew the Dark stretched to Rome itself?'

'Are those spiders venomous?' Dog asked. 'I have been bitten. Hurts like fire too.'

'No,' Kag replied, 'but if you don't get them cleaned and treated they will fester. Can you imagine a hundred such bites?'

'The Praetorians can,' Quintus muttered.

'Then let us get out of here,' Dog said. 'There will be a decent *medicus* in the Flavian and I might have to employ him permanently.'

There might have been, but Drust realised they weren't about to reach the Flavian when the road ended at a blank brick wall. You could see the barrelled arch where the tunnel had once been – and probably still was beyond the bricks – but there was no way through.

'Blocked,' Quintus said. 'Like I said.'

'What now?' Kag said wearily, and Drust remembered the open area. There had to be another way up.

Ugo shifted slightly and grunted. 'It seems those hopper spiders haven't stopped the Praetorians. Some of them are still upright and headed this way – I can see some lights.'

'Trapped,' Kag said and Quintus gave him a sideways scowl.

'Ha. As long as we know we're trapped, we still have a chance to escape.'

They moved quickly back to where the tunnel roadway opened out; the oncoming lights were closer and Drust eyed them warily.

Kag stepped off the road, holding up a new-fired torch and reassured by the firmness under his feet. He stopped, crouched and then turned to them.

'It's an old quarry,' he announced. 'From when Romulus was a youth.'

'Quarry?' demanded Dog, scowling, and Kag told him it was worked by slaves who dug in the half-dark for blocks of *tufa*, the original stones that built the city. They moved off, half stumbling over the uneven ground, which swelled and dipped like desert dunes.

Quintus dipped and came up with a handful of dirt, red in the torchlight. He grinned at them all.

'This is what they wanted later,' he said, 'when *tufa* was no longer enough.'

He let the dirt trickle through his fingers. 'Red *pozzolana*.'

'Now I know this and I know nothing,' Ugo muttered. 'Save that we had better run or turn and fight again.'

'It's the main ingredient of pouring stone,' Quintus told them. 'This stuff built the harbour at Ostia and elsewhere. It built the Empire – and we should fight.'

'The way we did in the dunes east of Dura,' Drust added grimly, and they looked round, remembering.

It was a simple plan. There would be the focus of a light, a glow that would bring them like night insects. It would be held by one man – Kag in this case – crouching on one knee and clearly at the end of his strength, abandoned by the others.

They would close in with snarls and nastiness, set to inflict some damage, enough to pain but not to kill – enough to sate them for the spiders and the big rats and the shock of a harder fight than they'd thought to find.

Then they would drag Kag off to face Verus, using it as a good excuse to get out of this underworld of shrieking horrors.

It was almost as Drust had seen it in his head, a trick they had used many times before, from the bracken wilderness of the lands beyond the northern Walls to the sand-sighing deserts of the lands east of the Empire.

Men are the same everywhere. They came up, cat wary and crouched, turning this way and that until they heard the laboured breathing of the kneeling man, saw how his head hung like a whipped slave.

'Where are the others?' demanded the leader.

'Gone,' whispered Kag defeatedly.

'You'd better tell us. The Winter Man is right behind us and he won't take that for an answer.'

The Winter Man. It did not take Drust much in the way of wits to work that out, which is where the plan changed in a heartbeat. He rose up, yelling, and ploughed over the red dirt slope and down the far side in a staggering run.

The men reacted as he expected, all the same – they whirled, backed off a few paces, brought weapons up. The leader gave a snarling order which was lost in an ending of whimpered scream, because Kag had sprung from kneeling in a thrust that took sharp steel into the base of his belly, just above where his cock began.

Then Kag did a complete forward roll, the sort of flash move a good *lanista* would beat you with a stick for attempting. *While you are turning arse over tip in the sands, your opponent is dropping a net on you and sticking you with a fucking great fork – stay on your feet, you* stupidus...

Drust bulled into the man who saw the opening, was about to stick Kag in the side. He gave a yell at the last which made the man spin round from Kag and thrust at him, a perfect legionary move, high up as if over the rim of a shield he did not have.

Drust step-hopped sideways, letting the sharp steel cut air and slamming his full body into the man at the same time as he thrust up. His *gladius* went in under the chin, came out the bridge of the man's nose, and he screamed out a bubble of horror and blood; his falling tore the sword out again and Drust turned, looking for another opponent.

Quintus arrived, laughing and slashing, with the Dis Pater horror of Dog behind him – but what broke the Praetorians in the end was none of that. It was Ugo, piling over the top of a ridge of *tufa* and red dirt, pausing only to throw back his head and howl out to his German gods, spreading his arms to show that he had a *dolabra* in either fist.

They started to run and were cut like ripe wheat; Ugo brought down two with as many strokes, vicious back-breaker swipes. Quintus made a mistake, the sort of left-or-right choice that Fortuna forces on you, with all the fickleness of that bitch goddess. It got him a slash across the thigh that flushed red all down his leg and set him cursing – not with pain, that came later – because he knew what he had done wrong.

All eight of the Praetorians died, leaving the Brothers pooled in the sputtering wan light of their dropped torches, panting and glazed at having survived yet again. The blood was reeking, and even as they watched, something coiled out of the ground.

'Gods above and below,' Kag spat, backing away. They looked in horror as more of them, glistening white, thick as a finger, long as a forearm, curled out of the ground. It made them back off even further, making for the solid ground of the *tufa*, where they could see the blind, white worms roiling and curling in the blood pools.

'I would not step down there if I were you,' Dog advised Quintus as he fell to examining the thigh wound. Quintus spat curses at him for what he was doing and Dog merely grinned and tapped his own scar, making Quintus recall the pain he had caused when fixing it.

'This place is worse than the Dark,' Ugo mourned, resting a bloody pickaxe on either shoulder. Drust, who had been worrying at the nag of the Winter Man and his imminent arrival, suddenly saw the weapons.

'Where did you get them?' he demanded and Ugo frowned, then smiled and lifted them. He wanted to clean the clot off them in the red dirt but wasn't going to step anywhere near the milling writhe of white worms, who were now slathering themselves in the slush of blood.

'I went over that little hill to hide,' he said, 'and found them there with a lot of quarry stuff – are those worms poisonous, do you think?'

'I wouldn't eat one to find out,' Kag answered laconically.

'I mean – do they bite and can you die from it?'

'Unlikely. They look like worms, same ones who deal with all dead things, only these ones have grown large and pale in the dark. I don't think these Praetorians have been dead long enough, so they will deal with blood until they are riper.'

'Best work these Praetorians did,' Dog noted scathingly. 'This is a sad sign. Are these the best Rome has to offer in the way of fighting men? I can beat any of them with a meat skewer.'

Drust just wanted to lie down and close his eyes in the silent darkness. To hear his heart and how it was still beating – still fighting. To tell himself that he had made it yet again and that he might just make one more.

Instead, he reminded them all of the Winter Man and how it could be no one but Verus; the thought of that white worm lurking in the shadows made them all jerk attentively.

'Show me this quarry stuff,' he told Ugo, and they followed, skirting the mass of worms, until they got to it, a litter of two-wheeled carts, shovels, pickaxes, baskets – all the materials you would need, Drust thought, to start heaving *pozzolana* out of this old quarry.

And it was new.

'Well, it seems there's a fresh demand for pouring stone,' Quintus said, grimacing now because the pain had arrived and the leg would grow stiff enough for him to drag it soon; he needed to be lying down with poultices on it to stop any blood-rot.

'The Emperor is building a new aqueduct which will have his name on it,' Kag mused. 'It is to serve the new baths he is also building with his name on it. That will take a lot of pouring stone.'

'So where are the slaves working this, then?' Dog wanted to know. 'The overseers and the guards?'

They all looked at one another and said it virtually in unison. 'The Ludi Romani.'

The Great Games were about to start, the Emperor's own, and everyone employed by him in Rome got two weeks off to enjoy it. Everyone but slaves, but without overseers or guards, they couldn't work either – but they had to have a way to get in and out.

'Find it,' Drust said.

Chapter Sixteen

It was a shaft with stairs carved out of the *tufa* and the holes to take the poles of lifting cranes up through a double-doored trap in the floor. It was greased and opened quiet and easy, up into one of the disused rooms of that old edifice, the Temple of the Divine Claudius. The room had been one of a cluster which had originally schooled some of the smarter Imperial slaves – they saw the discarded desks and benches. Now, instead of slates and rote, this room had baskets of red dirt, more tools, and a little track with moveable carts for running the *pozzolana* out to bigger ox-drawn wagons in the dead of night.

Best of all, the door out brought them to the street, with the bulk of the Flavian on one side, the squat travertine square of Ludus Magnus on the other, and the Sweating Post fountain offering a chance to splash water.

We look like slaves now, no doubt of it, Drust thought. Clothes filthy with red dirt and *tufa* dust, sweat and worse, cloaks ragged at the hem and some of us nursing wounds bound with rags; Kag limped fiercely and even the balm of the fountain failed to bring a smile.

'What now?' Ugo asked, mournful about being told to drop the *dolabrae* beside the other builder's mess before they came out into the street; but he saw the sense in it when the milling crowds round the Flavian rippled away from them.

'Curtius,' Drust said. They looked like slaves and, if not exactly gladiators, then some ragged form of trainer, and that excited little attention and no censure around the Ludus Magnus. Curtius wasn't hard to find, but he was amazed to see the condition they were in and led them out to the trainers' balcony overlooking the little amphitheatre; it was busy with fighters and the entire *Ludus* buzzed back and forth with a scurry of people – the Games were a week old and took a lot of organising.

'What did you do – dig a hole and jump in?'

'Wrong way,' Kag muttered, wincing, and Curtius squinted expertly, unpeeled the blood-stuck binding and hummed to himself.

'Fresh. Through and through – clean cut but it sliced muscle, so you will take a while to get back from that. Needs attention – *gladius*, was it?'

Drust told him in fits and starts between swallowing wine and bread and olives. A *medicus* appeared, was introduced as Anaxi since the full version, Curtius said, was a mouthful.

'One of the best we have. He can Orpheus a man out of Hades with a skilful touch and some of his Ptolemy magic.'

Anaxi grunted, clearly used to Curtius. 'I am not an Alexandrian, I am from Palmyra. And I know mostly how slashed and stabbed a man needs to be before you knock him on the head and mark him as six.'

He was light-fingered and expert, cleaned, stitched, slathered ointment and rebound the worse of the wounds with clean linen windings.

'What happened to Lentulus?' Curtius asked and Drust told him.

'I do not know if he still lives,' he added. 'I hope so – he kept his word and was braver than he first appeared.'

Curtius merely grunted. 'I knew he was a follower of Mithras,' the rut-faced old *lanista* mused, 'but I did not know he was so far up the ladder. That explains why Antyllus was so deferential to a barber – is the general dead?'

'A mercy stroke – Verus had already killed him,' Dog growled, shying away from the *medicus*, who scowled and waited patiently, saying nothing. Reluctantly, Dog let him work.

'You will have a mighty great scar for a mighty long time,' the *medicus* told him. 'Try not to pick the scab of it off or you will have a face like a bad cobbler's thumb. Well, a long-dead bad cobbler's thumb.'

He took up his bag of tools, nodded to Curtius and strode off.

Curtius watched the fighters for a time, then sighed. 'That Brasus – he has been tagged yet again, the stumble-foot. By the *retiarius* he is matched with for tomorrow.' He drank moodily. 'They will both be sixed... Did you find what Lentulus had hidden?'

Drust unshipped the scroll case from his shoulder and sat it on the table for Curtius to look at with a rheumy, jaundiced eye. He put his hand in his lap and clasped it, feeling it shake and trying to hide it.

'That it? Doesn't look much – what's in it?'

'Notes, letters, accounts – enough to bring down a lot of important people and save a lot more. We have to get it to the Emperor and no one else.'

'We?' Curtius spat back suspiciously. 'There is no "we" in this. Is that pale knife-man still out there?'

'He is,' Quintus said and added a pungent curse involving the fickleness of Fortuna.

'Well then,' Curtius replied. 'I can offer you some treatment for what ails you, some food, a little wine, and if you like, a pallet for the night in a safe cell. Beyond that – I am a little old for taking on killer knife-men.'

'Nothing like that needed,' Drust answered, 'but I have to talk with my brothers first. Then I will ask for your help.'

Curtius looked bemused and even more suspicious, then glanced at the sky and the head of the gilded bronze Nero peeping over the rim of the amphitheatre and throwing sunrays off his crown. 'Well, the Colossus Nero says I should have some lunch. When I come back, you had better be ready to ask the favour I will almost certainly refuse – it is a busy day. Forty good men will walk the *harena* tomorrow and only two will leave.'

They watched him walk, a stiff affair of battered knees and ankles and one bad hip, and then Drust turned to the others.

'We will never get this into the hands of the Emperor,' he said, 'simply by walking up to the purple seat at the Games tomorrow.'

'A score of Praetorians and assorted flunkeys will get in the way of that,' Kag agreed. 'So what's your plan?'

Drust took a breath and told them, aware of the tremble in his hand.

'There is only one way for the likes of me to stand next to the Emperor with a bundle of scrolls. That's if I am being awarded the Palm of Victory and the right to present written petitions to young Alexander in person.'

There was a stunned silence, then Dog's voice, swaddled by the fresh pack of bindings, said what they all thought.

'Wait – what? Palm of Victory? For what?'

'Winning the Circle of Treachery.'

There was a pause, then Dog laughed and winced. 'Jupiter's cock – you have made me burst one of these new stitches.'

'Are you serious?' Kag demanded. 'How would you even do that?'

'You'll be sixed,' Quintus growled morosely. 'Even with Dog.'

'Not Dog, not with that wound,' Drust said quietly. 'Nor Kag, nor Quintus, for the same reasons. I do not want to ask the last man standing, but I must.'

For a moment they stood, until Ugo felt the eyes on him, blinked once and then spread his face in a wreath of grin.

'I will stand with you. Fuck Fortuna in the arse.'

'Gods above and below,' Kag exploded. 'Pull your thinking out of your sponge-holes, the pair of you – you are too old, too slow... and besides, you will have to bind yourself to an owner. Take the oath. Become a fucking slave again in all but name.'

'With thirty-eight other fighters, younger, stronger and desperate to live,' Dog said. 'That's not a battle you can win. I have seen you fight recently, Drust, and have seen some god-touched moves from you. But you would have to be a true son of Mars to win this. You will get yourself sixed.'

He stopped, looked Drust steadily in the face. 'You will get Ugo sixed.'

'Ho,' Ugo rumbled, annoyed. 'My exit through the Death Gate is between me and Mars Ultor, no one else.'

'Not that German arse-sponge, then?' Kag spat back. 'The one you kept calling out to in the Dark?'

'That was there, this is here,' Ugo growled, half embarrassed. 'One is fine for making the sky flash and bang in a forest. The other is the god of the *harena*.'

'This is madness,' Quintus shouted. 'What does it profit us if you die? What of the plot against the Emperor then? The only blessing of the gods in it is that you won't find anyone willing to throw two old farts like you into the *harena*.'

Even as he said it, he knew; they all did. Curtius would. He had Brasus the Dacian and his second, some *retiarius* who was only marginally better. Here he would save money, save them, and still keep the numbers up.

'Look,' Drust said. 'The only other way is for us to run and the Empire is not wide nor long enough for us to escape. Even beyond it is no longer safe and we will never – NEVER – be able to return.'

There was silence at the truth of that, then Kag scrubbed his head with irritated confusion.

'Better odds than what you propose,' he began, but Drust stopped him with an upraised hand.

'It's not like I don't have a plan.'

They waited. Nothing came. When they realised nothing was about to, Quintus flung his hands in the air and walked a half-circle, growling curses.

'If the worst happens,' Drust said into the outbursts, 'then take the scroll case and work out another way to do it. Or run and hope everyone loses interest with the deaths of Ugo and me.'

'Either way, we are face down on the bed with the gods lining up at our arse cheeks,' Dog mushed bitterly.

'We have already assumed that position,' Ugo said, quiet and calm. 'We did from the moment Fama put our foot on the road of this enterprise.'

'Not a goddess,' Drust replied, smiling.

'A literary conceit of Ovid, or so I have heard,' Quintus agreed and managed a poor copy of his old grin.

'We'll give the case to Kisa when you are dead,' Dog said and managed a lot of venom through his swaddled face. 'Maybe he can think of something – but it will be too late for you pair then.'

'Always is for the Horatius,' Ugo responded, then looked round their raised eyebrows. 'What? He was the lad on that bridge, wasn't he?'

'The very same,' Kag said and clapped his good hand on Ugo's forearm. 'Well done, giant of the Germanies – thing to remember about that heroic defending is that two others were with him and no one remembers their names.'

'Herminius and Lartius,' Drust corrected soberly. 'And no one wants to recall them much because they were the ones who ran away.'

There was silence after that, broken by the return of Curtius, belching and wiping his mouth. He looked round them all and spat an olive stone over the balustrade.

'I have seen twenty miles of bad road that looked better than your faces. This must be serious.'

Drust put it to him and could feel the others, tense as hauled hawsers, hanging on the answer. Curtius, to his credit, never put any of the arguments against it, just tilted his head sideways a little, like a bird working out how to smash a snail to get at the food.

'This is a wild throw of the dice,' he said eventually, 'but if you are set on it...'

'Ulpius Ralla,' Kag said desperately. 'What will he think when a pair of oldsters turn up as part of his contribution to the Emperor's Games?'

Curtius rasped a hand over his stubble, then shook his head. 'Three pairs he promised and three pairs will appear – he won't know any of their names, let alone their faces.'

'His name is probably in those scrolls,' Dog pointed out.

'Which make clear he was misled and by whom,' Drust answered, then turned to Curtius.

'Have you a place to hide this? Make sure it is safe – I'd hate to win through after all only to find you have forgotten which drawer you put it in.'

Curtius took the case, looked at him, then Ugo. 'Win through. You make me laugh, Drust, so you do.'

'There is a plan,' Kag said bitterly. 'Or so I have been told.'

Curtius looked round them all, then back at Drust. 'Well, *auctoratus* – swear the oath, hand on heart.'

Auctoratus – the name struck a chill through Drust. A voluntary gladiator, a man who had chosen to be bonded like a slave. That's a long way to fall from being a freedman and a citizen, he thought. What would Praeclarum say about it? He felt the amulet of her pearls under his hand and hung round his neck. I will see her soon enough... Then he said the oath.

Uri, vinciri, verberari, ferroque necari – I will endure, to be burned, to be bound, to be beaten, and to be slain.

291

The words tumbled out of both of them like poor tin on a marbled floor.

Kag gave a groan and looked at the sky. Quintus threw up his exasperated arms once more and Dog stood silent and still.

'Go back to The Place and make arrangements to leave with everything of value you can carry,' Drust said with a half-smile. 'Just in case. You can come back later and watch us – I will get Curtius to leave you tokens – but if you see us fall, run fast and far.'

'Fuck you,' Dog spat back bitterly. 'Who are you to give orders now? You have made yourself a slave.'

Kag took him away, and Quintus, after a moment, offered his wrist to them both. 'You are mad-brained, the pair of you,' he said. 'Farewell until we meet in Hades.'

Drust slept in the familiar dark of a slave cell, but he only knew it was sleep when he woke from it. To him it was a grey, heaving sea whose swells swamped him then broached him to an ugly surface. Somewhere in it he recognised the truth of her loss, that she had gone with a last soft sigh and yet he was now losing her in pieces over a long time – the way she had warmed one side and now he could not feel it, the scent that seeped away from the little bag hanging round his neck like an amulet. Each one of them, those missing pieces, overwhelmed him with great greasy waves of realisation that she was gone forever, and they came more and more often in dreams.

Dreams is what I am when I am too weary to be me…

He woke when Curtius arrived with Ugo, blocking the light; the door had been left unlocked and open, a small sop to the idea that they weren't truly slaves. Curtius also brought wine, bread, olives and a hard salt cheese which Ugo claimed was excellent.

They ate and then Curtius went to the privy with his sponge-stick, leaving Ugo and Drust in an uneasy silence, which Drust eventually broke.

'I am sorry to have dragged you into this,' he said. 'Fortuna alone knows if we win or die, but the odds are not good. If you want to stop this at any time, just say.'

Ugo put down his wine and wiped his mouth. He sat for a moment, then took a breath.

'All of you laugh at me for the times I seem to become more German than Roman. You were raised in a slave cell, you remind me. You know the *harena* better even than Subura.'

He passed a hand over his head – freshly shaved, Drust saw with a lurch of old recognition; it was what he did when he fought in the ring.

'I am the white crow,' he said eventually. 'I am neither Roman – even after all this time – and the Frisii would not know me. You know the same feelings – I saw you north of the Wall in Britannia. They were your people, but they did not know you nor you them. Same with Dog, same with us all.'

He looked Drust steadily in the face. 'When first I came here I was a boy, led into the atrium of Servillius Structus's home inside The Place. The same one we wander around in now. It was raining and the *impluvium* was running with it, down into the pool. The only thing I could think of then was that this Roman had a hole in the roof – back home in Frisia, we'd all be out trying to patch it.'

He stopped, took a breath. 'I know better now – but every time I am there I look up at this square hole in the roof and realise that the only place I do not feel like a white crow is this family we have made. Is that not worth fighting for? Dying for?'

They were silent for a time, then Ugo shifted, farted and smiled. 'Besides – there is a plan. When do I get to hear of it?'

'Time for the *armamentarium*,' Curtius said, making a lot of noise coming through an open door. They followed him down into the sweating, fetid depths of the *hypogeum*, the underbelly of the Flavian. It was the fourth day of the fourteen that formed the Ludi Romani; tomorrow the Maximus would start the racing and the Flavian would unveil a *harena* where thirty-eight men would die.

For now, it was lunchtime and the *hypogeum* heaved like a maggot nest, stank of blood and animals, shit, piss and sweat – the last dripped like rain from the vaulted roofs of tunnels and chambers, and the heat was as killing as anything in the sands above their heads.

The *armamentarium* was close to the *spoliarium*, where they brought the dead and stripped them. It meant the armour and weapons didn't have far to travel along a line of slaves who examined the pieces for serious damage and cleaned the worst of the blood and final shit off. Then the corpses were tipped down a blood-slicked chute to somewhere even deeper – Drust remembered it, walking it with the Sardinian *medicus* who had been set to teach him how best to kill a man – and the weapons and armour went back to the *armamentarium*.

In the chamber of the *armamentarium*, Curtius elbowed through the throng until he stood beside a man wearing nothing more than a loincloth and a wrap of cloth round his head.

'Ruga – still here then? *Hoplomachus* for the big one,' he growled. '*Murmillo* for Drust.'

Ruga looked them up and down, wiped sweat off his eyebrows and then nodded. 'Titus – fetch the armour out of rack seven. Decius – rack twenty-eight.'

Drust wasn't sure about the *murmillo*, but Curtius had argued that it was his best chance of staying alive – the singular weapon of the *murmillo* was the *gladius*, which was practically part of Drust's fist. When his hand didn't shake.

On his left leg Drust would wear an *ocrea*, and he would be hefting an Army shield, the curved rectangle of *scutum* which had helped win an Empire. He looked almost like a legionary, save for the lack of body armour, the single greave, the *manica* – a sleeve of ring mail and padding on his right arm – and the helmet, the *cassis crista*, a heavy bronze affair with a grill designed to stop anyone shoving sharpness into your face.

It was battered and heavy, suspicious with old stains, but he collected all the metal and leather bits of it and grunted with the armful of weight, wilting while he waited for the others. He heard Curtius complaining about the state of the gear Ugo had been given.

The *hoplomachus* typically fought with bare chest and dressed only in a loincloth, the *subligaculum*, held up by a broad belt. He had greaves on both legs, from the middle of his thighs to his feet. On his right arm was a metal arm guard, the *manica*, and he had a helmet made to look like the ones Greek *hoplites* had once worn, with a feather on each side and a crest with a falcon stamped on it.

As if all that wasn't enough, he had a small, round, bronze shield commonly known as an *aspis*, for no reason anyone could remember. It let him hold a spear in his right hand and a *gladius* in behind the shield.

It was the spear which was annoying Curtius. It was supposed to be the *dory*, the famed weapon of the old Greek warriors of Sparta and the like, seven feet of shaft, a leaf-shaped blade with razor edges, and a spike at the butt end.

This one was short by three feet and had no spike. It was clear that it had been chopped off at some point and the repair had been a simple smoothing of the cut end.

'I want my spike,' Curtius growled. 'Bad enough that the shield has a frayed holding strap without you shorting my lad of three foot of reach.'

Ugo took the weapon, hefted it for balance, then twirled it like a small stick. He grinned.

'No, leave it. The long version is a waggling arse of a thing. I prefer this.'

'If you lose the tip off it, you'll have no back-up spike,' Curtius warned, and Ugo nodded, still grinning.

'I have a sword and a shield,' he replied. 'All you need.'

'Your funeral,' Curtius said morosely.

'I like that hat, all the same,' Ugo added, nodding to the affair in question. It was a glory of a *secutor* helmet but with the front made into a golden cat mask designed to leave the mouth and chin free. Between the ears, across the forehead, was a blue enamel shape with one of those Ptolemy signs called an *ankh* tricked out in black, the loop of it between the brows. The eyes were carefully slanted cut-outs.

'Belongs to Tiridates,' Curtius said brusquely. 'Greek, but from Oxyrhynchus. He fights with a *khepesh* – you know what that is?'

'Sickle-sword,' Ugo answered. 'A Ptolemy affair – I have seen it. Bit like the bastard offspring of an axe and a *spatha*. Well, Fortuna smile on him.'

'He fights tomorrow paired with Alafai the *retiarius*. The pair of them are the Emperor's favourites,' Curtius said sternly. 'I would not be so free with Fortuna's blessings on them.'

Ugo shrugged. 'Mars Ultor is the lad for the *harena*. Women have no place in it – no offence, Drust.'

'None taken, giant of the Germanies. Old Severus saw to that when he ended women fighting in the *harena*. I do not believe Praeclarum, may she sun herself in Elysium, was unhappy with the edict.'

'You go on, before you fall down,' Ugo answered, looking at Drust bowing under the weight of the equipment. 'I will be here for a while, making sure this son of a diseased sow gives me a better *hoplomachus* shield or has the hold strap on this repaired.'

'Fuck you with a three-tined fork,' Ruga said amiably. 'I know you by reputation – you both escaped from under the *harena* once – but if you are dancing in the ring tomorrow, then you are slave again. So watch your mouth.'

'I'd rather watch yours suck cock. I hear you can take the gilding off Colossus Nero.'

Drust listened to their fading exchange as he wobbled away through the throng, trying not to bang anyone too hard in case it jogged something loose and he had to find a way to pick it up again.

The corridor was busy with beast handlers, sweating their way between levels to sort out the cages with lions, tigers and the rest. Somewhere an elephant squealed and Drust moved like an ungainly barge through the sea of movement.

He saw the man come up the corridor. Saw him because he thought of Dog right away – the man had a hooded cloak, a real Army *caracalla* in waterproofed leather. In the next eyeblink he knew Dog would never walk with his head down and his hood up down here, any more than he would in the Tartarus that was Subura. He had no need to hide… but this man did; in a sweltering furnace of heat like the fetid breath of a dragon, this man hunched himself into a cloak.

He knew it even before the man raised his head to check the way ahead, sliding sideways to avoid the rushing flow of other people, sinuous as a desert snake.

Pale face, eyes that flicked endlessly, searching the corners. A bland face remembered only for the washed-out brows and lashes by any who caught only a glimpse of it passing on a dark street – but Drust knew Verus, had stared at him once in the shadows behind Julius Yahya and could never forget it.

Their eyes met like a clash of steel – Verus made a lunge forward, slid round a hurrying slave, collided with another and shouldered him off-balance. People yelled their annoyance. One reached out a hand to grab the cloak and Verus half-whirled; there was a sharp cry and blood flew.

There were roars of outrage and warning, but most of the people in the tunnel eddied away like water from a flung stone, leaving Drust standing, arms full of gladiator gear. He was appalled at how paralysed he was, watching Verus come at him like a rush of snow wind through the milling shadows. He heard voices shouting for the Urbans, the Vigiles – anybody.

A few steps from Drust, Verus was balked by a reddened pig-face attached to a half-naked body composed of bulged muscle from working the haulage windlasses. The pig-face snarled angrily, then squealed when Verus, his face as blank as carved travertine, stepped sideways and slashed him a second smile under his chin.

It seemed to Drust that he was kicked hard in the belly by the sight of spraying blood, a shock that struck him from crown to sole and back again. Me, he thought. That will be me…

He flung the armful of gear at Verus, having the grace of the gods to hold onto the hilt of the *gladius*, so that only the sheath joined the spray of lumber which took the knife-man in the face.

Verus reared up like a frightened horse, cursed, shook off a grasping hand and whirled in a circle, making the crowd shy away from him. He stumbled through greave and arm guard, kicked a helmet and hopped, cursing again, for Drust was a set of bare feet vanishing round a corner.

Drust ran by instinct, by smell, taste and the knowledge garnered from too many years ploughing through these fetid spaces. He yelled and when that failed he used his elbows, but a man with a naked sword sprinting in a crowded space left him trailing shouts of anger. Good, he thought, let Verus deal with that – yet he knew, by the increase in volume and the higher pitch, that Verus was close.

He tasted the foul air and sprinted left, banged through some double doors and skidded on the stinking tiles, slick with fluids and blood and entrails. He hop-stepped over two sprawled bodies and slammed into the sweating mass of a fat Dis Pater, his death-mask helmet under one arm and his hammer parked in the belly cavity of a disembowelled dwarf.

'Hoi – you shouldn't be here. Get the fuck out.'

Drust knew the *spoliarium* was a dark hole of bloody secrets that the people who moved in it liked to keep to themselves. The 'mysteries' they called it, as if there was some secret, magical, divine revelation that should not be divulged to the general public – but gladiators and *lanistae* and beast fighters sometimes arrived to claim the body of one of the fallen before it ended up down the Hole, and they knew the charnel-house truth.

He watched slaves lever the lolling body of a dead lion down into the Hole, a square pit in the floor leading to even darker and more fetid depths, where it would be skinned for the pelt, the claws and fangs removed for sale as souvenirs, and the remnants dragged off to a pit of lime, reduced to slurry and washed out through the drains into the Tiber at the end of the day. All the bodies ended up down there, he knew; 'never swim in the Tiber' was a catechism dinned into every denizen of Rome from a young age.

He knew the depth of the Hole well and considered it, but could not bring himself to leap in. The fat Dis was working up to a fury now, greasy face contorted; Drust waved the *gladius* and glared, which made him back off and let Drust duck round him and head for the door he knew was on the far side.

It was the only other exit besides the Gate of Death, which opened into the ring and only when the sweating servants of Dis were dragging the dead by chains and a hook through the heels. He heard confrontation behind him which made him sprint the harder, skidding dangerously.

He lost his footing completely just at the door, slammed into the jamb and tumbled out into the tunnel beyond, scattering more hurrying slaves, who shouted at him. He was getting to his feet when he felt something clamp on his ankle and looked down to see a fallen Verus, one hand gripping him like a crocodile out of a river.

He yelled out, tried to scrabble away, kicked with his free foot and felt the calloused sole of his naked foot slam something soft, heard a grunt; the grip did not slacken. Drust hauled and screamed for help, panicked beyond reason at the thought of this spiderous killer working his way up from ankle to knee, to thigh, knife ready for the killing blow...

The grip slackened and Drust started to scuttle away, hit the wall of the tunnel and used it to lever himself up. Verus, knife out, closed with a triumphant snarl – only to fly sideways and slam into the far wall.

'Now, now,' said a reasonable, smiling voice and, blinking with surprise, Drust saw a huge man in a sweat-darkened tunic. He had the fleshy good looks of a Greek – tight-curled black hair, big olive eyes with large lashes, a sculpted nose, a richness of lips and a solid chin.

Verus got to his feet and Drust wanted to call out a warning to the Greek, but someone beat him to it. 'Tiridates – watch, he has a knife.'

Tiridates leaned left and let the knife hiss pass him, then reared back as it came at him again; Drust saw he was surprised by the speed of it, that he had a new calculating look on his face. Drust didn't wait to find out more – he was away like a rat down a pipe, turned left and half staggered through the throng.

The barrel-arched tunnel, wider and less thinly populated, let him scuttle round one bend, round another – choice of three ways there, perhaps Verus would be fooled – and follow a wafting balm of cool, wet air.

It grew stronger as he reached the vaulted entrance where water splashed and gurgled, a garden of cool which every slave contrived to visit on some pretended task, if only to keep from fainting. There were no flowers or perfumed fountains here, all the same – it stank of rank farts and richer shit, a product of the elephants whose cages were dragged in for transport up into the *harena*.

You could not work that sort of weight and bulk with men trudging round a windlass, so they had worked out how to use water – the giant paddle wheels ground and squealed when the overseer bawled for release, and the water outflowed down over them in a spray and was carried away by channels beneath.

The chains tensioned, the cage creaked up, and Drust took a moment to scoop up some of the water and dash it over his sweat-streaked face and hair.

It was a mistake to have paused; even as his vision cleared to blurry he saw the pale shape arrive at the door, pause to stare round, whipping his white head like a questing hound. He had lost the cloak and his tunic was stained with darkness, from sweat or worse – he looked to have fallen more than once in the *spoliarium* and Drust felt a savage triumph at that. He wondered what had happened with Tiridates.

Verus spotted Drust as Drust spotted him, moved forward as Drust backed off. Others shifted away and those who had no business here made for the door; a slave called out and the overseer turned and scowled.

'Give me what I want,' Verus said hoarsely, and Drust tried to grin at him, but his top lip stuck to his teeth, the only dry thing on his whole body.

'You need me alive,' Drust taunted, 'so what will you do?'

Verus lunged, Drust parried and the blades rang – but Drust was still recovering when the knife sliced his forearm; the sight of the blood made him yelp.

'I need a throat and a tongue and a mouth,' Verus spat back. 'I do not need eyes, or ears, or fingers or toes... tell me what I need to know and save them all.'

'Take this elsewhere,' the overseer declared. He was a big man, porridge-fed, with a face like a badly made dumpling and some extensive man breasts sweating onto an impressive belly. He was used to being obeyed, but Verus gave him a scowl and a snarl and told him to fuck off.

'Fetch the Urbans,' the overseer ordered a slave. Join the pack who have already done just that, Drust thought bitterly. Do I see any? No, I do not...

Verus took a step to the right, into the path of the hurrying slave, who sensibly veered off and cowered. It was all Drust needed; he stuck the *gladius* between his teeth and sprang for the bottom of the vanishing elephant cage, clawed round the small grill holes and clutched, hoping the beast would not move a foot and crush his fingers.

He looked down and grinned at Verus's face. It would have been a perfect moment had he not nicked the corners of his mouth on the sharp blade; by the time he managed a swing onto the next level up, leaving the elephant to rumble on up to the light and the sand, the sweat was stinging those little cuts worse than the slash on his forearm.

There was a slave on the walkway – it's what the narrow ledges were for. Each cage needed a slave to ride on the outside, hanging onto the chains and the lifting hook. The slave was needed to open the cage door to let the beast out – and to open the trap that let the ramp spill the beast up and into the amphitheatre. Then he had to close them all again, jerk the rope to signify it was done, and the cage would be lowered back to the loading level. Rinse and repeat – on days like these, Drust knew, there was sweat-oiled labour and everyone was a greased cog in an old machine.

He nodded to the slave as if they both had every right to be there, one with a naked sword in one hand, then teetered his way round the loading shaft on the walkway. It led to the next loading shaft, a smaller one that took the cages for the bears and the tigers, the lions and whatever else would fit easily in them. There were a score of such shafts, circling right round the centre of the amphitheatre; if the overseers got it right they could introduce a swarm of tigers and lions and wolves all at the same time, hauled up by muscled slaves working a windlass.

He heard the ratcheting of a cage coming up, just as he heard the slave he'd left behind squeal, a fading, falling note; he was chilled to the marrow at the sound and all the sweat sluiced like ice water on him.

Verus loomed into sight, panting and black with sweat and dirt. He had swarmed up the chains and ropes like some scuttling spider and now he was sliding inexorably towards Drust, who could only poise on the narrow walkway and wait for him; there was nowhere else to go.

The snow head was stained with black streaks of grease, but Verus seemed unperturbed by a feat which could have got him crushed in a dozen different and painful ways; Drust cursed Fortuna for not having done it. That bitch goddess hates me...

Verus closed in, struck hard with the dagger, a blow designed to spear Drust's sword arm and numb it enough for the *gladius* to fall. Drust parried it, knowing the man was fast; he just managed to block the second strike, failed on the third, but did enough for the knife to pink him and draw blood, no more.

'Give it up,' Verus snarled, panting; he dashed sweat from his eyes with his free hand. Drust saw the cage come up, looked into the bewildered face of a slave riding on top. Then, just as the green-eyed mask of a tiger came level, he hurled the *gladius* at Verus and sprang onto the cage.

It rocked furiously and the slave yelled out; the tiger was already scared and flattened itself to the floor of the cage, squirted out some rank piss and yowled. Drust was exultant, turned to look in triumph at Verus and saw the man leap like one of the jumping spiders.

Verus caught the bottom of the cage with one hand, swung up the other and had to drop the knife to get a grip. The slave was yelling at Drust and Verus in equal measure; below, Drust knew, sweating men at the windlass cogs would be straining to turn and raise the extra weight.

They got it up to the ramp level and Drust heard them locking it off; their angry queries echoed up the shaft but were drowned out in the background drone of all the other shouts and yells and roars. Verus scrabbled from hanging to clinging onto the side wall of the cage and the tiger slunk round, snarling at him. The cages were thickly barred and the spaces too small for fangs or talons, let alone paws; no sense in having luckless slaves mauled every other day.

'What the fuck is this?' the slave demanded, raising up his goad, and Drust lunged at him, grabbed him by the front of the tunic.

'Run,' he said. 'The man coming up is a maniac, a killer. He will snap your neck like your ma does a chicken.'

The slave didn't like the look of Drust, but the man with the strange lashless, browless face streaked with grease and sweat looked like he matched that description.

'I will get whipped if the job isn't done,' he bleated.

'You'll die if you stay,' Drust replied and plucked the goad from his nerveless fingers.

The slave leaped onto the narrow walkway and slithered expertly down it, looking backwards. When he judged himself far enough away, he spat a foul curse at Drust and went off to the next shaft, screaming for help at the top of his voice. Drust turned to Verus, busy working his way along the far side of the cage.

'Watch for the cat,' he warned viciously, then poked the goad through the bars. The tiger, starved and angry and already petrified, felt the sharp prick of it and yowled, went into a frenzy of snarl and slash. Verus, already clinging on, lost one handhold and hung for a moment, a long, glorious moment where Drust offered unfeasible reward to any god who would make him fall the forty feet to the floor.

It didn't happen. Verus got his hand back, then went down the side of the cage and back to hanging underneath, where the goad couldn't reach him. He worked his way, hand by hand, along the bottom of the cage to the front, then flipped himself onto the wooden ramp. He stood, bent over and panting, looked up and pointed.

'I will nail you up like I did your spy,' he said between gasps. 'The *mavro* who thought himself a silent killer. I showed him the truth of that.'

'You have no knife,' Drust said as he stepped off the cage onto the walkway and took two steps to the lever on the wall. Verus watched warily, more concerned with the goad which was as good as a spear. He wants me to throw it, Drust saw. Perhaps he has the skill to snatch it out of the air and then turn it back on me.

He had no need to do that, would not be parting with the goad anytime soon. If Verus wanted to get to him, he'd have to leap back onto the top of the cage and come at him from there. It could be done from the ramp and Verus had seen that. There was much he had missed, all the same.

This is my place, Drust thought savagely. This is my Dark and I know how the beasts in it all work...

He pulled the lever and there was a dull clunk of sound which made Verus crouch and spin. The double doors above his head spread upwards like wings, showering loose sand, bringing the hot blast of the *harena* and the deafening, howling roar of the amphitheatre. The tiger spun and yowled, frantic and afraid, and the shadow of Drust arriving back on the top of the cage made it crouch flat and look up.

'Say farewell, Verus,' Drust yelled over the din. Then he hauled up the cage door.

There was a moment when the scared tiger and Verus looked one another in the eye. The former didn't want to leave the cage – but Verus didn't know that. He knew nothing. He ran.

He managed to reach the lip of the ramp, managed to get right into the brassy glare and blaring crowds all round him, where he stood blinking. Then the tiger reacted to running prey and the last punch of the goad; Verus was poised on the lip of the trap, pale eyes seared by the transition to the blinding light, when a black and yellow shape, moving like a hurled spear, slammed into him, yowling, ripping and biting.

They vanished out of sight in a roll of snarling, shrieking sand. The crowd went wild and even through the closing trapdoor Drust could hear how they appreciated the moment. He could hear it after the trapdoors had shut and he had given the signal for the cage to go back down.

He heard it for a long way down the shaft.

Chapter Seventeen

They were too late for the Forum parade, but managed to attend the *cena libera*, the formal dinner put on by the sponsor of the Games. Since this was the Emperor, it was lavish with whole suckling pig, rabbit and hare, fowl and fish – though the boy himself was not present. Ugo would not eat hare, which he considered sacred, but he liked the red mullet because it changed colour on dying.

No one ate or drank much all the same, just went through the motions of it while the great and good admired them, assessed them and made bets. There hadn't been a *perfidiae harenam* for years and no one, not even the fighters themselves, knew what to expect.

'No referee, no reprieve,' Curtius said between chews. 'It's a brawl – don't listen to the arse-sponges who threaten you with the goad if you stay with your back to the *harena* wall. They just want you to get out where the audience can see. Cover your arses, lads.'

'Good advice,' said a sonorous voice and they looked to the owner of it, who was sipping from a silver goblet. It was the Greek from the tunnel, Drust saw – Tiridates – who looked Drust up and down with an amused smile on his fleshy lips.

'I remember you,' he said. 'You scuttled off like a rat down a pipe with that white-haired madman in pursuit. A pity – I would have snapped his neck in another eyeblink.'

Drust doubted it but said nothing. Tiridates laughed and he did it like Quintus would, a genuine toss of the head laugh, straight out of an amused core through an open throat. He offered the cup and Drust took it, managing not to hesitate; it was a gladiator concoction, one of those they swore by, a distillation of bone ash in thin wine which was supposedly a tonic. Drust did not want to dwell on where the bone came from.

'I hear he is dead,' Tiridates said, taking back the cup – it had his own face on it, Drust saw, embossed cleverly in silver.

'Every bit of him,' Curtius agreed. 'Seven pieces, not counting an eye which is still out there, staring at the sand.'

'What happened to the tiger?' Quintus demanded, and Tiridates looked at him with that smile which was starting to irritate Drust.

'Got speared in the end by Camillus,' Curtius answered. 'The *venator* who calls himself Hermes.'

'Pity,' Quintus growled back, 'I'd like to have offered it a treat.'

Tiridates saluted him, then looked round them one by one with that superior smirk. Behind him, his pair-partner, Alafai, was looming over a senator's wife and making her sweat.

'A strange affair,' he said, stroking his fleshy, freshly shaved chin. 'I don't know the why of it, nor much care to – but I liked what it revealed.'

He flung one arm around Alafai's neck and tucked the cup inside his snowy tunic. Something fluttered and he made a swift, easy gesture which almost hid the skill, plucked it from the air, crushed it in his fist and let it fall on the table. 'Until tomorrow,' he said. 'I do not think I will have much trouble.'

'Arrogant cock,' Curtius mumbled, watching the pair move off. The brilliant moth, wings crushed to powder, turned frantic circles on the table, dying in a pool of wine.

Curtius sighed and looked at them one after another. 'He's right, though. Twenty-five contests, no losses, and only three of the men he fought got a let-off. There are others out there tomorrow who are not as good, but a lot better than either of you ever were. You should give this up – Verus is dead and there must be another way to get to the Emperor.'

'Verus is dead,' Drust agreed, 'but you should not assume that the threat dies with him. Julius Yahya may have others – and he is growing more panicked hour by hour. If there is another way, we have no time left to find it.'

He looked at Ugo. 'I would not eat or drink anything here, giant of the Germanies.'

Ugo looked stricken and blinked, then squinted accusingly. 'You drank.'

'After Tiridates and from his cup.'

Ugo shook his head sorrowfully, even as he realised Drust was joking. 'This is not what the *harena* used to be like. There is little gravitas and less honour these days.'

It was exactly what the *harena* had always been, Drust thought, but kept it to himself. It was an entertainment of blood and sand for the howlers of Rome, regardless of status or riches. It was dressed up with ritual and pomp, but in the end that's all it was.

All they had to do was survive until the end of the next day. The trick in that was to want to.

–

The next day dawned sultry and grey-pink over the Capitoline, where there was not one procession at the start, but two – one for the Emperor, the other for his mother. Both of them had their own musicians, and at least, Drust thought, they are blaring and thumping the same tune, though it was almost drowned out by a madness of cheering.

It was the first day of the races and the Forum Romanum was filled with howlers in tunics the colour of their favourite faction – the Mother of the Empire, in her *quadriga,* veered off once she was through the Forum Romanum and Sacred Way, then headed through the Forum Boarium, trailing all the garish roarers behind her and heading for the *carceres*, the starting gates of the Circus Maximus nearby. She looked magnificent, balanced upright in a racing chariot driven by a lithe youth, both of them diplomatically wearing eye-wateringly expensive cloth of gold.

Not once, as far as Drust could tell, did she look at her son, who rode alongside her in another *quadriga*, a heavier one more suited to his appearance as a triumphant general.

Those who followed him were in their best tunics or dresses – some even braved the heat and stubbornly wore a toga – carrying cushions and baskets and wineskins. Behind came the *editor* presiding over the games, who followed the Emperor with a group of priests, their ritualistic displays escorting carts with statues of Jupiter Maximus, Mars Ultor and others.

They processed into the ring and round it twice while the crowd cheered and howled at what was about to happen. Then they stood in the heat while the priests allowed the gods their moment, and finally were allowed into the undercroft shade while the front seats sorted out their cushions and cool drinks.

The show would begin with a series of sham combats with blunt weapons. Then there would be a few novelty acts, beast hunts and the like, which would at midday be replaced by the *noxii*, those criminals marked for slaughter by beasts and blades. In the afternoon, when the heat had died a little, would come the main event.

They had a deal of time to wait in the undercroft, while the illusion of shade vanished in a fetid heat that drove them to strip off their gear and make their way out and up to the tiered seats, where Dog and the others had been ticketed. Curtius came with them; there was no sign of the scroll case and Drust did not ask where he had hidden it.

The others were pleased to see Drust and Ugo again, especially when they dropped linen bags into their laps, full of food filched from the feast the night before.

'Oho – I love these,' Quintus declared. 'Roasted mice in honey and poppyseed.' He grabbed a handful stuffing them in his mouth, chewing with relish.

'Better than chickpeas,' Kag agreed and offered the bag back to Ugo after taking out some pastries. Ugo shook a mournful head.

'Drust said not to eat or drink anything. In case Julius Yahya had poisoned it.'

'A little more advance in your warning would have been good,' Quintus said, his chewing slowed. Drust laughed.

'He would hardly poison the food and drink at that feast – too many tasters, too many high and mighty.'

Curtius was squinting myopically against the glare; above, the sailors from the Misenum fleet, used to running the ratline rigging of ships, were busy as apes throwing out the shade of the massive awning. Even torn and threadbare here and there, it was still welcome.

'I think Brasus won,' he said. 'Can you see better than me, lads? He was up against a decent Gaul called… I forget his name. But he has won a few…'

'Is Brasus the *hoplomachus*?' Kag demanded and Curtius nodded. Kag shrugged.

'The *hoplomachus* got a let-off.'

Curtius sighed. 'Well, I made an offering to Mars Ultor to keep that Dacian arse around for a little longer – but the Ludi Romani devour fighting men. The Emperor's purse is deep for deaths. Brasus will fight once more in these Games and I do not think he will make it.'

Drust sat and raised his head to a brief cooling breeze; the sky was growing darker and he thought it might rain. He said so and Dog frowned.

'I hope not. That's not the best I have seen the sand; it will turn to porridge in the wet. Like that time at Alba Fucens.'

'It was Beneventum,' Quintus argued. 'Ended up like a comedy act – if I had worn shoes they'd have been sucked off my feet.'

'That's the one. It was Alba Fucens.'

They argued it back and forth and it was all to fill the space with sound so that they would not have to think on what was going to happen once the lunchtime follies had run their course; they were on the last act of it now, showering the crowd with tokens and even launching them from a small ballista so they'd reach the top tier.

Once Manius and Sib had done this, Sib throwing wooden balls up for Manius to shoot with blunted arrows; the balls bounced into the crowd, each one with a token. It seemed an age ago…

Drust lived because other men bled. This was his world, a stinking menagerie of death that he had once thought he could escape. With all they had gained – The Place, a slice of old Servillius Structus's enterprises, a measure of notoriety and fame – he'd thought he had succeeded, but it was illusion.

This was where he was destined to be, dragged back to it by Mars Ultor or the harpy claws of Fortuna, or even Venus – a dozen gods might decree it. I have seen the light fade from a man's eyes many times, he thought, and each time the last puff breath, the final birdwing flutter of a heartbeat simply marked the primal truth of my existence. I can wear a toga and pretend otherwise, but I am a slave of the *harena* when all's said and done.

He must have said the last out loud for he felt their eyes on him and opened his own.

'The sand is in your blood?' Curtius asked wryly. 'Maybe. As long as your blood is not in the sand, Fortuna smiles and shows you her best tits.'

They laughed, but it was strained. Did they yearn for something else, something not filled with the iron-reek stickiness of blood or the high, thin stink of fear? Did

Dog look at his hands and wonder if they were meant to hold something other than his twin swords? Did any of his tremble?

They all wanted to ask Drust about his plan, but did not. When they embraced, it was clear everyone imagined it would be the last time. Just as he was leaving, Drust stopped, turned and grinned at them.

'Ladle,' he said. Let them make what they could out of that.

He explained it to Ugo when they climbed back into their gear, now slimed with the cold grease of old sweat; Ugo grinned, shook his head in mock wonder and then laughed. When they shuffled into the dark tunnel that led to the *harena*, the Gate of Life wasn't open, so Drust could stare blindly into the darkness and wonder if it perhaps went on forever, so that he would walk and walk until he grew tired.

When he stopped and looked back, there would be darkness where he had come from. He would sit down in the darkness – perhaps even stretch out, close his eyes and rest. Perhaps there would be no beasts in this dark… perhaps Praeclarum would guide him to the light of a field in Elysium.

Sconced torches were lit, blowing away the dark and making splintered shadows while they waited, fetid with their own rankness and whistling, nervous breath. There was perfume too, from incense brought by some for a last offering to some god. Ugo crouched with a handful of aromatic smouldering twigs and washed his head and face in the smoke, muttering prayers. He offered it to Drust, who shook his head. What god would he pray to? It seemed every one he had sent prayers had fucked all the Brothers over in the end.

There was always an end to the tunnel and always a man waiting to die beyond it.

For now, they waited here for the trumpets to blow and the Gate of Life to open. The figures loomed and shifted, some doing a little dance from foot to foot, others jumping on the spot to settle their gear. Drust saw one he knew, a Greek called Dyad, who had chosen the name because it was a symbol meaning 'power' to those who secretly worshipped Pythagoras. The crowd knew him as Silver-Arm for the ornate shoulder-to-wrist guard, the *manica*, he wore. He was a *retiarius*, a net man, and had won a score of fights.

Then there was Tiridates, who looked round and caught sight of Ugo, head and shoulders above those visible in the blood-dyed dim.

'You are doing this after all?' he asked, and since no one answered him, heads turned. Tiridates smiled, his face dancing with shadows and flame.

'You think you can stand on your own without falling over at your age? You should be home, dozing.'

'I'd leave it is what I'd do if I were you,' Ugo grunted back.

Tiridates laughed. 'Fair enough. Couple of hours and you'll be fine – no, wait, which way does time run again?'

'Are you crazed?' an anonymous voice asked, and Tiridates snorted, then slotted on his helmet.

'Am I the one with the grey hairs fighting alongside my granda?' he demanded in a voice made metal by the golden cat mask.

Ugo leaned over him like a falling pillar. 'Beware the old in a place where the young die.'

There were chuckles at that until a voice boomed out, making them wince.

'Get ready. Remember, there is no *summa rudis* in this fight, no let-offs, no mercy. It is the last pair standing who will win – or the last man if your pair-brother gets killed. You kill your man or he kills you. If you cling to the edge of the ring, men will come and make you fight in the middle.'

The man, a referee normally, was dressed as Hermes and carried a hook on a stick which he waved meaningfully.

Someone snarled at him. 'You come at me with that and I will stick it down the bloody stump of your neck.'

The referee adjudicated at contests when the fights were normal. This was not normal and hadn't been done in so long that most were hazy on the rules. The one thing everyone was sure about was that no one else was about to get into the *harena* with forty desperate, skilled fighters and try and poke them with a sharp stick.

The trumpets blared. The double gates ground open, letting in the sear of light and the great blaring roar, like some waiting beast. They shuffled forward out onto the sands, walking stiffly, the clench in their arms and legs louder than a hungry baby's wail.

Out in the ring, they moved swiftly, left and right along the curved walls, giving the crowd no more notice than if they were flies that swarmed horseshit.

Drust blinked in the sunlight, took a deep breath that sucked up the faint ammoniac reek of the polluted sand, a smell so familiar it brought a physical stab in his core. He looked at Ugo, who looked back and grinned, then put his helmet on, becoming featureless and sinister.

Soon there would be the scent of blood, Drust thought, fresh as forge iron. The gates banged shut, the thunderous noise of the eager crowd faded to small echoing shouts, and they waited for a distant figure on a far balcony. Drust slid into the cave of his helmet.

The Emperor stood, raised one hand and waved. Trumpets blared – the crowd drowned everything out with a huge roar that buzzed Drust's ears.

The pair stood, backs to the wall, weapons ready, watching the pair on the right, the pair on the left, and only a score of feet between all of them. The pair on the left were moving even before the musicians took the trumpets from their lips. Easy meat, that's what they think. The old farts – take them out quickly, early blood…

They are moving for me, Drust thought wildly.

The leader was a *retiarius* with a dark blue kilt held up by a broad belt, two greaves to the knee, bound in padded wraps and the elaborate arm guard with its flare at the shoulder. His head was bare save for a loop of ribbon, the ends hanging down past his chiselled cheekbones. He was grinning, the net looped over one shoulder like a cloak. He hefted the three-tined fishing spear and closed in while the crowd roared; he'd have been more impressive if he hadn't been barley-fed, the diet aiming for layers of fat rather than muscle – but he was still fast on his feet.

The other one was a *hoplomachus*, armed and dressed like Ugo, a shapeless head encased in iron, a big shield, yet he had somehow managed to get a *spatha*, a long sword.

I am in trouble here, Drust thought, and hoped Ugo was watching his back from the pair on the other side. It came to him that they might not last long enough to work the plan.

The *retiarius* flicked the net off his shoulder with an easy gesture, whipping it at Drust, who blocked; the lead weights rattled off his shield and he would have been ready to respond save that the *hoplomachus* was coming at him with the longsword.

He parried it, letting the longer blade glissade off, then surprised the big armoured man with a fast respond, a stroke that might have taken him under one man-breast if he'd not shied away from it. Drust drew blood all the same and felt a leap of triumph at that.

It was short-lived; the air inside his helmet was coarse and the sweat ran in his eyes. It was always the problem with enclosing helmets and big shields; you either finished your man quickly or ended up puking on your knees, drowned and blinded in sweat.

He had lost sight of the *hoplomachus* – he had no edge-vision at all – and moved away from where he had last seen him until his back slammed into something solid. He heard voices and shouts behind it, loud enough to be heard over the howling crowd, and he knew it was one of the grilled doors leading into the *harena*; behind it were the beast handlers and the referees with their goads. He knew that because he felt one in his back, propelling him forward as a voice shouted at him to get to the middle.

The *retiarius* closed in, then stopped in confusion, looking at a cushion which had impaled itself on his upturned fork. Let no one tell you that there is any refinement in the expensive front seats, Drust thought. Everyone is the same at the Games and the only difference was that the cushions at the front were better.

He couldn't tip the neck guard of the helmet back far enough to look up, but that was just as well; the *retiarius*, frowning, was shaking his *fuscina* to free it of the cushion, while more debris was showering down – fruit, vegetables, empty lunchboxes, wineskins and anything else they could hurl, all accompanied by bestial curses. The crowd were disgusted that they could not see.

Drust lunged at his opponent, blurry with stinging sweat tears; his shield slammed the man and he yelped, lost interest in the impalement on his trident and backed off. There was a flash at the edge of the eyeholes in Drust's helmet and he reared back into the grille, just avoiding the slash of the *spatha*. He felt the goad in his back and his anger made him whirl and stab through the square opening; the man with the goad looked astonished as the *gladius* went in his throat and out again, leaving him coughing blood and sinking to his knees.

'Fuck you,' Drust muffled out, then had to turn back to the *retiarius*, who had freed the trident and had it in one hand, close to the butt end. He was good with it too, flicking for the face, then the foot.

There was a deep clanging sound and the *hoplomachus* appeared in Drust's vision, staggering sideways as he dropped his longsword. Even as he straightened up, a second blow came whistling round and this one took him in the throat, just below the helmet.

Drust saw Ugo appear in view, swinging the cut-off spear like a long axe. It confused the *retiarius* entirely; this was not how a *hoplomachus* was supposed to fight. Neither is one supposed to have a fucking *spatha* like your pair-brother, Drust thought savagely, then sprang forward.

He stepped on the trailing edge of the net, the *retiarius* hauled it in and Drust went over, feeling his ankle tangle. In a fury he rolled into it, slashed the *retiarius* in the knee, just above the padded greave, then stuck the *gladius* in the man's instep.

He was levering himself upright when Ugo gave the man a massive two-handed blow across the belly, slicing the broad belt and going downward into the thigh. Then he thrust the point of it into the man's face, straight into the gasping O of his mouth. The lips seemed to close obscenely round it, were cut in half when it came out. He vomited blood and fell to his knees.

Drust finished him with the usual blow to the back of the neck, then stuck the sword in the sand and fumbled until he had the helmet off. He saw Ugo do the same and they stood for a moment, gasping in dusty air and wiping the salt-stinging sweat from their eyes.

'The other ones?' Drust managed to gasp.

'I killed one. The other felt a pair come up behind him and backed off.'

Ugo looked back to where he had been. 'He's gone down, I think – we'll have this new pair to bother about soon.'

'You hurt?'

'Sweaty is all. I see you sixed a referee.'

Drust was not at all sure whether 'no rules' included that, but he saw the angry faces behind the grille, heard the accusing voices. He would have spat at them but he had no moisture, and was also sure they wouldn't be opening that grille and stepping into the *harena*.

Around them the fights went on; several men were down, others were dancing in the middle of the *harena*, a couple of pairings were taking a watchful break like Drust and Ugo, who picked up a wineskin thrown from the front seats and shook it, then grinned and put it to his lips.

'That has some decent swallow in it,' he declared and passed it over for Drust to drink. It was *calenum*, the patricians' favoured tipple, and the two gladiators drank it down and flung away the skin. Then Ugo hefted the spear and nodded in the direction of a pair who were coming closer; they were dressed in leather – mostly strap – carried two swords and wore full-face helmets. Fast and deadly then, working as a team. Young enough not to be gasping with sweat in their eyes, Drust thought.

'Time,' Ugo called out, almost gleefully – then he stepped forward and threw the spear. It was never meant to be thrown, wasn't balanced and missing nearly half its length – but it arced the scant few feet, hit one of the swordsmen in the chest and bowled him backwards with a shriek. When he stopped sliding and the sand settled, the spear stuck out like a new tree and his pair-brother stared, horrified.

Drust wished he had saved some of the wine to pour on his face and sluice away the paste made from sand and sweat, but there was no time – he closed in on the stricken lone fighter, who looked, licked his lips and backed off.

'Rear.'

Drust allowed himself a swift, darting look and saw two more fighters coming at them from behind, hoping to sneak in; Ugo had turned on them and scooped up the dropped trident. Drust cursed, then lunged at the lone man.

The man had lost faith when the spear skewered his pair-brother and now he committed the worst crime of all – he ran. After a few steps, Drust gave up chasing him, let him run into the howls and debris from the crowd. He'd only find more enemies in a ring, he thought, and turned back to help Ugo.

He had shuffled through the glaring white sand for a few steps when he heard a change in the crowd, a subtlety he was attuned to over the years. When he whirled, it was to see the lone fighter charging at him, sweated face snarling.

Bastard, Drust thought, he faked a retreat – a decent ploy but there were no *tiros* in this affair. He dropped to one knee and let the man slam like a bull on his shield, then levered with all his strength and a huge roar to help it.

The fighter went over his head, trailing sand and yelps. When he crashed to the ground, Drust heard all the air leave him in a rasp, but gave him no time to find more; he thrust the *gladius* in his neck once, twice, three times, then risked a look to see how Ugo was doing.

One of his opponents was down, but the big man was bleeding from the head and a slash across the thigh. The man against him might have been a *murmillo* when he started out but he had long since ditched anything heavy and was now armed with a long *spatha* and a spear. When Drust arrived at the edge of his vision, he backed off, panicked, but it did him no good. Drust and Ugo closed on him, slashing, stabbing, banging him with Drust's big shield until he went down. Then they rained blows on him; Ugo finished him off with the rim of his *hoplite* shield, a crushing blow to the skull.

They stopped, panting and gasping, looking around. There were bodies everywhere, but still a lot of men struggling and dancing. None of the Dis were out with their hook-and-chain servitors dressed as denizens of Hades; no one was going to be dragged off by the heels, not in this frantic affair.

'Ladle,' said Drust, the password for his plan. Ugo blinked and dashed sweat from his eyes.

'Time to die,' Drust urged. Then he sank down as if the last man had mortally wounded him. Ugo remembered the ladle, the way Drust had used it to flatten Mus from winning the cauldron contest. He grinned and keeled over facing the opposite way; now they had almost a circle of vision covered, and looked, lying in the dirty-white, blood-flushed sand, as if they had bled out.

They lay for a long time, feeling the heat, but there was cloud so no glaring sun to broil them. They got back their breathing and it would have been perfect, Drust thought, if they'd had a flask of water or a skin of decent wine.

In the end, he grew worried about Ugo, strained to hear the man's breathing over the noise but couldn't. Perhaps he really had bled out; he'd seen the wounds on the German and they looked leaky. So he risked asking and had back a grunt.

'Still here. Good idea, this – but Silver-Arm and his partner are headed this way. Looking to get to someone on your side.'

Drust could only see two figures, one supporting the other who was clearly done for – it seemed Dyad Silver-Arm and his pair-brother were looking for two easy kills.

'When they get to a position,' Drust hissed, 'take them from behind, like you would a two-as whore. Six them both.'

'Not honourable,' he heard Ugo mutter. 'That's Dyad and the other is the Gaul, Caccuso. The one they call Mountain of Heads. They are darlings of the crowd.'

'Six them,' Drust hoarsed back and hoped the big arse would do it, not rise up and challenge them both.

He did it better than even Drust had hoped; Caccuso stepped over him and when he did Ugo rammed the *gladius* up between his legs. It must have hurt because Caccuso screamed like a scalded pig and then died, rolling over and over and spraying blood; blue-white coils unfolded from under his kirtle. Ugo was right – it was no way for a hero of the *harena* to die, but fuck him, Drust thought savagely.

Silver-Arm was fast; he hadn't won so many contests by not having reactions like a hunted leopard. He spun and struck and Ugo gave a grunt; Drust saw the blade come out of Ugo's side trailing rubies, and the big German dropped to one knee.

Drust's leap up took the Greek by surprise; he'd thought only Ugo was faking it and the appearance of a second man almost froze him, long enough for Drust to hammer home a blow into the kidneys, a hard, frantic thrust that slammed the hilt on Dyad's flesh. The Greek reared away, but still had the presence to block Drust's second slash with the polished scales that gave him his nickname.

He was finished, though, and knew it. He went to one knee and tried to get up, failed and dropped his sword, went to both knees and bowed his head. 'Bless me divine number, you who generated gods and men. For the divine number begins with the profound, pure unity until it comes to the holy four; then it begets the mother of all, the all-comprising, all-bounding, the firstborn, the never-swerving, the never-tiring holy ten, the keyholder of all.'

Pythagoras. Drust wondered if there was any truth in it, then drove the point of the *gladius* down into his neck and the voice gurgled to a close.

'Six is the only number for you now,' he said, letting him fall face forward, then risked a swift look to see if anyone was closing on them. The two behind were no danger; one was a limp ragdoll shape on the white sand, the other was struggling with a new pair of fighters.

Ugo got to his feet, straightening up so that the blood sluiced down and dripped off his knees. There was a moment when Drust didn't want to believe it, but he knew – as he knew Ugo knew when their eyes met.

'I hope this Pythongrass is not god,' he growled. 'I am not good with numbers.'

'Count breaths,' Drust said, helping him up by one blood-slathered arm. 'In, out, in, out – that's easy.'

'Last pair,' Ugo said and his grin was bloody. Drust looked and saw it was true – the last pair had killed their only opponent and were now taking the plaudits of the crowd with raised hands and half turning in circles. There was no one left to worry about except Drust and Ugo.

And Tiridates and his pair-brother Alafai did not seem too bothered.

Ugo blew out blood and spat. 'I will get it to one,' he said. 'Beyond that is beyond me. Burn me well – don't let me go in the Hole.'

'Ugo...'

The big German took up the *hoplite* shield and the trident, stood upright and started forward at a staggering, weaving trot. Alafai saw him and called out to Tiridates, who stopped acknowledging the cheers and turned; even across the distance between them, Drust could see the uncertain eyes behind the enamelled splendour of the cat mask. These were supposed to be long dead, hadn't been seen upright for a long time. Ladle, Drust thought. No rules...

He charged after Ugo, shuffling through the sand, half weeping as he saw the big German veer sideways, dragging Alafai to one side. They closed and Alafai was ready, sword up, shield up – then Ugo hurled his *hoplite* shield like a discus, and the man had to block desperately. This was nothing like rules, not anything he had experienced before. By the time he had recovered, Ugo was on him; Alafai thrust his sword into Ugo's belly, but that was all part of it, Drust knew.

Ugo's trident took the man in the face, lanced into both eyes and smashed the nose. They went down in a welter of gore and sand and the crowd loved it with massive roars.

Drust felt numb. Tiridates stared his cat mask at the locked bodies, busy kicking themselves out of the world, then he turned murderously towards Drust, waited for him in the centre of the ring, oiled with sweat and other men's blood. He had no more than a loincloth and leather harness, the cat helmet, the long-handled, wickedly curved *khepesh* in one hand and a longer, leaf-bladed spear in the other.

Drust was bone-weary. He dropped the shield, which was too heavy for him to lift now, and saw the smile on those too-full lips, left bare where the masked helmet stopped. It was a sneer that said how Tiridates would kill this man – he could imagine no other outcome. Only a handful of nail-gnawed people up in the tiers knew that this was more than a passing bloody fancy to occupy an indolence of afternoon.

Tiridates shifted to keep Drust in front of him. He held himself with an easy confidence, assured in the superiority of his weapons and skill, and if he thought about how Drust, the aged and least of fighters when he'd been in his prime, had got to this point it did not dent his arrogance.

His reach was longer; he was younger and had no debilitating wounds – none at all, Drust saw, beyond a scratch or two a cat might have done. Drust had to stop himself from giggling at that thought; Tiridates still had the helmet, so he must be feeling some heat – but he also had that *khepesh*, an ugly weapon which he twirled to show his wrist was supple and strong.

Arrogance is good, Drust thought. It replaces thinking…

He continued to drift around the man, maintaining the same distance and letting the tip of his *gladius* dance, as if he knew how to work some mind-magic, as if he was assessing where he would strike with it. He stopped beside the slumped bodies, never taking his eyes from the cat mask; there was nothing at his feet but the annoyed buzzing of flies.

The sun came through as if Sol Invictus himself took a ringside seat for this final contest. It hammered the sand, even managed to mute the crowd; Drust felt sweat squeeze out all over him, run down his neck, drip down the inside of his arms. Tiridates must be feeling it, he thought, but he was desperate for that to be true – the cat mask stayed blank, the lips under it still smiled and there didn't seem more than an oiled sheen, as if he was fresh from a massage at the baths.

Then there was a grunt, a small puff of sound, no more. Drust broke his glance to look, saw the bubble form and break on Ugo's lips, saw the glaucous eye, slitted as if half asleep.

Tiridates leaped, the *khepesh* lashing out at Drust's neck. It was a perfectly delivered blow, the weight of Tiridates' arm right behind the brutal head of the machine as it whirled towards him. The blade is only sharpened on the outside portion of the curved end, Drust told himself. They stopped using it a thousand years ago – it was typical of this flash arse-sponge to be using it now.

It meant you had to get the blow just right to cut, otherwise you were using a massive hammer. That will do, Drust thought – but he was already sliding away from it as it came round, hadn't forgotten about the spear, and when it came thrusting in Drust went to the outside in a staggering flurry of sand. There was nothing finessed or elegant from him – he felt tired enough just to lie down and gasp – but he slammed the pommel of the *gladius* against that arm, blocking the blow, before it could even be fully retracted.

It blew numbness into Tiridates' spear hand; the weapon dropped from fingers that wouldn't work, the arm simply fell to his side and the lips beneath the cat mask made an O. He was lithe and fast all the same, sprang back, whipped the *khepesh* again in a flailing scythe to keep Drust away.

Tiridates kept his distance, circling in a crouch while the crowd jeered and howled. Drust was happy to let him; his breath rasped painfully in his throat, black and grey circles seemed to pop at the edges of his vision, and he dashed the sweat out of his eyes with his free hand.

Tiridates flapped his own free arm, willing the blood into it, willing the fingers to work. I should be on him now, Drust thought, when I have the advantage – but he had no such thing. He was barely upright.

When Tiridates was sure his fingers had grip, he came forward in a dancing rush, *khepesh* held in both hands, but in such a way that Drust had no idea whether he would swing from above his head or from one hip to the other.

He had a choice to move right or left, behind or in front. Moving in front meant a lot of energy he did not have, but it also meant his sword could come into play. Moving behind was less risky but futile.

He allowed Tiridates to strike, closing so that the double-handed blow would hit high up near the man's clenched fists, having travelled hardly any distance. They collided in a grunting sweaty mass and Drust's blade slashed across the gap between the base of the cat helmet and his neck. He felt the jar, heard metal grate but no sign of blood – then the blow thumped him in the ribs, lifted him up and sent him spinning sideways into the sand, rolling over the prone bodies.

Tiridates seemed unnerved by what had happened. He danced on the balls of his feet on the far side of the bodies, as if trying to convince the howling crowd – or himself – that he was still in control. There was blood on his neck, Drust saw.

Drust could barely wobble to his feet. The only reason the next blow missed him was because the move was one he knew and he could let the hissing wind of it pass him with only a slight bend, pivoting on one hand – under it he felt something hard and realised it was Ugo's *gladius*.

The crowd roared with delight as they separated, Drust now shambling like a head-down bull being led to slaughter. Drust saw figures flitting behind Tiridates and to the left; he risked a look and they were behind him too. For one belly-sinking moment he thought it was the last act, the final snap-finger gesture of a mad boy-emperor who had brought in more pairs to keep the entertainment going. Then he realised it was Dis and all his masked helpers with their hooks and chains, coming to knock the fallen on the head and drag out the clearly dead.

They won't come near us, he thought dully; this has to be finished by one or the other. He straightened, hefted a *gladius* in either hand and waited. Tiridates wobbled, the crowd was on its feet, shouting and screaming a war cry of its own, hurling cushions and hats. Tiridates gripped the *khepesh* with both hands and moved in, fast. Furious and bold – and it might work. Drust tried to will his legs to work, to throw himself out of the way of this boulder with a blade, who baby-stepped over the corpses in his path, teeth bared in a feral grin.

'Ladle.'

It was a last burbling roar from Ugo and Tiridates yelled, jerking away from Ugo's thrust, the sickle-sword flailing. It was a weak punch of Ugo's dagger blade, did no more than slide an inch into the ankle, but it made Tiridates hop and then – seemingly slowly, magnificently – crash to the ground in a spray of sand.

Drust stumbled forward as Tiridates rolled over, and his slash struck something solid, so that Tiridates howled like a burning cat – Drust saw his hand, *khepesh* and all, whirl through the air and flop in the white sand. Jumping spider, he thought wildly, and jabbed with the *gladius* again and again. He missed more than he hit, but one of them shoved the point into the base of Tiridates' remaining, desperate hand, thrown up to defend his face. Drust felt the point grind against bone, and he shoved and twisted the blade while Tiridates screamed.

The push of the *gladius*, with Drust half-fainting his weight onto it, finally pinned the hand to Tiridates' face while he struggled. He managed to break away, one hand skewered on his cheek, straight through the cat-face helmet, the *gladius* waggling where it had been torn from Drust's flabby grip.

Tiridates was struggling to rise, brought up his right hand to pluck the sword free, then saw the blood-raggled stump and realised he had no hands left to fight with. He knew something was wrong, but he was like the moth lying in a viscous pool, struggling to fly but unable to understand why it couldn't.

Drust took Ugo's *gladius* and knelt beside the Greek, seeing the fear, hearing the whimpering screams. With a grunt, he put the blade to one of the beautiful, astonished eyes under the cat face and leaned on it. Tiridates thrashed for a moment, managed to tear his hand through the webbing of his fingers, the other sword still in his cheek. He waved the freed hand wildly as if asking for mercy, then all his limbs flopped to stillness in the slow flush of blood.

Like a moth crushed into a pool of wine.

Drust's last few marbled steps up to the Imperial platform were in a mist. The Emperor took up a prominent position on the podium at the centre of the narrower side of the ring on the north side. He – and the other great and good – were raised above the podium on a dais. There were four columns, each surmounted by a statue of Victory, supporting a canopy and the whole thing was known as the *cubiculum* – the bedroom – because it permitted the Emperor and his guests to recline like Romans instead of sitting like barbarians.

Senators sat, however – they had their own prized *curule* seats, signature of their rank, which they could move about – but the Emperor lay in a *bisellium*, richly ornamented and with room for two people, although only one person ever occupied it. Except for today. This was where Drust would plant his sweating arse, once he had stumbled through the marble and porphyry, gilded tesserae, the orichalcum and the polite mouse-scuttering of applause.

The applauders in their broad and narrow purple stripes turned in their *curule* chairs and politely called out blessings as he passed; the guards were stolid in polished gilding and only their eyes moved – save one.

He was the most polished, most gilded of all, with his crested helmet tucked under one arm. He had fashionably styled hair and a twist of a smile on his lips as he held out his hand. Drust stared blankly; they had cleaned him up as best they could, stuck a fresh tunic on and bound his head wound so that he had a clean bandage, now slightly stained. He looked like a hero and felt like a dog turd.

'Some fight, I see,' Honoratus declared and had appreciative chuckles. Drust saw the clean, smelled the slight whiff of hair oil, was dazzled by the polish and personae of all these golden Palace Rats, and could not think of anything else through the strange veils of mist that seemed to be draped on him.

'Some don't,' he answered, and Honoratus, Prefect of the Praetorians, lost his smile, twisted though it was. He gestured sternly at Drust, who realised he wanted the battered leather scroll case, supposedly with the permitted petitions from Drust and his friends. Drust clutched it more protectively to him and Honoratus scowled.

'Let it be,' said a voice, gentle yet firm. 'He did not wade through all that blood simply to get close enough to kill me.'

'Might just have bribed a Praetorian,' said another, and the Emperor turned to gently chide the man, calling him Philostratus as he did so. Drust had no idea who the Greek was, but the boy-emperor kept a lot of philosophising Greeks around. He liked this one if only because of Honoratus's blood-bag face at the comment.

Boy-emperor. It was used scathingly by those who thought him too young and unlikely ever to be out from under his mother. He was trying hard to grow chin-hair on a bland boy's face, which looked like a child's drawing on an egg. He looked quizzically at Drust and stroked his chin as if he had the beard of Socrates. Then he indicated for him to sit, another great honour besides the monstrous purse, the laurel wreath, the symbolic victory palm branch and the wooden sword of freedom.

For this fleeting moment they were head to head, close as brothers.

'Here, give me your petitions.'

'Not petitions,' Drust heard himself say and then told him what the case contained and who was behind it all. Watched the dark-olive skin – not as *mavro* as the others in his line – turn the colour of creamed wheat. Drust sympathised – no good thing to learn of your ma's perfidy; he sat and wobbled while Alexander plucked one scroll and read it, then took out another. Drust was aware of the onlookers, at how puzzled and uncertain they were. The Praetorians were the same; there was something wrong, but they had no idea what and did not want to get foot-stamped more by this boy with the power of life and death.

The Emperor finally looked sideways at Drust and called out, seemingly to no one at all, 'Bring wine – more water in it.'

A cup was thrust into his hand. Drust sat and sipped – the wine was Falernian and snow-cooled; he wished they had ignored the instruction on the water, especially when Alexander finally raised his head and looked at him.

Boy or not, the eyes, once olive, had gone to cinders that shrieked of chains and pain and blood. Drust did not envy the conspirators.

'You have done well.'

There was that one eyeblink in time when we all thought we were making a difference, Drust thought, but we were just altering the pattern of things for the briefest of moments, leaving nothing truly changed. We have been involved in the destinies of five emperors for more than a decade, he remembered – we'd even thrown one in the Tiber – and all the time doing it we'd had one thought, one desire: leave us alone.

Drust sat at the scarred table in the Place, staring at nothing, talking mainly to himself. In a little while he and Kag, Dog and Quintus – all that was left of the original Brotherhood – would troop off with Kisa and the others to the funeral of Ugo.

The sky was slashed with pyre smoke from those who had rescued their own slaughtered comrades before the Hole got them. Under the smoke, the Games went on. Couriers had gone out north with the fate of Julius Yahya in their pouches. Senators unlucky enough to have been in the Imperial box had found themselves gripped by the shoulders and hustled away; others would be scurrying for safety.

The crowd around to hear Drust's victory proclaimed in the Forum Romanum was big and loud and colourful – Murena was racing and some big thug from Britannia, the new favourite of the Emperor, was fighting.

'Who won the big race?' someone had asked on the day Drust had been littered out of the Flavian, surrounded by the Brothers and Curtius, with other gladiators as escort.

'Who fucking cares?' was the answer. Drust heard it through the litter curtains and the fog of pain and treatment.

Drust, Lion of the Flavian – in a week the graffiti would be overwritten by screeds to the darlings of the chariot, or the latest hero of the sands. The world would roll on over Julius Yahya and Drust both.

'You will always be the Lion of the Flavian now,' Kisa offered when Drust growled all this out. 'Your gods who walk the fields of Elysium—'

'Can fucking stay there,' Kag interrupted savagely, and The Place fell silent. We had all been Brothers of the Sand, walking in the light, putting the Empire to rights, Drust thought. Had it all truly been just sand and dust? What would happen now? Would Julius Yahya make it to a trial in the senate? Would the Mother of Empire have enough strings to pull him out? Would she risk letting him get that far?

Would she leave us alone?

Drust sat and made patterns in the spilled wine, seeing the hilt of the *gladius* within touching distance of his little trembling finger. The hand only shook when it was empty of sword, he had realised, but the *gladius* was never far away and frequently he found it in his hand at the most innocuous times, and would stare at it, not knowing how it got there, scarce able to feel it in the same way you could not feel a wedding ring.

He asked the question, as he asked it every night since her death, sleepless and unsure.

Have I done enough? Can I lay it down now?

Historical Note

This follows on from *The Red Serpent* by about six months, taking place in AD 225.

Alexander was made Emperor when he was fourteen, taking over from his murdered cousin Elagabalus, who was eighteen. He was always referred to as 'boy-emperor', mainly because his mother had acted as regent until he came of age, and established herself so thoroughly that it was hard for Alexander to work his way out of her shadow – which he never fully did.

In AD 235 Alexander himself would be murdered, an act which plunged the Roman world into what historians like to call the Crisis of Empire, a fifty-year period during which there were at least twenty-six claimants to the title of Emperor, mostly prominent Roman generals who assumed Imperial power over all or part of the Empire.

The act which decided Alexander's fate was a march up to the Dark to confront the German tribes, following an expedition against the Sassanids, inheritors of the broken Parthian kingdom. On both occasions, Alexander showed too willing to pay for peace rather than fight – it might have been sensible, but it turned the Roman Army against him.

The story of Drust, Kag and the others begins in the vast German forests which formed part of a primeval woodland system that once carpeted the entire north of Europe. In Scotland there are remnants that permit some idea of what it must have been like – Abernethy, Glen Affric, Inshriach Forest and others.

On an average overcast day these are dark, forbidding places, full of strange noises, and anyone wandering into them today will feel, for all their enlightened knowledge, exactly as did the Romans; this is an alien environment, quite possibly inhabited by strange beasts and stranger people.

The fact that the Romans refer to these Germanic forests as 'the Dark' is an indication of how they – and the legionaries especially – disliked such places; the legacy of the slaughter of Varus in the Teutoburg Forest ran bone-deep.

In comparison, the Brothers' return to Rome takes them to haunts which, they discover, are every bit as dark, forbidding and full of beasts as the German forests. They also come to realise they don't know Rome as well as they thought.

Which brings us to underground Rome. You can get tours nowadays of some of what archaeology has revealed, but a vast network of tunnels, aqueducts, sewers, drains, quarries and secret temples – like the Mithraic one below the Circus Maximus – remain to be uncovered. The massive white worms, the jumping spiders, the rats big as lapdogs are all true and current, incidentally.

The last vicious acts in the lives of the Brothers of the Sand take place in these hidden places – and in the great glare of the *harena*, the sands of the Flavian Amphitheatre. The *perfidiae harenam* is an invention of my own, but such grand multi-gladiator events did take place, a great and expensive slaughter paid for by Emperors, the only people rich enough to afford to buy so many deaths for the delight of the audience.

The names and fates of many of these fighters have come down to us through the centuries, but for each lauded gladiator a hundred or more lie unmarked and long forgotten. This is the group Drust, Kag, Dog and the others belong to. They deserve to have their brief glories observed, their story told.

Glossary

General terms

Ala Flavia

We know for sure that the *Ala II Flavia pia fidelis milliaria* was garrisoned in Heidenheim from some time around AD 90–110 and moved to Aalen around AD 155–60, where it stayed until the middle of the third century. But where the *ala* (regiment) actually comes from is more difficult to trace. The name 'Flavia' points at an assembling under Vespasian (AD 70–79) or his sons (Titus AD 79–81, Domitian AD 81–96). The earliest mention is on a military diploma from AD 86 where it already has its full name *pia fidelis milliaria*. It is possible that the unit was created in the aftermath of the Batavian rebellion in AD 70; that would make it the oldest *ala milliaria* known.

Auctoratio

Most gladiators were slaves but some were volunteers. The *auctoratio* was the swearing of a legal agreement by free men who joined a school through adventure or debt for a contracted period, by which they handed themselves over as slaves to their master and trainer, agreeing to submit to beating, burning, and death by the sword if they did not perform as required. Gladiators were expected to accept death.

Aurehahn

Wood grouse, better known to Scots everywhere as the capercaillie. And, yes, it had a weird call.

Caesar's House

The one Roman everyone knows, Julius Caesar grew up in the worst area of the city, for all that his family was considered a cut above. The truth is that the Caesar residence was in Subura, which became the Roman slums, and his house was probably swamped by them rather than a residence deliberately chosen to be among the plebs. Long gone, its site and design is now speculation; best guess is that it was on the Argiletum – today's Via Cavour – close to the Porta Esquilina.

Chariot racing

To the ancient Romans this was Formula One meets Champions League. Chariots drawn by two horses were called *bigae* and those drawn by four horses *quadrigae*. *Trigae, sejuges* and *septemjuges* (three, six and seven horses) were less usual but not unknown. In Nero's time as many as ten horses might be used, and he himself is said to have driven one such *decemjugis* at the Olympic Games. Nero is also remembered for having introduced camels instead of horses to provide a little variety, while the young emperor Elagabalus tried elephants. There were, at this time, four factions defined by colours – Red and White were state-owned, Blue and Green privately owned. Support was fanatical and the Romans even had a name for the delirium – *furor circensis*. Fights between rival teams are well recorded, particularly one in Pompeii which caused several deaths and the teams to be disqualified for ten years, although the ban was later lifted thanks to the intercession of Nero's wife. In later Byzantium, the races were even more intense, more political and more riotous.

Collegium

Collegia could function as guilds, social clubs or burial societies; in practice, in ancient Rome they sometimes became organised bodies of local businessmen and even criminals, who ran the mercantile/criminal activities in a given urban region. The organisation of a *collegium*, ironically, was often modelled on that epitome of law and order, the senate. There were *collegia* for all sorts – the Collegium Centonariorum was for junk collectors, the Collegium Communionis Minirum for actors, the Collegium Saliarium Baxiarum for cobblers. The Collegium Bacchus, for worshippers of the god of wine, was banned in 64 BC. Any profession or organisation could set up such a college – the Collegium Armariorum was the one formed by the gladiators.

Colossus Nero/Colossus Solis

A massive gilded bronze statue, originally of Nero and destined for the vestibule of his planned Golden House, this no longer exists but is estimated to have been between 98 and 121 feet (30–37 metres) tall. Vespasian renamed it in honour of the sun god and Hadrian ordered it moved closer to the Flavian Amphitheatre – twenty-four elephants accomplished this – where it stood for centuries (the last record of it was in AD 354). It eventually gave the name 'Colosseum' to the Flavian Amphitheatre and, together with the Meta Sudans fountain known colloquially as the Sweating Post (see below), was a tourist attraction even in Drust's day.

Conditor

A rough translation is 'builder' and it was applied to those slaves responsible for maintaining the chariots, from wheels to yokes. The best of them could build one from scratch and were highly prized.

Conticinium

A particular time of Roman night/early morning defined as 'when animals cease to make a noise'. The wee small hours.

Dis Manibus

A standard phrase of dedication to the Manes, the spirits of the dead. Effectively they are being warned that there's another one on the way. In the gladiatorial amphitheatre it was an actual person, also known as Charun, the Roman form of Charon, the Greek demigod who ferried the dead across the Styx. Pluto, the Roman god of the underworld, was also used. Traditionally a man masked as someone from the underworld, accompanied by masked helpers, would use a hammer to 'test for signs of life' by smacking them out of the near-dead. Then the helpers would hook the body by the heels and drag it off through the Gate of Death to the *spoliarium*. Those who had survived left the way they had entered, through the Gate of Life.

Draco standard

The *draco* was first used by the Roman cavalry during the second century AD, possibly with the introduction of Sarmatian cavalry into the Roman army. Arrian, who was writing circa AD 137, described it as a Scythian invention which was adopted by Roman cavalry – he probably meant Sarmatian. The Romans began to use the *draco* in cavalry games, the so-called Hippica Gymnasia. These were described by Arrian as glamorised versions of training exercises, performed in decorated armour. It is possible that the *draco* was introduced simply because it was outlandishly foreign. Later, it was adopted by all military units – the *Historia Augusta* mentions that the mother of Severus (AD 193–211) dreamt of a purple snake before his birth (Freud may have made more of that). In the reign of Gallienus (AD 253–268), legionary troops are said to have paraded with a *draco* among the standards of the legions.

Fama

The personification of popular rumour – the Greeks knew her as Pheme and she was more a poetic personification than a deified abstraction, although there was an altar to her in Athens. The Greek poet Hesiod portrayed her as an evildoer, easily stirred up but impossible to quell. The Athenian orator Aeschines distinguished Popular Rumour (Pheme) from Slander (Sykophantia) and Malice (Diabole). Virgil described her (*Aeneid*, Book IV) as a swift, birdlike monster with as many eyes, lips, tongues and ears as feathers, travelling on the ground but with her head in the clouds. Romans became more familiar with her through the popularity of Ovid – in the *Metamorphoses* she inhabited a reverberating mountaintop palace of brass.

Flavian Amphitheatre

Now better known as the Colosseum (or Coliseum), it was originally known as the Flavian Amphitheatre since it was built by the Flavian dynasty. Commissioned in AD 72 by Emperor Vespasian, it was completed by his son Titus in AD 80, with later improvements by Domitian. Located just east of the Forum, it was built to a practical design, with its 80 arched entrances allowing easy access for 55,000 spectators, who were seated according to rank. The Colloseum is huge, an ellipse 188m long and 156m wide. Originally 240 masts were attached to stone corbels on the fourth level to support an awning, manned by sailors from the Misenum fleet, to provide shade on hot days. Its name came from the nearby massive bronze statue (see above).

Fortuna

A goddess who was the personification of luck in Roman times and, naturally, one much worshipped by gladiators. She was usually depicted with a *rota fortunae* (a Wheel of Fortune) and a Horn of Plenty, and could be represented as veiled and blind, as in modern depictions of Justice. The first temple dedicated to Fortuna was attributed to the Etruscan Servius Tullius, while the second is known to have been built in 293 BC as the fulfilment of a Roman promise made during later Etruscan wars – which is the same time that gladiatorial contests are thought to have been created.

Harena

Literally, 'sand'. Possibly Etruscan, which was believed to be the origin of gladiatorial contests.

The Ludi

Games in general, and festivals involving games. Games could be private, public or extraordinary – since gladiators were so expensive to train and keep, they fought three or four times a year and, unless the giver of the games paid for it, there was no fight to the death. Contests were, in fact, one-on-one and regulated by a referee, usually a former gladiator. Criminals and prisoners could be damned to fight in the arena, with the hope of a reprieve if they survived a certain number of years. These men were trained in a specialised form of combat. Others, untrained, were expected to die within a short time. There were also volunteer gladiators, ones who either enlisted voluntarily as free or freed men, or who re-enlisted after winning their freedom. Even *equites* and, more rarely, senators sometimes enlisted. The word 'gladiator' simply means 'swordsman'.

Ludus

The gladiator 'school'. It's estimated that there were more than a hundred gladiator schools throughout the Empire. New gladiators were formed into troupes called *familia gladiatorium*, which were under the overall control of a manager (*lanista*) who recruited, arranged for training and made the decisions of where and when the gladiators fought. There were gladiator schools near all the major cities around Rome, and one which has stayed in history is that of Batiatus in Capua, where Spartacus was trained. But the most famous gladiator schools of all were those in Rome: the Great Gladiatorial Training School (*Ludus Magnus*), which was connected to the Flavian Amphitheatre by a tunnel; the Bestiaries School (*Ludus Matutinus*), which specialised in training those who fought, handled and trained exotic wild beasts; the Gallic School (*Ludus Gallicus*), smallest of the schools, which specialised in training heavily armoured fighters; and the Dacian School (*Ludus Dacicus*), which trained lightly armoured fighters in the use of the specialised curved sword.

Mavro

A Greek word meaning 'black' or 'dark'. When applied to people, it is simply a statement of fact – it is neither derogatory nor insensitive. However, in the third century, the Severan dynasty who hailed from North Africa were considered strange and exotic, not for their skin-tone, but for their cultural heritage, exacerbated by marriage into an even more exotic Syrian family of sun worshippers. *Mavro* gained a note of disdain as a result.

Missio

A gladiator who acknowledged defeat could request the *munerarius* to stop the fight and send him alive (*missus*) from the arena. If he had not fallen he could be 'sent away standing' (*stans missus*). The organiser of the games took the crowd's response into consideration in deciding whether to let the loser live or order the victor to kill him. The referee, usually a *summa rudis*, or freed gladiator, made sure nothing happened until the decision was made.

Mithras

According to the Roman historian Plutarch (c. AD 46–120), Mithraism began to be absorbed by the Romans during Pompey's military campaign against Cilician pirates around 70 BC. The soldiers carried the belief with them from Asia Minor into Rome and the far reaches of the

Empire. Syrian merchants imported Mithraism to the major cities, such as Alexandria, Rome and Carthage, while captives took it into the countryside. By the third century, Mithraism and its mysteries permeated the Roman Empire from India to Scotland.

Munerarius (Editor)

The giver of the games. It could be a member of the nobler orders of Rome who put on the show privately (a rarity post-Republic) or in his official capacity as a magistrate or priest, but it was more likely the state organising games whose dates and functions were set in the Roman calendar. Outside Rome, *munerarii* were generally municipal and provincial priests of the Imperial cult, or local governors.

Numerus/numeroi

A *numerus* literally means 'number' and originally referred to units of the Imperial Roman army who came from barbarian allies, were not integrated into the regular army structure of legions and auxilia. Such units were of undetermined strength and their organisation and equipment probably varied according to the unit's ethnic origin. The term was also applied to semi-permanent detachments of regular army units.

Munus (plural munera)

Meaning 'the show', the term also has a connotation of 'duty'. It usually lasted for three or more days and, under special circumstances, for weeks or months. Provincial games rarely lasted more than two days, but Titus's games in Rome for the inauguration of the completed

Flavian in AD 80 lasted 100 days. The classic Italian *munus plena* included *venations* in the morning, various noontime activities (*meridiani*), and gladiatorial duels in the afternoon.

Omnes ad Stercus

A gladiatorial term, liberally scrawled on walls all over Rome. Best translation is 'it's all shit', but 'we're in the shit' can also be used, depending on context. It is not, as internet translations coyly have it, 'get lost' or 'go to hell'. In the context here, it is used as a password challenge, the response being *Sodales, avete*, which roughly translates as 'welcome to the club'.

Six

The number tagged against a gladiator's name in the school he was part of when he died. Origin unknown – but to be 'sixed' means you are a dead man.

Spoliarium

The room that lay behind the Gate of Death, where all fallen fighters and beasts were dragged by men dressed as servitors of Dis Pater using a hook and chains. It was a charnel house where slaves stripped off armour and weapons for reuse, then stacked the human bodies for a while until they were claimed for burial. If unclaimed, they were tipped down the Hole.

Sweating Post

The colloquial name for the Meta Sudans, a large fountain near the Colosseum, constructed about the same time and designed to look like one of the *meta*, the conical markers at either end of the Circus Maximus around which chariots would turn. The fountain echoed that function because it acted as a turning point for triumphal processions, which would turn left there, leaving the Via Triumphalis for the Via Sacra and on to the Forum Romanum. The water in the fountain was designed not to jet out but to flow down the cone, which seems to have given it the name Sweating Post. However, that is also the name for the conical training aid where generations of gladiators sweated with heavy wooden practice swords.

Urban Cohorts and Vigiles

The Urban Cohorts (*cohortes urbanae*) were created by Augustus to offset the power of the Praetorians in Rome. Near the end of his reign (27 BCE - 14 CE), Augustus created the first three urban cohorts, likely recruiting them from the existing Praetorian Guard which was also stationed in Rome. The precise date of their foundation is not known, but the first reference is from Suetonius, detailing how each member received 500 sesterces in Augustus Will. They acted as a police force in Rome and other cities of the Empire.

The Vigiles (*cohortes vigilum*) were also formed during the reign of Augustus to act as the city's permanent firefighting service. It was not the first time such a force had been created for the likes of Marcus Licinius Crassus, one of Rome's all-time richest men, had spotted the chance of making money by offering low prices for burning buildings and then having his team of slaves extinguish the fire so that it could be saved for redevelopment. If the property owner refused the offer, then the fire was left to rage on unabated.

The Vigiles were contemptuously dismissed by the better-paid, better-trained and better-armed Urban Cohort s as 'little bucket men' because their equipment included the wherewithal to fight fires – leather buckets and axes. The Vigiles had the power to enter any home or business and make sure the owner had obeyed fire regulations.

Wine

Rome's drink of choice and as varied as the people who drank it. Some were named according to vintage and others according to how they were made and the ingredients used. Lots of historical writers throw Roman wine terminology around like drunks, without actually knowing much about it. So I share my considerable, in-depth and painfully earned research…

Falernum

The most famous Roman wine was a *fulvus* white. It was best drunk aged, although it was reputed to last no longer than twenty years in the amphora. It is the one most abused by writers who have it drunk by legionaries in local bars, and if it is spilled is almost always red. *Falernum* was the Château d'Yquem of its day and unlikely to be affordable to anyone like a legionary.

Calenum

Similar to *Falernum*, this had a lighter taste and was apparently the favourite of the patrician class.

Albanum

There were two types: dry and sweet. It was regarded as a quality wine that needed fifteen years to mature.

Massilitanum

A smoky, cheap wine that was reputedly healthy but not very tasty. An absolute acquired taste. A decent analogy would be whisky drinkers trying Laphroaig for the first time.

Momentanum

Needed at least five years to be drinkable and even then it was unremarkable, according to Martial.

Mulsum

The apéritif of choice. *Mulsum* was wine combined with honey, either during or after fermentation. Columella recommended the addition of the honey during brewing, although Pliny the Elder felt it should be added to a dry wine before serving.

Passum

Raisin wine. Made from half-dried grapes left on the vine, *passum* was a sweet drink.

Conditum

Wine mixed with pepper, honey and seawater, this was a beverage adopted from the Greeks, who got it from further east. Cato recommended the use of Apician grapes.

Lora

Sneered at as the wine of slaves, *lora* was made from the leftovers of wine production. Grape pulp would be mixed with water and pressed a second or third time.

Posca

Not strictly a wine, this was a vinegar-based drink, popular with travellers. The vinegar was carried in a flask and added to water, making a reputedly refreshing beverage. The custom arose because of vinegar's disinfecting properties, as a way of making unreliable water drinkable. To improve flavour spices and honey were often added. It was the drink of soldiers on the march – and given to a dying Christ on the cross by one, so not exactly the cruel taunt portrayed in the Bible.

The Gladiators

Hoplomachus

This gladiator was distinguished by his short, curved sword. Like a *Thrax*, he wore high leg guards.

Murmillo

A fighter apparently named after a Greek word for fish. He wore a crested helmet and carried a tall shield.

Retiarius

This was the most distinctive-looking gladiator, a bare-headed, unshielded fighter whose main protection was padding and a shoulder guard on his left arm. He used a net to ensnare his opponent and a long trident to impale him.

Rudiarius

A gladiator who had received a *rudis* – the wooden sword that marked him as retired and no longer a slave – was an experienced volunteer, especially worth watching. There was a hierarchy of experienced *rudiarii* within a *familia* of gladiators, and *rudiarii* could become trainers, helpers, and arbiters of fights, the referees. The most elite of the retired gladiators were dubbed *summa rudis*. The *summa rudis* officials served as technical experts to ensure that the gladiators fought bravely, skilfully, and according to the rules. They carried batons and whips with which they pointed out illegal movements. Ultimately the *summa rudis* officials could stop a fight if a gladiator was going to be too seriously wounded, compel gladiators to fight on, or defer the decision to the organiser. Retired gladiators who became *summa rudis* often achieved fame and wealth in their second careers as officials of the combats.

Secutor

Translates as 'follower', this was the man usually sent in to fight a *retiarius*. His armour was distinguished by a helmet with small eyeholes that would presumably impede the trident's prongs.

Thrax

The Thracian was another type of fighter equipped like a former enemy soldier (from Thrace in northern Greece). He fought with a small rectangular shield and his helmet bore a griffin crest.

The Gear

Fascia

A band of cloth or leather that protected the leg below the knee and provided padding beneath a greave.

Fascina (or *tridens*)

The long, three-pronged metal trident that was the hall-mark of a *retiarius*.

Galea

The helmet worn by all gladiators except the *retiarius*. These were domed and often featured decorative crests and visors pierced with eyeholes.

Galerus

The distinctive metal shoulder guard of a *retiarius*. It curved up strongly from the shoulder, away from the neck, so that neck and head were protected but the fighter's head movements were not restricted.

Gladius

The straight stabbing sword that gave its name to the gladiator. For many years it was also the potent weapon of the legionary, until changes in fighting style brought about a longer pointed sword with more reach, the *spatha*. The *gladius* was relegated to light infantry and the cavalry also adopted the *spatha*, though with a blunt point so they wouldn't accidentally stab themselves in the foot. All of these were also used by gladiators.

Ocrea

A metal leg guard that ran from the knee (or above) to the shin and protected mainly the front of the leg.

Parma

A round or square shield that was smaller and lighter than a *scutum*.

Pugio

A dagger, weapon of last resort of a *retiarius*.

Rudis

The wooden sword or staff symbolising a gladiator's *liberatio*.

Scutum

A large rectangular shield (curving inward so that it formed part of a cylinder), carried by a *murmillo*.

Subligaculum

A traditional loincloth worn by gladiators (the chest was almost always bare).

Brothers Of The Sands

Beasts Beyond The Wall
The Red Serpent
Beasts From The Dark